THE
DARKLING HALLS
OF IVY

EDITED BY LAWRENCE BLOCK

A LAWRENCE BLOCK PRODUCTION

Special thanks to Bill Schafer and Ken Laager at Subterranean Press for generously allowing the use of the beautiful cover for this edition.

Contents

Something to Skip

A Foreword by Lawrence Block

After two years as an English major at Antioch College, in Yellow Springs, Ohio, I landed a job in the summer of 1957 as an editorial associate at a literary agency. I had just sold a story to a magazine, and my duties each day consisted of reading stories by writers every bit as hungry for success as I, and with even less likelihood of attaining it. Moreover, they were willing to put their money where their words were, and paid $5 a story to have their work considered for representation by my employer, the World-Famous Agent. (If a story ran over 5000 words, the fee was higher—another dollar for every additional 1000 words. The fee topped out at $25 for a book.)

Of course the boss never laid eyes on the stories. The eyes laid thereon were mine, and the long detailed letters explaining why, their obvious talent notwithstanding, this particular story didn't work and couldn't be repaired—those were my work, and each time I wrote one, I earned one of the five dollars they'd paid.

"But I look forward eagerly to reading your next submission!"

Right.

The job was the best education a new writer could have, and I dropped out of school to keep it, and wrote and sold magazine fiction when I wasn't dashing the neatly-typed dreams of hopeless hopefuls. I decided, though, that a year was enough, and in the fall of 1958 I was back in Yellow Springs, ready to put in two more years as a student and walk away with a bachelor's degree.

Not in the cards, I'm afraid. By then I was writing and publishing paperback fiction, and spending a disproportionate amount of time drunk or stoned, and completely at sea in my studies. And how are you gonna keep 'em down on the campus after they've seen Greenwich Village?

I tried to drop out after a month or so, realizing I'd made a huge mistake, but I was persuaded to stay.

Bad move.

I couldn't get through *Paradise Lost* or *Roderick Random,* and was utterly baffled by a course I'd enrolled in to satisfy a core requirement that began with "a quick refresher on Newtonian Mechanics before moving on to Quantum Theory." I never even took high school physics, and I had no idea what the hell they were talking about. I figured a Newtonian mechanic was a guy who could help you out if your Newton's engine was misfiring. I figured Quantum Theory had something to do with the beads that served as currency for Native American tribes. I figured . . .

Oh, never mind. Come summer I fled to a furnished room in New York and resumed writing books. I was midway through one called *Campus Tramp* when a letter came from the Student Personnel Committee. It said they thought I might be happier somewhere else, and you know what?

They were right.

And here I am, late in life, typing these words in my office in Room 108 of the Leonora McClurg Center at Newberry College, in (duh) Newberry, South Carolina. I'm spending the semester as writer-in-residence, conducting both a fiction-writing workshop and a literature course, *Reading Crime Fiction for Pleasure.*

How did that happen?

Over the years, I've occasionally entertained the notion of a sojourn in academia. It has long been a compelling fantasy, replete with ivy-covered walls, a book-lined study, a glowing hearth, eager students—and you can take it from there. Not the least of its virtues as fantasy was that I needn't worry about ever having to see it fulfilled. A fantasy brought to life is almost always a disappointment—and yes, that's probably true even of the naughty little three-way you've been secretly drooling over for years.

My own guilty pleasure was safely unattainable, because what institution of higher learning would stoop to hire some clown whose highest credential was a high school diploma?

Shows what I know. On a whim, I shared the fantasy in a newsletter. And one thing led to another, and almost before I knew it I'd been offered the very gig I'd been dreaming of.

But could I accept it? Did I really want to put my life on hold for a third of a year while I took up a position for which I was clearly unqualified? And wouldn't it get in the way of my real work?

I'll spare you an account of my mental backing and forthing. In the end I decided that John Greenleaf Whittier was right to proclaim "*It might have been!*" as the saddest words of tongue or pen, and that in this particular instance I'd rather regret taking a chance than not.

And then there was Patrick O'Connor's example. Pat was a remarkable fellow, worldly and erudite, an editor and publisher, a renowned dance critic and a qualified ski instructor. At one point in his later years he had an opportunity to be certified in some arcane specialty—as an appraiser of something or other, if I recall correctly—and was wondering whether it was worth jumping through the requisite hoops.

"Patrick," a friend told him, "I think you should do it. You may never do anything with it, it may have no practical effect on your life, but it's just the sort of detail that really fleshes out an obituary."

It was the prospect of teaching that got me thinking about *The Darkling Halls of Ivy*.

In recent years, age has taken a toll of my energy and imagination. Fewer stories come to mind and most of the ones that do remain untold. Now would be the time to throw myself into a hobby, but perversely I've sold my stamp collection, purged my library, and lost interest in accumulating anything, irrespective of its capacity for sparking joy.

So I've looked to fill the hours with activities that would provide the illusion that I was still a writer, without obligating me actually to write anything. Through the miracle of self-publishing, I've made almost my entire backlist available in ebook and print-on-demand paperback form. (It consists in large part of pseudonymous work I'd tried to keep secret for decades. Go figure.)

I've filled even more hours enlisting narrator/producers for joint-venture audio self-publishing, and teaming up with translators to self-publish German and Italian and Spanish editions.

And, perhaps the last refuge for a non-writing writer, I've compiled anthologies.

What could be simpler? You round up a batch of excellent writers, provide a theme, and get out of their way. They write the stories, you contrive to put them in some sort of sequence—alphabetical order is always safe— and write a thousand words or thereabouts as a foreword, so that readers will have something to skip.

If there's a tricky part, it's finding a suitable premise. Even in a cross-genre anthology like this one, the stories ought to have something in common. But you don't want everybody writing the same story.

The eighteen stories in *The Darkling Halls of Ivy,* as you'll see, are as individual as fingerprints. They have, as far as I can make out, only two things in common. They're all set in the world of higher education, and they're all to be found at the darker end of the spectrum.

Oh, and one thing more. They're all excellent.

And, to reiterate, there are eighteen of them.

I mention that because in recent years my anthologies have almost always consisted of seventeen stories. I'd be hard put to tell you why. I can't deny a distinct fondness for the number 17, but it's well below the Mendoza line for obsessions. But there are seventeen stories in *In Sunlight or in Shadow,* seventeen in *Alive in Shape and Color,* seventeen in *At Home in the Dark.*

One of the writers I invited to *The Darkling Halls of Ivy* was the remarkable Peter Lovesey, a cherished friend with whom I've largely lost touch in recent years. I wasn't surprised to learn he had way too much on his plate to write a new story, but was happy indeed when he suggested I might consider reprinting an earlier one—and happier still when "Bertie and the Boat Race" turned out to be a perfect fit for *TDHOI*.

Thus the volume you hold in your hands—or view on your eReader—does in fact contain seventeen new stories, with an additional classic tale for lagniappe.

Hmmm. Maybe I'm not as far below that OCD Mendoza line as I might prefer to think . . .

Requiem for a Homecoming

by David Morrell

"Did they ever find who killed that female student?" Ben asked.

Despite the heat in the crowded pub, he still shivered from sitting in the open convertible during the homecoming parade. After twenty years living in Malibu, he'd forgotten how cold autumn nights could be in the Midwest. He took for granted the people he'd waved to hadn't the faintest idea why he was in the parade. They'd cheered for the actor on the movie poster propped behind him, not the screenwriter whose credit was in fine print at the bottom.

"Female student?" Howard asked.

Ben and Howard had been graduate students in the English department back then. Now Howard taught here, and Ben had accepted the guest-of-honor invitation (despite a screenplay deadline) so he could spend the weekend with his long-ago friend.

"The one that got stabbed in the library," Ben answered. "On homecoming Saturday. Our final year."

"Now I remember," Howard said, lowering his beer glass. "Of course. Her."

"Are you guys okay?" a female voice asked.

Ben looked at the waitress, who had purple hair and a ring through her left nostril. She gestured toward their nearly empty beer pitcher on the table.

"We're good," he answered. "Thanks."

As she pushed her way toward the next booth, the din of the celebrating students gave Ben a headache.

"So far as I know, they never proved who stabbed her," Howard said.

"There was a rumor," Ben said. "About Wayne McDonald."

He referred to an assistant professor, who'd joined the faculty that autumn. A week after the murder, the assistant professor had died when his car veered off a highway and flipped several times before plunging into a ravine. The deaths so close together may have been a coincidence, but after the police discovered that the murdered student had come from the same college where McDonald had recently earned his PhD, there was talk that they'd been connected in other ways, that McDonald had killed her and committed suicide.

"Nothing was proven," Howard said. "All of that happened twenty years ago. What made you think of it? Coming back to campus?"

"Do you remember her name?"

"After so much time?"

"Rebecca Markle," Ben said.

"How . . . ? You must have looked it up on the Internet."

"Didn't need to. I never forgot how terrified everybody on campus felt after her body was found in the library. When I moved to Los Angeles"—Ben had received a scholarship to the grad-school film program at USC—"I kept thinking she was in a place she could take for granted was safe. How surprised and helpless and afraid she must have been when the attack occurred. The first screenplay I sold began with a version of what happened to her."

"I noticed," Howard said.

"Do you remember what she looked like?"

"From photos in newspapers twenty years ago?" Howard shook his head.

Ben pulled his wallet from his jacket and removed a photograph. The edges were bent, the color faded. It showed a young, attractive woman, thin, with long blond hair, expressive eyes, and an unhappy smile.

"You keep her picture in your wallet?" Howard asked.

"From the yearbook back then. After the college invited me to be guest of honor this year, I cut it out."

"What on earth for?"

"There was a memorial section for the five students who died that year. One drowned at the reservoir. One committed suicide. One had cancer. One got drunk and fell off a balcony at a frat party." Ben paused. "And Rebecca got stabbed to death in a secluded section of the library. You still don't recognize her?"

"No."

"She was in the modern-novel course we took that term."

Howard sat straighter. "What?"

The din of the celebrating students seemed louder.

"Wayne McDonald taught that course," Ben said.

"I remember he taught it, but not who was in it. There must have been a hundred students. Why didn't the police make a big deal about her being in the course? It would have been another connection between her and Wayne."

"Are you sure you guys are good?" the female voice asked.

Ben turned toward their now-weary-eyed server. "I bet you could use this booth for people who drink more than we do."

"I hope you don't mind. Tips can be generous at homecoming. The more people I serve . . ."

"Here's something to make up for us hogging the booth." Ben gave her more than what she'd probably receive all week. "I used to work part-time in the kitchen here. I know how hard it is to pay tuition. Howard, if you're not tired, I'd like to walk around the campus."

After the heat of the pub, the night's chill stung Ben's cheeks. He zipped up a jacket Howard had lent him and shoved his hands in its warm pockets. The noise of the crowd remained in his ears as they crossed the street toward the college.

Arching tree branches obscured a quarter moon. A gentle breeze scraped leaves across a path.

"The trees are bigger," Ben said. "But the ivy on the buildings looks the same. How's your family?"

"Our daughter graduated from here two years ago." Howard referred to his stepchild. "She works for an advertising firm in New York."

"Great. And your wife?"

"No better."

"Sorry."

"Depression isn't anybody's friend."

Their footsteps crunched through the leaves.

"The reason the police didn't make a big deal about Rebecca Markle being in that class is they didn't know," Ben said. "Her name wasn't on the list of students taking the course. She wasn't registered."

"How do you know?"

"I dated her."

Howard turned to him in surprise.

"She and I sat next to each other at the back of the lecture hall," Ben said. "We got to talking. I asked if she'd like to go to a movie. We had a few beers afterward."

"You never mentioned it."

"It didn't seem important. All she talked about was Wayne McDonald, how brilliant he was, how she could listen to him forever. I never asked her to go on another date. I forgot about her until I saw her photo in the news-paper and realized who'd been killed."

"What about the police? Did you tell *them*?"

"Working part time in that pub earned barely enough for my dorm fees. You know how I paid my tuition—selling uppers to guys in our dorm who waited too long to study for exams or write term papers. I helped them pull all-nighters."

"I always wondered where you got the pills."

"The police would have wondered, too. How long would it have taken them to make a drug dealer a suspect? They could've decided I was furious because Rebecca refused to go out with me again after she discovered how I earned money, or they might have decided I shut her up after she threatened to tell the police I sold drugs. Neither would have been the truth, but by the time the police realized it, my reputation would have been dirt. I'd just received a scholarship to USC. I couldn't risk losing it."

The night breeze turned colder. Ben pushed his hands deeper into the jacket's pockets.

"And you've been thinking about her ever since?" Howard asked.

"I remember her sitting across from me in the pub we just came from. The same booth, in fact. Tonight, *you* sat exactly where *she* did twenty years ago."

"You're creeping me out."

"I'm going to write about her again, but this time, it won't be only a brief scene. It'll be about a man who feels guilty because his ambition might have let a murderer escape twenty years earlier. He comes back for his college homecoming to find who did it."

"You're here doing research?" Howard asked.

"And to see *you* again. It's been a long time."

"Yeah, somehow we could never get our schedules to match," Howard said. "Sounds like an interesting movie."

"Well, it has a lot of twists. For example, the main character's best friend dated the murdered woman, also."

In the darkness, Howard peered down at the murky leaves. On the street far behind them, car horns blared. Engines roared. Students whooped. The night became quiet again.

"I didn't date her," Howard said.

"She pointed at you in class. She told me you went out with her."

"It wasn't a date."

"She told me she hoped I wasn't going to try what *you* did."

"It wasn't what it sounds like."

"What *was* it then?" Ben asked.

"I often visited Wayne during his office hours. You knew that."

"You were his favorite student."

"He hadn't adjusted to being a faculty member," Howard said. "He missed being in graduate school. He liked hanging out with me. A couple of times, he invited me to his apartment to have dinner with his wife and three-year-old daughter. I said 'office hours.' Actually he met students in the cafeteria at our dorm. It was obvious he was avoiding his office. It was also obvious he had something he wanted to say to me. Finally, he told me there was a female student who wasn't registered for his classes but was showing up for all of them. He told me she'd followed him from his previous college, that he'd given up a job offer there because of her."

Another horn blared in the distance. More students whooped.

"Why did she follow him?" Ben asked.

"Wayne swore he hadn't been involved with her. He'd been hired as an instructor in his last year at the previous college. Rebecca Markle had been one of his students. He said he'd treated her like any other student, but she thought he meant more than what he was actually saying in his lectures, that he was sending her coded messages, telling her she was special to him. Remember how he made eye contact with every student as he lectured. He scanned back and forth, making it seem he spoke directly to each of us."

"A gifted teacher," Ben agreed. "What did he want you to do?"

"To talk to her, one student to another, and persuade her to leave him alone. Not only *him*. He said his wife had seen Rebecca outside the apartment building where they lived and outside the nursery school where his wife dropped off and picked up their daughter. They were scared."

The night's chill made Ben shiver. "After Rebecca was murdered, did you tell the police about what he'd asked you to do?"

"No."

"Why not?"

"That would have made him a suspect, and I didn't believe he killed her. Where are you going with this, Ben? Is what *I* did any different from what *you* did, keeping quiet because you were afraid the police would suspect *you*?"

"Sorry for being intense. You remember how I used to get when we were students and I was working on a story. Where am I going with this? Back to the hotel to get some sleep. Tomorrow will be busy."

———— • ● • ————

First came an alumni breakfast, where he told good-natured Hollywood gossip about what happened behind the scenes of the films he'd written. Then he gave advice to actors in the theater department. Then he spoke at a lunch for major donors, emphasizing how he wouldn't have had a career if not for the excellent education he'd received here.

At the football stadium, he met numerous dignitaries in the college president's skybox. When he'd been a student, he hadn't been able to afford to go to a football game. This was the first game he'd ever seen that wasn't on television. Even from the top of the stadium, he heard the crack of helmet against helmet.

When the second half started, he pretended to walk toward the near-by men's room, passed it, descended stairs, and reached the car-crammed parking lot. In autumn sunlight that made him squint, he walked past brilliantly colored maple trees toward the library. Having written a film about electronic surveillance, he noticed cameras on various buildings, cameras that hadn't been there twenty years earlier and that might have recorded Rebecca Markle's movements.

Ben passed the English/philosophy building and climbed the stately steps to the column-flanked doors that led to the vast library building. Inside the echoing vestibule, he needed a moment to orient himself after not having been here for twenty years. Then he shifted to the right, passed through an archway, and entered an area where numerous computers occupied rows of tables. On homecoming Saturday while a football game was in progress, only a few students studied the screens. There were cameras here as well. If they'd been installed twenty years earlier, they'd have recorded Rebecca Markle passing through this room and perhaps have revealed someone following her.

He went to the back of the room, passed through an arch, and climbed stone stairs. More cameras. He could have used an elevator, but he'd once written a scene in which a character got a nasty surprise when stepping from an elevator, and the intensity of writing that scene had stayed with him ever since.

On the third landing, he passed beneath another camera, walked along a narrow corridor lined with books, turned a corner, proceeded along a further corridor of books, and entered a small, square, windowless area that had a desk and a wooden chair. He'd visited here several times during his final year. In his imagination, he had returned here many times since.

It was here that Rebecca Markle had been murdered.

He peered down at the floor. She'd lain in her blood after the killer had attacked from behind, reaching around her, plunging a knife into her chest.

Plunging repeatedly.

Footsteps made him turn toward the only entrance to this area.

Howard appeared.

"You followed me?" Ben asked.

"Didn't need to."

"Oh?"

"If you're researching Rebecca's murder, the logical place for you to be is here, at 3:30 when the medical examiner estimated she was killed," Howard said. "I watched the library entrance from the far side of the English/philosophy building."

"You could have been a detective instead of an English professor."

"Or someone in a movie you wrote. Do you seriously think I killed her?"

"I never suggested that."

"Like hell. You set me up last night. 'Did they ever find who killed that female student?' you asked. You must have enjoyed listening to me pretend I didn't remember who Rebecca Markle was. Then you forced me to admit I'd gone out with her. It wasn't a date. I was trying to help Wayne."

"Okay," Ben said. "It wasn't a date."

"I can play your game in reverse. Last night, you gave all sorts of reasons for me to believe *you* killed her. Maybe she threatened to tell the police how you earned your money. Maybe you couldn't bear the thought of USC finding out and cancelling your scholarship."

"That would have been a powerful motivation," Ben agreed.

"It would have made more sense than any motive you tried to invent for *me*."

"I don't believe you killed her."

Howard looked surprised.

"But role playing helps me write stories," Ben said. "If this were a detective movie, you'd be a suspect until somebody else seemed likely."

"So you're convinced Wayne did in fact kill her?"

"He had a sort-of alibi because a few people remembered seeing him at the football game. But according to the rumor, he slipped out the same way *I* did. I bet when I go back to the game, no one will realize I've been gone."

"He'd need to have brought a knife," Howard said. "I can't imagine him cold-bloodedly planning to murder someone."

"If only there'd been cameras in the library twenty years ago," Ben said. "They might have shown someone following Rebecca, just as today they showed *you* following *me*. But I don't believe she was followed."

"You think the attack was random?" Howard asked. "A predator saw her alone in here? An attempted rape turned into murder?"

"Or perhaps someone was already waiting."

"I don't understand."

"Perhaps Rebecca came here to meet someone."

"Now you're back to Wayne. No one else had a motive," Howard said. He took a step forward. The tiny space felt even smaller.

"I shouldn't have come back," Ben said.

"Maybe not," Howard told him.

"Would you like to know how my script would end?"

"Never make your audience impatient."

"The audience would suddenly realize that seemingly casual remarks made earlier were actually clues. There'd be a quick cut to a previous scene. 'How's your family?' the detective asked. 'Our daughter graduated from here two years ago,' the apparent suspect answered. He meant his stepchild. 'And your wife?' the detective asked. 'Depression isn't anybody's friend,' the apparent suspect answered. A quick cut to another scene would show the apparent suspect talking about spending time with the assistant professor, his wife, and their three-year-old daughter."

Howard stepped even closer.

"Yes, I spent a lot of time with Wayne and his family," he said.

"And with his wife and his daughter after Wayne died," Ben said.

"Dammit, *somebody* had to. People assumed Wayne was the killer. They avoided his wife. Their little girl wasn't welcome at the nursery school any longer. I was the only person who showed them kindness. She wanted to leave town, to take her daughter and live with her parents in Minneapolis while she tried to recover from Wayne's death and figure out what to do next. I told her if she ran, people would believe they were right to suspect Wayne. She had to stay, to show them they were wrong."

"You were in love with her?" Ben asked.

"From the first time I saw her."

Ben peered down at the floor where Rebecca Markle had lain. "Yes, I shouldn't have come back."

"So how is your screenplay going to end?" Howard asked.

"Wayne's wife . . ."

"Yes? What about her?"

". . . could have asked Rebecca to meet her in the library. Rebecca wouldn't have expected any trouble here. Afraid for her family, Wayne's wife begged Rebecca to leave her husband and child alone. When Rebecca refused, when she turned and walked away, Wayne's wife . . ."

"Pulled the knife from her purse?" Howard asked. "She planned it?"

"As a last resort. After she saw Rebecca at the day-care center, she was desperate."

"In the story," Howard said.

"Yes. In the story. Then maybe Wayne suspected what she'd done. Maybe he saw blood on the sleeve of a blouse or a sweater his wife had been wearing. Maybe he became so distressed he couldn't concentrate until a week later he lost control of his car and . . ."

"In the story," Howard repeated.

"Yes. In the story."

"What's that movie where everybody sees the same thing but every version is different? It's Japanese."

"*Rashomon.*"

"I remember we watched it together. Your story could be like that. Different versions of what happened. None truer than the other. Me killing her, you killing her, Wayne killing her, a predator killing her."

"But not Wayne's wife?" Ben asked.

"Definitely not Wayne's wife. She couldn't have done it. She had an alibi. She was at home, taking care of their little girl."

"Yes, to meet Rebecca, she'd have needed a babysitter," Ben said. "Someone she trusted. Someone who maybe saw blood on a sleeve when she returned home. Someone who never mentioned it to the police or contradicted her when she told the police she'd been taking care of her little girl at the time of the murder."

"Hard to find someone she could depend on that much," Howard said.

"Yes, hard to find." Ben peered down at the floor again. "I think I talked the story to death."

"When we were students, that used to happen to you."

"I'd better get back to the game. The college president has a lot more donors he wants me to convince to be generous."

"Good luck with them."

"I'll do my best since this is my last homecoming."

An Even Three

by Reed Farrel Coleman

Susan Kiner gazed out her classroom window in Striker Hall at the cloyingly scenic setting of Halleyton College and groused to herself about how far she had failed to come.

"Nice place to be buried," she'd said to Henry Corbin during her interview. Corbin was her former student and current Dean of Humanities at Halleyton.

She kept a pleasant expression as she watched Henry laugh off the remark. Susan was sure that like everyone else, he was chalking it up to her famously prickly personality and sarcastic sense of humor. "She makes Dorothy Parker seem like Mother Teresa. Susan's a handful," she had once overheard a Vice Provost at Arizona State say to a donor. She knew Henry still bore some scars her biting remarks had left when she was his thesis advisor and lover at UW, Madison. But Susan had been perfectly serious, because buried is what she was. This small liberal arts college surrounded by the endless evergreens and grass-carpeted mountains of northern New England was her last stop, the pine-scented sarcophagus in which her career in academia would be put to rest.

Her late husband, the Nobel Prize-winning economist Max Schlegel, used to joke during Passover Seders that the holiday should serve both as a celebration of the Jews' emancipation from slavery in Egypt and as a testament to how many times his wife had failed to get tenure.

"Dear, Jesus, Susan, talk about being passed over. First Wisconsin, then

ASU, and NYU. You've missed the cut more times than a shaky handed surgeon." And that was before it happened again at Princeton. Comments like that helped account for Max no longer being part of her life.

Now as she waited for her Ethics 1 class to show, the flavor of her own bile soured the last pleasant grace notes of her morning latte. *Bitter.* She had much to be bitter about. Sure, at the beginning of her career, when she was just learning how to navigate the maze of departmental politics, she bought into the bullshit that women did not get tenure, especially in philosophy departments. But the bitterness was less about her own complicity and more about the way she had degraded herself in order to move her career along. It killed her to think about the men she had forced herself to sleep with in order to get their votes for tenure, the men who always had excuses when the votes in her favor fell short. Their bad teeth and body odor, dandruff and ineptitude. *God, their ineptitude!*

She saw her reflection in the pane of glass. *I'm still pretty sexy for an old bird,* she thought without joy. And for a woman in her late fifties, Susan Kiner certainly was still awfully attractive, in the vein of the mature Lauren Bacall. Unfortunately, pretty continued to be a curse for smart women. The #metoo movement hadn't changed that. Her male classmates and colleagues thought she hadn't seen the bathroom graffiti or heard their whispered locker room witticisms. Of course she had, from her first day in graduate school until her last days at Princeton. *The woman who put the pussy in PhD The girl who put the cunt in Kant.* Where had her looks gotten her? Where had the politicking and bad sex gotten her? Where had the scholarship and publications gotten her? Halleyton fucking College, that's where!

The creaking of the huge oak classroom door broke her bile-infused trance. She turned away from her fir-tree-framed reflection to see a procession of sleepy-faced eighteen- and nineteen-year-olds zombie walk to their seats. There were twelve of them, seven girls and five boys. Eco-friendly coffee cups in one hand, unfortunately ironic cell phones in the other. Susan had to confess she liked the small class size. You could do some actual teaching in a small class, really get to know your students this way. She dispensed with introductions and got right to it. This had always been her style. *Attack!*

"The Trolley Dilemma, have any of you heard of it?"

A girl in the front row raised her hand and spoke without waiting to be acknowledged, "Is that anything like a subway dilemma? Because in New York, we face that all the time."

A few of them laughed. Some rolled their eyes. Some were still panicked at the thought of being away from their helicopter and bulldozer parents for the first time.

"Nice," Susan said, "but no. So, on to the Trolley—"

"Aren't we going to introduce ourselves to each other?" It was a slender boy in the second row, handsome. His demeanor was that odd late teenage combination of shy and cocky. "It's rude, isn't it, to just start this way?"

Susan could feel her guts burning. She had no respect for modern students, students who grew up in a participation trophy world. Students who couldn't sit on the toilet without wearing a safety belt or a motorcycle helmet. Spoiled, coddled, risk-aversive little twats whose feelings got bruised more easily than the orange flesh of an overripe mango. The burn in her belly and her expression of it is what had been the final nail of her coffin at Princeton. *Don't react! Don't react!* It had become her mantra a little too late to save her job there.

When he was interviewing her, Henry Corbin recalled several stories that were part of the lore of Susan Kiner. She smirked when, with a nervous cough, Henry broached the subject. *He would never have had the balls to bring this stuff up when he was my student*, she thought, *or when he was in my bed. But now that he's got me pinned and wriggling . . .*

"Susan, did you actually throw a student out of your classroom for arguing with you about causality?"

She laughed, remembering the incident as clearly as if it'd happened ten minutes earlier. "I was using the example of a shooter, a gun, a bullet, and the victim's resulting death. This kid interrupts me to say, 'The victim didn't die from the bullet wound. He died because he believed the bullet would kill him.' She laughed again. "I told him to get the fuck out of my classroom and that if he ever said anything so unreasoned and stupid in my class again, I'd fail his ass. Kid got an A and the rest of the class got the message. Philosophy class isn't a place for bullshit. It's exactly the opposite."

Susan could see that Corbin was genuinely horrified at the obvious glee she took in relating the story. She enjoyed his discomfort.

"And the Valencia Captree Award, did you really—"

"Ah, yes, Valencia Captree." Susan's face fairly glowed at the mention. "When I was an undergrad at Columbia, there was a question on my metaphysics midterm asking us to define a believer. Our prof, Mitch Schare—you remember Mitch. Anyway, he read the answers aloud before returning our booklets. Valencia Captree defined a believer as 'One who doubted the existence of God.' To this day, I have never heard a stupider answer to any question and that's saying something. So for years, I'd give out the Valencia Captree Award to the student who gave the dumbest test answer of the term. It was all in good fun."

Her pleasure was short-lived. Corbin's expression turned icy. "Not here, Susan. No Valencia Captree Awards. No kicking kids out of class. No cursing. You use the pronouns students ask you to use when addressing them. You warn them if the subjects you are going discuss involve race, religion, sex, and/or violence. We believe in safe spaces and microaggressions at Halleyton."

"You're kidding me, right?"

But one glance across the desk and she knew Corbin wasn't kidding. "I owe you a lot for helping me get my degree and for introducing me to the joys of earthly delights, but I don't owe you my career. You're brilliant, Susan, but you're a pain in the ass. This is your last roundup. I think we both understand that."

That was months back and though she didn't much like the rules she accepted that they were going to be strictly enforced and that she had better toe the line.

"There are five people tied to the tracks of a trolley line," she said to the class, the stern warnings during the interview with Corbin now only a vague memory.

A boy in the back seemed perplexed. "Trolley. What's a trolley?"

"Like in San Francisco, man," a girl in the class answered. "Like the light rail system between here and town."

"There are five people tied to the tracks of a trolley line," Susan began again. "If nothing is done to divert the trolley, the five people tied to the track will surely die beneath the wheels of the trolley car." She was careful not to point at any one of the students. "*You* are alone, standing by the track switch, but notice that there is a single person tied to the track onto which you would divert the trolley. Your choice is clear. If you don't act to divert the trolley, five people will die. If you do divert the trolley, one person will die. Your dilemma is clear. What decision do you make and why do you make it?"

These kids are bright, she thought. They asked the right questions. *Can we know anything about the people tied to the tracks? What if the five people tied to the main track are all violent felons and the one tied to the side track is a cancer researcher?* She actually enjoyed the discussion in spite of the fact that she had taught this class and used this example for over thirty years. She stopped the discussion when there was a natural lull, taking that as a cue to do the perfunctory introductions, explain about tests and papers, and to give the reading list. She ended by saying, "We will return to the Trolley Dilemma throughout the term to see if your attitudes are changed by your reading and research on the subject."

When she headed to her office, Susan Kiner was optimistic that this green and pleasant land wouldn't be the soul-crushing purgatory she feared it might be. Her optimism lasted until about four that afternoon when there was a knock on her office door. It was a contrite, embarrassed-looking Henry Corbin. Contrite and embarrassed, but displeased. She gestured for him to sit, but he declined. The air went right out of her.

"Okay, what is it, Henry? I thought my two classes went very well."

"I had a visit from one of your Ethics students."

"Which one?"

He shook his head. "Who is irrelevant. It's what that matters."

"In English, please, Henry. Or does the code of conduct not permit you discuss things I am not allowed to discuss? Am I supposed to intuit the substance of the complaint through your body language?"

He laughed in spite of himself. "Frankly, I find the complaint ridiculous, but . . ."

"But the parents of these students pay a fortune, education and the rules of normal human behavior be damned."

"Something like that, yes. The Trolley Dilemma, you should have warned the students that there was potential violence involved in the discussion."

"You're putting me on, right?" She got up from her desk and looked behind the door, checked her bookcases. "This is like *Punked* or *Candid Camera,* right? You're recording this, hoping you'll get a rise out of me to show at some faculty dinner."

"I wish it was a joke and I hate even having to bring it up, Susan, but I'm serious. There are six potential deaths involved in the Trolley Dilemma, violent deaths. Keep that in mind in the future. Fortunately, I've convinced the student not to make the complaint a formal one."

She was tempted to demand to know the complaining student's identity and at other points in her career she might have been willing to go to any length to force it out of him. *What do you think the president of the college and the executive board would think of their Dean of Humanities if I told them you enjoyed choking me when we fucked? Or that you used to beg me to let you watch another man fuck me while you masturbated.* But she didn't go there except in her head. She was grateful to Henry and she already thought she knew who the student in question was. Drew Bishop was the handsome boy from the Ethics class, the one with the shy/cocky affect and the one who was disappointed at her rudeness.

"Thank you, Henry, it won't happy again. I'm sure you understand I'm a little new to this level of oversight. Forgive me."

He seemed heartened by her response. "No need for that, Susan. You know how much I admire you. Why don't you come for dinner tonight? Peg would love to see you."

"Thanks for the invite, but I have to say no. Another night, okay? I've got plans."

She hadn't had plans until Henry Corbin walked into her office. She had them now because, finally, she had had enough. She had taken all the crap she was going to take and the time had come to give it back.

Men liked to think themselves enigmatic creatures, mistaking their own emotional confusion for complexity. Susan Kiner had a very different view of the male of the species. Women were complex. Men were simple and the younger they were, the more they believed themselves complicated masters of the universe. That made them easy targets. She had only a solitary target in mind. Step one was to find out if he was straight. Given how Drew returned the admiring glances of the girls in class, Susan was confident he was straight. If he was gay, that would make things more difficult. Not impossible, but it would mean getting at least one more person involved. She had no desire to do that nor would she let herself be pushed.

She would take her time. It was her experience that hurrying things along led to mistakes and that a quick victory was also an unsatisfying one. No, she would not be rushed. She would no longer suppress nor swallow, accommodate nor accept the indignities, the hurts, the lies, the false promises, the rejections, the faithlessness, and disloyalty visited upon her. She would let the burn in her belly smolder, let it rage until it would nearly consume her. Then, and only then, would she take her revenge. As her late husband had found out, there would be nothing micro about her aggression.

Absurdly, wonderfully, Halleyton made itself complicit in her plan. Due to the small size of the student body and the school's philosophy, the kids were compelled to visit with their individual professors in the professors' offices for a half hour every two weeks. Susan had made sure to schedule Drew early in week two, but at the end of the day so that there would be no appointments to follow.

"Hello, Drew, please have a seat," Susan said, without looking up from her desk.

She listened, making sure to let him sit in silence for a bit. Silence, she had found over the course of her career, was very telling. Some silences were loud and expressive. Some still and uncomfortable. Most people, Millennials in particular, were ill at ease with silence. She wondered how long it would be before he pulled out his pacifier cell phone to occupy himself. One thing she noticed immediately was the overwhelming blast of Drew's grassy cologne. *Teenage boys and cologne! It took them until their mid-twenties to understand that a little bit went a long way.* But she was encouraged. *He wants to impress me, to be attractive to me. Boys and older women.* She had always thought Freud a bit of a pompous clown, but she had to confess that maybe he had something right about men and their mothers.

Susan and Max hadn't had children. That was one decision they got right. They both understood there would never be enough oxygen in the room for a child of their making. There was barely enough breathable air when they were in a room together. Funny that she should think about Max—a man with a Nobel Prize and a Nobel Prize-worthy cock—with this boy sitting across from her. But then again, no. The bedroom was really the only honest place in a house. The one place where all the artifice, awards, and degrees became moot. The place in the house that gave completely different meanings to supply and demand and to the categorical imperative.

She looked up. "Hello, Drew."

He tried not to smile, failed miserably. He was already hooked, but she was going to slow walk it. They made some small talk, then moved on to the readings she had assigned and to a discussion of how to approach his first paper. Before he left, she made a point of apologizing for failing to do proper introductions during their first class and for not warning the students about the violent nature of the Trolley Dilemma.

"Oh, that's okay, Professor Kiner."

He was hooked, alright.

After their second class, she had "accidently" let her hand brush against his as she passed him in the hallway. After the third class meeting of Ethics 1, she dropped some papers on the floor as he was leaving. Dutifully as a dog, he stopped, turned, and helped her gather them up. When she thanked him, she made certain there was more in her voice than simple appreciation. She let her stare linger. But it wasn't until their third office visit that she moved beyond the occasional longing look and flirty comments.

"Drew, I know this can get me fired, but . . ." She was properly hesitant. "Would you like to have dinner with me tonight? Oh, God . . ." She acted embarrassed, her face blushing red. "Please, I'm sorry if—"

"I'd love that," he said. The hero saving the damsel from distress.

Dinner went uneaten that evening. Susan even enjoyed herself some. She had forgotten about the staying power and endurance of young men. He was unskilled but enthusiastic and not utterly inept. Mostly he was smitten and that was the point.

"Please, Drew, you can't tell anyone about us. I mean it," she whispered, licking his ear, playfully biting it. "We'll both be kicked out of here and I can't—"

He squeezed her tight, stroking her hair. "Never."

On his fourth office visit, she locked the door behind Drew and cleaned off her desktop. Drew didn't need to be told what to do. In bed the next night, she asked him a favor.

"I need some help with a paper I'm working on."

She had him interested. "A paper?"

"I still do get published, you know."

He looked a little panicked and was quick to apologize. "Sorry. What's it about?"

"The Ethical Dilemma of Suicide."

His eyes got big. "What is it you need me to do?"

She swung her legs off the bed, but slyly stopped herself, leaned back and kissed him hard on the mouth. Only fifteen minutes later did she finally climb out of bed.

She brought back a list of publications. "I'm so busy, I can't do all the research I need to do. If you help me, I'll name you as one of my co-authors and you'll have your first publication credit."

His eyes got big with excitement. "Really? You'd do that?"

"For you, lover, anything. Oh, and one last thing." She handed him a second piece of paper. "This is a suicide note written by a student at MIT and it presents the dilemma perfectly. You'll see. Do me a favor, make a file of it on your computer. My office printer isn't working and this is the only copy I have."

He put the research list and the copy of the handwritten letter on the nightstand before pulling Susan back into bed.

It was the day after the Ethics 1 final exam when she put the terminal steps into play. The timing was perfect as there was a snowstorm predicted for the morning. The snow would help obscure any potential mistakes or evidence left behind. For two weeks now, they had been meeting for nighttime walks in different wooded areas off campus. He was initially hesitant, but Susan knew how to deal with that.

"But, Sooz, aren't you afraid we'll get caught?" he asked, looking over his shoulder during the first of their little hikes.

"I'm a little ashamed, Drew, but I've got an intense fantasy about having you out in the open air." And before he could say another word in objection, she dropped to her knees.

He never again asked about getting caught.

That last night, they met at a rocky spot called Blind Bend. She got there ahead of him and when Drew arrived, Susan handed him a glass of champagne.

"To us, lover."

"To us."

They clinked glasses and drank. She poured him another glass.

"What are we celebrating?"

"Our paper on the Ethical Dilemma of Suicide . . . it was accepted for publication." She hugged him tightly, kissed him.

"That's fucking great, Sooz. Wow!"

"I'll tell you what's great, the way your mouth tastes of champagne. One more glass and I'm going to make you feel like you've never felt before."

He drank that glass in a single gulp. She saw the recognition in his eyes that something wasn't right. She saw it and felt a cold burn inside, a jolt more electric than handing out a thousand Valencia Captree Awards. Drew became unsteady, his eyes rolled up into his head. It appeared to her that his wobbly legs were losing their will to hold him upright.

"My head is all cottony, Sooz," he said. "Your face is . . . droopy. I don't feel good."

She was laughing now, enjoying the fruits of her labor.

"Why . . . why are . . . you laughing?"

That halting question was to be his epitaph. His eyes closed. Gravity grabbed him by the hair and yanked him toward the center of the earth.

Susan unfolded the tarp she had hidden behind a big glacial boulder, rolled Drew and the champagne bottle onto it, and carefully pulled them down the hill to the light rail tracks. This is why she had chosen Blind Bend. When the train came around the curve, it would be impossible for the engineer to see the body on the tracks and to stop the train. Susan had timed it and tested it with a road kill raccoon. She checked her watch. *Ten minutes.* She removed Drew's gloves and formed his right hand around the neck of the bottle. Pressed his lips to the bottle top, poured some more of the drugged liquid into his mouth and onto his coat. She dropped the bottle far enough away from the tracks to make certain it would be found intact, then folded up the tarp and made her way back up the hill to watch.

At her perch, she collected the plastic glass from which Drew had been drinking and checked for any other objects that might give her away. When the light rail train blew its horn, Susan smiled and said. "Hello, Trolley. Goodbye, lover." Susan found the little split of untampered champagne she had poured her drinks from and made a silent toast to the sacrificial lamb who had died in lieu of all the assholes who had conspired to steal her career and dignity from her. The horn blew again. Brakes screeched and . . . Snow was already falling as she made her way back to campus.

Because Drew had died so near the end of term, the memorial service was held the first week of the spring semester. Susan sat to Henry Corbin's right on the other side of the aisle from the kid's family.

"Did you know he was so depressed?" Corbin asked in a whisper.

She shook her head. "I had no clue."

"He was apparently obsessed with suicide. The police found all sorts of research on the subject on his computer and a file with a suicide note."

"That's terrible."

"He mixed himself up quite a cocktail in that champagne bottle and just laid down across the tracks. Made sure he did it where the train couldn't help but kill him."

"So sad."

There was a loud sob from behind them and they both turned to see Ella Farnboro nearly fainting with grief. Ella had been in Susan's Ethics 1 class with Drew.

"That bitch!" Corbin's whisper had grown fangs.

Even Susan was taken aback. "Bitch?"

"She's the one who complained about you and the violence of the Trolley Dilemma. She's complained about every one of her professors for either being racist, sexist, ageist . . . There seems to be no end to what that girl finds offensive."

"Why put up with her?"

"Her father's an important alum and a huge contributor to our endowment. Three and a half more years of that girl and I think I'll do what Drew did."

Susan said nothing. She felt no guilt. Whether Drew had been the real offending party or not was beside the point. She did, however, enjoy the notion of ridding the world of Ella Farnboro. Ella would make it an even three. There was a certain symmetry in groups of three that appealed to the human aesthetic. It certainly appealed to hers.

She stifled a laugh, thinking about how cleanly she had managed victims one and two. At least there had been some perks and challenges in murdering Drew. Max . . . Max had been almost too easy. Twenty-five years

Susan's senior, he had been suffering the onset of dementia. That, along with a chronic heart condition—"He didn't have one," Susan was wont to say—made it all rather simple. No one raised any questions when it was determined Max's death was due to his overmedicating himself.

She looked back once more at Ella the Grieving and smiled on the inside. Susan Kiner had returned to Halleyton unhappy at the prospect of a second term of teaching the brats, a term without intrigue or plans. Ella had rescued her from her fate and for that much she was grateful to the girl. Halleyton was, as Susan anticipated, a burial ground. Only it would not be hers.

Writing Maeve Dubinsky

by Jane Hamilton

We were seniors at our failing liberal arts college in the Midwest when Maeve Dubinsky materialized. Miss Dubinsky, the updated, inclusive version of the grim reaper suddenly in the room. Why shouldn't a woman be Death? It was surprising how swiftly the end came, the shameful revelation of mismanagement of the endowment, the trustees themselves blindsided, the new President out of his depth, the Congregational college founded in 1848 so far from its ideals. We were in our final semester. When I say *we* I'm referring not to all my classmates but to Ito Flores, my boyfriend, and me. It was said that we were the most gorgeous couple on campus, the seventeen acres where the lawn upkeep had been suspended. Ito and I the last great blooms. I record our winning the virtual beauty contest with the disdain it deserves. The lovely and the plain alike hoped to get out before the place, come May, was a jungle.

That semester Maeve Dubinsky had been hired at the eleventh hour to teach our Advanced Fiction Workshop. You've heard of Maeve Dubinsky, right? She was replacing a prominent writer who must suddenly have fabricated an emergency, who had the good sense to stay away. Maeve Dubinsky, half Irish Catholic, half Polish Jew, age fifty-nine. When we got the bulletin about her as the replacement we glanced at her memoir that chronicled various abusive situations in her childhood. We could hardly look at the pages, the beatings and worse of the Irish father and uncles, and the torment raining down upon her from the Jewish grandmother. It wasn't the violence in her life but her claim to suffering that bothered us, the triumphant tone of the book. She was a young woman in her author photo, her hair pulled back, her head filling the frame, as if she were an animal who'd come right up to your face to sniff you. There was a novel covering the same terrain, Irish and Jewish abuse, both books published decades before to "critical acclaim." The kiss of death, it is said of such praise, Miss Dubinsky having to pick up teaching jobs where she could. Or, quite possibly she'd exhausted her subject matter, nothing more to report.

At first there were ten of us in the workshop including Ito Flores, my Ito a quarter Japanese, half Mexican, the last quarter Northern European with a splash of an unnamed Native American tribe. My mongrel was six foot two inches, he had large dark eyes with soft black lashes, his sleek braid suggesting both the tidy peacefulness of a woman and the warrior impulse of a horseback-riding Native. He'd been raised in a middle class mixed neighborhood in Chicago, Mister United Nations moving down the street in his macho, yet graceful way. His mother taught in a tony suburban private school which he attended, Ito prized and at home in the world.

Through no fault of my own I am a White Anglo Saxon Protestant from Madison, Wisconsin. Emma Louise Howard. A super-duper hoarder of privilege. Tall, slim but not skinny, with a sweet little bosom and excellent legs. At the risk of tedium, because there is nothing more tiresome than beauty, I once overheard my high school drama teacher saying to another faculty member that I was the most exquisite girl—no, exquisite person, he amended—in my school. A student body of 2100. He surely meant beautiful inside and out. I had always tried to be as kind as possible. I loathed haughtiness. Even while being crowned Prom Queen and cast as Eleanor of Aquitaine in *The Lion In Winter*. A human being gets the goods by the luck of the draw and must use her gifts wisely. My mother's words. *You were made to be admired*, a friend of mine said in a matter-of-fact way. We both knew she could have stated her idea about my purpose in a crass manner. I had and still have a nimbus—yes, a nimbus—of auburn hair, creamy skin, heavy-lidded green eyes, a noble profile. As a girl I was partial to my mouth and beginning at about age ten I could imagine someone wanting to kiss it. I used to stare at the curve of my lips in the mirror. So: good for me! I understood that I needed to study hard in order to honestly reach my goals. Maybe because of the attention people paid me I had always been shy. I loved books and by first grade was determined to be a writer.

On the fiction workshop roster, in addition to Ito and me, there were two Chinese students, full pay, and a boy from Detroit, Jesse Pearlwater, who had been groomed for the liberal arts by an organization that finds promising inner city kids who have a chance of academic success. Jesse, hounded by bad luck, coming from a city in crisis to a college that no one knows is on the brink of extinction. In our class there were also four average English majors from places like Edina, Minnesota. The bank of silent girls, we called them. And last, there was Iris Irvington. Iris was a junior from Davenport, Iowa. She was a good listener, quiet but friendly. It was known that she was a writer of great talent but she didn't behave as if the Associated Colleges prize for a short story, which she'd won the previous year, glory with a thousand-dollar check, made her any different from the rest of us struggling to put words to paper. She had pale brown hair, and glasses of a shape I can't recall. There was nothing about her that drew attention, a slightly overweight young woman in a sweatshirt with the name of our doomed college on the front, and baggy pants. In truth, I can hardly bring her face to mind. It seemed likely that she'd never had a girl or boyfriend. That's not something I knew for sure, but the stories I'd read of hers in Intermediate Writing Workshop were often about characters who were achingly lonely. She was clearly writing what she knew.

Did Ito and I have talent? I had been told that I did. In my college years thus far I had earned praise for my poems and stories, my memoir, and my one-act play. Ito was a studio art major with the goal of studying Urban Planning at the graduate level. He could draw any given thing with vibrating exactitude, he was an uninhibited dancer, his poetry was spare and tender, drums were a favorite instrument, Ito artistic in every sphere.

When Maeve Dubinsky came into Fuston Hall 203 on the first day of class we all gaped at her. It was impolite but we couldn't help it. We thought, not out of a mean spirit, but from genuine curiosity: *What is it?*

Her young author photo no longer pertained. She had long messy grey hair, a tremendous amount of volume in that wiry heap. A middle-aged woman who needs to retain her badge of girlhood? It's an embarrassment. Unfortunately, there is no way to render her precisely and in the same stroke be generous. We'd later laugh at the two small silver barrettes at either side of her head, as useful as two paperclips meant to hold together a bed of kelp. There is more. I'm afraid the hair was not the only cause of our disbelief. Steel yourself. She was wearing a blue and white gingham dress, like Dorothy on the yellow brick road. White knee socks and old-fashioned blue cloth tennis shoes.

Who dresses like this? We all looked at each other with the question spinning in our eyeballs. It was an unseasonably warm January day but even so we might have inquired further and wondered who wore such a garment in winter?

On that first day Miss Dubinsky read a short story out loud to us, which took a full hour. You will think: Emma Howard is a writer of fiction, she is making much of this up, overloading the details, the sign of an amateur. In addition to the absurdities I've mentioned it's a fact that Miss Dubinsky had unpleasant-looking crooked grey teeth, and an almost lisp, a thickness in her s sound. Was there not one good thing about our teacher, for the mother who insists that if you can't say something nice remain silent? One feature or aspect that wasn't repulsive? She appeared to have good eyesight, no need of glasses.

I very much enjoyed being read to, Ito on most nights reading a chapter from a gentle British mystery. But listening to Maeve—as we sometimes called her to ourselves—listening to her reading a *New Yorker* story from the 1950s was nearly intolerable, not least because she'd laugh ahead of the lines she knew were going to be amusing. When Lisa Lee's phone rang in the middle of the story Maeve looked as if she were going to draw two pistols from her gingham pockets and shoot Lisa dead. Lisa cried, "Emergency!" and fled. We all wanted to drop the class but we were too nice to do so. Ito said later, "We should want to help her, Babe."

"Oh, my god," I replied.

We wanted a refund but we understood that the college could barely put food on our plates. Lisa Lee was the only student callous enough to get out.

No one said anything when the story time was over. Maeve wiped her eyes at the poignant conclusion, her hands pressed to her flat chest. She then passed out the syllabus. During the fifteen-week semester we each would have the chance to workshop three stories. We were to meet with her to discuss our rewrites. (The spinning eyeball alarm again: under no circumstances were any of us going to be closed up in an office with her.) There were published stories to read in addition to our classmates' work, and finally, we were to keep a journal in a physical book using a pen or pencil. With our antique implements we could write about anything, Maeve said, anything at all. The assignment was meant to sharpen our observational skills. To allow for slow time, she said. *Put your goddamn phones down for ten seconds*, she meant, *look out to the world, pay attention*. We'd have to hand in the notebook periodically but if there were pages that were too personal we should staple them together to indicate NO TRESPASSING. I did not raise my hand to say that that was the kind of thing we'd had to do in junior high.

Right away I understood to what purpose I'd use my journal. Or, I thought I understood. Because of many circumstances, Ito being a transfer student, and my off-campus study program the year before, he and I had only met in September. Our love was new. I was in that concerning phase where—so in love was I—I was in danger of losing my identity, my self submerged, erased by the splendor, intelligence, and goodness of Ito Flores. Ito is typically a surname in Japan although it is occasionally given to a girl. Flores of course means flower. My girly man posy. I loved him so much I believed that the power of my feeling could kill me. That is a dramatic statement but it felt true. Now and then, however, all that feeling bored me to tears, bored me also practically to death. Containing the strength of my love and the tedium of it, the two forces together, was my current high wire act.

After class that day I went to the library, sat down at my carrel and began to pour out my heart to my handsome new soft blue leather-bound notebook. I knew that I would have to staple all the pages together but I also knew I was writing them for Miss Dubinsky. I was quite sure she would peek. She struck me as the kind of person who, like Iris, had had little or no experience with sexual love. And so, I would tell her the story of Ito Flores and Emma Howard. Ito was by no means my first boyfriend but he was my first truly grand passion. I'd write for my own pleasure about seeing him across the crowded room, his noticing me, the dance we did around each other before we came together for a prearranged meeting. We'd decided we'd walk silently through the arboretum, agreeing that we would not speak as a way to get to know each other. For some time we walked in the September twilight. When we came to the river's edge we faced each other. He took my right hand. I touched his cheek with the left. Next, for several hours, we stood at the river's edge and kissed. There was, as if at our command, a full moon. Miss Dubinsky would probably not think such a marathon make-out session possible but I would disabuse her of her fixed ideas. *Uh, Miss Dubinsky? A pair of lovers actually can stand upright for nearly three hours and kiss the shit out of each other.* By the river Ito and I admired each other fully and profoundly. We cried. We laughed. But we did not speak.

We waited for three weeks to have full-on sex, which in college time is half a century. For three weeks we talked continuously—or possibly it was I who did most of the talking—the anticipation of bed nearly shattering us. When we finally got down to it we proceeded with extreme slowness so that the experience was inter-galactic in nature, *if that makes sense, Miss Dubinsky.* I thought I should add some details in my journal for verisimilitude, or to pique her interest should it have flagged. I wrote about how once, when Ito had gone down on me, he had spread my lips so carefully, licking along my inner labia before he lashed with just the right pressure at my clitoris. He then lifted his head and said, "Emma." He repeated my name twice more. "This," he said, "is where I want to live."

That sentiment, romantic and grandiose, amid the animal pleasuring might make deep waters run in Miss Dubinsky.

I did not *share* my writing with Ito. My good boy didn't scribble in his journal but instead put down algebraic equations, the numbers and symbols looking like kanji. He made a staff on one page, hummed an original tune, and wrote down the notes as he went. On the next page he drew my hands and feet. No one would ever object to Ito interpreting the rules in his own creative style.

In my journal I had a great deal to say about him, about his upbringing in Chicago, his being a dazzling fish in the waters of his upper crust school, and about how being in love can so easily become overwhelming, how it can make a woman obsessive, terrifying to herself and to others. *Do you love me anywhere near as much as I love you? Will you love me for all time? Am I a hundred times more wonderful than all your other girlfriends put together? If your love dies I will perish. Reassure me, reassure me, reassure me!* I wasn't suicidal but I could imagine being suicidal. It was my greatest hope that Ito would never know how unhinged I sometimes felt. Emma Howard, raised by a feminist mother and father, held captive by love.

For about two weeks I wrote faithfully in the notebook. I also composed a story about being a United Parcel Service delivery person over Christmas, something that I had experienced. I'd ridden in the brown truck over winter break with a driver named Ray, running packages to the doors until December twenty-fourth at nine p.m. Ray was a fifty-eight-year-old man of few words, a man who'd driven a UPS truck for thirty years. I'm fairly sure he'd never had a helper of my caliber, *the angel* he called me, but not in a creepy way. My story was a love letter to him.

The first few weeks in our three hour Wednesday afternoon class we workshopped the silent girls' stories, we discussed Eudora Welty, Hemingway, Amy Tan, and James Baldwin. Miss Dubinsky was doing her part for diversity. She gave mini-lectures on setting, character, and plot. When no one raised a hand to answer her questions she'd quickly give up trying to draw us out, bloviating about the writers she'd met when she was at Yaddo a hundred years before, and when she taught at Columbia, that era in New York City hobnobbing with Mr. Shawn, she called him, as if she'd been published by *The New Yorker*, as if she hung around in the office halls bumping into people she considered celebrities but who meant nothing to most of us. As if our classmate, Jesse Pearlwater of Detroit, Michigan, would be impressed by the obvious fiction of Maeve Dubinsky having drinks with Norman Mailer. Presumably in her pinafore and tennis shoes.

For the first several weeks of class we slumbered and we slept.

I think it was somewhere in the timeframe of week three when I realized that A., I hadn't written in my journal in a few days because of more pressing assignments, and B., I couldn't find my journal.

I did most of my work in the library, treating my assignments as a job, my homework a location I went to daily. When my allotted time was up, I'd return to my home for domestic pursuits, exercise, and enjoyment. It was commonplace to claim a carrel in the library for a semester, to keep your books and supplies on the shelf of your real estate. I certainly would not have meant to leave my journal in the library and at first I didn't consider that negligence possible. It was somewhere in my room or in the house I shared with three other woman and our various love interests. I confess to being a slob, and it wasn't unusual to have to turn my living quarters upside down trying to find the lost object. As most things did, I figured it, too, would turn up.

On the occasions when we'd see Maeve eating in the cafeteria, always by herself, we'd turn around, go out the door, return to the house, and order a pizza. I don't know that we ever saw her with a colleague. She once arranged for a session in the union lounge where she planned to read us another *New Yorker* story from the archives. No one signed up. The other class she taught, Introduction to Creative Writing, was for freshmen, people we didn't have much contact with, students who probably also kept their distance. There was a single time when we were trapped by her. I remember exactly when it happened. Week five. It was the night before Iris Irvington's and my workshop, she and I the last to put up our first stories for discussion.

Ito and I were in a booth at the sandwich hangout downtown. We sometimes sat on the same side of the booth because, always, we wanted to be close to each other, to touch all down the sides of ourselves even while eating. Obviously, there was plenty of room for another customer. When Maeve came toward us with her tray, when she laughed nervously and asked if she could join us, when she'd already set the tray down and slipped in across from us, Ito said, "Miss Dubinsky! It's great to see you!" I stepped hard on his foot.

He asked her how she was enjoying her time on campus so far.

She made chortling noises, saying everyone had been welcoming, that the weather was brutal as she'd expected, but sub-zero temperatures were very good for getting work done, didn't we find that to be our experience, too? I asked her what she was working on. At that point she unbuttoned her heavy brown cowhide coat with darker fur at the collar and cuffs. She was wearing a pink cashmere sweater with a series of cashmere ruffles down the shoulders.

If we were looking at her it was also true that she was staring at us. It was as if her smile were an auxiliary eye, as if her optic nerves couldn't take in all that was Ito and Emma, and therefore she had to outsource some of the job to her mouth, her smile hard and wide. I was aware of the fact that the bitter cold had made my cheeks red, and that Ito's cross-country skiing had darkened his skin, his cheeks also flushed. There was the usual nimbus of my hair, and Ito's shiny black hair which was unbraided and draped sleekly over his shoulders—well, we were undoubtedly a breathtaking spectacle. Her gaze radiated more than wonder and admiration, though. Miss Dubinsky was doing the common activity that sometimes I had sensed other people doing: undressing me in the mind's eye, and next undressing Ito, and, in Maeve's case, mashing us together as if we were a Barbie and Ken doll.

I had to ask her again what she was working on, snap her out of her clumsy reverie, or maybe I asked if she kept her projects private, which, I said, was understandable.

While her lentil soup grew cold she told us about her Polish Jewish aunt, how she'd been a great ceramicist, and how she'd gotten herself, and Maeve's mother and grandmother, as well as some of the artistic bowls out of Poland in 1940, how for a time they all were hidden by a stranger—that whole awful narrative, many of the relatives dead in camps, most everything lost. Maeve was working on a history of that aunt. A story that is no longer exactly news. I'm sorry to say it, but I so am over World War II. Ito was very good, asking her follow-up questions, and murmuring how interesting her family was. As if that consideration wasn't enough, he went on to say, in a confiding way, that he had Japanese relatives who'd been in an internment camp in Washington State. I swear Maeve choked on nothing when he said that. She choked on her loneliness, and on her gratitude to Ito for hearing her story and having something in his own background that resonated with hers. Then, more terrible than all the accumulated Maeveness, plus her Holocaust tale and the choking, what did she do? She invited us to her apartment for dinner.

"I'm sorry, what?" I said.

"She's invited us to dinner!" Ito stamped on my boot.

Thankfully she did not set a date, and Ito, who now controlled the subject, was able to put it off, saying I was in a play, which she should come and see, and he was working on his final portfolio for his major.

Before we left her with her cold soup she said that the most rewarding aspect of teaching was getting to know young people like ourselves, and keeping in touch through the years.

Ito said, "That's fantastic."

We staggered up the hill from town to the library clutching each other, incapable of speech. "That didn't happen, did it?" I finally said. We both answered my question, "IT DID NOT HAPPEN." We embraced for about five minutes before we parted. I know we can't use certain words for relatively trivial purposes, and yet, while the sandwich episode was not like witnessing a shooting, it felt like an attack. It was definitely an emotional assault. Hands to our mouths—disbelief—*hold me again, please hold me.*

Shortly after that I was again digging around on my carrel shelf. There was my journal between the *American Heritage Dictionary*—Emma Howard the last living student to use a real dictionary—and my *Norton Anthology.* How many times I'd looked on the shelf! I didn't think someone had taken it. Rather, I thought, What a disorganized numbskull I am. I sat down to write about being at the cafe with Miss Dubinsky, shuddering as I went. And thankful she'd talked so much we did not have to watch her eat.

This is how a workshop was organized in that time and place. Every person received the stories that were up for workshop twenty-four hours before the class. (The learning platform for sharing called Moodle had gone south and because the college had lost much of its IT staff we had to resort to the old-fashioned way of getting our stories to each other.) Twenty-four hours was time enough to read and make comments, to prepare for discussion. Iris and I, as I said, were the last students in the first round to go up. Ito's poignant narrative about being a mixed-race boy at a fancy North Shore school had already been universally praised. I had lavished time and affection on my UPS story about Ray and was pleased with it. Because Ito and I were busy people we didn't realize that Iris hadn't sent us her story until the morning of the workshop. She and I did not have a texting relationship. There was no answer to the urgent email I wrote to her, and for the first time Ito and I showed up for Advanced Fiction Workshop without having done a critical component of the homework.

When we walked into Fuston Hall 203, the mood of the class was noticeably different than it had been in the previous weeks. The students were alert. Miss Dubinsky, at the head of the conference table, was smoothing her papers as if she'd failed to iron them the night before, as if ironing were required. I had the sensation that everyone was looking at us, seeing us, but at the same time not looking at us.

I laughed. *What's going on?*

The students tittered. *Nothing!*

Ito and I said we hadn't gotten Iris's story. *Oh! Huh! Sorry. Mistake. Everyone else has it.* Iris muttered her apology into her laptop. She said she had extra copies and would give them to us at break. Class began. Miss Dubinsky was wearing a kilt and a white blouse, placing herself into yet another absurd tableaux, this one well past the yellow brick road, the maiden lady a member of The Scottish Dance Society, the Highland Fling one of her specialties. First, we discussed the assigned Raymond Carver story. Second, my UPS piece. I no longer remember the title. People spouted the usual workshop trash: I love the way you_____. I adore the part where_____. My favorite line is_____. I only wish there were more of_____.

In the middle of the responses Miss Dubinsky asked the class what the difference between a vignette and a story was. When no one answered she seized the teachable moment and gave a mini-lecture on the subject. At the close of her topic she said that if I wanted to take the piece from vignette status to story level I would have to create fully developed characters, tension, and plot. And provide insight. As it stood it was a delightful, she said grinning hard, little sketch.

There was then a fifteen-minute break before our discussion of Iris's story began, a break that often stretched to twenty-five minutes. Everyone except Ito and me left the classroom for the vending machines, the bathroom, or the lounge to relax with their phones. Without looking at us, Iris slid her story in one direction across the table to Ito, and in the other to me. He and I never sat next to each other, maintaining the illusion for the students and for ourselves that we were independent people.

When Iris was gone he said, from across the room, "Maeve is full of shit, Babe. It's a great story."

I shrugged. Like I could care. No one had understood the stoic beauty of UPS Ray.

"I mean it," he said. "Great!"

"Read," I instructed.

When I flipped through the pages of Iris's oeuvre to see how many of them there were I was stopped at page five, a paragraph catching my eye—an expression that in this case felt literal, as if my eye had been snagged on a hook.

When Christian was making love to Pearl he found himself saying short sentences that he didn't know he believed until he'd uttered them. When his face was very near her lips, which she'd spent half her paycheck to have waxed, he always opened his eyes. He loved the velvet brown of the outer part, the girlish ramparts protecting the pink inside, the pastel Easter color of a soft animal's ear, his tongue roving her privacy before he allowed himself the delicate bulb that for him had swollen, that large bold small thing! That for him puffed itself, that for him strived and also perhaps begged. He heard himself say her name. He heard himself say, "This, Pearl, is where I want to live."

I had stopped breathing.

Pearl gripped his hair, her head tipped back, unable to do more than groan. She would later remember how reverently he'd spoken to her, and she wept, thinking that she, too, wanted him to live in the folds of her body, how she wanted to keep him there, he her secret, his very self lodged in her most private part, the pearl of her own Pearlness, and how it hurt her now, to have to see him in the world, as if she had somehow lost him, as if she had by her own mistake made him available to everyone else.

I looked in what was surely a twisted, open-mouthed way across the room to Ito. He was reading intently, his brow furrowed. I found it difficult to breathe, much less cry out. There seemed nothing to do but turn to the beginning. The title was "Writing Christian & Pearl". The story concerned a Swedish man of extreme height and handsomeness, and his lover, an African American woman from inner-city Detroit named Pearl. Such tricky fictionalizing! Ito the Swede, and I the black character. The twenty pages were a chronicle of the couple's immense charm and attractiveness and their intense love for each other, how, for instance, they had to sit side by side in restaurants, how they'd had a silent date and kissed by the river, how ravishing they were when they ravished each other, and how they seemed to be the New Jerusalem, the Swedish God with the Nubian Princess. Imagine their golden-skinned children who sadly would not be legacy students at their failing college. Everything that I had written in my journal was foundational material for the story, material that was as if tinder which Iris had blown on to make the blaze.

The story was not from the point of view of an omniscient narrator or from the close third of either Christian or Pearl. The love narrative had a frame around it, the couple's story told by an ungainly Irish American college girl named Polly Flint. Polly tells us that she finds herself imagining the particulars of this man and woman's relationship for several reasons. First, she is homely and fat and fears she will never find love. But, because she's a writer, because she believes in her own power, she knows that creating Pearl and Christian will allow her, blow by blow, to actually experience their passion. And second, as to her power, she wants to take on the challenge of probing the inner life of an African American girl from Detroit. Polly intends to see if she has the talent to inhabit a person very different from herself, Polly having grown up in a split-level ranch house in Davenport, Iowa. Most of the action takes place in Pearl's bed—the couple never gets up to eat or go to work or take a piss. In between bouts of love-making Pearl tells Christian about growing up in a neighborhood in which there often were not basic services, including running water. She describes missing a bullet not once but twice, how her little brother thought church had the same meaning as funeral, and how the family across the street who found a goat in a park brought the animal home to live in their yard. War erupted when the Bosnians from half a mile away tried to get her back. Iris was not plagiarizing from the story Jesse Pearlwater had put up a few weeks before but the setting was identical.

When Pearl is not telling stories to Christian or fucking her brains out she is obsessing about him and questioning his love for her to the point where she feels both invisible and monstrous.

The last paragraph starts with Polly closing Pearl's journal, which she has found in the cafeteria. Polly then sits down to write the love story that we are presently reading. She admits that so searing is her wish for love, she would rather be Pearl than Polly Flint; she would trade her own privilege, her debt-free student status, her intact family, all of it for poverty, if she could have Pearl's beauty, and if Christian would love her. Further, Polly Flint will run the risk, as she imagines what it is to be Pearl, of making every woke reader outraged. She will do so for the rapture she'll feel if only for the time the writing is taking place. It is worth selling her soul to be delivered from her loneliness for the few weeks the story will preoccupy her.

Before I could scream at Ito, Ito who was still reading down at the end of the table, some of the students had come filtering back from break time. If Polly, the fictional writer, was courageous, Iris, the real live person, was a coward. She had not been able to bring herself to give the story to Ito and me ahead of time. She had shamelessly swiped my journal. I set the pages aside and busied myself with my phone, looking at no one. I would not cry. I would not haul Iris from her chair and scratch her eyes out. I would not tear off my clothes and simulate masturbation, although it was tempting. I didn't once look up to see what, if any, was Ito's reaction.

When the class resumed, and Iris had read the first page of her story out loud, which was the charge of the person in the hot seat, and when Miss Dubinsky asked, "Thoughts?" I said nothing. Lucy Wan started up about the terrific writing, how her mind had been blown by Iris's powers of description. As other students spoke in a similar vein I was considering my options:

A. The stripping and gyrating.
B. More subtly, go to the bathroom, remove my panties, return to Fuston Hall 203. Sit across from Miss Dubinsky, hiking up my skirt and opening my legs underneath the table, flashing my professor.
C. Leave the classroom, go downstairs, pull the fire alarm.
D. Leave the classroom, go to the Dean of Academic Affairs. Report the case of cultural appropriation so gross on the part of Iris Irvington as to warrant disciplinary action.
E. Also in the Dean's office report Miss Dubinsky, a professor who should not have allowed the story to have been workshopped.

When four or five people had done their drooling I raised my hand.

"Emma?" Miss Dubinsky said. She was rosy, Miss Dubinsky as if in the flush of youth. I had the abrupt realization seconds before I spoke that she had already read the story when she'd appeared at the sandwich shop the evening before, that Ito and I were very much on her mind when she barged into our booth. She'd been living in the story, living in my vulva, as she sat before her lentil soup.

I began slowly. Having played a queen on stage was helpful, Eleanor of Aquitaine a master of control. I explained that we lived in a time when certain kinds of people could not write about other kinds of people. You could call this censorship, I said, you could call it a limitation to the imagination, or you could call it a timefulness. The fact remained that specific groups of marginalized people owned their stories. Period. The fact was, persons of privilege were not allowed trespass into that narrative material. Therefore, Iris appropriating the details of a black woman from inner-city Detroit was automatically off limits to her. I paused. I asked Jesse Pearlwater what he thought about the story, since Iris was blatantly stealing his material. In five weeks Jesse may have said three but no more than four sentences. He observed that Iris had not gotten some of the street names right in his neighborhood. That was the extent of his complaint.

"Really," I said.

I maintained that even though Jesse seemed not to mind about the appropriation I minded, and all of us, as writers, should mind. I said that Iris must withdraw the story. She ought not to have written it in the first place. She, of all people, had to understand this principle by which all of us who were writing now must abide.

"That is so interesting, Emma, thank you," Miss Dubinsky said. She then launched into a mini-lecture about The Imagination and how it must not, in her view, be shackled.

I interrupted. I said, "You cannot use that loaded word in this context, Miss Dubinsky. That is a word reserved for the slave trade and for African American men in prison. It is a word as charged as the N-word. Further, the imagination is not shackle-able. It can rove wherever it wants but in the light of day it has to respect boundaries and be dignified. It is shameful to use that word in the casual way you've just done."

Miss Dubinsky had never looked more pink as she wound herself up into the standard harangue: What would happen if no one could write outside of their racial, gender, or class grouping? Where would Tolstoy be, Shakespeare, Henry James, Harriet Beecher Stowe?

I did everything I could to keep the lid on until finally I said, "Please stop talking."

Miss Dubinsky was startled. It's hard to believe but maybe no one had ever told her to shut up.

I said, "We are living in a special moment in history. This is the moment where marginalized people are beginning to be heard. It is their time to speak of their own authentic experience."

It was as if it were only Miss Dubinsky and me in the room, everyone else having faded into the plaster. I was saying that she and I, no matter how hard we tried, no matter how earnest our attempt, could never understand the pain of those who were oppressed, who were still bearing the scars of their ancestors. I was speaking when Ito broke into the conversation. He said, "Hold up. We are here to talk about Iris's story. That's our work right now."

Miss Dubinsky and I, somehow having forgotten his existence, blinked as if the sun had come from behind a cloud.

"We can discuss appropriation, the pros and cons for like ever," he said in his smooth soft way. "Let's save it and get back to this astonishing, this *astounding* story." He held up the pages as proof. "I've got to say up front that I don't give a—" he considered language only for a second—"rat's ass about appropriation. And I get to be an authority because, Hey! I'm a minority. Big time. I think if you can get away with it, Iris, you can get away with it. Which in my opinion you've totally done. I bow down to you, girl."

Iris, also with color in her cheeks, looked as if she might cry, I assume from joy.

He went on. "No one's mentioned the erotic stuff but, YOW! It's erotic but not pornographic? Another big subject. The difference between those two things, one being Art, the other not. Women are pretty much a mystery to me—" he looked at me and to Iris, wondering at what must have seemed a mystical connection of ours, since in his mind I'd gone and told her about his masterful love tricks. He said, "You're an Artist, Iris, is the main thing, no questions asked." Miss Dubinsky looked close to orgasm.

"The thing is," he continued, "thing is, no one has said the obvious. This story is ABOUT appropriation. Am I right? It's meta! That's what makes it so brilliant. The writer, Polly Flint, is herself wondering if she can get away with it. She stakes a claim for the risk being worth it. Why? Because she's a writer. Because that's what a writer, the real deal, has to do."

I was staring at Ito. Who was this person? His hair was in a ridiculous man-bun. "No," I pronounced.

Everyone in the room was acutely focused, heads up, good posture, leaning forward: the lovers in real time were circling each other, one of them about to pounce.

"What do you mean?" Ito said. "You know I'm right, Emma. I happen to know you don't believe what you're saying. You do not believe in this appropriation horse shit. You are fully on the side of team imagination."

Had I never heard him speak before. "Team imagination?" I said with scorn. I may have looked as if I were going to retch. "Would you care to know what I believe? Would you? What we are talking about here is a violation of a culture that has suffered beyond our capacity to—"

He put his hand up, that hand, his long slender fingers the one instrument capable of stopping my speech. "Okay, cry me a river, I get it, I do. Let's say the river has been cried, all right? River, check."

No one in the class said that they, too, felt the river had been cried and had been checked. No one said anything.

"Back to the story," he was saying. "As far as Art goes, as far as the Artistry of this story, I do have a problem with it. The feelings of the lover, of the woman Pearl? I don't believe that someone as gorgeous and smart and confident as Pearl is would be so lost, so unmoored. She's got the love of a good man." He looked warmly across the room at me as if smoke were not coming from my nostrils. "Her whole shtick just doesn't seem credible. I guess Iris wanted some tension in the relationship to make it interesting but—I don't buy Pearl's sense of inadequacy."

"Right, right," I said loudly, looking at Iris. "That seems completely false to me, too."

Iris's fleshy mouth was pulled down, her eyes wide, as if to say to me, *What are you talking about? These are* your *feelings.*

Miss Dubinsky was shaking her head mournfully. "Pearl's feelings of worthlessness in the face of this passion? My goodness. They are all too real. Any person who has been in love will understand Pearl's despair."

That was it, the final indignity. I started to gather my papers. I tapped the pages crisply on the table into a stack. That Miss Dubinsky was identifying with my own true reactions to Ito was not to be borne. It wouldn't be possible to sit for the rest of class. And yet I did not want to leave without a parting shot. It seemed, without more than a second or two of thought—it seemed necessary to direct my quiver at Miss Dubinsky. The creature, the witch. I put my manuscripts and book into my satchel. I would not attack her dress. Nor her hair nor lisp. Not her endless mini-lectures or her outdated pedagogy. Standing up, I put on my coat. Dressing was the opposite of my first inclination to strip but it seemed to command as much attention as the other would have. I adjusted my satchel strap across my chest. I settled my hair. I assumed Ito was watching me along with everyone else.

"I read your novel," I said to Miss Dubinsky. I put a glove on. "I don't believe, Professor—is that your title?" I waved away my concern.

Ito called, "Emma—"

"I'm speaking," I said, attacking the consonants, the same verbal approach required when training a dog to SsssssssiT-ah. I forged ahead. "I don't believe that a person who wrote your novel," I was putting on the other glove, "a book that rehashes worn material, that is stylistically uninteresting, a book that has no fresh ideas. That the author of that novel has any business—none—teaching writing at the college level."

Such quiet! I dug around in my pocket for my hat. "I guess I do see your point about appropriation, though. Iris here could have written your story in a more compelling way. If you can't live, I guess you're lucky if at least you can write." I laughed. "Imagine Iris stealing your journal! And writing your novel! Well! I guess we'd all have to be grateful! Wouldn't we? Iris."

When all that exclaiming was done I put my hat on and walked out of Fuston Hall 203.

There's not all that much more to tell.

Is this a story or a vignette?

I went to a friend's house who lived way off campus, turned off my phone, and hid in a nook by her bedroom. When Ito found me I cried so hard he could not accuse me of cruelty or any other charges he may have wanted to bring against me. Eventually I learned that after my grand exit Miss Dubinsky had withered, that she had basically melted into the floor, nothing left but the giant gold safety pin of her kilt. Most of the students had shoved their belongings into their backpacks and gotten out. Iris, and of course Ito, stayed behind to tend to our teacher.

I hadn't decided what course of action to take about dropping the workshop or continuing, when the college shocked the entire community by, in effect, halting the semester. Ending the history of the college. There would be two or three more weeks of classes instead of eight, at which point we'd all call it quits. The situation was a collapse of epic proportions which I have to say in a moment of lunacy I felt responsible for, my outburst in Fuston Hall 203 the little last piece to break the college. Or maybe it was Maeve and I, both of us with the hood and the scythe. The college already worn out by identity politics; our argument, had I taken it to the Dean, would have been like a mercy killing.

Seniors would be given their degrees, and arrangements had been made with a nearby state university to absorb students who were willing to go to a strange campus and enter courses there mid-stream. I never saw Miss Dubinsky after that infamous class and have never tried to look her up. I leave the poor woman in a heap on the floor of Fuston Hall 203; it is fair use of my power to edit out Iris and Ito's kindness to her.

In those weeks before we left campus, at some point I reread "Writing Christian & Pearl". I could see that it was a smart and beautifully written story. Iris had taken morsels from my journal and enhanced them, made them throbbingly erotic and sad. I admitted, finally, that I loved Pearl in the story more than I loved myself. Pearl understood her own character and was in touch with her confusion about how to be in the world, which was complicated and interesting because of the privilege that had been thrust upon her. Moreover, her humility was real. She was both sharp and empathetic. Christian was every bit as good and therefore as dull as Ito. I also faced the fact that I was no writer. For a long time that seemed the worst of the fallout, the understanding of my average abilities a touchstone, a thing I return to again and again, as if it is a rabbit's foot in my pocket—almost a comfort. I have not since then tried to write anything other than grant proposals and this summary of my experience with Maeve, this confession, call it, my crying a river. Advanced Fiction Workshop wounded me and made me ugly, or it revealed my inherent ugliness. So: good for me! The goddess with a chipped nose and missing arm. Ito and I broke up right after we left campus—I don't recall who did the dirty work. Iris is currently getting her MFA. Four years later I now work for a nonprofit in Chicago that funds projects specifically related to climate change. It's rewarding, trying to be useful. I'm doing what I can because, after all, I hate to think of every bit of this foolishness coming to an end.

Alt-AC

by Warren Moore

Roger Patterson—well, *Doctor* Patterson, but the ink probably hadn't dried on the degree yet, and his dissertation hadn't been on the university library's shelves long enough to gather dust—saw the Senior Scholar curse as the bus pulled away from Valley III dorm and headed to the Kalamazoo airport. Patterson couldn't hear the curse over the sound of the diesel engine, and he wasn't exactly a lip reader, but the older man's body English indicated an oath, and probably not a minced one, either.

He walked up the sidewalk, toward the man who stood there, luggage still in his hands. "Don't worry," Patterson said. "There'll be another one along in about fifteen minutes. Maybe ten, since it's Sunday morning—getaway day." There were still some sessions left, this last day of the International Congress for Medieval Studies, but most of the attendees had read their papers and were hurrying home to their research, or their summer classes.

Or like Roger Patterson, to his job search. There were still a few positions for medievalists that hadn't been filled. At least, there were rejection letters he hadn't yet received.

"That's what I told myself fifteen minutes ago," the Senior Scholar said. "So I had one more conversation. One more request for an article. One more request for a letter of rec. And now I've cut it too fine, and I'll miss my flight."

"Maybe not," Patterson said. "I drove. If you want a ride, I'll be glad to take you. It's only about fifteen or twenty minutes, and unlike the shuttles, I don't have to stop at the Radisson."

"Would you?"

"Sure. Just let me bring the car around." And in a couple of minutes, he had done just that. He took the Senior Scholar's bags and set them in the back seat of the beige Taurus from the motor pool. Thank God for the department—it didn't matter that Patterson had just finished being a grad student; they let him take the car and even threw in the fleet credit card. It was only about a four-hour drive back to Muncie. It probably would have taken at least as much time to fly, counting the drive to Indianapolis, and free beat the hell out of even a cheap airfare. The trunk held more than an overhead bin, too.

In fact, he was doing better than a lot of his peers. Ball State had already agreed to take him on as contract faculty for the next year. "We take care of our grads," the chair had told him. It was true, at least for a while. But on the other hand, it wasn't tenured, or even tenure-track, and if enrollment dropped, if the courses didn't make? You can't teach courses that aren't there, and besides, the grad students were even cheaper labor.

The Senior Scholar identified himself as Wayne Beggs, a history prof from a land-grant university out West. "I'm Roger Patterson, from Ball State. I defended a couple of months ago." He accepted congratulations from Beggs, but braced himself for the question he knew was coming.

Sure enough: "Have you been on the market?"

On the market. Patterson heard the phrase all the time, and he didn't like it very much. It made him feel like a haunted house, or a slightly bruised avocado. And it sounded so simple—like you put yourself out there, and crowds of shoppers would flood the aisles looking for someone just like you, a freshly-minted expert on Early Middle English verse sermons who could also teach freshman comp if need be. (And the need would almost certainly be there. Senior Scholars had moved past *that* brand of hazing after tenure. Patterson wondered when Beggs had last taught World Civ Before 1500.)

The reality? It was more like an overcrowded animal shelter, with the gas chamber just down the hall. Instead of the two weeks Fido might get, it was more like three years—three hiring seasons, really, when most of the job announcements came out in September, and most of the cuts had been made by the Modern English Association meeting in January. If it was a good year, there might be twenty-five tenure-track positions for all of English Lit from Caedmon to 1500. And Patterson knew that the previous year had seen twenty dissertations on Chaucer alone. Add in the less popular work? And the related fields—gender studies, environmental criticism, race studies, and some probably too new for him to have heard about at his distance from the Ivies—it was no wonder that every position drew a hundred applications or more.

Of course, most of those positions were never within Roger Patterson's reach. Hiring departments marry up; new PhDs marry down. Ivies hire from Ivies or Oxbridge, or just raid schools lower on the food chain for established scholars. Big Ten schools and the "public Ivies" take the next batch, and so on down, with new blood from flagship schools going to Directional State U, or maybe a small, liberal arts college.

But Roger Patterson was from Ball State, and a couple of weeks before he had driven to Kalamazoo, the Director of Grad Studies asked him if he had thought about community college positions. There was another lie at that link in the food chain: "Sure, you might *start* at the Swamp County School of Mortuary Science and Transmission Repair, but hey! You can write your way out!" Easy enough to say, but teaching four—or five, or six—sections of remedial comp each term ("Don't call it *remedial*—it's *developmental*." Bullshit: if you have to explain what verbs are, it's remedial.) not only limits your research time, but Swamp County's library is probably going to be a bit short on the work you need to read just to stay caught up.

Oh—and those student loans start coming due six months after graduation.

Roger Patterson suspected that he was on the ground floor of a pyramid scheme that Cheops would have envied. And like anything on the ground floor, there was a good chance now that he'd be swept up and dropped in a dumpster.

So why had he done it? Why does someone get talked into selling Amway, or essential oils? It's the promise—in Patterson's case, the promise of The Life of the Mind, the World of Ideas, or some other phrase with prepositions and capital letters. And maybe some people got there. Hell, *someone* had to.

And so he had begun, and had loved the time he had spent. For the two years of the MA, and the four of the PhD, he had felt special. Senior faculty had offered praise and encouragement. The undergrads he had taught—two sections a term—respected him. Sometimes, not knowing the difference, they called him "Professor Patterson," and although he'd corrected them (You never knew who might be listening, and you didn't want to sound arrogant in front of someone who might write your next job recommendation), he liked the way it sounded. Like a desperate gambler anteing up his rent money, Roger Patterson, like so many others, had stayed in the game, hoping he might catch the break that would let him walk out as a winner.

But he knew he probably couldn't stay in the game more than three more hands. The clock was ticking. Hiring committees look at the dates on a *curriculum vitae—résumé* is just too prosaic—and if that degree was more than three years old, eyebrows would rise. What was *wrong* with this candidate? Why were they still . . . *on the market*?

English was the worst, most people said, but history was only slightly better, if at all. So Patterson figured Beggs knew all that, and it wasn't the sort of thing one said in small talk at Kalamazoo, the profession's four-day hybrid of scholarship, family reunion, and fraternity beer bash. Even people in other disciplines knew about "Kazoo," and part of the conference's rep came from the sense of common passion and joy that marked the event.

Even a big college will likely have no more than a single medievalist in the English department, and another in History. The process of graduate school leads you to specialize, and after years of classes with other bright, interesting people followed by solitary scholarship, you might find yourself the only person in your building who even cared about what you read and wrote. So Kalamazoo had the appeal of people whose interests may not precisely match yours, but with 3000 or so people in attendance, you were bound to find someone you could talk to.

And so you didn't talk much about "the market," the thinning ice beneath a career you had dreamed about, the sort of career that was celebrated by the Senior Scholars who were seeing one another for the twentieth year or more.

Instead, if you were Roger Patterson, you said, "Not really. I put a few applications out there, but since I hadn't defended yet, I knew there wasn't much chance. I'll go in earnest this fall."

Beggs nodded. "It was different when I started—in the late seventies, it was a seller's market. I had four offers in hand a week before I defended. So I took the one I liked, and I've been there for forty years now.

"It's been a good career," he said. Patterson agreed, and Beggs continued. "And thank God, it isn't over yet. Just ten years ago, I would have had to retire at seventy, but I'm not tired of it yet, so why should I stop?"

Patterson knew that was true, too. One of the reasons there were so few jobs available was that no one wanted to take the rocking chair and the Emeritus status anymore. Why should they? A university, or even a small college, was a fine place for a tenured professor. You could teach classes that coincided with your interests; you could live in the house you bought decades before, knowing the value had gone up: "Just a short walk from campus!" If it was a university town, there was prestige, respect. You could be a pillar of the community.

And if the workforce had changed as the years passed, if the comfort of your position was subsidized by the grad students and part-timers who dealt with the core classes, by the Roger Pattersons, well, it wasn't *your* fault if you were Wayne Beggs. It was just how things shook out. When the government and the accreditors added new rules, new regulations, and new hoops through which to jump, then you stayed busy with your research and your writing. Someone would hire administrators for those chores, and if the new Assistant to the Vice-Provost was making more than you, well, they kept you from being bothered. Sure, the Assistant's salary meant that you couldn't replace Carothers when she retired (or moved into administration herself), well, that was okay, too. There were always folks who would teach those classes for less money, because they wanted the experience or wanted to add a line to their résumé or just thought it might be a nice change from selling insurance. If you were Wayne Beggs, things may have changed around you, but you didn't make a big deal about it. "If you thought about it at all," Patterson silently added.

For all the talk about radicals on campus, professors weren't keen on making waves before they got tenure. You didn't want to cross the wrong people, a chair or a Dean, or God help you, a donor. And by the time you got tenure, well, things were pretty comfortable, really. Best to attend the Faculty Senate meetings, enjoy your library privileges, and go to your conferences each year.

And so, in its own way, Kalamazoo was a microcosm of the academic humanities. You might be a Roger Patterson, hoping someone would take a flyer on someone without a pedigree before you passed your sell-by date, or you might be a Wayne Beggs, with the time to read and think and write. Well, not as much of the last as had once been the case. "I know it's hard," Beggs said. "The last time I was on a hiring committee, we had more than a hundred applicants for a Visiting Assistant position." Beggs didn't add that a VAP was about as low as one could get on the academic totem pole and still get insurance. Patterson had been in the game long enough to know that. Beggs also didn't mention how many of these applicants had more publications, and at better journals than he had over the course of his decades at the university.

"What kind of publications do you have?" Beggs asked Patterson.

The younger man's eyes flickered to the rearview mirror as they moved through Kalamazoo's streets and the university receded behind them. "Well, what I really have are presentations, mostly. But I have written some reviews, and a couple of encyclopedia entries, and I've received some interest about the thesis."

"University press?"

"No," Patterson said, telling a painful truth. Placing a thesis outside the academic publishers didn't count much *on the market*. It didn't matter that the subsidies those academic publishers used to get were dwindling or disappearing altogether. In fact, so were the publishers themselves. Administrators called it "sculpting", the process of setting budget priorities, and if it came down to a choice between running a journal that went to a couple hundred libraries or a new scoreboard with hi-def replay screens at the stadium, it wouldn't go well for the journal. After all, that stadium was "the front porch of the university." Alumni didn't get misty-eyed remembering that festschrift in honor of the Religion professor at State.

It really *was* kind of medieval, Patterson thought—but didn't say—as he went on describing his work. There had been the nobility and clergy, and you could have had a nice life at court or in the monastery. But there had been a hell of a lot more peasants, planting, harvesting, spinning, shearing. It was a pyramid, all right: an enormous base and a tiny capstone, with no levels between the two.

And as Patterson spoke, describing his work with what you call "the elevator pitch" when you're *on the market*, he wondered if the older man ever thought about how unlikely it was that Patterson—or the hundreds of other would-be academics—would ever have a chance to live the life Beggs had enjoyed.

The peasantry had known that as well, and occasionally tried to do something about it. England had seen the Peasants' Revolt of 1381, where John Ball had preached to the commoners,

When Adam delv'd and Eve span,
Who was then a gentleman?

And for a short time, the peasants had managed to frighten the nobles, and had even slain the Archbishop of Canterbury. But their leader, Wat Tyler, had made the mistake of trusting the teenaged Richard II for a parley. When they met, the nobles killed Tyler "for his ill manners", the King declared the concessions he had made to be void, and a few hundred deaths later, the Revolt ended as most of them do. Adam and Eve notwithstanding, the gentles remained gentles and the peasants remained peasants, and so now.

But that was medieval as well, wasn't it, Patterson thought. Each of us—he, Beggs, all the others on the shuttle buses to the airport or attending a last session or trying to shake off a hangover from the traditional (and infamous) Saturday night dance—occupies our spot aboard Fortuna's wheel. Some of us ride at the top. Others fall as the wheel lowers them. Beggs was not atop the wheel, but he *was* high enough to enjoy the view. Who could begrudge his wanting to extend his ride?

And while Roger Patterson might hope he caught the wheel on the upswing, he had to be ready if it didn't move at all. "So I'll give it two or three years," Patterson said, "and if that doesn't work? There's always alt-ac."

Alt-ac. The word had come into conversation a few years earlier, and as jobs in the Humanities became ever scarcer, the term had become more common. It was a short form of "alternative to academia", and it meant the world of employment beyond university walls. Alt-ac could be public or private sector, anything from grant writing to being a staff writer for a quiz show. The *Chronicle of Higher Education*—the weekly newspaper for the small town that is higher ed—was running features on Philosophy PhDs who worked as hospital ethicists, rhetoricians turned advertising consultants, historians who became archivists for Coca-Cola. The message was unstated but constant, the smiling faces in the accompanying photos showing the reader, "See? It's okay! Yes, you spent a third of your life or more training for a job that probably won't exist—well, not for *you*, anyway—and you know that the professors who taught you will shake their heads sadly when your name comes up ('Patterson? Fine student, I thought, but just didn't seem to have what it took. He should have thought about community college . . . ' After all, if you didn't get hired, you must be lacking something. Q.E.D.), and you had to walk away from your Mr. Chips dreams and wonder what might have been for the rest of your life, but you took those lemons and made lemonade, didn't you? It's okay!"

But in those same issues of the *Chronicle* were articles about "shaking the alt-ac stigma," about not feeling as though your time holding up the top of the pyramid had been wasted. No one came out and called it the booby prize, but when you were *on the market*, the neologism chilled your blood, just a little bit.

But since Patterson had used the term himself, Wayne Beggs spoke approvingly. "That makes a lot of sense, Roger. And I'm glad to hear more people seeing that alternative. Everyone seems to think that all you can do with a PhD is teach. But you know, you can pick up a lot of transferable skills along the way."

Even as Beggs spoke, Patterson wondered, *What does he know about it?* A generational accident of timing had meant that Beggs got to live his dream, a dream Patterson wanted as well. He'd bet the old bastard never had to *transfer* anything but a wayward phone call.

All the same, Patterson agreed with what Beggs had said; sucking up is one of the valuable skills one learns in grad school, though it's called *professionalization*. "Sure! I have research skills. I can write and speak effectively, and I've demonstrated that I can stay self-motivated through a major undertaking. All of those are saleable talents, right?"

Beggs nodded, smiling in a way that looked like what it was—a half-hearted act of encouragement.

They had reached the airport. Patterson helped Beggs get his bags from the back seat. The men shook hands and said they'd look each other up at next year's Congress. "Next year in Kalamazoo" didn't have the same ring as "Next year in Jerusalem," but it seemed to say something similar about enduring hard times.

Patterson watched Beggs walk into the terminal and pulled away, but instead of finding his way to the southbound interstate, he looped around the airport's service road, eventually finding an unoccupied cell phone/observation lot near the runway's end. Sunday of Congress Weekend might be a busy flight day in Kalamazoo, but it didn't mean that there would be many people watching the planes depart on a Sunday morning. He parked the car, and pulled the trunk release lever.

As he circled to the back of the car, he thought of the transferable skills he had described for Beggs. He hoped he wouldn't have to use too many of them, but he had put them to work already. One could research verse sermons, or the Peasants' Revolt, or improvised weapons from the Irish Troubles or the ongoing unpleasantness in Iraq. And if you minored in chemistry as an undergrad, and knew where to find an army surplus store in Indiana—well, those were skills too, weren't they?

In the distance, he saw a plane picking up speed as it neared him, gaining the speed for the takeoff that would carry the passengers to Detroit, where they would catch other planes to take them back to their own universities and their own careers. Patterson lifted the homemade RPG launcher to his shoulder, saw, heard, and felt the regional jet draw nearer, felt the urge to fire the rocket. He waited another second, saw daylight between the plane's landing gear and the runway, and pulled the trigger, above which he had written the words *Wat Tyler*.

Later, Patterson would notice that his ears were ringing, but he guessed he hadn't thought about the noise at the time. It was too exciting.

The rocket hadn't gone exactly where he had wanted it to go—he thought he had aimed at the cockpit, but if anything, it was even better. The shot veered to the left slightly, and sheared into the plane's right wing. There must have been a fuel tank there; even at his distance, he could feel the heat from the flash. And as what was left of the airplane made a 45-degree roll to Patterson's right, the remaining wing clipped the ground and made the fuselage pinwheel at an angle skewed away from where he stood. He thought he may have felt the heat from the second fireball then, but it could have just been imagination, and besides, he had places to go.

As he reached the interstate, he wondered if Dr. Beggs had been on the plane. He hoped not—the man had seemed nice enough. But then he got back to thinking of the job search. Yes, he would give the market a serious run this fall, and he figured that there would be thirty, maybe even fifty jobs for medievalists over the next couple years that wouldn't have happened otherwise. And fewer people applying as well.

That was one of the things they had said in the alt-ac articles. You may have those transferable skills, but you also have to be entrepreneurial.

Einstein's Sabbath

by David Levien

Ensign Loew struggled with his necktie, the thin end hanging down longer than the thick, while Riddle, his roommate, watched. Riddle, who was tall, a bit pillowy around the middle, and indistinct, never encountered such problems when on his way to chapel on Sundays. But this was Friday evening, and Ensign Loew, who was also tall but not quite so as Riddle, and who had grown gaunt and angular over the past two years due to shipboard food that hadn't suited him and wasn't plentiful besides, had a Sabbath dinner to attend.

Ensign Loew glanced over at his roommate, who sat on his bunk—his bed, rather, now that the war was over and they were in civilian accommodations. Riddle's shoes left black polish smudges on the gray blanket. He was smoking a cigarette, and a flurry of ash had fallen on his chest. Ensign Loew considered saying something about it but didn't. Riddle wasn't one of his men, after all. Having gotten out of the navy at the end of the war, Ensign Loew wasn't really an ensign anymore either, but while the effects of the South Pacific sun had fled his face for a pallor more befitting the Princeton winter, some changes were harder to negotiate than others.

Checking the mirror again, Ensign Loew weighed undoing the necktie and trying again for a third time, but with no faith in better execution, tucked the longer end into his pants instead, and then turned to locate his coat. The months after the war and his discharge had passed in a blur, and by autumn he'd found himself reenrolled at the university studying architecture. Chapel attendance was mandatory for all undergraduate students, and the Jews in the student body were so few there was no distinction or allowance made for them. Ensign Loew didn't mind. In fact, he liked it. He found the Collegiate Gothic structure stirring, and sitting with the others and listening to the soaring music of the pipe organ while ignoring the prayers altogether was not objectionable. But the other Jewish students did object. Their complaints fell on deaf ears in the dean's office until an august voice came to their aid in the form of Albert Einstein, who resided in town and was a professor at the Institute of Advanced Study. When his eminence volunteered to host Jewish students on Sabbath eves in lieu of chapel, how could Dean Brown or President Dodds, no matter how rankled, refuse?

Ensign Loew had been reluctant to attend the gatherings, being far from observant. Since the start of the war, religion had ceased having any meaning to him at all. So the Sabbath, even at Einstein's, had been an occasion he'd been eager to avoid, and most of the first semester had passed. But a grievance had grown in him over the months, one that demanded action. So when Cohen, a physics student, cornered him in the library and beseeched him to come, he stopped turning away from what he knew he must do and accepted. Now that the moment was upon him, Ensign Loew felt his hands clenching in anticipation at what would happen. He looked down at them, tremulous and still slightly red and waxen, before he slid into his coat, settled it on his shoulders, and turned to go.

"Your cookies," Riddle said, stopping him.

They weren't cookies, but how could Riddle know what was in the box? Ensign Loew stopped, picked up the white Fischel's bakery box tied with red string, nodded his farewell to Riddle, and walked out the door.

The afternoon cold had come fast as the sun dropped behind bare trees, and the hand that held the bakery box was stiff with it, while the other was jammed deep inside a coat pocket. The last of the season's dry leaves scraped along the sidewalk, and when Ensign Loew stepped on them, they crunched under the hard soles of his shoes in a way that reminded him

unpleasantly of Japan. As he turned onto Mercer Street, Ensign Loew considered the mounting assignments he had due in his Concepts of Structural
Design class. He'd missed the first few deadlines, asking for more time, but
it seemed he was frozen. He would sit down at the drafting table with his
bumwad and T-square and pencils, and nothing would come forth. The
assignments were clear enough, but he was suddenly unable to draw a decent line. This had never happened to him before. He'd always been able
to draft. He could sketch decent approximations of anti-aircraft emplace-
ments, bunkers, and latrines on the flap of a K-rations box while under fire
in a tossing Higgins boat with everyone vomiting around him. But now, in
a quiet studio with good light, he couldn't reliably finish a side elevation for
a garden shed. After surviving the madness, and on the precipice of living
the life he had intended, it all appeared to be collapsing within him now.
He'd blamed his hands at first, but was through kidding himself. He finally
knew who was truly to blame, and what to do about it.

Professor Einstein's house was a small white pattern-book cottage of no ar-
chitectural significance. Ensign Loew stopped at the wrought-iron gate on
the edge of the sidewalk by the footpath that led to the front door and con-
templated turning away. Through the front windows he saw people moving
about in the living room bathed in golden light. He didn't see Professor
Einstein. It wasn't fully dark yet. It wasn't too late. He paused and considered retreat, but as he lifted his hand from the gate latch, the front door of
the house swung open, as if by magic, and a small middle-aged woman appeared. The sounds of crystal and silverware being arranged escaped from
behind her. She beckoned him with a wave. Ensign Loew steeled himself to
his task and walked toward the house.

Her name was Maja. She was Einstein's sister and welcomed him with
a firm handshake. If she had taken any notice of his palm, she didn't show
it. She had whitening wavy hair and formidable brows, and wore a black
dress with a long chain necklace that held a locket. He told her his name,

and she cut off any final prospect of escape when she commanded: "Come in, Loew."

The inside of the house was warm and smelled of roast chicken, chopped liver and potatoes, and something else Ensign Loew couldn't place that made it seem the province of older people—mothballs, perhaps. Maja fairly tore off his coat and draped it over the stairway banister with a few others.

"I'll take your cookies," she said, reaching for the bakery box.

"They're not cookies," he said.

"Heavy," she commented, wresting the box from him and bobbing it up and down by the string. He allowed himself to be ushered past an impressive grandfather clock and into a small living room occupied by about a dozen other students.

The undergrads stood around awkwardly, holding small glasses of fruit juice and adjusting their spectacles. They all turned, a collection of Semitic features and bright brown eyes, to greet Ensign Loew, or at least to see who the new arrival was, as the actual greetings he received were murmured at best. He nodded back, noting the stiff collars, the awkward ties and scratchy wool lapels of the assembled, and imagined he looked just as uncomfortable. He saw that only two of the attendees were women, likely Evelyn College girls, with wiry dark hair, thick eyelashes, and ripe red lips. They wore modest ensembles of black sweaters over long heavy skirts that brushed the floor and both women looked fairly mortified to be there. They offered their help repeatedly to Maja, and Helen, a kind-eyed American woman who seemed to be a secretary or maid of some sort, in the handing out and collecting of beverages.

Ensign Loew caught eyes with Cohen, who was over at a sideboard that held refreshments.

"Punch?" Cohen offered.

"No, thank you," Ensign Loew said. He noticed a bottle of rye whiskey along the back edge of the table. But he saw it was still sealed, and as much as he would have liked a highball, he didn't care to be the one seen cracking the bottle.

"Oh, just have one," Cohen said of the punch.

"All right," Ensign Loew said, accepting a glass of the syrupy apricot-colored liquid.

"So, you made it," the young physics student observed.

"I did."

"It's a good group . . ."

"Yes."

"You'll see."

Ensign Loew looked around at the eager young students.

"It's a Jeffersonian style dinner—one conversation, table-wide. The talk can range from science to metaphysics to current events. Last week we played a very diverting word game after dinner," Cohen volunteered, assuming the role of anxious interim host. But there was a stunted, anticipatory air in the room, as at a show or circus when the main act has not begun yet.

Finally, there was the sound of footsteps in the hallway and everyone turned. Ensign Loew knew well what the man looked like, but only from photographs. Though rarely seen and certainly not known, his presence was felt throughout the town. Some said he smiled on small children in the streets or gave a nod to shopkeepers. Ensign Loew thought he'd caught a glimpse of him once, crossing in front of a bus on Nassau Street in overcoat, scarf, and hat, but when the bus had cleared the figure was gone, leaving him doubting the possibility. Now, though, here he was, the man himself, in his own living room, appearing before this chosen lot in ivory shirt and black cardigan, his spray of white hair rising above mirthful eyes and rosmarus mustache. The assembled, a field of sunflowers, finished their slow rotation toward him.

"Ah, I see you have all successfully negotiated your Sabbath's journey," Professor Einstein said. He spoke humbly and simply in proper German-accented English.

"I just came over from Walker, it's much closer than the Mount of Olives to Jerusalem," Cohen answered, perhaps hoping to distinguish himself from the others who only smiled, somewhat slavishly. Cohen's comment didn't fill Loew with jealousy as much as wonderment at the ability to make such a remark. The professor merely gave a generous if unimpressed nod at the reference.

"Shall we move to table?" A dark-haired woman, not yet thirty years old, who had emerged from the kitchen proffered an invitation. She was taller and more slender than Maja, had smoke black eyes and spoke with just a trace of a European accent. The contingent moved slowly but willingly toward the dining room.

"Margot," Cohen whispered as they walked. "His daughter. Stepdaughter, I believe, but daughter just the same." It was known that Professor Einstein's wife had passed but that he lived among women.

The dining room's focal point was a beautifully set long table with eight carved mahogany chairs, supplemented by wooden folding chairs for the overflow of guests. There seemed to be no hierarchy by which the seats were assigned, save Maja at the head nearest the door to the kitchen, while Professor Einstein sat in the middle of the span, Helen on his left, Margot on his right, and several undergrads, like the disciples they were, fanned out on either side of him.

Maja said the *Barucha* and lit the candles. Margot recited the *Kiddush*.

"Hirschhorn, come make the *HaMotzi*," Professor Einstein instructed a big-bodied young man with thick plastic-framed glasses who stood and said the prayer. When he went to slice the bread, Professor Einstein put his hand around Hirschhorn's on the knife handle and guided the cut.

"Enough of this silliness, let us eat," Professor Einstein said, retaking his seat.

"What silliness?" Maja said, her voice leavened with pique.

"For me the Jewish religion, like all others, is an incarnation of the most childish superstitions," Professor Einstein said to the group, in a way that made it clear he and his sister had been over this ground many times.

"Yet we gather like this?" one of the girls asked, strong of voice but innocent as a deer.

"Exactly," Maja said, as if her point were proven.

"Back at the Luitpold-Gymnasium—"

"It was the boys' secondary school," Maja interjected, with the irritation of one who's already lost an argument.

"We learned the Catechismus Romanus, the short catechism." He saw the looks on their faces. "Despite what you think, I actually enjoyed learning the stories of Christianity, especially the ones about the Nazarene. Anyway, one day the teacher, a Catholic priest, held up a large spike and said, 'These were the nails with which Christ was crucified by the Jews.' All eyes in the classroom fell upon me. I burned with embarrassment. It was my first taste of the venom of anti-Semitism. And after our recent frightful dose, we must now, more than ever, exercise our affinity." Professor Einstein ate a small morsel of bread and nodded for his daughter to serve him green beans but no meat.

Ensign Loew felt himself rapt at the tale and suddenly doubting himself and his ability to do what he'd come for.

"So you don't believe in God?" the girl asked.

"Oh, but I do, Miss Ginsberg. Not in some providential god concerned with matters of man, of course, monitoring our actions and tallying our failings—but rather in Spinoza's God, who reveals Himself in the lawful harmony of the natural world."

The conversation grew more secular as the meal continued. Was the food overcooked or heavily salted? Ensign Loew wasn't sure, but he liked it. The wine—would real people think it too sweet? Maybe, but he found it agreeable to drink. As Ensign Loew ate a small plate and drank two glasses, the conversation ranged from politics, to the Nuremberg trials, to something new for sale called Tupperware, to the latest ill-fated battle in the "Cannon War" with Rutgers. Everyone, it seemed, had an opportunity to participate in the talk—everyone except for a certain older visitor, who had joined the group several moments late, a tiny wizened German physicist down the table for whom Professor Einstein had recently secured a visa—and Ensign Loew. The physicist spoke no English, and so ate in silence,

answering any questions specifically directed toward him with a muted "ja" or "nein." Ensign Loew didn't have such a handy excuse. Instead, he concentrated on the wine. He was vaguely aware of some discussion about a new bathing costume that had emerged in France that summer, when Professor Einstein had an idea and spoke to his sister.

"Maja, go and fetch—" he began, before slipping into German and saying something that brought a smile to the physicist's face. Maja disappeared from the room. In a moment she returned with the bottle of rye, which she opened. She poured several fingers into a schnapps glass for the physicist.

"Anyone else?" Maja offered.

Ensign Loew gestured to the schnapps glass in front of him and it was filled. There were no other takers. The physicist and Ensign Loew raised their glasses to each other in fellowship.

"Hey-ep," the physicist said, and drank his down. Ensign Loew followed suit, feeling the exquisite burn of the whiskey in his chest.

"Again, Maja," Professor Einstein directed. He seemed to know his guest. Maja, out of politeness, offered Ensign Loew another as well, and out of politeness he pretended to consider before accepting. She set the bottle down and took her seat.

"Hey-ep." There was one more refill, but before they drank again and before Maja could secure the liquor, the physicist vanished with a nod, and the bottle, through the dining room door, leaving Ensign Loew on his own and perilously close to drunk. He turned his attention back to the conversation in time to learn that the French bathing costume in question was known as the "bikini," and with that the topic shifted to the atomic testing that was under way at Bikini Atoll.

"I read that at the end of the war an army pilot was dispatched to fly over Hiroshima to provide an accurate report after the bombing," said Ginsberg. "From eighty miles they observed smoke rising from the city."

It was visible from the water, too, Ensign Loew thought, swallowing the last of his rye and refilling his wine cup.

"As they got closer, the level of destruction became clear," she continued. "Practically all living things, human and animal, were literally seared to death. And this is what we're testing? What can possibly be learned from such *tests*, Professor? Isn't it just further demonstration of our superiority over the Russians and others trying to develop their own atomic weapons?"

The assembled awaited answers in gripped quiet. Ensign Loew was at once annoyed by the questions and attracted to the interlocutor's pluck and intellect.

"Excellent questions, dear," Professor Einstein began in a voice that communicated complete understanding. He patted at his mustache with his napkin. "Are any of you chess players?" he asked, and did not wait for a response before continuing. "I fear when it comes to modern arms, all sides have reached a state of *zugzwang*—that is, the condition where any move destroys one's own position . . ." He sighed, gave his mustache a last pat, and placed the napkin on the table. "Let us go sit in the parlor."

With a general thumping and scraping, the group repaired from the dining room. Those who'd been seated on the folding chairs brought them along as if by a preordained yet unspoken directive. Ensign Loew, occupant of one of said folding chairs, followed suit. The dedicated living room seating had been arranged into a large circle, which was augmented by those who'd carried their chairs. Though it was now technically well past sundown, Helen and Margot came from the kitchen with cookies and pastries, including rugelach, on silver trays, as well as a coffee service. Maja reclined on the sofa. It seemed her work for the evening was finished. A few of the students went outside to the front porch to smoke cigarettes and pipes. Only after everyone else had been offered did Margot arrive at Professor Einstein in his wingback. Ensign Loew watched as he selected a rugelach from Fischel's and took a bite. With an exclamation of delight he finished it and took another.

"Do we have any more of those?" he asked in a low voice.

"Yes, in the kitchen, Papa," she said.

"Good. Be sure to save me two for tomorrow, my dear."

Ensign Loew felt a small wave of pleasure that Professor Einstein had liked the item he'd brought and which Riddle had mistaken for mere cookies. This was followed by a larger surge of self-disgust in Ensign Loew at his toadying impulses. Professor Einstein dusted off his fingers as he finished chewing and reached for a violin case on the floor next to his chair.

"Perhaps a bit of Mozart?" he said, looking at his daughter. "Sonata in B-flat." She went obediently to an upright piano against the wall and lifted the dust cover to reveal the keys. She seated herself on the bench and paused with impeccable posture before nodding to her father, who had the violin cradled beneath his chin.

They began to play a plaintive and sonorous duet that was quite accomplished for such a casual gathering. The students sat spellbound and were transported to another time and place, a Europe from centuries before. The professor's playing was dexterous and sensitive. It seemed to Ensign Loew that the man's capacities had no bounds. Then they launched into an allegro portion, trading off passages between them, their eyes sparkling with delight as they communed without words. When the music ended, the young people applauded. Professor Einstein smiled while Margot gave a shy bow. Ensign Loew wanted to restrain himself from joining in, but this became yet another failure as he found himself clapping vigorously, banging his hands together hard and long until hot pain shot through them and everyone was staring at him. He finally stopped. He'd never been at a gathering like this before. Perhaps it was this conflict within him more than all the noise that drew Professor Einstein's attention.

"Thank you for your indulgence," he said, closing his violin case, then turned toward Ensign Loew, his gaze illuminated by a preternatural curiosity. "The new face among us, you appear of the age. What was your billet during the war?"

Ensign Loew felt the attention of the room upon him again and cleared his throat before saying, "I was with the Third in the Pacific."

It grew very quiet. Enough of them knew what the Third had been up to in the late stages of the war. All of them knew it had been rough.

Professor Einstein, naturally, possessed a more specific knowledge of the actions of the Third, as he did about virtually everything.

"And what was your job?" he asked.

"Combat engineer in the Construction Battalion."

"A Seabee?" It was Cohen again. He sounded surprised. Cohen and Ensign Loew had made small talk numerous times, but it had never been discussed.

"Yes. I commanded a squad of men and machines that could carve a landing strip or barracks out of jungle in a matter of days," said Ensign Loew. "Hours, if we had to." He'd also seen airstrikes blow his work back into its natural state within moments, but didn't speak of this. He thought back a little over a year, when his fondest hope had been for the squad to be able to complete a project without having to put down their tools and take up their carbines. He'd seen the enemy's incendiary bombs burn everything in their path, including the air.

"You were quite young for that kind of duty," the professor observed.

"We were all young," Ensign Loew said. He thought of his best friend, Phillips, who had been on a gasoline barge just off Tinian with a dozen others, none older than twenty. It had gone up after an enemy plane's strafing run. He had watched it burn from shore. There had been no survivors.

"Do you have a girl?" Professor Einstein asked.

"I had one when I shipped out, but not when I returned."

"I see. And what are you studying here?"

"Architecture"—Ensign Loew felt unable to stop himself—"but it's not going all that well."

"No, I imagine it isn't," Professor Einstein said, as the twinkle in his eye flattened to a knowing that unnerved the young ensign. The professor then turned away from him and talked to others for a bit, but a pall had been cast over the evening.

Ensign Loew sat in his isolation and continued to sip, slowly but quite steadily, the *Kiddush* wine, and before long realized he was indeed drunk. He also realized that several of the guests were preparing to take their leave.

People were standing and stretching. There was a general folding of chairs, offering of thanks, and locating of coats. There was talk of next week. Ensign Loew realized with dismay that he'd spent his chance badly.

"Well, I'm going to call it a night," Cohen said, clearly suggesting Ensign Loew follow suit. But instead of leaving, Ensign Loew took this opportunity to go to the powder room in the front hall, where he splashed water on the back of his neck in order to rouse himself. It was time to face what he had come for, and he was resolute that he would do it in front of whoever was left in the house, he *preferred* an audience now. But when he emerged from the bathroom, he found the parlor empty. The guests had departed and even the ladies of the house were no longer present. Only Professor Einstein remained. He was still seated as he had been before, but now a scientific journal rested open upon his lap. He looked small, vulnerable, and all of a sudden showed his age.

"The others have gone," Ensign Loew remarked.

"Yes," Professor Einstein agreed, "but you're still here. I detect something simmering in you, young man. Do you have something you wish to discuss?" With a hand the professor offered the chair across from him.

"What I have to say is best delivered standing," Ensign Loew said. "I've written you letters. I don't suppose you got them."

Professor Einstein nodded slightly. "You're Loew, the young former officer. You have tried to contact me. Your correspondence is in my office."

"But you wouldn't see me. You gave me no answer at all." Ensign Loew felt himself begin to tremble with something akin to rage.

"Well, my work, my schedule, they did not permit."

"Of course," Ensign Loew said. He felt his Adam's apple push down as he swallowed with force. He took a deep breath. "You, your discoveries, you're responsible for all of it," he blurted. Professor Einstein looked at him inscrutably.

"You are aware I did not work on the project," Professor Einstein said.

"*Your* paper on Brownian motion supported atomic theory."

Professor Einstein nodded.

"*You* deduced that tiny amounts of mass could be converted into huge amounts of energy."

"True."

"Without these things, they would have never been able to . . . You signed the letter that secured the funds. You birthed it. *You* are the father of death. And you have a debt to pay." Ensign Loew was aware of how volatile he sounded, of how he was leaning forward, and it was true that in that moment he wasn't sure what he was capable of. But the older man was unperturbed.

Professor Einstein slowly closed the journal and met Ensign Loew's eye.

"As you might imagine, others have come to see me on this matter. But you've built quite a case against me, young man. If I were inclined to explain myself, I could tell you that nuclear fission would have been discovered without my work. I could also tell you that had I known the Germans would fail in their efforts to develop the atomic bomb, I would never have written that letter to the president."

To continue on would be ungracious, but all grace in Ensign Loew had been stripped away by the war. "You did what you did, don't try and sidle away from the credit now."

"You know I did not create this power. I merely helped unlock it."

But Ensign Loew wasn't prepared to stop.

"If you could have seen it—what you've done . . ."

"But you have seen it, haven't you," Professor Einstein said. "Would you like to sit down and tell me about it? Because otherwise, if continued, this behavior of yours that you displayed tonight will surely tax your liver."

Ensign Loew felt himself staring at the older man, his eyes locked onto those shining dark orbs. If his knowledge of the world didn't approach Professor Einstein's, and of course it didn't—that much was clear to him now, because the great man's knowledge seemed infinite—then by virtue of what Ensign Loew had endured, it was at least equal in this one narrow area. Despite himself, Ensign Loew found himself sinking into a chair.

"All right," Ensign Loew said, steadying his voice. He wished he had more rye, or even some water, but he wasn't willing to wait any longer. "We were one hundred miles out when we saw the flash. At fifty we saw the column of smoke."

"Rising from the city."

"There was no more city."

"The liberated atom spares nothing in its way," Professor Einstein said, as if to himself.

"The sky was red and solid with smoke and dust, a great canopy of it, and then the rain came, thick and black. We could see it hitting land in the distance. There was heat. It went on like that for days, while they kept us on the ship. Then the orders came down to go ashore and try and rebuild some roads, and we took to the landing craft . . ." Ensign Loew paused for a moment, unsure if he could go on. Then he did.

"The first thing we noticed was the quiet. There was no sound. No voices, no vehicles, no birds. Of course there were no birds, there were no trees, not a single blade of grass was left. The ground had been burned into a dark crust. It crunched under our feet in places. Then we discovered we were walking on charred bodies." Ensign Loew paused, but Professor Einstein said nothing and allowed him to continue.

"On the outskirts we saw a few naked people, walking toward us, still staggering around even though more than a week had passed—an old man, a woman with a baby. We tried to look away. It was as if some strange thing had deprived them of their clothes. One sailor thought they must've been in a bathhouse when the blast hit, because they were all naked. And they were all Negroes."

"Negroes?"

"Negroes. It made no sense. Maybe they were prisoners. We asked: 'What happened to you?' When they answered, we realized they were Japanese. Some spoke English and told us 'After the blast, this is the color we turned.' We passed through the smoke of crematorium fires, which had begun to be stoked day and night, to dispose of the dead, until we reached a makeshift military hospital and saw the patients had the patterns of their kimonos burned right into their skin. The Japanese doctors were treating them with vitamins and other things that did no good. They asked if

American doctors had a cure for the bomb's effects on the human body. All we could say was: 'We don't know.' Then they asked if the American doctors were coming. We said yes, even though none were coming."

Professor Einstein remained silent as Ensign Loew's words cascaded forth, of their own accord now. "It was a pitiful sight, Professor: people in agony, slowly dying. Not soldiers, but women, the aged, children . . ." Now his words tapered off. How could he describe how their heads were swollen, how their noses and their lips, their very skin, just peeled off, revealing bone? He found his voice again. "We gave them water. We thought it was the humane thing to do."

The professor shook his head sorrowfully.

"But as soon as we did, they vomited it out. And kept vomiting, blood. It all rushed out, until they were dead."

Ensign Loew stopped talking. The metronomic ticking of the grandfather clock was the only sound in the room. And then it, too, stopped. The clock had wound down. For a moment there was only silence. Then the professor spoke.

"Those are radiation burns on your hands."

"There weren't any gloves."

"But you helped anyway." Professor Einstein put aside the journal and leaned forward. "Young man, if it is of consolation to you, and I am not sure that it will be, the human nervous system requires one-thirtieth of a second to register, and one-tenth of a second to flinch; thus, for those who were close to the detonation, the blood in their brains was likely evaporating before they could feel anything."

"And for those whom I just told you about, who lived and suffered?"

"All those who live suffer, it is the way of the world," Professor Einstein said with great sadness.

A long, dreadful pause ensued. Why had he thought this man, this one man, could provide him with answers or absolution? Because now that he was here in front of him, Ensign Loew saw it: There were no answers, none for him, anyway, none that he could hope to understand. Ensign Loew didn't know if the professor was on the verge of throwing him out or perhaps falling asleep in his chair, before he finally spoke.

"Your hands, they are improving?"

"They are."

"As your hands have healed, so will your soul. You have crossed through the wasteland, but you emerged. You must forgive yourself. You don't have to forgive me, but you must yourself."

Ensign Loew looked up at Professor Einstein and blinked.

"Now, you don't want to think about this too much anymore, young man," Professor Einstein continued, fervor in his voice for the first time of the evening. "Do you understand me?"

This was a possibility that hadn't previously occurred to Ensign Loew.

"What should I do?" he asked, an utter fool before the older man.

"Extinguish it from your memory. Somehow. You can. Forget this idea of causality. If it exists, it cannot be known. There is no absolution. But neither is there punishment. Instead, you will accept all that happened, and you will move forward. Meet another girl. Marry. Find something in which to place your faith, whether it be love or the immutable purity of design. Create. Build. Lead your life in a way that does those whom you witnessed some honor. It is the only choice for you. For everyone who was here tonight."

There was nothing further to say between them. The young man sat there, unexpectedly calm. After a while, Einstein seemed to notice the quiet and picked up a small brass crank from the table next to him, stood, and accompanied the younger man to the foyer. Einstein opened the glass casing and used the crank to wind the clock, slightly adjusting the minute hand as his guest put on his coat. The ticking resumed. Loew nodded to his host and stepped outside into the cold, starry night. Einstein looked after him, raised his hand in a slight wave, and then closed the door softly.

As Loew walked down Mercer Street, exhaling thick clouds of breath, he was enveloped by a great sense of lightness. The shame of his complicity, his survival, began to recede at last. He hoped he would find a way to draft again. He believed he would. He reached his dormitory, ready to resume his studies, having stepped out of the crumbling order of history and finally ready to reenter the realm of the living in all its mundane beauty. He never returned to Einstein's for another Sabbath, and indeed they never spoke again.

In memory of
Robert E. Levien,
Princeton '45, USN ret.,
1923–2014.

The Degree

by Joe R. Lansdale

Thanks for the mail vibe, Len, and I'll do my best to address your question in full. I realize it may have been merely a polite way to begin a communication, and may not have been something you were truly hoping to be answered, outside of some brief homily, and believe me, you'll get that, but perhaps with a bit of window dressing. You have stepped in it now.

I'm not too far ahead of you in the game of life, cousin, but since you asked, here's part of my answer, and we'll call this the standard part of the lecture, so to speak, the homily, and then I can only offer my observations and personal experiences. Grab the seat cushions and wait for it.

If you want some kind of career, and you suggest you want the same kind I'm striving for, you have to plan for it.

Yeah. I know. There it is, the dead fish under the sofa, but in the main, that's all I got.

Now for a bit of that window dressing I mentioned.

In a way, I suppose you could say I have been planning on my career since I was quite young. Or rather my parents were planning on it for me. Dad always said, "Unless you want to live on the bottom of the food chain, be one of life's targets, you best put your nose to the grindstone."

I'm sure you've heard that from your parents, or some version of it, and maybe that's why you're asking me what to do, because of our similar backgrounds. I am what you soon will be. A college boy, but I have dreams.

My family didn't really have the money for the university. We aren't on the lower rung of the ladder, as you know, but neither are we at the top of it either. We hope to rise, and fear falling below, which is a solid kind of fear, of course.

I took out loans for my education. If you can avoid that, and I doubt you can, as I know your family's financial situation is similar to our own, then you should. Loans can eat at you. You think, well, I'll pay them off with the better money I'll make from having a degree, but that doesn't necessarily follow. There are pitfalls.

I been studying for a while now, and I'm still not finished, and I owe tons already. The final bill will be staggering. I may be forced to do what I trained for well past my prime, and that might even mean a part-time job, and even then, I don't know I can pay it all off, so I have to decide to enjoy my work, and be happy with that. I do think about rising in the business, becoming worth a lot more than average, but I can only work for that, not count on it. I may be stuck with field work all my life, or at best, rise to middle management, and at worst, I may be sweeping the place out, wherever that place might be, as where I will be stationed in the end is currently unknown, of course. No guarantees.

I'm not squawking, I hasten to add, but those are the facts, and you, cousin, will be facing the same situation. The American Dream is an opportunity, not a promise.

For years free college was talked about, or letting debts go, but frankly, the government has too much tied up in so many other things that government loans are not something they want to drop. Private loaners, and I have used both government and private, aren't in a forgiving mood either with the way things are these days.

I like the work I'm training for, as I've had a taste of it in the labs, but again, who's to say? It can also be stressful. I have days when I feel overcome, but I soldier on. Not everyone can. Keeping up grades, studying, doing lots of physical training. It's a tough gig.

A fellow I met on campus and became good friends with, Jason Rone, he got so overwhelmed with his studies, the lab projects, that one day he went up to the Top Tower, as they call the highest building on campus, and jumped.

There were people who saw him do it, and they said on his way down he was flapping his arms like wings, as if he was suffering regret and hoping to take off like a bird. He didn't manage to do that. They said he yelled one word that he stretched out to last until he was all the way down, splattering on the cement.

The word was *Shiiiiiiiiiitttt.*

That's kind of funny in a way. Jason was always a kidder. He said to me not long ago, "Wouldn't it be a severe fucking to my government loans if something happened to me and they just had to eat it?"

Looking at it that way, his jump was a kind of joke, and he cheated them out of their money. I'll miss him. He could make everyone in lab laugh.

Still, I'm sticking with my educational plan, and jumping hasn't occurred to me as a solution. I don't know if I'd have the balls to make that choice anyway. Better to owe all my life than to end it, right?

Environmental studies are a much harder degree than I imagined. When I was young, I figured it would be easy enough. Everything seemed easy then, as I was only thinking about it, not doing it.

My first class is my favorite. It's the lab class and we get a chance to get our hands dirty, so to speak. With all the environmental problems, and the fact that most are caused by overpopulation, learning how to lower the population, minimizing our footprint as they call it, seems an absolute necessity.

And you got all these people, immigrants coming in, and you got assholes having babies one after another, so something has to be done. I've nothing against babies, but some people just shouldn't have any.

Lab class is easier than the real thing. They bring specimens and experiments to you. You don't have to go out and find them. All you have to do is what you're taught. The labs are training for field work, but it's not real field work. Still, it gives you a taste.

When they bring in the lesser citizens or non-citizens, to lab class, the ones they nab from the other side, I find that I can overpower my experiment rather quickly. I got some size on me, but it's the training that counts. Sure, the lab's streets and building walls are merely facsimiles of the actual areas where the lesser lives dwell, but to learn how to do the job right, you have to start somewhere. Way I see it, I do what I'm supposed to do, it's just one less doorway or cardboard box with feet sticking out of it. If we ever reach zero population status, then I suppose I might be out of a job after years of study, but with the way things are going now, all the people, many of them working shit jobs, the Spartan method, as it's called in class, is one way to fix things.

The Spartan philosophy, or at least parts of it, are the main basis for what we do. You should study that before you come to the university. You may know about it, but know it well. And if you are unfamiliar with it, here it is in a nutshell.

Spartans in ancient Greece, if they could sneak up on and kill one of the peasants, it was fine. But they had to show their stealth skills, not get caught, and if they managed that, well then, killing was acceptable, sanctioned by the government. Spartans considered it training for the army, living off the land, using stealth skills to kill. That's why they call us Environmental Spartans.

We are an army of sorts, but I always feel that I'm part of something bigger than myself when I'm in lab and I catch my experiment, subdue them, and then strangle them with my preferred jujitsu choke, sometimes a garrote.

The children are easy, but you have to chase them more, and they can be quick and elusive. There's not as much room for them to run in the lab setup, but it gives you a feel for what you'll be doing once you get the old sheepskin. In the outside world, they won't be brought to you on a platter, so to speak, and they'll have more room to run.

Another thing, and the lab instructor pounds this into you. You got to watch thinking of them as being like you and me, as they are not. Remember, many are non-white, others are dirty, and practically savage, so, hey you do what you got to do. It's the job.

And keep this in mind, as it's important. They are a resource. Sometimes

I look at them and see them as the same as me, but I know that's my empathy, which is high and something of a nuisance. I try to make their deaths brief, and I try to keep in mind I've taken a potential breeder and moocher off the street, and have provided some nice cuts of meat.

Believe me, I've thought about training to be a butcher, but if we manage to do as we are trained, reach the logical end to all that training, that meat could be limited, though, of course, some of them would be kept for breeding purposes to keep some kind of supply, so you can't say all babies made by those shitters are bad. But controlled breeding is different than willy-nilly breeding, and then them being out there trying to get over the wall into the main population. Some think they're as good as us.

There's the first bell. I have ten minutes before the second bell and class.

Got to run. I like to warm up before I go in. I don't want to get caught on the back foot, so to speak. One of the experiments got the better of a lab partner last week, put him in the hospital. The experiment was a tough one, girl about seventeen with a stutter, but I got her. I got her good. Used my hands. Oh, I train with the sniper rifle, all the other weapons. The flame thrower is fun, I admit, and man is it efficient, but it's messy, and you can catch the lab walls on fire and frequently the meat is so damaged there's no gain. That's a weapon for elimination, not utilization.

Silly accidents can happen with the flame thrower, as well. Yesterday, guy in class was putting the cook on one of the experiments and burned his own eyebrows off, which was kind of funny. If that wasn't enough, a week ago another fellow using the flame thrower, set the professor's desk on fire, which did not go over well, but afterwards a lot of us had a laugh about it, and the meat was recoverable, and each of us were allowed to have a piece of it. It was charred in spots, raw in others, but digestible. Our professor called it a ritual, not a meal, but it just made me hungry.

Here's a note of warning, as you may not have heard. You remember Gabe, my age, big guy? Bigger than me. He and I used to hang together. Good guy. He could cuss the vermin about as well as I have ever heard it done. The other day he twisted his ankle bad in class, during a lab exercise with one of the outsiders. Well, more than twisted it, he's really messed it up. I see him with that limp, it's hard to imagine him staying at our level. And you got to do that. You got to take care of yourself so that you have a better chance of quickly recovering from an injury.

I hate the situation Gabe is in, and if he doesn't heal up quick and solid, they may release him onto the street, behind the wall. On the other side he'll have the shit population to avoid. If he can avoid that, well, he is open game for us then.

I hope he heals up. That's all I can say. The environmental corps have rules, and those rules were made to make society work, to keep it on a certain economic and racial level, keep out the invalids and malcontents.

I believe that, Len. I do. We can't have inferior folks out there breathing air and shitting turds. That's not good. I don't even think it's biblical, though I haven't read the book to know. I will, of course. Eventually.

Now, keep in mind, Gabe hasn't fallen to that level, the level of inferiority, but he is pretty bad off, and I have a feeling how it will turn out. Already, I'm trying to accept that he won't be one of us much longer. It's like when you have a relative who has some kind of disease, and you know they're dying, and they know it too, and you don't plan for it, but gradually, you start to wean yourself off their declining energy. They are, at least for you emotionally, already dead. It's nature's way of accepting inevitabilities.

I think about the fact that I could end up that way as well. We're all an injury shy of being infirm, and that's almost as bad as having the wrong skin color. People with diseases, malformation and so on, they just don't fit in to a progressive society, do they, Len?

So, I think about that, sure, but I have learned, through certain mantras we are taught, to slip it to the back part of my brain, as if it is behind a fence. And again, I've got those empathy problems. I have to think of it like feeding rats to snakes. They are the rats, and we are the snakes, and snakes are survivors. So are rats, but that's why we have the environmental corps. To make those rats part of our reptilian survival.

Damn, forgive me for comparing us to snakes. We are far better than some cold reptile. But, empathy or not, the rats are the rats, and you have to know rats can bite back and breed constantly.

We have the government behind us. They don't.

We have our degrees and our training. They don't.

We are doing something beneficial to the world. They are not.

They are the problem.

We are the solution.

We come from a better class of people than they do. They kill, it's murder; we kill, it's legal assassination. Remember, nits make lice.

This brings me to one last note. You asked about Aunty Cecily, why you haven't seen her around, and I have saved this information for the last, as I thought it would be a good conclusion to my suggestions to study hard and train hard and to stay super fit.

Aunt Cecily, she got a little short on memory. Too much had to be done to maintain her, so, they put her on the other side of the fence. She didn't last long.

Weep not for Aunt Cecily, for she had ceased to be the person we knew by the time my mother, her sister, helped put her over the fence. She wandered right into them, Mother said, and it was quick, and when Mother knew it was certain, she looked away and we have written her off. This will be the last time I mention her name.

There's the second bell. Got to go for sure now. Must end this, and therefore, let me close with this. I didn't really give you much in the way of advice, but I hope it helps you to understand it can be done, and that it's worthwhile work, and I'm glad you're interested in following in my footsteps, as you say. Well, those footsteps have taken a short trip as of now, but I wouldn't mind doing well enough as a student, and later in my job, so that you might see me as a role model of sorts. Last bit of advice. Stay healthy, for heaven's sake.

The American Dream may in fact be, as I said, an opportunity, not a promise, but it is alive and well.

Hang in, cuz,
Charles

Rounded with a Sleep

by A. J. Hartley

"*Knowing I loved my books, he furnish'd me*
From mine own library with volumes that
I prize above my dukedom."

—Prospero, *The Tempest* by William Shakespeare

"You've been told this before," said the department chair wearily. "Several times, and not just by me. These issues predate my appointment, Herb. They were in your file long before I got here," she added, as if he might be missing the gist. "This mystic, guru approach to teaching in which the students sit at your feet and drink in your wisdom . . . It's just not how things are done anymore."

"Have the students complained?" said Herb. He was serene, confident.

"Some have, actually. The better students. They say they feel dazzled by your brand of knowledge but don't feel like they are really learning very much about Shakespeare."

"My brand of knowledge," Herb echoed.

"I mean," she faltered, "that what you are doing is out of step with their other classes. The students don't feel a sense of connection, like you aren't involved in the same conversation as they are having with their other faculty."

"Well, there is that," said Herb, smiling.

The Chair's eyes flashed. She was generally good at keeping her emotions in check but Herb knew he had touched a nerve.

"Their other classes are talking identity politics, canon formation, and a whole range of theoretical and critical approaches you don't even acknowledge! I'm told the only critics you refer to are Pope, Dryden and Johnson. Tell me you are including some twentieth century approaches at least."

"We may touch on a little Empson," Herb remarked airily.

"*William* Empson?"

"Correct," he replied, smiling in that way of his which made you feel like a dog being patted on the head for bringing him his slippers.

"That's almost a century old, Herb! You know how much literary study has changed in that time? Good God, think of how much the world has changed."

" 'Beauty is truth, truth beauty,' " Herb pronounced. " 'That is all ye know on earth and all ye need to know.' "

"Keats?" spat the Chair. "We are talking about updating your teaching to something resembling the world these kids actually live in and you give me fucking Keats?"

The expletive was a rarity in the Chair's mouth and Herb counted its appearance as a victory.

"I have no time for fads," he said. "My business is truth in art, truth unaltered by the passage of time, by trendy politics or educational innovation. Shakespeare, as Ben Jonson observed, is not of an age but for all time."

"Nothing is for all time, Herb."

"Not if your vision is clouded by the whims of academia, no. But some things transcend craze."

"Meaning your brand of culture is the only one that matters," said the Chair, her lips tight, another nerve touched.

Herb Martin watched her. Though she was quite still her body positively vibrated with suppressed energy like a steel cable drawn tight. He had assumed that her calling him on the carpet—an annual ritual since she had taken over the job—was just more bureaucratic bean counting, but this felt different: personal. The idea pleased him, reminded him of how powerless she was, despite her position, in the face of his seniority. He knew she would love to get rid him, bring in some cultural critic type who specialized in Shakespeare and "marginalized peoples" or—God help him—performance theory, but Herb wasn't going anywhere, and the more frustrated that made her, the better he liked it.

"We seem," he said, "to be at an impasse. This is the way I teach. It is the way I have always taught. The way I was taught . . ."

"And that's the problem, Herb. We have moved on."

"I have not," he said simply, adding before she could interject her full-throated agreement, "because I see no need to move on, no benefit in change for its own sake. You think my methods are Victorian . . ."

"Not just your methods, your content too."

"That is as it may be," Herb said, the world's most elegant steamroller, "but that is because I think the Victorians were right: their insight, their sensibility, their pride in a tradition."

"A straight, white, male tradition."

"A tradition of excellence to which all could aspire."

The Chair barked with derisive laughter.

"How generous of you," she said, "to invite the lowly to join the club which celebrates the things which confirm your authority."

"You're welcome," said Herb, smiling like a plaster saint.

The Chair gritted her teeth and sat there for a moment, hands palm down on the desk top as if she was holding it in place. Then she took a breath and opened a manila folder which had been positioned at her elbow ready for use like a dueling pistol.

"Let's talk about your syllabi," she said, as if he had just walked in and the previous debate had not happened. She scanned whatever damning evidence was inside the folder before stabbing a crucial paragraph with her hard, thin finger and enumerating the specifics.

"Non-standard format. Whole weeks left without specific reading assignments. No student learning outcomes itemized. Unclear grading criteria. Nothing keyed to department or college mission statements."

She looked up expectantly and Herb smiled as if she had complimented him. He had been teaching Shakespeare for forty years, from before Darnell College—or anyone else—had deemed standard syllabi format or student learning outcomes an essential component of higher education. His gaze flicked from the chair's unwavering and slightly alarming blue eyes, landing on her immaculately arranged books on her dustless shelves. Alphabetized, he noted. Very efficient.

"My classes are unique," he said. "They don't fit the patterns of other teachers."

He didn't say *lesser* teachers, but the adjective was there in the slight curl of his lip and the Chair saw it.

"You can't just randomly assign grades at the end of the semester!" she shot back. "You know how many student grievances I've had to field for you over the last two years?"

"Not random," he said, unflustered. "The students write a final paper and their grade is based on that combined with their attendance."

"That's the entire grade?" said the Chair, peering at him in disbelief. "No exams? No reading quizzes? No presentations or group work?"

God, thought Herb. Group work! Like asking monkeys to build a steam engine.

That was one of his long-dead mother's phrases, bless her toxic little heart. And why a steam engine? He had no idea.

"No," he said.

"You can't do that, Herb! Apart from anything else it means you have nothing on which to base midterm grades . . ."

"I don't assign midterm grades."

"You have to! It's college policy. If you don't, the students have no idea how they are doing in your class until the end!"

"They should be doing their best work regardless."

"They aren't doing any work till the end! You mean they should shut up and listen and then reproduce what you told them!"

"I am the expert. They are the students. They are supposed to learn from me."

"Oh, for God's sake, Herb!"

"Are you suggesting I should be learning from *them*?"

"You know, that might not be such a bad idea, if only so that you learned how to navigate the campus's online data entry system instead of pinning grades to your office door!"

"We always used to . . ."

"We don't now! It's a privacy violation if everyone in the class can see everyone else's grade. If you need to be shown how to use the computer system," she added, suddenly weary, "we can do that, but it is your job to use the tools the school has provided. And I mean *your* job. I don't want to hear that you have been asking your colleagues to do it for you."

That was Tommy Kirkland, little snake. Blabbing out of school when he had been asked a favor by a man he should have considered a venerable mentor. The technical writing teacher had only been at Darnell two years but was already the golden child of the department. Won grants. Herb had never applied for a grant. He taught his classes and wrote little articles which appeared in minor journals edited by men he'd known for decades, and he had assumed that *that* was his job. But somewhere between being tenured before the Great War, or so it seemed, in the days when polite if dusty rumination about old books had been *de rigeur*, the goal posts had moved. In fact, they had not so much moved as turned into something else entirely, like a basketball hoop or, as he frequently complained, a cash register.

"I'm not a baby sitter," he said, mustering a little righteous indignation. "And I'm not a corporate drone! I'm a senior faculty member and an expert in my field."

In fact this last had never really been true. Herb never admitted as much in public, but he knew it nonetheless. The profession had left him so far in its wake that he wasn't sure he really was in the same field as the new Shakespeareans with their theory, their identity politics and their steady dismantling of all he had taken for granted. Academia had, he sometimes declared, lost its way, and if Herb Martin had never become the North Star of his field, that was the fault of his impoverished profession, and its loss, not his.

"Your expertise is appreciated," the Chair said, not so much weary now as exhausted, so that the closest thing to disagreement she could muster was the carefully evasive passive voice. He *was* appreciated. Just not by her . . .

"I don't feel particularly appreciated," said Herb, sensing weakness.

She sighed, tipped her head back so far her face pointed to the ceiling, and closed her eyes. She breathed, then returned.

"Can I level with you, Herb?" she said, leaning forward and putting both elbows on the table.

The shift in her tone, the way the fight had suddenly evacuated from her face, unnerved him a little, but Herb still thought he had won, so he nodded and said "Of course," in a breezy, confident sort of way.

"This isn't coming from me," she said. He knew something had flashed across his face because she shook her head, raising one hand as if warding off a fly. "I don't mean you personally are being targeted by the dean or the provost. This is not about your five-year review."

Herb's five-year review: the document in which he was supposed to include his detailed plans for publication and other scholarly activity for the next half decade: and the document in which he had written simply "More of the same, I suppose." It had not been well received, and had led to a conversation almost exactly like this one just three months earlier.

"It's about the college," she said.

"Arts and Sciences?" said Herb, intrigued.

"No," she replied, looking, he thought, almost upset. Herb felt a prickle of glee. "I wish it were just the unit. But no. It's Darnell. The whole school."

"What about it?"

"Things aren't going well, Herb," she confided. "Financially. Enrollment is way down and I'm hearing whispers that our accreditation is being suspended pending the resolution of certain fiscal issues."

Herb frowned.

"Fraud?" he asked.

"Nothing like that. Just debt. We've been borrowing heavily for years, and the tuition hike has not brought in the necessary funds."

Herb sat back, relieved. This was all above his paygrade. He borrowed her gesture from before and waved the matter away.

"It will be all right," he said. "Universities have these ups and downs."

"It's more than that . . ." she began, then redirected. "The point is that we are under the microscope, particularly in terms of whether students graduate on time and whether they think they do so with skills that are directly applicable to the work place."

"Perhaps if we went back to teaching traditional literary study and its attendant values, students would see the worth of the program!" retorted Herb, rediscovering his righteous ire. "We are about the development of the human, about expanding their horizons, about reflection and analysis . . ."

"Critical thinking and communication," the chair cut in. "I know. Though I'm not sure how sitting silently through your lectures for sixteen weeks hones their critical thinking skills."

"I'm modelling how to think so that they can see . . ."

"They don't see that!"

"I can't be held accountable if students misread the value of what they are learning . . ."

"But that's the thing," the chair cut in. "You can. You are being. We all are. I realize you dislike the idea that what we do is somehow akin to vocational training and that we are being made to jump through the same hoops as the business school . . ."

"By people who don't respect or understand . . ."

"What we do, yes," she cut in, "but this is where we are, nonetheless. We need to be able to show that students are learning—and *believe* they are learning—applicable job skills. This is higher education in the twenty-first century, Herb, and if you can't swallow your pride and get with the program, there will be consequences, not just for you, but for all of us."

Herb frowned.

"What kind of consequences?" he demanded. She was bluffing. He was a tenured full professor. He was on the edge of an honorable retirement and emeritus status. He knew the Chancellor personally. If she thought she could ease him out, dock his salary or send him back to teaching freshman comp, she had another thing coming.

She gave him a considering look then sat back, defeated.

"Let's not get into that," she said. "Just . . . try not to fight every request to get on board as if it's a matter of principle that goes to the heart of what you think you do."

"Well, I'm not so sure . . ."

"Herb!" she said, with such force that he blustered to a halt and gaped at her. "Just fix the damn syllabi, okay? Now if you don't mind, I have a meeting."

Herb left the Chair's office in an indignant haze. As he walked the slightly buckled floors of the oak-paneled corridor which wound back to his office he rehearsed his usual speeches about the corporatization of education, the bloated and unnecessary ranks of middle management nonentities, and a brace of other familiar talking points invoked privately to justify ignoring whatever directive he had just been given. These were among his favorite mantras. He believed in them. It did not occur to him that the moral high ground on which he stood had been shifting for decades and might never have been his.

His slow but reliable train of thought was momentarily derailed as he rounded the corner and found someone standing at his office door. Waiting. Herb hesitated, considered turning back before he was seen, but the man looked up.

Man was right. Herb had assumed it would be a student, but this person was close to his own age, clad in a charcoal gray suit, sharp looking and slightly too shiny to be respectable.

Shark skin, suggested some largely dormant part of Herb's brain, resting its case as the man turned to Herb and gave him a broad smile full of sharp-looking teeth.

"Professor Martin," said the man. He looked positively delighted to see him and Herb, unused to such a greeting, fell back on formality.

"Is there something with which I can help you?" he asked.

The remark made the shark-man's smile wider still. His teeth sparkled.

"More of an explanation, really," he said. "From me. I'm Tony, by the way."

He pronounced his name, then extended a strong, tan hand. In its grip, Herb felt positively frail.

"You seem to have the advantage of me," he remarked, knowing that he sounded unfriendly and not caring.

"I do," said Tony, holding Herb's eyes a fraction too long and savoring the second word as if it had real and slightly menacing significance. Then he smiled again, grinned, really, and any whiff of coolness evaporated. "I just wanted to confirm that I'll be sitting in on your Shakespeare class this afternoon."

Herb, who had put his hand in his pocket for the office key, stiffened.

"In what capacity?" he asked frostily, his eyes on the door handle.

So the Chair had not been bluffing. They were watching already.

Herb shoved the key into the lock and twisted it hard, applying his shoulder to send it juddering open.

"Just a fan," said Tony.

"A *fan*?" said Herb, giving him a withering look. He disliked the word at the best of times.

"Of Shakespeare's," said Tony, "though I've heard great things about you too. The great Herbert Martin. Quite the intellectual powerhouse in your day."

Herb considered him coolly for a moment, then pushed his way to the padded leather chair behind the stained ancient desk. It was piled with equally stained and ancient books and strewn with papers covered in his own neat copperplate. The computer sat among them like a space ship from an alien world.

"Well, I'm glad to have achieved such renown," he remarked dryly. "But I'm afraid I don't permit auditors. The class is closed to the public."

"Ordinarily, yes, I know that," said Tony, still smiling, undaunted. "But this, brother man, is a rather special case."

"For you, perhaps," said Herb, sitting heavily, and turning to face his visitor who was still standing in the doorway as if waiting for the invitation to sit which he would not receive. "I'm afraid my policies are nonnegotiable."

"Yes, I thought as much," said Tony, "which is why you'll find that I have been added to the class roster."

"I beg your pardon?"

"I'm registered for the class. I'm what you might call a nontraditional student."

So saying, Tony produced a piece of computer printout with a couple of signatures in blue ink.

"The course began three months ago," said Herb, staring at the printout blindly. "You can't add it now! The semester is almost over."

"Even so," said Tony, flashing his hammerhead smile once more.

"Even so what?" said Herb. "Even if your registration is legitimate—and I don't see how it can be at this stage of the term—you'll fail for sure. You've missed everything. Even if you did a decent final paper you can't possibly meet the requirements of the course. You can register for next semester if you wish."

Herb pushed the paper back toward the other man, but he didn't take it, and it teetered on the edge of the desk between them like a wounded bird.

"That's just fine, brother man," said Tony, his smile fixed as his level stare.

"Fine?" said Herb, unsure if he had scored his point or not.

"I don't mind failing. I just want to be in the class."

Herb stared at him.

"If you had wanted to be in the course you should have come in August."

"You misunderstand me," said Tony easily. "I mean I just want to be in the class *this afternoon*."

"I don't follow."

"You are teaching *The Tempest* today, yes?"

Herb shook his head as if to clear it.

"Is that relevant?" he asked.

"Oh yes," said Tony keenly. "Absolutely. That's why I want to be there. I'm very . . . *connected* to that play."

"Be that as it may," said Herb, "you can't add a class in the final week of the semester. I'm sorry, but that's my last word on the subject. Now, if you don't mind, I have a class to prepare."

That was a lie, of course. The class Herb was about to teach would be exactly like every other *Tempest* class he had ever taught. He lowered his eyes to his desk and made a show of pushing some papers around and flipping open a book.

Tony did not move or speak. He loomed but Herb ignored him. Then the other man leaned over and pushed the computer printout squarely into Herb's field of view. Herb inhaled, pursed his lips and sat back, giving the other man a defiant stare.

"Again," said Tony, smiling again, "you misunderstand me. I paid for the class. The whole course. You are, of course, free to fail me for nonattendance thus far, but today I will be attending your class. As I said, I was simply notifying you so that we wouldn't have to have this conversation in front of the other students. I know how much you hate to be embarrassed in public, brother man."

And with that, he turned on his heel and left.

Herb fumed. He called the registrar's office and used phrases like *what is the meaning of?* and *preposterous and disrespectful*, but the registrar told him that her hands were tied.

"You can file a grievance and you can fail him, but you can't forbid him from attending a course for which he has registered and paid unless his presence is disruptive, threatening, or . . ."

But Herb had already hung up.

He considered taking the matter to the Chair but knew that would not help, and might make him look impotent, even foolish, all of which set a burner under his irritation until he was beside himself with rage.

Just why the matter bothered him so much, he couldn't say, though he knew it was dimly related to his previous argument with the Chair and to that broader sense of powerlessness, of being part of a profession the world at large respected less and less. It was maddening. He was at the height of his powers as a teacher, a prominent (well, fairly) expert on the world's most famous and studied author but he had no control of his own professional life. He blamed all those trendy scholars with their impenetrable jargon and their smug, leftist agendas: it was no wonder the profession had a bull's eye daubed on it by the media, the politicians, the odiously titled *business community* . . .

And so he spent the intervening hour before class.

A part of him doubted Tony would show, assumed that—his point scored—the man would vanish from Herb's life forever. After all, why would anyone spend a semester's tuition on a single class? Even a professor like Herb who had a pretty high assessment of his gifts in the classroom knew it made no sense, and that bothered him.

That's fine, brother man . . .

Something felt wrong, off somehow, as if the world had wobbled on its axis and reality as he had always known it had shifted subtly, and not for the better.

It was with an unsteady hand that Herb opened the door to the familiar seminar room. He tried to look nonchalant, flashing a vague smile around the room at his eight students: in the old days there had been three times that many. Most classes would have been cut if they had been so clearly under-enrolled, but he was senior and this was Shakespeare, a course the department's mandate promised to offer annually, whether it was in demand or not. The thought bothered him, and his smile flickered. Then his gaze fell on Tony, and it stalled entirely.

Tony was wearing the same sharky suit as before, but he looked older now, older even than Herb, so the slick, sharply cut fabric looked doubly strange, like a costume, though what he was supposed to be, Herb had no idea. Tony met his eyes and his smile expanded ingenuously, as if their shared presence here meant that their former disagreement had been re-solved and swept away.

Herb sat unsteadily. He felt hot and his breathing was labored. Nor-mally he would begin by calling the names on his attendance sheet, but he didn't want to draw attention to Tony sitting smug and shiny in the corner, so he fumbled with his books and then said simply,

"Right. *The Tempest.*"

The students looked at each other and then at him. After taking atten-dance Herb usually walked around the classroom talking, tossing out quo-tations and critical references without pause for the allotted time, allowing five minutes at the end for questions. There rarely were any. Despite his comments to the Chair about how he assessed student participation, there really wasn't any, and what Herb called participation everyone else called attendance.

Good word, *attendance*. It suggested being present and, well, attend-ing: listening, but also simply waiting, like Prufrock's attendant lord, hov-ering around Hamlet poised to be instructed or, more likely, to applaud the scene's true star.

But today Herb was, in the parlance of his students, off his game. He felt unsteady, rattled, his usual bravura performance of erudite scholarly wizardry labored and creaky as his old limbs. His voice wobbled. He tried to push on through but he knew they heard that uncharacteristic hesita-tion, and while he thought some of them pitied him a little, he knew that most were glad. As the Chair's insinuations about complaints made clear, a lot of them didn't like Herb very much. They thought him old-fashioned to the point of irrelevance, certainly, but that they might have indulged as an old man's eccentricity. No, they disliked him because they thought him arrogant, condescending and dismissive of anything he didn't already know. By extension they also found him tacitly but definitely misogynistic, homophobic and racist, not because he espoused such positions in his lec-tures, but because of what they thought of as the *vibe* he gave off, the little smirks and sneers which accompanied his pronouncements like punctua-tion marks, and because he never allowed such matters to sully the poems and plays on which he held forth. For Herbert Martin, Shakespeare was still the glory of a western canon which was straight, white and male, a canon expressly bent on promoting its own values over all others, belittling, dismissing and destroying as it went . . .

Did he know this? Not in, as it were, so many words, but did the possibility smolder deep in his twisted, angry and ineffectual little heart? Did it stoke his sense of unappreciated greatness, of a career wasted in a no-name institution, casting pearls before the undergraduate swine who gobbled up whatever might "check the boxes" required by the inane professions they would stumble into, jobs which would pay better than his faster than it would take him to craft his next monograph, while his junior colleagues and resentful Chair watched him like circling vultures, casting lots for who would get his office when he finally accepted the destiny he had been refusing for years? Oh yes, it did that all right. Sometimes he wished he could poison the ink on the pages of the books they pored over in class like the villain in that Umberto Eco novel, kill them off like rats, even with the texts they could never understand. But then he would think that continuing to teach them all that they hated was poison and triumph enough, and the cinder of his heart would flare and spark with malicious joy before cooling again.

He kept such thoughts tightly under wraps, or so he thought. He suspected that some of his quiet loathing leaked out but that didn't concern him. He was the esteemed professor; the opinions of his students were of no consequence. If the truth were known, he took the same attitude to the Shakespeare texts which were the bedrock of his career. He felt no particular liking for them, no abiding interest, certainly no passionate conviction about their worth. Taken together they were simply data about which his job circled like detritus in a drain. They were facts and quotes, riddles to which he knew the answers. He might have been lecturing on the workings of a washing machine, diagraming ley lines or explaining the syntax of some dead language. It wouldn't make any difference to him. Perhaps it never had. From this point in his life it was hard to remember. He looked back from time to time, but it was like peering down a railway tunnel, long, straight and dark. He knew that somewhere there was a point of light, a place where he had entered the tunnel, but he couldn't see it, and had not been able to see it for so long that he no longer thought of it as a real part of his existence, as if he had been in the tunnel forever and always would be.

So Herb trotted out his *Tempest* lecture, steeped as it was in scholarship that was a century and half old, painting a picture of the aging wizard Prospero as the benign patriarch punishing the guilty for their own good, dispensing wisdom and justice before turning his back on the desert island and on magic, returning to his dukedom in Milan with his enemies following, humble and contrite in their manifest sins. He didn't talk about slavery, colonization, racism and genocide, though they were central to what other professors talked about with regard to the play, nor did he sully his depiction of Prospero with charges of puritanism, abusive parenting and Machiavellian political manipulation. Prospero was Shakespeare, he said, a self-portrait of a man looking back on his artistic career at the moment he stepped away from it. And though he didn't say it aloud, Prospero was also himself: wise and potent, a mystical figure whose authority was absolute and incontrovertible even in age. *Because* of his age.

"Antonio doesn't ask for forgiveness."

The remark came without preamble: no raised hand, no throat-clearing cough asking permission to speak. It just rolled out wide and flat and challenging.

It was the old man who had shown up for the first time that day: Tony.

Of course it was. Herb faltered then gave the newcomer a level stare.

"I'm sorry?" he said, smiling faintly.

"Prospero's brother," the other replied unapologetically. "The man who usurped his dukedom and arranged for him to be packed off with his daughter to the island."

"I am aware who Antonio is," said Herb. "Whether a villain asks for forgiveness or not is immaterial. He is defeated by Prospero who reclaims his rightful office from him."

"And Antonio says nothing."

"What is there to say?" asked Herb, genuinely unsure.

"He could say, 'yeah, you're right, brother man. I was an ass to steal your dukedom, and God has clearly smiled on your efforts to outmaneuver me here. I confess my crimes and acknowledge your rightful place.' But he doesn't say that."

Herb blinked uncertainly. He felt suddenly unsure of his footing and where this was heading.

"So?" he managed after a lengthy pause. "I'm not sure I see what . . ."

"I'm saying Prospero wins by doing what was done to him," said Tony, flashing his shark smile. "He was thrown out of Milan so he came and took over this island, enslaving Ariel and Caliban, ordering his daughter about before wrecking his enemies on the coast with a storm. Then he manipulates the king into a marriage alliance, using his daughter as a pawn—literally, as it turns out—and retaking his dukedom from his brother by force. This isn't about *moral superiority*. It's about might, not right, and everyone knows it. That's why Antonio doesn't speak for the rest of the play. He's been beaten, but he's no more a villain than Prospero is, is he, brother man?"

Herb winced at the phrase, then bridled.

"The play is full of villains," he intoned. "Prospero is not one of them. The villains are Antonio and Sebastian, not forgetting Caliban, Stefano and Trinculo who plan to kill Prospero and take the island for themselves!"

"Yeah, but that was never gonna happen, was it?" said Tony unruffled. "A jester and a drunken butler wresting control from a master magician and his army of spirits? That's like asking monkeys to build a steam engine, right, brother man?"

Herb stared, the hair on the back of his neck prickling. The only person he had ever heard say that outside of his own head was his mother. What was happening?

A curious stillness had come over the class. The students were watching, spellbound. It was rare enough for Herb's lectures to be disrupted by questions. His being contradicted was unheard of. The usual dusty calm of the classroom had been replaced by something charged with possibility, with menace, as if they were waiting for lightning to strike right there in the drab, familiar room, exploding out of nothing like magic.

As when first I raised the tempest . . .

But Herb hadn't raised it. This interloper had. Waltzing into his class-room and questioning his insight, his authority? It was outrageous, intol-erable.

Slowly, his old joints creaking, Herb heaved himself to his feet.

"You, most wicked sir," he boomed, "whom to call brother would even infect my mouth,

> For this, be sure, tonight thou shalt have cramps,
> Side-stitches that shall pen thy breath up; urchins
> Shall forth at vast of night that they may work,
> All exercise on thee; thou shalt be pinch'd
> As thick as honeycomb, each pinch more stinging
> Than bees that made 'em."

He had spread his arms in a wide open gesture to the heavens, palms upward and fingers splayed as if cradling an invisible globe above his head. The classroom's dull overhead fluorescents flickered and the pages of Herb's ancient textbook riffled in a sudden and inexplicable wind. As the lights stalled and died completely, the windowless room was plunged into sudden and absolute darkness, but only for a moment. Then the students' terrified eyes made out the faint phosphorescent glow of the professor, a greenish submarine light as from strange, electric creatures that lived in fathomless darkness. His eyes shone, bright and terrible, and his mouth opened wider than seemed natural, like an angler fish snapping and gulping down prey almost as large as itself. He scanned the faces about him, drew himself up to his full height and spoke in pride and outrage, his voice rattling the walls so that the class clasped their hands to their ears and shrank into their seats.

"I have bedimm'd the noontide sun," he roared, "call'd forth the muti-nous winds,

> And 'twixt the green sea and the azured vault
> Set roaring war: to the dread rattling thunder

Have I given fire and rifted Jove's stout oak
With his own bolt; the strong-based promontory
Have I made shake and by the spurs pluck'd up
The pine and cedar: graves at my command
Have waked their sleepers, oped, and let 'em forth
By my so potent art. You dare to question me!
You try to take from me this holy isle?"

The room shook. The floor buckled and desks flipped, scattering books and laptops, though the sound of the student screaming was drowned by the professor's bellowed words which filled every molecule of space in the room, and in their minds.

"I loved my books!" cried the professor, speaking now not just to Tony but to the whole class, "and sought to share them with you, ingrates that you are! I took pains to make thee speak, taught thee each hour one thing or other, when thou didst not, savages, know thine own meanings!"

"You taught us language," snarled Tony in the corner as he too got to his feet, "and our profit on't is, we know how to curse. A plague on you for learning us your language!" He turned his attention to the students then and spoke lower, or rather his mouth moved and the words appeared in their heads as if they had thought them themselves. "Why, as I told thee," said the words as they faded into clarity in their heads, "'tis a custom with him in the afternoon to sleep: there thou mayst brain him, having first seized his books, or with a log batter his skull, or cut his windpipe with a knife. Remember first to possess his books; for without them he's but a sot, as I am, nor hath not one spirit to command: they all do hate him as rootedly as I."

"WE ARE THOSE SPIRITS," responded the class together. "WE WILL NO LONGER SUFFER THIS HIS MONSTROUS TYRANNY."

And then they stood and found about them the little insignificant things—the pens and nail scissors, pocket knives and heavy, heavy books—which could, with purpose and a little bleak imagination, be turned to weapons, and they shuffled forward, breaking Herb's precious chair circle and falling upon him like hyenas on a blind and stricken wildebeest. And as they worked, Tony spoke Herb's words for him.

"But this rough magic
I here abjure, and, when I have required
Some heavenly music, which even now I do,
To work mine end upon their senses that
This airy charm is for, I'll break my staff,
Bury it certain fathoms in the earth,
And deeper than did ever plummet sound
I'll drown my book."

Herb's dimming eyes stared at him, rage and horror and desperation fighting for preeminence, but then, like Antonio recognizing when his brother had beaten him, the fight went out of him.

It was time. He hadn't seen it before—how had he not seen it before?—but the simple truth of it was undeniable now. Herb spoke again, his last speech, quiet now, barely more than a whisper, words of sadness and resignation.

"Our revels now are ended," he said, so quietly that he could not even hear his own voice above the storm. He pressed on nonetheless, in spite of the chaos and the pain of his wounds. "These our actors, as I foretold you, were all spirits and are melted into air, into thin air . . ."

And that was all he could manage. Professor Herbert Martin slipped quietly away, and the storm ceased, and the lights came on, and the students were sitting where they had always sat, looking bemused and a little bored, slowly paying more attention when they realized that the teacher had stopped talking.

There was some nervous laughter because they assumed the old man had fallen asleep, and someone made a joke whose humor soured quickly as the truth registered. A blond girl ran to the department office and the Chair came, cell phone pressed to her ear and calling for EMTs who would arrive six minutes later and eight minutes too late. Not that there would have been anything to do. It was, after all, time.

The Chair dismissed the students, said the teaching assistant would be in touch about the future of the course, what work was due and how final grades would be resolved. It was tragic, she said, though it felt more like a carnival ride which had suddenly become interesting without warning. There were even a few startled, inexplicable tears shed, though the room still felt charged with something other than grief, and beneath her earnest efficiency even the Chair seemed very slightly pleased. She turned to the teaching assistant who had always done most of the grading for Herb's classes.

"You'll be in touch with the class electronically, Tony, yes?"

Tony nodded, then recited from memory.

"We are such stuff as dreams are made on, and our little life

Is rounded with a sleep."

The Chair considered him quizzically, as if there might be something slightly wrong with him, then framed a knowing little smile and shrugged with one shoulder and the right side of her face.

"Quite," she said.

The Reasoners

by Ian Rankin

"It all begins with Kant, of course."

The young man's name was Richard Pormeroy. His accent was English and he wore a suit, neither of which really surprised Chris Digance, though perhaps they should. Pormeroy after all was a student in his mid-twenties, and they were in a building in central Edinburgh. Pormeroy was an M.Litt student, English Literature his field of study. His thesis, as he had explained it to Digance, concerned the post-Orwellian dystopian novel. It wasn't just his shapeless tweed suit that made him look as though he'd just stepped out of London in 1948. He had a floppy fringe which rested on the upper rim of his round spectacles. His face was long and pale, his fingers nimble as he undid one lock and then another before pushing open the heavy wooden door.

The two men stepped into a musty room lined with groaning bookshelves, the books predominantly leather-bound and not intended for bedtime reading. Digance didn't doubt that Kant would be there somewhere.

"*The Critique of Pure Reason*," he stated. "Published in 1781."

"Almost right," Pormeroy said with a thin smile that spoke volumes to Digance. Privately educated, maybe even at boarding school, somewhere in the south of England. Wealthy parents—almost certainly "old" money rather than new. There was a self-satisfaction to the smile, a sense of clear and absolute entitlement and an understanding that its wearer would be the cleverest person in the room, or at any rate the best-educated. Digance tried not to bristle. He himself Pormeroy would regard as lower-middle class; at least one parent in a profession but go back another generation and you'd find council housing and caravan holidays, scrimped Christmases and a fear of quarterly bills.

Pormeroy closed the door after them and even seemed to consider locking it again. Instead, he pocketed the set of keys, giving the pocket a little pat afterwards.

"I mean," he said, "that you are correct as to the title of Kant's work and the date of German publication. But The Reasoners' Club is, so far as we can ascertain, actually named after the great philosopher's second book— *The Critique of Practical Reason*. You will appreciate why."

Pormeroy broke off, fixing the visitor with an inquisitor's gaze.

"Because the club favours the practical over the pure?"

Pormeroy's widening smile told Digance he'd passed this test. "The Reasoners' was established in 1820 to further Edinburgh's reputation as a city of enlightened thinking. David Hume, alas, pre-deceased the society's founding, but would have found favour here, having been an influence on Kant."

"As was John Locke."

"But Locke was *not* from Edinburgh."

"So we don't talk about him? Didn't he influence Hume?"

"To what extent?"

"I'm . . . not entirely sure. I just read it somewhere."

"And your knowledge of the philosophy of Immanuel Kant?"

"I know about *a priori* knowledge versus *a posteriori*."

Pormeroy took his time folding his arms. "Enlighten me," he said, eyes glinting behind his spectacles.

"Okay, I'm not a philosopher," Digance eventually admitted. "I can't say I understood very much of it. But then Kant isn't why I'm here."

"Though without Kant neither of us would be exactly *here*, would we?" Pormeroy unfolded his arms and stretched them either of side of him. Digance did what was expected of him and studied his surroundings. The room was cramped, thanks to a large rectangular table at its centre.

There was no carpet, just a wooden floor whose varnish had long faded. Leaded windows looked out across a courtyard. This was the room given by the University of Edinburgh to The Reasoners'—given in perpetuity, according to Digance's research. There were a dozen chairs around the table, whose surface was covered by a layer of dark green leather. On top of the bookshelves sat busts of venerable past members, and any sections of the wood-panelled walls not taken up by shelving had been filled with framed portraits. Digance recognised the faces of Arthur Conan Doyle and Robert Louis Stevenson.

"They were both members, naturally," Pormeroy said. "As was Sir Walter Scott—though long after he'd ceased to be a student."

"It's not just for students then?"

"Let's just say we finessed our constitution to allow entry to the greatest novelist of his age. Many others came here to speak, but could not hope to be admitted as members."

"I was hoping to see the club's constitution actually."

"All in good time." Pormeroy had folded his arms again. "So this tome you're working on . . ."

"As I said in my letter, it's a history of secret societies in Britain's ancient universities—the Athena in Oxford and Minerva in Cambridge, the Classique in St Andrews, and so on."

"None of us are so secret though, are we, otherwise you'd never have found us? None would have replied to your initial query?"

"I'm grateful that you did. The thrust of the book isn't going to be critical, if that's what's worrying you."

Pormeroy snorted. "I'll be gone from here next year. It'll be someone else's problem by the time you publish."

"You'll remain a member though?"

"Oh yes, once The Reasoners' has you in its grip, it never lets go."

"I think I read that there are over three hundred members."

"Living ones, yes, that sounds about right."

Digance gave the room another look. "They don't all attend meetings though."

"First refusal goes to the student body. That's why we need to be particular. We have a core of twenty-five. We *can* squeeze them all in if need be."

"Male to female ratio?"

"That's not a factor, Mr Digance. We *do* have female members."

"How many right now, if you don't mind me asking?"

Pormeroy took his time weighing up whether to answer. "Just the one student," he eventually admitted. "Here on merit, I assure you. We've tried to recruit more women during my tenure, but they . . ." Pormeroy sighed and gave a shrug.

"Meetings are monthly?"

"That's correct."

"With occasional distinguished speakers?"

"Right again."

"And on evenings when there is no outside guest . . . ?"

Pormeroy pulled out a chair and seated himself, placing his hands on the table, palms down. "We debate, we discuss, we cogitate. The aim is enlightenment, and at this moment in history I'd say that's a far from ignoble endeavour."

"I wouldn't disagree."

"You're not going to find anything out of the ordinary, I'm afraid. No initiation rites involving sacrifices, no invocations to cthonic powers, not even a *soupçon* of dressing up."

"There would have been a time though," Digance mused, nodding towards the portrait of Sherlock Holmes's creator. "Didn't Conan Doyle and his fellow medical students experiment with chloroform and the like? And Stevenson was known to enjoy various pleasures. Then there's Thomas de Quincey—didn't I read that he spent a few evenings in the company of The Reasoners' Club?"

"True enough, but I can assure you that recreational drugs play no part in our discussions. We may wander towards a bar at the end of the evening, but all we provide in this room is tap water."

"The stories aren't true then?"

"What stories?"

"Well, the late 1960s spring to mind . . ."

Pormeroy slapped his hands against the table and rose to his feet. "Not a critical book, you said?"

"Not as such, but I can't ignore salient facts from the club's history."

"Is that so?"

"And John Chambers is a salient fact, wouldn't you say?"

"I'm disappointed in you, Mr Digance. You write for a magazine of repute. I wouldn't have taken you for a member of the gutter press."

"A member of your club disappeared into thin air. It was a *cause célèbre* at the time. There's no way I can ignore it if I want my book to be in any way authoritative."

"I'd like you to leave now." Pormeroy was gesturing with a hand.

"You said it yourself—you'll be gone from here by the time I publish. This should be something we can discuss freely and frankly, leading perhaps to a greater understanding. Enlightenment, you might even say. Besides which, it's ancient history. The club has changed. You even allow the odd woman through the sacred door."

"Out!"

"Can we arrange a further meeting first? I won't be in town long and I'm still keen to look at your membership roll and constitution."

"Out!" Pormeroy repeated, his voice growing louder. He walked to the door and flung it open. A young woman stood there, looking startled. She held a glass jug of water in one hand.

"For tonight's meeting," she explained. Pormeroy's face softened.

"So thoughtful, Emily," he said. Then, turning to Digance, voice hardening again: "Goodbye, sir."

Digance had found a sheltered spot in the lee of the building opposite, from where he could watch the members of The Reasoners' Club arrive. He counted nine of them, to which he added Pormeroy and the young woman called Emily. All he could see through the illuminated second-floor windows were occasional shadows. At one point he walked across the courtyard and stood below one window, but all he could hear was nearby traffic. When a female face appeared at the window he retreated. After two hours, the group started filing out. A few carried backpacks into which they were sliding sheets of paper, presumably notes from the discussion. Pormeroy and Emily were the last ones out, Pormeroy pausing the check that the door was securely locked. They headed for the archway, beyond which lay the city's streets and bars. Digance debated whether to follow but decided to head home instead. But as he passed beneath the arch he saw that she was waiting for him.

"I told them I'd catch them up," she explained, holding out a hand for him to shake. "I'm Emily Brond."

"Chris Digance."

"I know. Richard spent half the meeting talking about you."

"Oh?"

"Warning us from talking to you."

"Yet here you are."

"I prefer to make up my own mind. Besides which, he only aroused my curiosity." Her smile extended to her gleaming eyes. She was petite, thick dark hair spilling from beneath a black beret. Vermilion lipstick and plenty of kohl around her eyes.

"Did Pormeroy say why I'm here?"

"Writing a book. He's afraid it will be salacious. Can I buy you a drink?"

"As long as it's not in the same bar as the other Reasoners."

"I think we can manage that." She hooked her arm around his and they walked the short distance as though they were old friends. Their destination was a side-street, the pub small but quiet. Live folk music was advertised but there was no sign of any musicians. He tried paying for their drinks—a couple of gin and tonics—but she waved the offer aside and led him to a corner table.

"Are you an undergraduate?" he asked.

"PhD actually. I'm older than I look."

"What are you studying?"

"Philosophy. David Hume."

"You're in the right city then."

"And I've got the world expert on Hume as my supervisor."

"Really?"

"Professor Grierson."

"I've heard of him. He's a club member, isn't he?"

She looked at him above the rim of her glass. "How do you know that?"

"He listed it in *Who's Who*."

"You really *are* a journalist, aren't you?"

"Sometimes."

"Richard says you work for some London arts and politics magazine. Is that where you're from?"

"Yes."

"Me, too. Muswell Hill."

"Streatham—before it was gentrified. Did you do your undergraduate degree here?"

She shook her head. "Bristol."

"And how do you like Edinburgh?"

She took a moment to respond. "It feels . . . leaden. Like there's this weight of tradition pressing down on it."

"Of which The Reasoners' Club is part."

She gave another smile. "Probably why I joined. Wanted to see if I could dust off its cobwebs."

"And?"

"Too many busy spiders." She paused. "Is your book really going to go for the jugular?"

"I just want to demystify these closed little worlds, or maybe explain to a wider audience what their attraction is. That's all I wanted from Pormeroy—to maybe gain access to members past and present, get their take, learn a bit more about the club's aims and rules." He broke off to sip his drink. He heard a phone ping and watched her dig into her coat pocket. She studied the screen.

"They're wondering where I am," she said. "Better finish this and get moving." She waved her glass at him.

"I need to buy you one back."

"Another time maybe."

"Would you be willing to talk to me about the club? In confidence?"

"I'll think about it. Give me your number."

He reeled it off and she tapped it into her own phone.

"What else was under discussion tonight?" he asked as she started to rise to her feet.

"Personal versus public morality," she said. "As a journalist, you might have enjoyed it . . ."

Digance was stretched out along the sofa of his rented flat, his computer on his lap, jazz playing through its just-adequate speakers. He had tidied up his e-mails and done some FaceTime with his on-off girlfriend Agnetha. She was a corporate lawyer whose career always took precedence, something he hadn't minded at first. She was in Brussels tonight and would be in Berlin tomorrow. He had looked up flights from Edinburgh before dismissing the idea. This trip was already costing too much, mostly, it had to be said, because he had plumped for a nicer flat than was strictly necessary. It looked out on to some parkland and had formerly been the city's main hospital complex. Modern high-rise blocks had been placed between the original buildings and he was on the seventh floor of one of these. It was basically a glass box, but it was also a five-minute walk from The Reasoners' Club. And, for the time being, it was his.

He had just finished typing up his notes when a buzzer sounded. He went to the door and put his eye to the spy-hole, thinking a food delivery must have got the wrong address. But the man standing in the hallway didn't look like he delivered anything for a living. Digance slid the chain across before opening the door.

"Yes?"

The man was staring at the chain, as if feeling slighted. He held a photo ID up to the gap. "I'm Detective Sergeant Clifford. Just doing some door-to-door inquiries." He had tucked his ID back into his pocket and was holding a creased sheet of paper. "I'm going to assume you're not Ms Chen, but does she still live here?"

"Not as far as I know. I got the rental through an agency."

Clifford folded the piece of paper into four and looked ready to try scribbling a note on it.

"Be easier at a table," Digance said, unchaining the door.

"Thank you." The detective followed Digance into the living room. "Not from round here then?"

"How did you guess?"

"Not many locals would bother with the door-chain. Then again, better safe than sorry."

Digance had settled at the circular glass dining table, inviting the detective to do the same. Clifford flattened the sheet of paper and drew a line through the name Chen.

"Problem with these flats," he explained, "it's mostly short-term lets. Would you be one of those, Mr . . . ?"

"Digance. Chris Digance." He watched as Clifford wrote his name against the address on the sheet. "I've only been here a couple of days. Few more and I'll be on my way again."

"What brings you to Edinburgh, Mr Digance?" Clifford was dabbing sweat from his forehead with a large pristine handkerchief. "All these flats are like cookers," he complained.

"I've noticed." The window was already open several inches, allowing a little cooling and the occasional siren, shout or dog-bark from the outside world.

"Grand view you have. Must be spectacular in daylight." Clifford had risen to his feet.

"Can I fetch you some water or something?"

"I'm not lingering." He tapped the sheet. "Got another half dozen door-knocks in front of me tonight."

"Did something happen in one of the flats? Nobody said anything."

Clifford shook his head and sat down again. He removed a photo from his inside pocket and slid it across the table. "It was over a week ago.

Student by the name of Walters. Happened just out there at more or less this time of the evening."

It looked to Digance like a matriculation photograph. A young man, smiling, full of promise.

"Gareth Walters," Clifford went on. "Whacked on the back of the skull, died in hospital the next day. Bleeding on the brain."

"Bloody hell."

"He was in his final year. Staff say he had a brilliant future ahead of him in the sciences. Not an enemy in the world."

"Meaning no suspects?" Digance watched as Clifford gave him a look. "I'm a journalist," he explained. "I'm not news though, so don't worry."

"I'm not the worrying type. But you're here on a story?"

"I'm researching student societies." Digance broke off and looked at the photo again. "Would he have been a member of The Reasoners' Club?"

"What's that when it's at home?"

"A sort of secret society—well, not *secret* but they don't take many members. I'd think it's popular with science students though." He watched as the detective made a note to himself. "So it was just a random attack, is that the thinking? I mean, if he didn't have enemies."

"Sometimes it's our friends we have to watch out for, as they say."

"True enough."

"No witnesses and precious few leads so far though. One thing I would ask is that you keep your eyes open—we've not found his mobile phone. Could be the attacker took it. Might have discarded it after."

"Or more likely sold it."

"We've asked around. Nobody on our radar's been offered it."

"You'll have been on to his provider though? To check his call records?" Digance saw the detective give him another look and raised his hand by way of apology. "Can't help myself—once a journalist, et cetera."

Clifford's hand retrieved the photo and replaced it with a business card. "In case you need to contact me." He saw that Digance was frowning. "Something wrong, sir?"

"The back of the photograph," Digance said. "I thought I saw something."

Clifford held up the picture of the victim's face, then turned it over. Two rows of numbers were written there.

"Just something we found on a scrap of paper next to his computer. I've been trying to work out if they mean anything. He liked doing number puzzles, sudokus, that sort of thing."

Digance nodded slowly, watching as the detective pocketed the photo and rose to his feet. "Better get going. Whole point of being here at this time is that people are more likely to be home. Thanks for your help."

"I'm sorry I couldn't do more."

"At least I can tick you off the list before I try to track down Ms. Chen. I don't suppose she left a forwarding address?"

Digance shrugged an apology. The detective offered a sigh.

"Wouldn't want to make my life any easier, would we?" he said, making for the door.

Once he was gone, Digance found himself standing at the window, staring out at the darkness. The park—he remembered it was known as The Meadows—was well-lit the length of its walkways and cycle-paths, but as you headed further into it the illumination faded almost to nothing. He switched his computer back on and searched for Gareth Walters. There were plenty of news stories; he wondered why he had paid them no attention. After twenty minutes he closed the screen and went into the bedroom, opening a bedside drawer and extracting a document folder. At the glass dining-table he sifted through the few dozen sheets of paper and faded newspaper cuttings. The piece of paper he had been looking for was folded in four, as it had been when he'd been given it. It had originally been posted, but the envelope had been destroyed. Rows and rows of numbers, covering both sides of the sheet, meaning nothing to its recipient, who had kept it anyway, kept it half a century before handing it on to Digance. Never a great believer in coincidence at the best of times, he sat and studied the numerals one more time, seeking a pattern, seeking enlightenment.

Julius Grierson explained that he was a Regius Professor, meaning he was by royal appointment.

"First such was in Aberdeen in 1497—appointed by King James IV. Not that my own tenure stretches back quite that far."

It was an overcast, mild morning and they were seated in Grierson's chaotic office on Buccleuch Place, tucked away in an old tenement building behind the newer and uglier university structures which surrounded George Square. There was a sofa, piled high with books, newspapers and what looked like a selection of bound graduate theses. Four chairs sat around a square wooden table. Digance imagined that tutorials had taken place here. Maybe they still did, but only if each surface was cleared of yet more books and paperwork. Nor was Grierson's desk any tidier.

"There's a computer under here somewhere," he had joked, settling into his chair. For want of anything else, Digance had perched himself on the arm of the sofa. There was a stuffed owl on a shelf behind Grierson, flanked by busts of Plato and Aristotle. Several paintings of David Hume had been hung on the wall above the shelf.

"Thank you for agreeing to see me," Digance said. A tray lay on the floor nearby. An electric kettle and three chipped mugs sat on it, but there was no offer of a hot drink. Grierson scratched a hand through his wiry silver hair and peered at his visitor over his half-moon spectacles. He then dug into a pocket of his baggy oatmeal cardigan and blew his nose on a paper tissue.

"I'm not exactly rushed off my feet," he said, "not these days. If I didn't visit the faculty office now and then, I swear they'd forget about me altogether. A few postgraduates to tide me over, but no lectures or seminars . . ."

"I met one of your students yesterday, Emily Brond. She's a big fan."

"Emily's bright, very bright. And sharp, too—the two don't always correspond."

"Brave, too—not many women have crowbarred their way into The Reasoners."

"Indeed not. In my day the constitution still didn't allow them. It was amended later, but it's shocking to think back to it. Mind you, there were lots of places in the city where women weren't welcome, from pubs to golf clubs. Changed days, praise be."

Digance nodded and tried to make his next question sound casual. "You joined The Reasoners' in 1968? I think you were nineteen?"

"Sounds about right."

"So you'd have known John Chambers?"

The professor's face darkened a little and his mouth turned down. "A bad business."

"He vanished after one of the regular meetings?"

"I think that's right."

"In the early summer of 1969."

"Fifty years past. I've always wondered what became of him."

"I'm guessing the whole Reasoners' Club would have been thinking the same—speculating, even."

"Oh yes. The police came asking, and the family, of course. And one or two newspapers. Is that why you're here—the fiftieth anniversary?"

"I'm not that kind of journalist. But it's hard to write about the club without saying something about a case that made it notorious for a short time."

"Notorious?"

"Brought into the public sphere as never before. I believe some members resigned?"

"A few. I was never sure why. It was hardly the fault of the club that he . . . Well, whatever happened."

"What do you *think* happened?"

The professor puffed out his cheeks and exhaled. His head seemed to shrink further between his shoulders. With his double chin, round face and heavy-lidded eyes he looked not unlike one of the portraits of Hume, and Digance wondered if they were perhaps distantly related.

"It was the 1960s," Grierson was saying. "I know the Swinging Sixties mostly happened in a couple of square miles of London, but Edinburgh was not immune. There were drugs, naturally, and the artistic community was flourishing. Galleries and clubs and happenings. The Incredible String

Band were from Edinburgh, you know. They played Woodstock but they started right here. John Chambers was . . . not quite a hippy, though I think their philosophy appealed. Working-class background, I seem to recall. Salt of the earth types who were happy to stay in their lane. That was never going to be enough for John. He dallied with left-wing protest, worked on a radical magazine. My feeling was, one day he simply stuck out his thumb and headed south, maybe ended up in Marrakesh or Nepal. Anything was possible back then."

"But to disappear so completely . . ."

"Anything was possible," Grierson repeated.

The text from Emily Brond had felt like a summons: *3pm—the café in Blackwell's Bookshop.*

She was already seated at a table when he arrived, pouring herself what looked like peppermint tea from a small teapot. He fetched himself a cappuccino and a slice of chocolate brownie, offering to split the latter with her. She shook her head.

"I'm not sure I should even be talking to you," she said in an undertone as he sat down. "Richard has been phoning around. Seems none of the other societies you say you're researching have ever heard of you."

"Maybe I've just not got round to them yet." She gave him a hard stare. "Okay," he said. "Let's say I've been economical with the *vérité*, but it's true that I'm a journalist."

"Richard double-checked that, too, just to be sure you weren't pretending to be Christopher Digance."

"Are you and Richard . . . ?" The scowl she gave him said it all. "So if I tell you something, does it stay between us?"

"Of course."

He opened his satchel and began to rummage. "My grandmother died a few months ago. I was given the job of going through her things—correspondence, photographs, all the clutter people leave behind. Her brother was John Chambers." Emily Brond's mouth puckered. "There were letters and postcards from him and plenty of snaps of them when they were kids. She really loved him and that love was reciprocated. It tore her in half when he went missing." He was placing a few of the photos on the table for her to see.

"What was your grandmother's name?" Brond asked.

"Gillian—but she's always Gilly in her brother's letters, just as she seems to have called him Johnno." He took a deep breath. "When I started looking at the case—the family kept all the cuttings from the time, plus various notes from the police investigation—I began to have questions. I wanted to know more about him."

"It was fifty years ago." She was examining each photograph in turn. "You really think there's closure to be had after all this time?"

"I don't know. But a couple of months after John disappeared, my family received this in the mail." He unfolded the sheet of paper with its row after row of numbers, watching as her eyes widened. She leaned back a little further in her chair, as if unwilling to get too close to the letter. "What is it?" he asked her. "Do you recognise this?"

"It's . . ." Finally she stretched out a thumb and forefinger, taking the sheet of paper from him and studying it. "It looks a bit like . . ."

"What?"

"Back at its inception, The Reasoners' Club used a code so members could send messages without anyone else being able to read them. God knows why, except that boys and their secret societies like that sort of thing, don't they?"

"You're telling me you can read this?"

She handed back the paper with a slight shake of the head. "But I could, if we had the club's constitution to hand. Each number relates to a letter. So 1 would be the first letter of the first word of the constitution and so on."

He turned the sheet over, noting that there was no number beyond 26. "It's the straightforward alphabet," he muttered.

"But only decipherable by those in the know."

"So if we had a copy of the club's constitution . . ."

"As handed out to every member past and present."

He stared at her. "You've got one?"

"In my flat."

"Shall we then?"

"Do I get to finish my tea first?"

Digance had started scooping up the photographs. "No," he said.

It was a top-floor tenement flat in Marchmont, just across The Meadows from Digance's rental. Brond ushered Digance into the untidy living-room then went back into the hall and tapped softly on a door, opening it and saying something. He tried to listen but couldn't make out the words. Then she was in the living-room again, closing the door before removing her jacket and backpack.

"Flatmate," she explained. "We won't see her. She's a bit under the weather. Do you want water or anything?"

"I'd rather get down to business if that's all right."

She gave a thin smile. "I prefer a man who takes his time," she said. "But if you insist . . ."

She left the room again and returned a minute later with a photocopied document. It consisted of about twenty sheets, stapled together. Digance removed a notepad from his satchel along with the coded letter. They cleared some space on the coffee-table and sat side by side on the sofa. Forty minutes later Digance leapt to his feet and strode to the window, staring out at the darkening street.

"Do you want that water now?" Brond asked. "I'm having some."

"Got anything stronger?"

"An old bottle of gin with about an inch left in it—no mixers though."

He shook his head and waited for her to return from the kitchen. She handed him his water and they both drank. He exhaled noisily.

"Bloody hell," he said.

"Bloody hell," she echoed. Then they sat back down and he lifted his notepad, beginning to read aloud.

"*An experiment gone wrong, that's what it was. LSD to free the mind, heroin to add extra punch. John overdosed and we panicked. This was the end of our dreams and careers. We were going to be surgeons and engineers and philosophers. All gone. That's why we hid the body, driving Owl's car to some woods in East Lothian. A peaceful spot, we convinced ourselves. No more drugs. No more sixties. But I'll never forget. None of us will forget. We will aim to be the best we can be, in memory of John. I know you can't read this but I needed to write it and send it to you. My confession. My penance. I just needed to say I'm sorry."*

"Owl," Digance muttered. "Your Professor Grierson has an owl in his office."

Brond gave a snort. "Half The Reasoners' Club probably do—it's the symbol of wisdom after all."

"All the same, I need to talk to him again."

"Why? What good's it going to do?"

He was sorely tempted to tell her about the other message, the one left by Gareth Walters, but right now his attention had to be on his own long-dead relative, who had been mourned without leaving a body for his family to mourn over. He ran a hand across his forehead.

"It was an accident," Brond was saying quietly. "Self-administered. They were young men and they did the wrong thing by not coming forward, but that's all we're talking about."

"They committed a crime."

"And?"

"And that needs to be acknowledged. Police need to reopen the case, interview all the club members from that time. Whoever Owl is, I can't see too many students owning their own car in the 1960s. That narrows things down. Maybe the handwriting on the note . . . or fingerprints or DNA . . ."

"To what end, Chris? Think it through." She placed a hand on his thigh. There was a sudden sound of wailing from the other side of the door.

"That'll be Chloe. I should go see if I can get her anything."

"What's the matter with her? Has she seen a doctor?"

"She'll be fine." She gave his thigh a squeeze before getting to her feet, leaving Digance alone in the room with the decoded letter and his thoughts. After five minutes, he went into the hallway. There was a groan from behind one of the closed doors, followed by a muted one-way conversation. He raised his hand to knock but thought better of it. Instead he gathered his things and left, sending a text to Emily Brond as he descended the stairs. The walk to his flat took less than ten minutes. Rain was starting as he took the lift to his floor. He wasn't sure why he had bought the bottle of supermarket whisky on his first day in the city, but he broke the seal now and poured a large measure.

Was Brond right? Now that he had his answer, what was to be gained by taking it further? He had barely known his grandmother, and the story of her brother was only ever told intermittently. Johnno had become family lore rather than existing as flesh and blood. But Digance had got to know him through those letters to his sister. Adventurous and, yes, maybe even impetuous. He had "borrowed" a motorbike at the age of fifteen and taken it as far as the west coast, until he had neither petrol nor money left. He told everything to Gilly, it seemed— up until he started university. In his letters after that time there was scant mention of fellow students and no mention at all of The Reasoners' Club. His handwriting had also deteriorated. Digance had wondered if some of the letters had been written under the influence of drink. Now he needed to add recreational drugs to the equation. He raised his glass in a silent toast to Johnno Chambers. Tomorrow he would talk to DS Clifford and show him the code. But there'd be another meeting before that. He pictured the owl which seemed to float above Professor Grierson's head and thought of the old man's words: *anything was possible back then.* Up to and including burying a friend, it seemed. Half a century might have passed, but Julius Grierson would still have to answer for it . . .

He carried a takeaway coffee with him to Buccleuch Place next morning. The whisky he'd sunk the previous evening had been followed by another, and now his head was telling him this had been foolhardy. He climbed the stairs with some effort, thinking that the Professor had to be fitter than he looked. Digance took a moment to get his breathing under control before ringing the bell. There was no answer so he tried the handle. The door was locked. He stooped down and peered through the letterbox. It looked as though the shutters had yet to be opened. A card on the door told him that office hours were 10-3. His phone said 10:28. The downstairs door slammed and he heard footsteps, but when he looked it was a bleary-looking male student. He ignored Digance and tried turning the door handle.

"It's locked," Digance stated.

"I've a ten thirty tutorial."

"Not today by the look of it."

The student went to the other door on the landing, knocked and entered, Digance following. A woman in her mid-thirties was inside. The card on the door identified her as Dr Ruth Mills, Aesthetics and General Philosophy.

"I've a 10:30 with Professor Grierson," the student explained.

"I've not heard him come in," she responded, heading to her phone and making what looked like an internal call. Digance felt he was wasting his time and began trudging down the stairs again, finishing his coffee as he reached the bottom. He sent a text to Emily Brond, asking if she had a phone number or home address for Grierson. She called back immediately.

"You're going to see him," she stated.

"Obviously."

"Why?"

"To ask him if he was in the car that night. If maybe he helped with the digging."

"Are you sure about this? Because I'm not—do me a favour and just give it a bit more thought."

"I mulled it over all last night."

"Please, Chris, give it another day. Where's the harm?"

"I'll see. How's Chloe by the way?"

"She's a bit fragile right now."

"It's not a physical thing then?"

"I'll talk to you later, Chris. Goodbye."

He realised he was heading back towards the café where he'd bought the coffee. Well, one more wouldn't go amiss. And the café was around the corner from his flat, so he might head back there for an hour, try to sort his head out. The skies were clearing and it was milder than it had been. The world whirred by him on bicycles and skateboards. Students and schoolkids flocked outside the café and the supermarket next door. Dog-walkers were heading home after their morning constitutional. One or two people even smiled and nodded, as though they recognised him. He took the lift up to his floor and was taking another swig from his cup as he noticed two figures outside his door. One was DS Clifford, the other a woman in police uniform. Both straightened their shoulders at his approach.

"DS Clifford," Digance said. "I was just thinking I needed to . . ."

Clifford thrust a sheet of paper out towards him. "I have a warrant to search these premises, Mr Digance."

"What?" Digance glanced at the warrant. "What's this all about?"

"Property stolen from a room in the university belonging to The Reasoners' Club."

"I've not stolen anything!"

"A witness recognised you leaving the building."

"When?"

"Last night."

"I wasn't there last night. This is insane."

"In that case, you won't mind if we take a look?" The question hung in the air as Digance looked from one officer to the other and back.

"You won't find anything." But he took the key from his pocket and unlocked the door. "Precious few hiding places in any case."

"We'll be out of your hair in no time then," Clifford stated. He headed into the living-room, Digance following. It shared a space with the kitchen, nothing separating the two. The female officer had made for the bathroom and bedroom, having first checked the hall cupboard.

"This is ridiculous." Digance could hear the fitted wardrobe being opened, the bedside cabinet. Clifford had made short work of the few kitchen cupboards, extending his search as far as the fridge and freezer. He waved the whisky bottle at Digance.

"Like a drink, do we?" He put the bottle back down on the worktop and moved to the sofa and the only comfortable chair, sliding his hands between the cushions.

"Who made the complaint?" Digance asked. "Student called Pormeroy by any chance? He doesn't want me digging too deep into his precious club. That's what I wanted to talk to you about ..."

He broke off at the sound of the female officer's voice. Clifford strode towards the bedroom, Digance following. The officer was indicating the underside of the bed. Clifford knelt down and took a look. Without changing position, he pulled a pair of thin blue rubber gloves from his pocket and slid them on with seasoned dexterity. Then he reached beneath the bed and pulled out two leather-bound volumes.

"I've never seen those before," Digance spluttered.

Clifford was studying the spines. "Early membership rolls, attendance records and minutes. Some very famous signatures in here, Mr Digance." The detective had risen to his feet. "Valuable signatures." The other officer was unfolding a large plastic evidence bag. The books just fitted inside. Clifford sealed the bag.

"You and me better have a wee talk down the station," he said. "Best bring your coffee with you though—the stuff we get is undrinkable."

The interview room was on the ground floor of St Leonard's police station, to the left of the reception desk. Digance knew now that the uniformed officer was called PC Collins. Clifford had left her to guard Digance while he fetched a mug of tea for himself. There was a camera attached to the wall above the door and a recording machine on the desk. Neither looked to have been used in recent memory. Clifford returned with a stained white mug and placed it on the desk alongside his notebook and pen.

"When is this supposed to have happened?" Digance blurted out.

"Yesterday evening between nine and ten."

"I was in my flat."

"Alone?"

"Yes."

"Pity."

"The college must have CCTV surely."

"We're checking it, though it might not prove conclusive. What *does* seem pretty conclusive is the two volumes found beneath your bed."

"Planted there by Richard Pormeroy."

"He's the young student who currently runs The Reasoners' Club? Specialises in dystopian literature but has a useful sideline in lock-picking?"

"An inquiring mind can find just about anything on the internet," Digance reasoned.

"Might explain how you were able to gain access to the club after hours." Clifford sipped from his mug.

"Except that I didn't. And my feeling is, newer locks might prove a lot easier to pick than old-fashioned ones which require big clunky keys. The place wasn't crowbarred open? No sign of damage?" Digance watched the detective shift slightly in his seat. "I'll take that as a no. One other thing I'm confident of—you won't find my fingerprints on either of those books."

"You could have worn gloves."

"You won't find any in the flat."

"Nevertheless . . ." Clifford paused for another sip. "Why would Mr Pormeroy want to frame you?"

Digance took a deep breath. "Because I was getting too close to solving a mystery. A relative of mine disappeared in 1969. A coded letter was sent to the family. I cracked the code and found out what had happened to him." He made sure he had eye contact with the detective. "The code was composed of a sequence of numbers."

Clifford almost appeared to be acting in slow motion as he placed the mug back on the desk.

"Say that again for me, please," he intoned quietly.

Clifford accompanied Digance back to the flat. He'd explained that there were no charges as yet, but the case was ongoing and it didn't mean Digance was off the hook. While the detective sat at the dining-table, Digance got everything ready. He didn't have Emily Brond's copy of the constitution, but he had the letter in both its coded and decoded forms. He reckoned there'd be plenty there to help him with the note Gareth Walters had left behind. While he got started on the note, Clifford examined the 1969 letter.

"Incredible," the detective muttered. "Just incredible."

"Is there enough there for a prosecution?" Digance asked.

"A confession would be better." Digance glanced up at him. "I mean, not from some anonymous source." Digance nodded and got back to work.

It didn't take long. When he had finished, both men read the message.

Meadows 8pm, need to tell Owlet I'm finished cheating on Chloe

"Owlet?" Clifford said, frowning. Digance kept his face from showing emotion. "Is that what the club members call themselves? Owls and owlets?"

"I'm not sure," Digance replied, even though he was.

"Chloe was the deceased's girlfriend." Clifford ran his hand along his jaw.

"Oh yes?" Digance kept his voice level. He knew now, knew that Emily Brond's roommate had not been ill—she'd been grieving.

"This is helpful, Mr Digance." Clifford waved the note at him. "Your role won't be forgotten, I assure you."

"Just remember to check for CCTV and fingerprints. CCTV from the college last night *and* from this block this morning. That's the only time those books could have been planted."

The detective nodded slowly, but Digance could tell he had more important matters on his mind. Murder trumped theft any day of the week . . .

He'd sent Brond a text. *You at your flat? Need a word urgently!* Not that he was content to wait for a reply. As soon as Clifford left, he headed for The Meadows, almost breaking into a jog as he crossed Melville Drive and headed up Marchmont Road. When his phone pinged to let him know

Brond was at home, he replied *5 mins* and kept moving. It was only when she opened the door to him that he realised the sweat was dripping from his hair.

"You look a state," Brond said. He ignored her and made for the living-room.

"What is it?" she asked.

"Close the door if you don't want Chloe hearing what I'm about to say."

"A man of mystery all of a sudden." When she closed the door and turned towards him, he could tell from her face that she knew what he was about to say.

"You need to promise me something," he began. "Promise me you'll talk to Grierson, use any power you have over him to get him to confess."

"To something that happened five decades back?"

"It doesn't matter how long ago it was. It's closure, and that's what I want."

"I assume you've something to offer me in return?" She took a step towards him, arms folded.

"I know about you and Gareth Walters. He was seeing you behind Chloe's back. He met you in The Meadows that night so he could tell you it was over. I've not seen the rage in you—not yet—but it must be there, hiding behind your eyes."

She gave a snort. "And how did Sherlock Holmes work all this out?"

"A message Gareth made to himself, using the Reasoners' Code, saying he was rendezvousing with you. He calls you Owlet. Grierson the wise old owl and you his favourite child. It won't take CID long to work it out. I'm giving you time to either run or concoct a story. And all I want in return is for you to have a word with the professor."

"That's big of you, Chris. And if I say no . . . ?"

When the door burst open it hit Brond firmly between the shoulder-blades, sending her flying. Before she could recover, a shrieking Chloe, dressed in T-shirt and running shorts, was on her, pushing her to the floor.

"You bitch! I knew there was something going on!"

Digance tried dragging her off, but Chloe was a woman possessed, her small clenched fists connecting time and again with Brond's face, a face that slowly did start to change, becoming infused with anger. She roared as she fought back, using knees and elbows and clawed fingernails. Digance felt lost, impotent. He straightened up, trying to decide what the hell to do. Then PC Collins was in the room, DS Clifford a couple of shocked steps behind her. Between them, they separated the two bloodied women.

"Let's try to be reasonable!" Clifford bellowed.

Ah yes, thought Digance—pure versus practical reason. But human affairs were a lot messier than most philosophy would allow. Chloe and Emily were glaring at one another, nostrils flaring, the breath coming from them in ragged bursts. For all her debating strengths, he doubted Emily Brond would be able to reason her way out of a prison cell. In fact, Digance was practically sure of it.

Noise Cancellation

by Tom Straw

===

F red Rogers can kiss my dimpled ass. Why the shot at a dead cultural darling? It goes back to 2002. At my Dartmouth graduation, I'm sweating
a microclimate under my polyester gown, and his folksy commencement
address got weirdly personal. He was describing the measure of true success. "It's not the honors and the prizes, and the fancy outsides of life which
ultimately nourish our souls." Then, swear to God, a thousand classmates
in folding chairs, and Mister Rogers says the next bit right to me. Full eye
contact. "It's the knowing that we can be trusted. That we never have to fear
the truth."

I felt stunned, then inspired as I kicked up my bachelor's in engineering
to a doctorate and started teaching Applied Acoustics and Signal Process-
ing at Eastrim College, a safety school in Connecticut. But six years ago I
started cursing Fred Rogers for getting in my head. That was when I did
The Bad Thing and started to fear the truth. That bastard's words visited me
as an accusing echo that wouldn't be silenced, always served up with pangs
of dread. Those spells were intermittent. Gut flutters when something
sparked a memory. I tamed the guilt monster by telling myself the deed
was done and obsessing wasn't constructive. But the fear. That's a different
animal. The fear is about what might come, namely discovery. But that's all
the stuff of projection. At least it was until the other day.

——— ·•· ———

"Simon? Are you in distress?" Just like Nicole to put it that way. Mannered, silver screen dialogue like she was in a Turner Classic Movie. "Are you choking? Shall we dial 911?"

"Choking" and "911" sent a ping of hushing alarm through the college president's dining room until the only sound was the low hum of Dean Drake's portable oxygen concentrator.

I waved off the roomful of owl eyes. "I'm fine, see?" I wasn't fine. The hanger steak hadn't seized my lungs, it was an offhand remark from Nicole Guidry. The professor of Victorian Lit, who claimed squatter's rights to any seat next to me since my divorce, speared a carrot coin and examined it with a twirl. "I received a visit this morning from a fellow who wanted to ask some questions about you."

"What sort of questions?"

"He warned me not to say. I'm sure he'd object if he knew I was even telling you about the meeting. He wanted dope on your background." Her French manicure goosed my coat sleeve. "Don't tell me Eastrim's star professor is going to work for the CIA."

"Hardly," I chuckled. "Why, was he from the government?"

"He wouldn't let on. But he had a letter from Dr. Zazueta to authorize cooperation."

When she nodded toward the president's table I set down my fork so she wouldn't notice it quaking in my hand. "What about my background?"

"Oh, matters of the mundane stripe. Family status, your history here since we became colleagues. Your projects." Then, with less notice than she had given her carrot, "He seemed especially keen on Sonic Quarry." Sonic Quarry. The two words that nearly got me Heimliched.

I didn't dare probe the subject. And forget sniffing around Dr. Zazueta. Not only was he chatting up the donor who was his guest of honor at the luncheon, if someone was stirring the embers of my dark past, I wasn't giving the coals any more oxygen.

Besides, maybe it was nothing. Maybe this would die on its own.

That's what I told myself sitting all night in my Ikea divorced guy's chair listening to the college bell two blocks away mark every hour. Between tolls, my head vibrated to the echo of a deceased kid-show host. *"Fear the truth . . . Fear the truth . . ."* At dawn I left the apartment to change the channel. I let myself into my acoustics lab, happy that the modest space at the School of Engineering sat in the rear of the building. My painted metal door near the dumpsters meant I didn't have to deal with colleagues or students to go to work.

My grant was to take sonic dampening to the next level by eliminating the need for headphones. I was experimenting with infrared beams that lock onto the user's ears and deliver noise cancellation through the air wherever he or she moved. It would be the *Get Smart* Cone of Silence, minus the cone. In a loud office or open plan environment like WeWork, this would be breakthrough technology. Plus every rock star performing live would be able to ditch the annoying earbuds. Blow jobs and my Rock & Roll Hall of Fame induction, to follow.

I set up the gear I'd fabricated, powered up the console, and positioned tripods holding the impulse transmitters and the acoustic camera. First pass, I maxed-out the levels. Too much energy. Smoke curled off the head of my test dummy, Sting.

Concentrated sound waves fried the infrared sensors on his temples and turned his ears into an ooze of molten neoprene.

What was going on? It wasn't like me to be so clumsy. Poor Sting would manage another round, but I couldn't find the stash of IR sensors. I speed dialed my lab assistant, who hid them God knows where, but he rejected my call. I left a voicemail asking why the hell he was two hours late and bolted outside to gulp air and walk off my jitters.

Except no amount of hiking could put distance between me and the drone of Fred voices trailing a yard behind my head. I quickened my pace so I could blow by the Admin Building unseen, but at the Founder's Steps I cut a sudden turn to climb them.

"Good morning, Ellen, is Dr. Zazueta in?" Impulse delivered me to the president's suite. Risky, but that's the way it is with me and impulse. I can't fight it. Sometimes impulse is instinct punching through the clutter with a message. Ellen checked her monitor to see if I was on the books.

During that blip the message reached me as a plan. Engage Dr. Z on some BS budget request. Give him an opening to heads me up about this guy asking about me—and Sonic Quarry. I wouldn't need to confront him. If he didn't mention it, it was probably a nothingburger. And, God forbid, if there was cause for concern, we could get the noise out then and there.

A flash in my periphery. The squat form of Dr. Zazueta, about to step out of his office. As I turned, he seemed startled by me and spun inside, avoiding my eyes. Before I got out a hello, his automatic door hissed closed. He dodged me. The fucking college president saw me and dodged me.

Ellen muttered some excuse about a conference call. I couldn't hear her over a rising crackle of decibels.

At noon, my lab assistant, Joshua Reese, called back sounding anything but repentant. "We need to have a convo."

"Damn straight. Where the hell are you?"

"Okay. Can you dial that down? I got sidetracked."

Like I need this now from my Millennial lab rat. "Doing what, downloading GIFs of your current mood?"

"That is so abusive, and no, some suit showed up and started pumping me about you."

My gut clenched. A jet engine roared in my brain like Sting's head absorbing peak dB. "Let's meet now," I said.

To avoid running into anyone from Eastrim, I picked a seafood joint on the Sound where I dock my Grady White. A chilly mist meant privacy outside on the porch. From our picnic table, Joshua blew on his fried calamari through his Verdi beard and surveyed the slips. "You can afford a boat?"

A nineteen footer, the sole property I got out of the divorce, hardly made me Richard Branson, but I wasn't there to talk boats. "Tell me about your visitor."

"Dude asked about a lot of things." His reedy voice projected the arrogance of a self-loather. "But I bet I know what you're stressing." The lab rat popped in the calamari and eyed me while he chewed, taking his time, enjoying this. Raised entitled, now empowered. But how? What could he know?

"I'm not stressing." I flattened my palms on the redwood to still them and faked nonchalance. "What is he, a reporter? A nice media presence might get me hired by a real university."

He flashed me his phone screen. "Found him on LinkedIn. Patrick Windom, LLC. Academic Forensic Investigations."

"What . . . is he investigating, did he say?" My own voice came to me muddied by static like a distant a.m. signal at night.

Without asking, he took an onion ring off my paper plate. "You didn't know Surali Gupta and I were sleeping together, did you?" His question was calculated to level me, and it did. His face showed smug enjoyment as he dredged my onion ring in my tartar sauce and watched me take slow, ragged inhales.

"I didn't. You and Ms. Gupta were in love?"

He shrugged. "Naw, just doin' it. We hooked up as study buddies back in your class, and one thing led to another." The onion ring lost its appeal, and he tossed it onto my scallops. "Sucked when she died."

"A tragedy." Surali Gupta got killed six years ago in an avalanche that buried the resort where her family was vacationing in the Swiss Alps. "She was gifted."

"Don't need to tell me. Her senior thesis was brilliant." Then he delivered the mail. "I read it, Professor Coe."

I refused the bait. "Her honors project was promising. She still needed to refine it."

"Refine, my ass. You stole it and published it under your name."

There it was. The Bad Thing, verbalized. I broke eye contact and set my gaze over his shoulder onto my boat, fantasizing about a drowned lab rat. "Did you tell this story to the investigator?"

"Dude. It's not a story. It's the truth." The hired help, calling the professor dude. "And no. It's smarter to have this talk with you first."

"Did he seem suspicious of—"

"—Of you plagiarizing the Sound Quarry project? From your dead honors student? He asked a lot about it. But suspicious? I guess there's one way to find out. Unless you don't want me to test that." Joshua Reese had danced right up to extortion, but left it unsaid. So slick that I resolved never to underestimate Generation Snowflake again. Then he nudged the ball. "I see Wüff Acoustics has an opening in Boston for a headphone systems engineer. I'm thinking it's time I broke out of academia." So much for slick. A fat guy in a Speedo working a slot machine was more subtle.

"Wüff is the new Bose. Openings are highly competitive."

"I'm chill. Wasn't their head of R&D your research assistant before me? If I were you, I'd make a call. Today." Without taking his eyes off me, he swiped one of my scallops and tossed it to a seagull. "And I've always wanted a boat."

Driving back to campus I opened voicemail from my ex, betting what it would be. Tracy's been on me to notarize a quitclaim deed on the house, all hers in the settlement. Bad bet. "Hi, do you know a . . . Patrick Windom?" A cinderblock landed on my chest. "He wants to talk to me after I get off work. About you, but he wouldn't say why. Call when you get this." Sleep deprived and blitzed, I scraped the dumpster, pulling into my spot. A yard of paint off my quarter panel. Stupid not to sleep. But how could I? Not under all this.

"He's an investigator," I said, putting her on speakerphone while I clicked links. "His website says he's an attorney with thirty-five years of HR experience at top universities. 'Unparalleled expertise in academic forensic investigations.'"

"You knew this would catch up with you." Not a scold, but resigned despair. My ex-wife knew it all. I had confessed to her when things were better, when I had a soulmate. Tracy bore the burden of my sin with me, even getting turned on by the hot collusion sex, chugging throaty whispers that I was her bad boy.

But our delicious dirty secret curdled into resentment. "You know your problem?" she ruled one night. "You lack impulse control."

Tracy decided if I was capable of this, I was not to be trusted. She had the house, primary custody of our son, and now the fate of my academic career in her hands. If plagiarism wasn't a vocational death sentence, robbing a grave for it was.

"I knew it could come. That's different from knowing it would." My answer sparked the same old harangue that lit the long fuse on our split. In our last-gasp years, one too many glasses of Merlot, and I was on the stand under her cross-examination, rationalizing my fraud. If those grillings accomplished anything they helped me burnish my justification.

My theft of intellectual property needed a better legend than opportunistic impulse if I were to live with myself. I gave up wishing I could go back in time; the proverbial bell could not be unrung. So I went back instead to reconstruct my defense.

I formed a saga of unfairness. Because it felt true.

Six years ago I'd been killing myself experimenting with a breakthrough in capturing sound. Since audio waves are vibrations, wouldn't the pulsations of spoken words oscillate off inanimate objects enough to be turned into sound, same as the gouges Edison put in wax phonograph cylinders? I tried pointing a high speed camera through a sound-proof window at various objects while "Fee-Fi-Fo-Fum" was spoken in the room. Then I magnified the video, processed the impulses through a playback algorithm I wrote, and, hot damn. What did I hear but "Fee-Fi-Fo-Fum," projected off a cellophane pretzel bag. I'd done it. I had discovered a method of turning common objects into audio amplifiers without needing a microphone.

The implications? Staggering, starting with eavesdropping. Imagine the giddy high-fives at the NSA when they got a load of my innovation.

I would never find out.

Just as I was final-proofing my paper, a team at MIT published *The Visual Microphone: Passive Recovery of Sound from Video*. It was my project, except they used a potato chip bag.

Someone beat me to the buzzer just as I was reaching for it.

The MIT crew got the accolades, the corporate underwriting, the NPR interviews, and the TED Talks. I spent a month in my pajamas in a darkened room.

Then Surali Gupta turned in her thesis, all dazzling teeth and fiery eyes.

"Professor, I definitely think this is a thing." My honors student had done the MIT crew and me one better. She demonstrated how you could turn passive recovery upside-down and noise cancel any unwanted sounds in a video. Surali proved you could process footage from a noisy, crowded room, spot-kill everything else, and isolate one, targeted conversation. For instance, our president and a world leader at a state dinner. Her accomplishment was radical.

Before I could share my reaction, she got buried under four hundred meters of snow.

I publicly mourned her loss. I led her candlelight vigil.

Then I put my name on her work.

It only seemed fair.

Fate had stolen my rightful glory. Fate then balanced the scales with the project I published as *Sound Quarry: Mining Audio from the Rubble of Noise*. Mister Rogers did not approve.

Fred's voice commingled with my ex's speakerphone diatribe. "My BP is through the roof over this, thanks to you."

"Don't talk to this guy. Cancel."

"And how does that make me look? No way."

"Well, what are you going to, you know, tell him?"

"The truth."

I stared at my son's drawing on the corkboard beside me. "Yay Dady" above a crayon stick figure wearing a cartoon crown in front of a cartoon college. My voice cracked. "Tracy . . ."

"I won't volunteer anything. But if he starts to dig, I refuse to lie. If there's legal action, I'm not going down with you as a co-conspirator." Before she hung up, she added, "And sign that damn quitclaim so my one asset can't be seized."

Home for a nap.

A nap wasn't happening. Neither was dinner. How could I eat?

I poured a Jameson to quiet the nerves while I Googled "Academic Fraud Punishment." Talk about key words.

"The consequences for cheating, plagiarism, and other forms of academic dishonesty could result in censure or termination from Eastrim College." Ironic. Verbiage lifted from MIT's policy. I didn't laugh. Branded with a scarlet letter P, I'd be lucky to find work as a middle school sub in Ely, Nevada.

The pisser is this. My fraud stalked me even though publishing *Sound Quarry* didn't exactly rain down the spoils.

Sure, it cinched my tenure. I also got a dedicated lab, the Chancellor's Trophy, and the glossy cover of *Eastrim Quarterly*.

But the dream-level stuff, the life changers, never came. My applications to bust out of academic Podunk and teach at the top universities . . . MIT, Carnegie Mellon, Cal Tech, Purdue . . . were met with silence. Even the only one I wanted, my alma mater, Dartmouth, had no positions available.

My second whiskey did me no more favors than the first. I paced in a stupor, fixated on why. After six agonizing years tweaked that this could rise up and bite me, why now? Had my ex shared pillow talk with that skeevy geology prof she was banging? Maybe my lab rat blew the whistle to blackmail a job out of me. Or was it Surali Gupta, getting a laugh from the grave with a back-up copy of her senior thesis surfacing? Last bells rang on campus, and I was still a walking fist.

Task orientation. A timely life hack to quell the fuss of voices. I logged on my Eastrim server to scrub any vestigial files linked to Surali Gupta I'd overlooked back in the day.

Access: Denied.

I pecked out the number for IT on the cracked screen my phone suffered at the rude conclusion of my call with the ex. "I'm sorry, Professor Coe, there's a temporary freeze on your account."

"That makes no sense." At least, I hoped not.

"It's under a review, per President Zazueta. I suggest you contact his office directly. Did I address all your concerns?" This time when I launched the phone, cutting-edge alloys were no match for Depression-era plaster.

I rushed back to my lab. Flashing lights filled my car.

Pulled over by Campus Security. For a nanosecond I wondered what smoking gun they turned up in my server account. But it was just some glorified mall cop warning me about driving without headlights. Jeez, where was my head?

In my office, I started snatching banker's boxes from the storage closet. They blocked me from my digital archives, but I could still scrub my physical files. The Sound Quarry research was so bulky it crushed the cartons at the bottom of the stack. The tower keeled over, spilling a shitload of docs. I gave them the kick they had coming. Then I raked them up by the armload to skim read and sort into piles: Keep or Shred.

While I sorted, I listed my options, a best practice when you see no way out. Option one: hang tough. This will blow over. Yuh, right. Two . . . run away. Load the boat with five-gallon jerrycans and make for Florida. I could also come clean. Purge my guts to Dr. Zazueta or on Facebook Live. Then there's the option I was too afraid to think of. Suicide. I craned toward Sting, still in his chair. What would cranking it to level eleven do to my brain? No. Best just to wait. See what came down, and leave it to impulse. Although, considering my crime of opportunity, impulse didn't always serve me so well.

Mister Rogers laughed and went all street. Called me impulse's bitch. Freddy Boy, pissed that I ignored him and wanted the fancy outsides of life. Fuckin'-A, I did. Now all I wanted was quiet.

Can't a man have his quiet?

About three a.m., an icicle pierced my heart. I found dozens of pages of Track Changes comments I'd embedded in Surali's thesis as notes to myself. How many other incriminating notes were nested in these hundreds and hundreds of pages?

Screw it. I quit reading and started a shredding party.

Basically, I became a machine, feeding the max number of pages at a time (sixteen, Christ) into the jaws of the shredder. The grinding of those teeth, the whirring of the motor, got to me. I blasted Classic Rock on my

Bose cans. But the voices of panic wouldn't be dampened. When Buffalo Springfield sang about paranoia striking deep, I killed the tracks and let the headphones muffle things. They muted the room but not my brain.

I should have slept, but had reams to go. I shouldn't have drunk, but I poured another. I shouldn't have plagiarized, but I doubled down, shredding evidence like a bookie in a raid.

I shoved in another stack. The machine's teeth became those of Fred Rogers, my damn conscience in a cardigan. *"It's the knowing that WE CAN BE TRUSTED."* How could he speak so gently yet be so loud? *" . . . That we never have to FEAR THE TRUTH."* I fed him another stack of files. *"FEAR THE TRUTH."* The shredder jammed. *"FEAR THE TRUTH, FEAR THE—"*

"Shut up! Shut up! Just. Shut. Up!" I tried to jerk out the stuck pages but tipped over the machine, spilling the confetti of my sin at my feet. In a fury, I ripped off the headphones.

Knocking.

Was that real? Four more raps on my metal door.

"Help you?" The man was backed by piercing sunlight. I wiped water from my eyes and made out the serious suit and tie.

"Professor Coe?" He gave me a scan under a salt and pepper brow like he was measuring me for orange coveralls. A grin to throw me off. I didn't reply. It didn't stop him. "Sorry just to drop in. I've been calling but keep getting no answer."

"Yeah, my phone. It's . . ." Roadkill back at my apartment. A business card showed up in my hand. Academic. Forensic. Investigator. Flashing neon. "Do you mind? I'd rather we had this conversation inside." I stepped back. Patrick Windom, LLC, strode in like the landlord, owning everything his gaze fell on.

I lurched into tour guide mode. Babbling. Beating back the cranial racket with my own voice. "My current project." Sweeping gesture. The acoustic camera, blahdy-blah. The IR outputs, blahdy-blah, the shock-mounted loudspeakers, blah. He was old enough to smile at Cone of Silence. Good sign. This would be all right. Yeah, I had this. If I could just keep my cool and not say anything stupid. He winced at Sting's fried neoprene. I kept yacking. As long as I stalled, I was still Professor Coe. Not much of a strategy. But I was in free fall.

My visitor head-bobbed at the setup. "Interesting." Liar.

Just like that he put his back to my experiment and helped himself to a chair. "Today, though, I'm more interested in going back." The investigator pulled a file from his briefcase. From where I stood, I could see my last name on the tab label. "Are you prepared to revisit your past?"

I was afraid to ask what Tracy gave up. I saw my little boy, weeping as his Dady got publicly stripped of his crown.

"You sure you don't want to sit?" I wiped a tear and shook no. "Let's proceed. I've been brought here to do some hard looking into your background. I'm done with most of it, but I can't close my inquiry without hearing directly from you."

In the orchestra pit of my skull, a violin screeched one, endless, sour note in a high pitch. I couldn't turn it off. "You . . . want to ask me about Sound Quarry."

His brows met. "I warn my interviewees to be discreet. But one thing we both know." He fixed me with The Look. The one Fred Rogers locked on me at commencement. "There are no secrets in academia." The *"FEAR THE TRUTH"* loop joined the shrill note.

Through the noise salad, the investigator said, "Too bad you can't invent some way to keep people quiet." He turned to look up for assent as I smashed the tripod down on his forehead.

The acoustic camera flew clean off its bracket. Stunned eyes locked on mine. His disbelieving mouth croaked out, "Why?" I bashed again to silence him. To silence everything.

Then a bash to silence my ex.

Then a bash to silence my lab rat. Then a bash to silence Surali Gupta. Then a bash, bash, bash to silence Fred fucking Rogers.

The campus bells tolled five when I got back from taking Sting's travel trunk for a one-way cruise on the Sound. You watch enough *Dexter*, you pick up a few things.

An hour later, I zipped the tripod, the busted camera, and Windom's briefcase into the nylon duffel with the bloody sponges and bleachy rags. Good poundage for my next water dump. I righted the chair and took in the lab. Maybe I was impulse's bitch. Maybe this wasn't a permanent solution. But I heard something I hadn't heard in six years.

Quiet.

Opening the door to go deep six the last of the evidence, I ran into Dr. Zazueta reaching to knock. "Good, you're still here. I promised Patrick Windom I wouldn't come by until he told you. Is your phone off or something?" The college president brushed past me carrying a canvas tote. I hurried after him.

"Told me what?"

"Mr. Windom was hired to vet you by Dartmouth. Your application was finally accepted. You're to be the new dean of the Thayer School of Engineering. Congratulations, Dean Coe."

The room started to tilt. I braced against the wall. "Sorry I ducked you yesterday at my office. Not a very swift move on my part, but I have a lousy poker face, and I was afraid I'd spill the beans." He handed me a bottle of Moet & Chandon from the tote. "I thought for sure you'd know by now. This morning Windom said he only had a few cursory questions to ask you just to dot an I and cross a T before he shared the good news. Strange. His rental car is outside. You haven't seen him?"

Dr. Zazueta's eye caught on a spatter of coagulated blood I'd missed on Sting's withered ear. He turned back to study me.

I stood speechless in the silence. Until Mister Rogers returned.

Fred had plenty to say.

Monkey in Residence

by Xu Xi 許素細

In the spring of 2017, just after the grave sweeping 清明 festival, the Government of the Hong Kong SAR[1] proudly announced funding for a new Academic Chair position—Monkey in Residence—to be given to the public universities. Its objective was to honor our famous ancestor, that half god, half mortal Monkey[2]. Monkey, as everyone knew, had sired several heirs and the dynasties of Monkeys that followed were, the government claimed, a significant family of special Chinese citizens from whom we should learn more about our own history, travels and culture. What better place than at those institutes of higher learning where young minds are molded and refined?

---

[1] SAR Special Administrative Region of the People's Republic of China, a.k.a. Hong Kong's postcolonial neocolonial status under its then sovereign ruler.

[2] Monkey is Sun Wukong, more commonly known as the Monkey King, a mythological figure who travels with the Buddhist monk Xuanzang to the western regions of China through Central Asia and India to obtain the sacred Buddhist texts or sutras. Monkey's story is told in the 16th century Chinese novel *Journey to the West* 西遊記 (Xiyou Zi in pinyin). The novel is considered one of the four great classical novels of Chinese literature, and is generally attributed to 吳承恩 Wu Chengen. Monkey's descendants in Hong Kong are a speculative family but judging by the growing population of monkeys in evidence throughout the city, this speculation may be less fictional than it appears.

All over the city, huge posters with the character "Monkey"[3] appeared, announcing a "logo design and naming contest" for the new Chair position. The electronic poster was also all over the internet and even had its own Facebook page.

猴

Money in Resident

Logo Dissent & Numbing Concert for new Char Prize $11,980.20

It took about a week, but the posters were eventually replaced with all typos fixed and the prize money corrected to $12,000[4]. A government spokeswoman blamed the errors on their communications department intern from one of the universities' English department, whose recently appointed Acting Head was heard to declare *my English is not very good, ha! ha! ha!* At least he was correct about that, his colleagues whispered, beleaguered as they were by the third Acting Head to be installed in less than two years. The government spokeswoman was however quick to add *this error is inconsequential as the Chinese language version is correct, and, after all, most in Hong Kong know Chinese, ha! ha! ha!* Laughter by the powers-that-be had recently become a trend, a fashionable way to soften bad or fake news. Most of us nodded in agreement, although a few running dogs dissented, those long-resident leftover colonial British or BBC's[5] who neither read

---

[3] Monkey: 猴 (hou), Mandarin, although in Hong Kong the Cantonese equivalent 馬騮 (maa lau) was what locals used.

[4] Hong Kong dollars in 2019 were pegged to the US dollar at the rate of approximately 7.8 to 1 USD, meaning the prize was worth a little over US$1,500, which strikes us as a paltry sum for some human to design a logo and provide a name for what was an extremely expensive salaried position for a Monkey (or human, for that matter).

[5] BBC: British born Chinese or the British Broadcasting Corporation. The difference is academic.

nor spoke Chinese. We wondered when these latter would get fed up and leave, sooner rather than later some wished, although others said why care as long as they fed our economy, *and anyway,* we whispered, *English and Chinese* (Mandarin and Cantonese) *are both our official languages, so we can be bi- or even tri-lingual, right?* Far more complaints were heard about the prize money. Where was the missing $19.80? Was this corruption or a mistake? Inquiring minds wanted to know on Weibo, Instagram, even on LinkedIn. Certainly along our vines the whispers spread across the city. Eventually, the government's Financial Secretary (FS) gave in after much pressure by the Dean of Business at HKU, the leading university. The FS was a graduate of HKU, but, as everyone knew, his myopic focus on the bottom line greatly surpassed his common sense.

Meanwhile, the excitement among Monkey's descendants was palpable.

"What are my chances do you think?" Monkey Fire Hero III asked. At age ten, he was eldest son of his generation and leader of the fire clan in Hong Kong. The grandeur and power of a Chair Professorship gleamed in his mind, although he was loathe to admit it.

His inner circle of younger male fire clan Monkeys were quick to say he definitely *must* be the choice. After all, who else was more brilliant, more virile, more important than he? Flattery, they knew, would keep him calm. His violent temper erupted whenever his face was lost, which happened often, given his propensity for pompous declarations about his power and achievements. They quickly diverted his attention by non-stop chattering.

"How do you think they'll make the decision?"

"Is it one at each, or just one position that all universities compete for?"

"You don't suppose they'll consider,"—this, followed by a wince—"*female* Monkeys, do you?"

"D'you think he has to be a graduate from one of the universities? Or if not, one who graduated with honors from a top international one?"

All the others tried to shush this last speaker. A young son-in-law who had newly entered the inner circle, he was unaware of Monkey Fire Hero III's sensitivity about his abysmal academic record. As recently as last year, their leader had gone to great lengths, *again,* to try to have his grades altered or redacted and to have an honorary PhD conferred on him by either Oxford or Harvard. Unsuccessfully, as it turned out, because there was no one left to bribe or do his bidding. *Really, at his age,* they all whispered, wondering why it should matter anymore? Luckily, their great leader appeared not to have heard, his short attention span interrupting, as always.

But their clan's Chief Financial Officer Dickson, a non-Monkey human, declared, "This is a ridiculous idea."

Dickson rarely spoke. When he did, the fire Monkeys listened. There was a long-ish silence, punctuated by teeth picking, spitting and banana peeling. When in doubt, fire Monkeys were given to the long pause. Finally, Fire Hero III himself spoke up. "Why should that be ridiculous?"

"Think about it," Dickson said. "How many Monkeys go to our universities in Hong Kong? Zero. Okay, maybe a few of the cross-bred Monkey-humans do, but they're mostly females so they don't count, because females can get away with treason. Most of the male cross-breeds hang out in the trees with you all. This government is just trying to placate you, to make you feel important so that you'll vote them back in at the next election. It's all about politics, all about the restlessness among the Intelligent Beasts. Who among the beasts caused the most havoc at the last election? The Monkeys, of course, since . . ." and here he glanced sideways at the others, "the smart humans know that Monkeys, especially fire Monkeys, are by far the most intelligent. So this is one of the FS's famous 'sweeteners'—toss them a bonus and they'll be content."

He took a breath, sucked on his inhaler, and continued. "Even you, honorable leader, attended the University for Intelligent Beasts on the Chinese exclave island territory, Feiyudao[6]. That's the natural order of things, where Monkeys stick with their own kind and return to the trees."

---

[6] Feiyudao (飛魚島) or Flying Fish Island is a speculative geographical location in the mode of Jonathan Swift's floating island Laputa, as depicted in the third book of *Gulliver's Travels*. Likewise, the University of Intelligent Beasts bears some resemblance to the Academy on Laputa.

The effort of speaking clearly exhausted him and he slumped back in his chair to continue gazing at the spreadsheets on his screen.

The long pause was interrupted, too soon, by the same young son-in-law. "Feiyudao? Do you mean Tobiuo-Shima?"

Once again, a noisy shushing followed. Didn't this kid know *anything*? Just because he had majored in Japanese—a serious mistake, many in the clan believed, for their leader's youngest daughter by his tenth concubine to have married this cultural traitor—he still was Chinese and should have known better than to refer to Pinnacle Point Island of the contested Diaoyus by its Japanese name! Especially within earshot of his father-in-law.

Finally Fire Monkey III spoke. "Thank you, Dickson. We will take your concern under advisement."

Meanwhile, at the University Institute of the City of Kowloon, or U-ICK for short, Jaspar Man-ming Mui, the now-former intern at the communications department of the Government of Hong Kong, was basking in subversive glory. In his dorm room at U-ICK, school mates surrounded him, notably two popular girls, Punny Li and Anita Chan, who had previously paid him scant attention.

"What made you do it?" they all wanted to know.

"I was inspired. It's like Professor Kendrick says, language is the tool of the user. Master the tool and you have power." On his walls hung the framed "erroneous" poster. He had ensured a large stash did not get destroyed, and already a frenzied international bidding war had begun for this latest collectible. The electronic version still existed in cyberspace, protected by a firewall so thick not even the hackers in North Korea could crack it.

Jasper was seated next to YK Tseng, his best friend and hacker extraordinaire, who already had a scholarship for grad school at MIT to where he was headed in September.

"What are you going to do now, Jasper?" YK asked.

It was no secret he could be placed on academic probation, maybe even expelled, and if so no other government university would likely offer him a place. His only recourse would be one of the private colleges. Unlike YK, he did not see his future at a university abroad. He shrugged, nonchalant. "No idea. Maybe I'll start a new bi-lingual news magazine and report on the corruption in government."

Punny, who majored in Veterinary Science, spoke up. "You two should start a new political party. All the democracy and independence parties have collapsed. Give people hope. This government resorts to such low tactics. Bribing Monkeys, imagine!"

Jasper beamed. He had been crushing on Punny all year but she barely knew he existed, until now. This was worth it. Who cared if U-ICK threw him out? There was more to life than a university degree. Of course, his parents thought otherwise but for the moment, he silenced his mind of their disapproval, and instead pictured Punny, her skintight jeans and panties around her ankles as he humped her.

Not to be outdone, Anita, who was like Jasper an English major, said, "The news magazine is a much better idea. After all, language is your talent, not politics." Punny shot her an angry look. Undaunted, she continued. "I'd help you with that and so would my friends at HKU." Her reference to the city's top university was deliberate. She knew it would flatter Jasper whose English ability surpassed most local students. His overall grades just hadn't been good enough to get him into HKU, and he had had to settle for U-ICK instead.

"We'll see," Jasper said. "Professor Wan has already 'sumoned' me to a meeting." He pulled up the email from the Acting Head of English. "Look, he has five spelling or grammar errors in two short sentences. Fuck his mother, why should I care what he thinks? He's a joke."

Everyone agreed, although Punny remained silent. Wan was a professor at Vet Science where she badly wanted a lucrative research post. He had promised to support her, so she didn't dare bad mouth him, even though she knew it was only because he wanted to get into her pants. But Anita spoke up, since the rumors around Wan had trailed him into English. "What's the matter, Punny, don't you agree? Or is Wan too, aah . . . salty-wet-horny around you?"

Punny blushed and fled the room. Jasper, who hadn't known this bit of gossip, felt his heart balloon pop. But, having slain her rival, Anita had already sidled up next to him in her micro skirt and filmy, skimpy top, a willing substitute for his gaze.

A noisy and confused debate ensued until YK declared he was hungry, and the group headed out to the nearby hawker stands at the wet market for late night soup noodles and congee.

By September, Fire Monkey III was installed as the first Professor Monkey in Residence in the city. No one was really surprised at this choice—what other Monkey could the government possibly have picked?—although what did surprise us was that U-ICK was the first university granted this honor. What an insult to HKU! After all, it had been in existence since 1911, and was a *proper* university, while U-ICK was a former Polytech that only gained university stature in 1984. *Furthermore,* the whispers along our vines breathed, *HKU has ivy-covered walls while U-ICK is mostly bare concrete, except for us morning glories.* It was a tut-tutting moment in academia. Even Fire Monkey III briefly pondered this curious situation, but being a Monkey, he quickly moved on to more important matters. And his number one concern was the greening of U-ICK. "Trees," he declared at his Distinguished Chair lecture, "this campus needs more trees and vines. It will improve the learning environment if students learn to live in nature. We must plant a rain forest on the roof of the rotunda at the top of the hill. That will be perfect."

The Financial Secretary, who was in the audience, leapt up to applaud Professor Monkey in Residence; trees were cheaper than buildings or labs and *anyone* could plant trees! All the faculty and most of the students also rose. The President, who had dozed off, staggered to his feet. He did not want a Professor Monkey in Residence, but the FS had forced this position on his university. President Ma was afraid Monkey would foment revolt among the hundreds of emotional support animals registered at the university in recent years. Already, the campus resembled a giant petting zoo, what with the Chihuahuas, Pomeranians, shih tzus, Siamese and Persian cats, geckos, cockatoos, parakeets, even kingfishers and cormorants, peacocks, plus the odd snake or two hanging out with their student companions. He had wanted to draw a line at snakes, given the poisonous species in the territory, but SPAS, the Society for the Prevention of Alienation of Snakes, had protested for twenty-five days, forcing him to cancel his vacation, until he succumbed.

President Ma's distress increased as applause thundered through the auditorium. How he wished he had never established his Institute of Cross-Border Veterinary Science & Technology. ICE-VEST, as it was known, had become his albatross. He had not expected the alarming demand for emotional support animals by the students, something most faculty supported. Their revenge. He had diverted salary monies out of other academic departments into ICE-VEST, and no one could replace retired or departed faculty. His hope was to tap into scientific research funds from China—swine or avian flu, hoof and mouth disease, mad cow, were these not worthy of study? Instead, he was mired in an animal farm, and soon a rooftop rain forest that would turn into a planet for apes!

"President Ma?" His assistant's gentle voice nudged him out of his daytime nightmare. Everyone else was seated, while he still stood, applauding weakly, lost in confusion. The mammalian ocean behind him snickered. The President sat down, defeated.

A week after Monkey's lecture, Jasper attended his hearing by the Academic Disciplinary Council. Professor Cyrus Wan, Acting Head of English, presided. The night before Wan had called President Ma, begging him to preside. "You owe me," he said. "I agreed to be Acting Head to force out as many professors as possible to get you more funds for ICE-VEST. I've already done that in three other departments as Acting Head. At *your* request. You can't throw me to the cockroaches now!"

"One last time," Ma said. "I promise no more."

"The media will be there. You know it. The *English language* media! How am I supposed to talk to them? I'll be a laughing stock."

"Don't worry, Wan. Just expel the little fuckhead for disrespecting our government, make a one-sentence statement and leave. Any other questions, just say no comment. You can do it."

Now, Wan was confronted by the student and Professor Kendrick of Linguistics. The proceedings were all in English, since Kendrick was British and all public universities were supposedly "English medium." He tried to focus on the case Jasper was making in his own defense. Kendrick chimed in about the "creative use of language" which the government had simply failed to appreciate. The other professors on the council nodded sagely, made noises about not stifling critical discourse. Wan could see the writing on the wall; they were not willing to punish this student.

Afterwards, outdoors on the grand concourse, Kendrick made statements to the press about freedom of speech and how no crime had been committed. Jasper was allowed to continue his studies and he and Anita produced their bi-lingual newsletter, much to the dismay of Ma and Wan. The first editorial offered great support to the proposal by Professor Monkey in Residence for the rooftop urban rain forest. Within nine months, the campus had become a jungle and Jasper and Anita staged a naked, communal lie-in beside the lily pond, where the fences were twined by vines of morning glories. Punny did not participate.

This all happened a long time ago, when Hong Kong still had several universities, before the city erupted in protests led by the Intelligent Beasts. It was a time when we knew change was in the air. After 2047, we no longer were a Special Administrative Region of China, governed by the Basic Law of "one country two systems." The first Monkey in Residence led to others, including several females, and in time, humans learned to swing on vines and ate the bananas, ferns and morning glories that grew abundantly in our sub-tropical jungle. The buses and subways and cars disappeared, as did the airport and planes, because some humans also learned to fly with the migrating birds and butterflies, while others joined the underground world of rats and snakes.

The universities whittled down to one, U-ICK, because most Hong Kong students flocked to the University for Intelligent Beasts. In 2022, after the roof of the rain forest rotunda collapsed, President Ma tried to flee campus in the wake of the scandal, only to trip over an emotional support boa constrictor whose companion student was out to lunch. The boa, agitated, encircled Ma and strangled him to death. Ma never witnessed the longevity of his ICE-VEST, eventually renamed the Academy for Monkeys in Residence or AM-Res. The renaming was essential, as Jasper and Anita noted in their bi-lingual online media, *Borderless Hong Kong,* because "cross-border" no longer held any meaning as humans and Intelligent Beasts were rapidly transforming into Humane Intelligent Beasts or HIB's through cross-breeding. When Monkey Fire Hero III finally passed away, at the ripe old age of forty-five, the whispering along our vines was that *perhaps he really was a baboon because everyone knows monkeys just don't live that long.* But it didn't stop the territory that had been Hong Kong from honoring him with the equivalent of a state funeral. After all, we wouldn't be the wonderful world we are now, if not for that first rooftop rain forest he planted. Despite the roof collapsing, weighted down by undrained water underneath, it accelerated the transformation of our city as nature claimed it back. Besides, he was the first Professor Monkey in Residence. For us, the vines of morning glories, we mostly want to tell the stories of the real heroes, even if they were just history's accidents.

Bertie and the Boat Race

by Peter Lovesey

People close to me sometimes pluck up courage and ask how I first became an amateur detective. I generally tell them it began in 1886 through my desire to discover the truth about the suspicious death of Fred Archer, the Tinman, the greatest jockey who ever wore my colours, or anyone else's. However, it dawned on me the other day that my talent for deduction must have been with me from my youth, for I was instrumental in solving a mystery as far back as the year 1860. I had quite forgotten until some ill-advised person wrote to my secretary to ask if HRH The Prince of Wales would care to patronise the Henley Regatta this year.

Henley!

You'd think people would know by now that my preferred aquatic sport is yachting, not standing on a towpath watching boats of preposterous shape being manoeuvred along a reach of the Thames by fellows in their undergarments.

The mystery. It has a connection with Henley, but the strongest connection is with a young lady. Ah, the fragrant memory of one I shall call Echo, out of respect for her modesty, for she is a lady of irreproachable reputation now. Why Echo? Because she was the water nymph who loved the youth Narcissus. The real Echo is supposed to have pined away after her love was not returned, leaving only her voice behind, but this part of the legend you can ignore.

She was the only daughter of a tutor at Christ Church College, Oxford, and I met her during my sojourn at the University. I was eighteen, a mere stripling, and a virtual prisoner in a house off the Cornmarket known as Frewin Hall, with my Equerry and Governor as jailers. My father, Prince Albert, had rigid views on education and wanted me to benefit from the tuition at Oxford. Sad to relate, he deemed it unthinkable for the future King to live in college with boisterous young men of similar age. Six docile undergraduates of good family were accordingly enlisted to be my fellow students. They attended Frewin Hall and sat beside me listening to private lectures from selected professors. I don't know who suffered the greatest ordeal, my fellow-students, the tutors, or myself. I was not academically in-clined. The only inclination I had was towards the stunningly pretty Echo.

I met her first across the dinner table, Papa having insisted that din-ner parties should feature in my curriculum. I was to learn how to conduct myself at table, use the cutlery, hold a conversation and so forth. Most of my guests were stuffed-shirts, the same studious fellows who shared my lec-tures, together with various professors and clergymen, but, thank heavens, it was deemed desirable for members of the fair sex to be of the party. Some of the tutors brought their wives. One—I shall call him Dr. Stubbs—was a widower and was accompanied by his daughter.

Echo Stubbs. My pulse races now at the memory of her stepping into the anteroom, standing timidly so close to her father that her crinoline tilt-ed and revealed quite six inches of silk-stocking—I think the first sighting I had of a mature female ankle in the whole of my life.

When I finally forced my eyes higher I was treated to a deep blush from a radiantly lovely face. Her black hair was parted at the centre in swathes that covered her ears like a scarf. She curtsied. Dr. Stubbs bowed. And while his head was lowered I winked at Echo and she turned the colour of a guardsman's jacket.

I shall not dwell on the subtle process of glances and signals that sealed our attachment. She didn't say much, and neither did I. It was all in the eyes, and the barely perceptible movements of the lips. She enslaved me. I resolved to see her again, if possible in less constricting company. I lost all interest in my studies. Every waking moment was filled with thoughts of her.

My difficulty was that she and I were chaperoned with a rigour hard to imagine in these more indulgent times. If my beautiful Echo ventured out of Christ Church, you may be sure her po-faced Papa was at her side. The only opportunities we had of meeting were after Morning Service at the Cathedral on a Sunday, when every word between us was overheard by General Bruce, my Governor, and Dr. Stubbs. So we spoke of the weather and the sermon while our eyes held a more intimate discourse altogether.

During lectures I would plot strategies for meeting her alone. I seriously considered ways of gaining admittance to the family's rooms in Christ Church by posing as a College servant. If I had known for certain which room my fair Echo slept in, I would have visited the College by night and flung gravel at her window. But in retrospect it was a good thing I didn't indulge in such heroics because we had lately been troubled by a series of burglaries and I might have suffered the embarrassment of being arrested. My amorous nature has more than once been the undoing of me and it would have got me into hot water even at that tender age were it not for a piece of intelligence that reached me.

The worthy Dr. Stubbs, I learned, was a rowing man. He had been a 'wet bob' at Eton and a Blue at the University. For the past two years he had acted as umpire at the Henley Royal Regatta.

I've already made clear my views on rowing, but I happened to be in possession of two useful facts about Henley. The first: that it was *de rigeur* that the fair sex patronised the Regatta in all their finery, congregating on the lawns of the Red Lion, near the finish. And the second: that the umpire followed all the races from the water, rowed by a crew of the finest Thames watermen. Do you see? I had the prospect of Dr. Stubbs being aboard a boat giving undivided attention to the races whilst his winsome daughter was at liberty on the river bank.

I devised a plan. I would go to Henley for the Regatta and hire a small craft, preferably a punt, without revealing my identity to anyone. I would furnish it with a hamper containing champagne and find a mooring close to the Red Lion. As soon as Echo appeared, I would invite her aboard my punt for a better view of the rowing. Need I go into the rest of the plan?

Now one of the unfortunates who sat with me through those dreary lectures in Frewin Hall was a runt of a fellow called Henry Bilbo, about five feet in stature, and he happened to be the coxswain to the College First Eight. I'd noticed Bilbo being treated with undue civility by Dr. Stubbs long before I learned of his connection with the Boat Club. If anyone else, myself excepted, arrived late for a lecture, he would be severely rebuked. Not Bilbo. He was an arrogant little tyke, too.

"You would appear to lead a charmed life, Henry," I remarked to him one morning after lectures.

"Oh, I have the measure of old Stubbsy, Your Royal Highness," he told me. "We rowing men stick together. He's relying on us to win the Ladies' Plate at Henley this year."

"Henley, when is that?" I affected to ask. I didn't want Bilbo to know how eager I was.

"The Monday and Tuesday after we go down. Don't you know, Bertie? It is the Royal Regatta."

"Only because my father condescended to be the Patron," I said. "Because it's Royal by name, it doesn't mean Royal persons are obliged to attend. Rowing bores me silly."

"Won't you be supporting us?"

"I have other calls upon my time," I said to throw him off the scent. "Do you have a better-than-average chance of winning?"

"Only if we can match the Black Prince," he told me.

"Who the devil is that?"

"First Trinity. The Cambridge lot. They've won it more times than anyone else. They're defending the Plate. But with me at the tiller-ropes, we should give them a damned good race. Dr. Stubbs has stated as much."

"He takes an interest, then?"

"He's our trainer. It matters so much to him that he's passing up the chance to be umpire this year. It wouldn't be sporting, you see, for Stubbsy to show partiality."

This was devastating news, but I tried to remain composed. "So he won't be on the umpire's boat?"

"Didn't I make that clear? He'll be on the bank, supervising our preparation. You really should be there to see us." As a lure, he added, "The adorable Echo has promised to come."

Trying to sound uninterested, I commented, "I suppose she would."

"She'll watch us carry the boat down to the water and launch it. She'll be all of a flutter at the sight of so many beefy fellows stripped for action." He grinned lasciviously. "Her pretty chest will be pumping nineteen to the dozen. Wouldn't you care for a sight of that?"

"Sir, you exceed yourself," I rebuked him.

He apologized for the ungentlemanly remark. I'd always thought Bilbo ill-bred, even though his father was a Canon of the Church of England.

After he left, I spent a long time considering my options. If Dr. Stubbs was to be on the bank, he would expect his daughter to be beside him. My punting plan had to be abandoned.

On the same afternoon, I announced my intention of calling on Dr. Stubbs at Christ Church. I sent my Equerry to inform him how I liked my afternoon tea: quite simple, with poached eggs, rolls, cakes, scones, shortcake and a plate of preserved ginger. Anything else spoils dinner, in my experience.

The beautiful Echo was not at home, more was the pity. She had left early to visit a maternal aunt, her father explained. I came to the point at once. "I understand, Dr. Stubbs, that you are taking a personal interest in the College Eight."

"That is true, sir. We have entered for the Ladies' Plate at Henley."

"I should like to be of the party."

"You wish to pull an oar, sir?" he said in some surprise, for I had never evinced the slightest interest in rowing.

"Heaven forbid," said I. "My intention is merely to accompany you and any other members of your family who may be with you."

"There's only Echo, my daughter. She likes to watch the rowing. We'll be honoured to have you with us, Your Royal Highness. I think I should mention, however, that I will be occupied to some degree with the College Eight."

"You needn't feel responsible for me," I assured him. "I'm capable of amusing myself."

He said, "I'm sure the stewards would be honoured if you would present the trophies, sir."

There was only one trophy that interested me. "No," I told him firmly. "I prefer to attend *incognito*. Once in a while I like to behave like one of the human race." I helped myself to another cake.

I could see that his mind was working over the consequences of this arrangement. He said, "I wouldn't wish you to feel encumbered by my daughter. It could be embarrassing—you, sir, in the company of a young lady. I could easily arrange for her to join another party."

Encumbered? "On the contrary, Dr. Stubbs," I said, "if anyone is to join another party, it is I. Your charming daughter's place is at your side, encouraging the crew. After all, they have entered for the Ladies' Plate. To have a lady in attendance is a good omen."

He said, as he was bound to say, that my presence was equally indispensable. "I just hope there's a Ladies' Plate to win on the day," he added. "At the rate the silver is disappearing from the colleges, I wouldn't bet on it. There was another burglary last night."

"Oh?"

"Yes, at Merton. A fine pair of candlesticks was taken. The fellow got in through a pantry window, apparently. He's deucedly good at squeezing into small spaces."

"Is it a youth, do you suppose?" I suggested.

I could see he was impressed by my acuity. On my way out, by the porter's lodge, I met Bilbo. He'd seen which door I came from, so I was forced to admit the reason for my visit—the ostensible reason, at any rate.

"You want to cheer us on?" he piped in disbelief. "I thought you regarded rowing as a silly sport."

"I wouldn't even call it a sport," I confirmed, "but one likes to support one's *Alma Mater*. Who knows? Perhaps I'll be so captivated by the sight of you fellows that I join the Boat Club myself."

He said, "It's back-breaking for the oarsmen, Bertie."

"But a sure way to impress the ladies."

"Indeed," he enthused. "Echo Stubbs treats me like one of the gods since I got into the First Eight."

"But you're only the cox," I commented with disdain.

"With respect, Bertie, that shows how little you know about it," he had the neck to tell me. "The coxswain is the brains of the boat. The rest of them rely on me to steer the best course, and that's no little achievement at Henley."

I could hardly wait for the regatta. Not for one moment did I believe Bilbo's boast that Echo held a torch for him. It was unthinkable. Apart from everything else, she was several inches taller than he.

The Ladies' Plate was decided on the Tuesday, and it started cloudy, but by lunchtime the sun condescended to appear and we had a perfect after- noon for the Aquatic Derby. Glorious Henley. That dimpled span of water with its wooded heights and enamelled banks was occupied by hundreds of floating picnic parties, whilst others promenaded along the river bank. There is no question that rowing brings out the most gaudy attire, and not only among the fair sex. If an invasion of crinoline had transformed the scene, it was matched by the effrontery of the coloured blazers and boaters on view. The scene was exhilarating, even for one without a jot of interest in the contests on the water. I will admit to having a *conquest* in mind.

Amid such gaiety I was able to move inconspicuously, scarcely recog- nized (for in those carefree days my likeness was not in every illustrated newspaper one opened). At leisure, I strolled the length of the course, sniff- ing the new-mown hay and rehearsing my overtures.

My thoughts were sharply interrupted at three o'clock, when a gun was fired in the meadows to warn those afloat to clear the course. A few minutes later the celebrated crew of London Watermen came dashing through the bridge, transporting the umpire ceremoniously to the start. What a pity it wasn't Stubbs.

The Ladies' Challenge Plate was the fourth race on the card. No pre-liminary heat had been necessary. It was to be a straight race between First Trinity and Christ Church, a distance of a mile and a quarter from the starting point above the Temple Island to the winning post opposite the Red Lion, below the town bridge.

The Oxford boats were sheltered under a large tent erected beside the river on the far side of the bridge. The scene here was in stark contrast to the merriment along Regatta Reach. An air of serious endeavour prevailed, the oarsmen preparing for the ordeal to come, nervously pacing the turf, saying little. The observers here seemed also to be infected with the sense of what was at stake. They stood at a respectful distance. I spotted Echo at once, looking ravishing in the Christ Church colours, standing with her father.

I doffed my boater and Echo gave a sweet curtsey. "Please," I said. "No ceremony. Let's all be family today."

Turning to Dr. Stubbs, I asked, "Are the crew in fine fettle?"

"The best I've seen, sir," he told me. "They've been here for a week, stay-ing at the Red Lion, getting in hours of practice."

"Not at the bar, I trust," said I, evincing a delightful laugh from Echo. "Shall we offer them our good wishes?"

"Oh, yes!" said Echo, with a shade more passion than seemed appropri-ate. She made a beeline for a diminutive figure in blazer and flannels whom I recognized as Bilbo.

"He's our cox," said Dr. Stubbs, as if I didn't know. "He steers a canny course."

"Is there some skill involved?" I said.

"Good Lord, yes. The steering is paramount. He'll be steering for the church."

I didn't understand. I hadn't heard that Bilbo had religious affinities. "Do you mean Christ Church?"

"No, sir. You misunderstand me. Henley Church is the object to have in one's sights until Poplar Point is cleared. We've drawn the Berkshire sta-tion and that should be to our advantage. He'll make it tell. You'll see."

Not choosing to add to the adulation, I passed a few words with several of our oarsmen, who would, after all, be putting their bodies on the rack to win the race. But I kept an eye on what was happening and I saw Echo blush deeply more than once. I hoped nothing indiscreet had been said. Finally, Dr. Stubbs himself went across to remind Bilbo that it was time to lift the boat off its trestles and take to the water.

Even I will admit that I was stirred by the sight of eight blades cutting the water in concert as they moved into the stream to row down to the start. But we couldn't linger. Stubbs had decided to watch the race from Poplar Point, a quarter of a mile from where we stood.

As we threaded a route through the crowd, with Dr. Stubbs leading, I turned to Echo and enquired if she was feeling nervous.

"Terribly," she admitted.

I leaned closer and confided, "If you'd care to hold my hand and give it a squeeze, I wouldn't object in the least."

She blushed and murmured her thanks.

I said, "Speaking for myself, the main excitement will be standing close to you."

She lowered her eyes. I have that effect on the fair sex.

Stubbs was right: Poplar Point was a fine vantage place, even if we had to stand shoulder to shoulder with others. I took out my binoculars. There were signs of activity from the umpire. The crews were poised for the off. I saw Bilbo take a hip-flask from his pocket and knock back a swig of whisky to calm his nerves. Dr. Stubbs enquired if I had a good view. I put down the glasses, eyed his daughter and said I could see everything I wanted.

At length the word was given, and the oars dipped in. The Black Prince had the better of the start and for two hundred yards kept a narrow lead. The Christ Church men remained calm, pulling splendidly, their blades scarcely creating a ripple. Bilbo put his megaphone to his mouth to raise the rate.

"If they can stay in contention, the Berkshire station will be in their favour towards the finish," I told Echo, exhibiting the expertise I had picked up from her father.

Some know-it-all turned and said, "They'll need it with this wind blowing. The Bucks station will be sheltered by the bushes. Christ Church are going to struggle."

Beside me, Echo was taking quick, nervous breaths. I felt for her right hand and held it. My own pulse quickened.

Christ Church came up level as they approached the first real landmark, at Remenham. I thought I heard Echo say, "He can do it!"

She was so involved in the race, poor child, that she ascribed a personality to our boat.

Steadily, with never more than a canvas between them, the crews approached Poplar Point. Echo was pressing so close to me that I could feel the steel hoops of her dress making ridges in my flesh. It was peculiarly stimulating.

Then a strange thing happened. Something fell into the water from the Christ Church boat: Bilbo's megaphone. It floated a moment before disappearing. Bilbo half-turned, and evidently decided he could do nothing about it. They had reached the critical stage of the course and they were definitely in the lead, but he was steering dangerously close to First Trinity's water.

The umpire picked up his own megaphone and his voice travelled over the water. "Move over, Christ Church."

"What's wrong?" I asked.

"He's in danger of fouling," said Dr. Stubbs in a strangled tone. "Move over, man!"

As if he could hear, Bilbo tugged on the rudder, but too powerfully, for our boat lurched to port, and was now in danger of running aground.

"What's his game?" cried Dr. Stubbs. "He'll lose it for us."

The Black Prince had drawn level. In fact, it was slipping by whilst our erratic steering was causing uncertainty in the boat. The crew were losing their form, bucketing their strokes, uncertain whether to reduce their effort as the boat veered off course.

"For God's sake, pull to starboard, man!" Dr. Stubbs bawled. Bilbo couldn't possibly hear.

Echo let go of my hand and covered her eyes. I put a protective arm around her shoulders. Her Papa was far too occupied to notice. The Christ Church boat was out of control. It glided inexorably towards the bank. People in punts screamed in alarm. Parasols fell into the water. The bows hit one of the punts with such force that the front of the eight rode straight over it. A man tumbled into the water.

The stern dipped below water level. It started to sink. Several of the crew freed themselves and leapt clear. I looked to see what Bilbo was doing, for his inept steering had caused this catastrophe, but he remained at his post, head lowered, as the water crept up his chest.

Meanwhile, the Black Prince rounded Poplar Point in fine style and cruised towards the finish, past the band of the Oxford Rifles on their raft and the cheering thousands along the banks and in the stewards' grandstand. The drama at Poplar Point had been unseen by those at the finish and they must have waited vainly for Christ Church to come into view.

My pretty companion was in distress. "Oh, Bertie, we must see if he's all right! We must go at once!"

We made the best speed we could down to the towing path. But movement was difficult in the throng of people anxious to observe the accident. We couldn't get close. Someone was being lifted from the water. There were shouts for a doctor.

"Who is it?" I asked. "What's happened?"

"The coxswain. He went down with the boat and almost drowned."

"Henry?" cried Echo. She fainted in my arms—some consolation for the lamentable end to my romantic afternoon.

"Hold on, sir," said Dr. Stubbs. "I've got some whisky here." He felt into his hip pocket. Then tried his other pockets. "Where the devil is my flask? Hell's teeth, I must have dropped it in all the excitement."

They took Henry Bilbo to the local cottage hospital. We visited him there and found him in a more serious state than any of us expected, in a coma, in fact. He would not respond to anything that was said. Some of the crew volunteered to remain at the bedside, but I deemed it wise to escort Echo and her father out of that place as soon as possible. I didn't care for the look of Bilbo, and I was right. He never recovered consciousness. He died the same night.

It was widely assumed that the wretched fellow had been too overcome with shame over his mistake to free himself from the sinking boat. In college circles, he was being spoken of as a martyr.

This was the point in the story when the detective in me first began to stir. I couldn't for the life of me understand why Bilbo had behaved so oddly. The more I thought about it, reviewing the events of that afternoon, the more suspicious I became that there was something rum about his death. I recalled watching him drink from that flask of whisky at the start, beginning the race competently in charge, but later dropping the megaphone over the side and, shortly after, losing control of the steering. Had he imbibed too much?

Without reference to anyone except my Equerry, I returned to Henley a day or so later and spoke to the doctor who had conducted the post-mortem examination. He appeared satisfied that drowning had been the cause of death. He insisted that the classical signs (whatever they may be) had been present. I asked if further tests would be carried out and he thought this unlikely.

"What caused him to drown?" I asked.

"The inability to swim, sir."

"But this was in shallow water."

"Then perhaps he was trapped in the boat. These matters are for the coroner to investigate."

"Trapped?"

"Conceivably he was exhausted."

"He was the cox," I shrilled in disbelief. "He hadn't even lifted an oar."

Far from satisfied, I asked if Bilbo's clothes had been retained.

The doctor said they had been destroyed, as was usual in such cases. The only item not disposed of was a silver hip flask. It would be returned to the family. I asked to see it.

"Returned to the family, you say?" I queried, turning the flask over in my hand. "To Bilbo's family?"

"That is my understanding. Is there something amiss, sir?"

"Only that the initials on the outside are not Bilbo's," said I. " 'A.C.S.' doesn't stand for Henry Bilbo. These are the initials of Dr. Arthur Stubbs, of Christ Church College."

I was in no doubt that I had recovered the lost hip-flask. Better still, it had been well corked and some of the liquor remained inside.

"If this does, indeed, belong to Bilbo, I shall see that his family receives it," I told the doctor. "If not, I shall return it discreetly to Dr. Stubbs. We don't want poor Bilbo's reputation being muddied for any reason." With that, I took possession of the flask.

On the train back to Oxford, I was sorely tempted to take a nip of the contents of that flask. What a good thing I didn't, because when I turned matters over in my mind, it seemed wise to discover some more about the liquor Bilbo had swigged prior to the race. Without speaking to anyone else, I took it the next morning to be analysed by Sir Giles Peterson, the leading toxicologist of the day, who was resident in Oxford.

Eventually he told me, "Your Royal Highness, I examined the contents of the flask and I found a rather fine malt whisky."

"Only whisky?"

"No. There was something else. The mixture also contained chloral hydrate."

"Chloral?" said I. "Isn't that what people take to send them to sleep?"

"Yes, indeed, sir. Many a nursemaid uses it diluted to subdue a troublesome child. It's harmless enough in small quantities, but I wouldn't recommend it like this. The whisky masks the high concentration."

"Could it be fatal?"

"Quite possibly, if one took about 120 grains. Death would occur six to ten hours later." He hesitated, frowning. "I hope no one offered this to you, sir."

I laughed. "Certainly not. Whisky isn't allowed at my tender age."

The laughter vanished later, when I considered the implications.

Somebody had laced Dr. Stubbs's whisky with a lethal dose of chloral.

By some dubious set of circumstances it had come into Henry Bilbo's possession. He had imbibed and rapidly succumbed during the boat race.

Who would have plotted such a dangerous trick, and why? One's first thought was that one of the opposing crew had sabotaged our boat, but I could think of no way it could have been done, and even Cambridge men are not so unsporting as that.

After pondering the matter profoundly, I arrived at the only possible explanation. I decided to share my thoughts with Dr. Stubbs.

I made an appointment and called at his rooms at six in the evening. But I was in for a surprise. Instead of the manservant, or Stubbs himself, I was admitted by Echo—the first I had seen of her since the fatal afternoon. She looked *distrait*. Beautiful, but *distrait*. And dressed in black.

"By George, I didn't expect to be so fortunate," I told her.

She pressed a finger to my lips. "Papa is asleep. He hasn't been feeling well since the regatta. It upset him dreadfully."

"But I made an appointment."

She nodded. "And I took the liberty of confirming it. I wanted a few minutes alone with you, Bertie." She ushered me into their drawing room.

I could scarcely believe my luck.

"What did you want to discuss with Papa?" she asked.

"Oh, it can wait," I told her, seating myself at one end of a settee.

She remained standing. "Was it about the flask?"

I confirmed that it was. I told her about the lethal mixture.

"Lethal?" said she in horror. "But chloral is a sedative, not a poison."

From the look in her eyes I knew for certain that she—my innocent-seeming Echo—had spiked her father's whisky, and I knew exactly why.

"Whoever was responsible simply intended to make your father sleepy," I suggested.

"Yes!" said Echo.

"You—the person responsible, I mean—that person planned that your father should feel so tired that he would lie somewhere on the river-bank and take a very long nap. You would be free—free to dance the night away at the Regatta Ball."

She nodded, her brown eyes shining.

"Only the plan misfired," I pressed on. "Henry Bilbo picked your father's pocket."

"Henry?" she piped, shocked to the core. "You're implying that Henry was a thief? Oh, no, Bertie!"

"Oh, yes," I disabused her. "I don't like to speak ill of the dead, but he was a bad lot, a burglar, responsible for that spate of thefts we had. He was just a titch, after all. Quite easy for him to get through small windows. I've no doubt that he was the one. And when your father came over to speak to him before the race, Bilbo couldn't resist the temptation. He saw the flask in your Papa's back pocket and slipped it out."

She put her hand to her throat. "Not Henry!" She swayed ominously.

I stood up and supported her in case she swooned again. "Come and sit on the settee. Your secret is safe with me, my dear."

She stared at me, aghast that I had worked it out. "After all, my pretty one, your motives were unimpeachable."

"Were they?" she whispered, wide-eyed.

I embraced her gently. "All that you wanted was some precious time alone with me whilst your father was out to the world. That *was* your reason for tampering with the flask, was it not?" I gently probed.

"You won't tell anyone, Bertie? Not even my Papa?"

"You can count on me."

Her response, like the Echo in the myth, was to present her adorable mouth for a kiss.

And in spite of the myth, Narcissus did not disappoint her.

That Golden Way

by Owen King

F reshman year, my roommate had a mental breakdown. His name was
Andy Patek and I'm pretty sure he never attended a single class. When I
arrived on move-in day, Andy was already settled and tucked into his bed;
he rolled onto his side, introduced himself, and shook my hand without
getting up. On the wall above his bed was tacked a poster of a cartoon surf-
er, muscular in board shorts, stretching out in a camp chair on a beach with
his hands behind his head, his face sketched to transmit absolute content-
ment: NO SHIRT NO SHOES NO PROBLEM, it read beneath the picture.
I asked him if he was feeling okay. "Man, it's just a lot," he explained, and
I nodded, thinking I understood—college was a massive change, you were
on your own and in charge of yourself—but pretty soon it was obvious that
I didn't.

Andy must have gone to the bathroom sometimes; I never saw it,
though. For the not quite three weeks that we lived together, whenever I
was in the room with him, he was either lying in bed asleep, or lying in bed
listening to his headphones and pointing his flashlight at the ceiling and
flicking it on and off, or sitting up a little. A few times I blearily opened my
eyes in the middle of the night to see him shining his flashlight—it was an
ultraviolet black light, so in the dark it cast a purple beam—and in those
moments it looked like Andy was pinned beneath some alien ray, and you
could imagine it drawing him smoothly, irrevocably upward from his bed
and into the belly of a UFO.

After the first week, I grasped that something was wrong, but I was eighteen. I had never dealt with anything like it and was uncertain what I should do. He was incredibly polite; and since he hardly left his bed, the floor on his side of the room was pretty spotless. I didn't want to hurt his feelings or piss him off. I didn't want to cause a fuss. When the room started to stink of body odor, instead of saying something to him, I bought a spray can of potpourri from the campus store and I spritzed it over him as he slept.

But I could see he didn't look good. As Andy got skinnier, his hair seemed to get bigger, like it was sucking up all of his remaining life energy; his bushy brown mop took on the wild, sagging, pasted together look of an eagle's nest. Purple hollows had formed under his eyes and his cheekbones stuck out in rails.

It seemed like he was waiting for something bad to happen, as if he was resigned to it, like the warden would be along soon to escort him to the electric chair. Grimacing at the ceiling, clicking the flashlight.

I knew Andy was from California, so I asked him if he missed it. He shook his head. "I don't miss the past. It's all about the future. And if you think about the future, and you care, you know, if you care about your fellow man, it's scary stuff. Because you can see the troubles and tribulations. I see them." Andy blinked at me with his eyes that could see the future. "Not clearly but I see them out there, coming up.

"And like, at the same time, I know—in my deep-down heart, I truly know—that if I follow that golden way, everything'll be all right. But it's major, scary stuff. It's like, faith is required, you know?"

What the fuck did that mean? I should have asked, but I didn't. "Right," I said.

One morning in our third week, I brought him a cranberry muffin from the cafeteria and he said, "Man, this is kind, but I don't know, you know," and gently placed it on his windowsill, as if it might explode.

"They have other muffins," I said, and I've spoken few words in my life that I wish more fervently that I could take back, because Andy suddenly started to weep. Tears ran down into the wisps of his half-formed mustache and he blurted, "No, no, no. I want this nice muffin here, man," but it remained untouched on the window sill when I came back from classes a couple of days later and the Resident Advisor pulled me aside to inform me that Andy's parents had shown up with medical professionals and taken him away.

I kept expecting someone to come and pick up his stuff, or call, or something, but no one ever did.

I had my own problems, too. I wasn't fitting in.

What was dispiriting was that college was so much like I had imagined. People actually did all the things pictured in the pamphlets. Guys in sandals really did play Frisbee Golf on the sunlit greensward of the quad; tall, slender girls really did walk around in white shorts and sunglasses with books pressed against their chests; there really were acoustic guitar jam sessions in the dorm lounges; late into the night, attentive study groups really could be glimpsed through open doors, young scholars sitting shoulder-to-shoulder on beds with their legs crossed and their feet bare, sharing an open volume across two laps; everywhere you looked in the cafeteria, there really were good-looking clusters of people laughing and eating pizza. College really was college, ivy-covered walls and the freedom to be yourself.

But I was the same guy I'd been in high school, grinding through three drafts of every paper, doing the assigned reading and all the suggested reading, and then reading ahead. I didn't like to think of myself as shy; I liked to think of myself as careful. If you've ever seen a horserace, you've marveled at the way the horses gather on the inside, long knobby legs chopping clods from the track, barrel bodies jostling for space, one loose shoe from calamity. If I was a jockey I'd have gone on the far outside. I wanted to win, but I didn't want to crash, and I didn't see why I had to risk it in the first place. That was no life for a horse.

In my mind I tried to make a virtue of my instinct to maneuver toward the sides and edges and away from the crowd. From the last row in the lecture hall I had the best view of the chalkboard, the full panorama of the lesson. From the corner of the party I could see everyone in the room and observe how the different mini-groups interacted, and then, if I eventually wanted to interact with someone (okay, a girl), I'd have a better sense of what I was getting into. Maybe I didn't need the freedom to be myself because this was me.

Then again, there was Andy Patek. My roommate had lost his mind, completely unraveled in the course of three weeks, and I'd brought him a cranberry muffin.

What had happened to him wasn't my fault, but it was obvious I should have done something sooner. My college was one of the great institutions of American learning, founded by a railroad magnate back in the days when there were railroad magnates, and I'd worked hard to gain a scholarship. When the lights were out and I looked across the room at his bed, which I had neatly made, and at his poster of the cartoon beach bum—NO SHOES NO SHIRT NO PROBLEM—I wondered at all my striving, if it was a worthy end unto itself. I felt an absence in myself, a cavity in my chest on the upper left.

I imagined a poster of a cartoon me in a camp chair on a cartoon beach. I was slumped and glowering. NO FRIENDS NO LIFE A PROBLEM, the legend beneath said.

With his blanket on his bed and his flashlight on the window sill, left behind like all the rest of his possessions, Andy Patek didn't seem gone, exactly. (I'd eventually thrown out the cranberry muffin.) He just seemed like he was away, which is different. People who go away sometimes come back.

In early November I met Greta at the Party Room.

In an attempt to develop some sort of social life I had made myself a regular at the Friday and Saturday night parties held by the three guys who lived in the suite down the hall from me on the fourth floor. That was our dorm's Party Room; you paid five bucks for a Domino cup and could drink as much watery Coors from the beer ball as you wanted.

My regular move was to drop my five in the plastic pumpkin by the door, grab a cup from the cup tower stacked beside the pumpkin, ease my way through the press to the beer ball in the right hand corner of the room, fill up, and then slide all the way along the wall to the room's far left hand corner. In that corner there was a huge, industrial-sized coffee can that the suitemates had found in the trash behind the cafeteria. It was three times as wide as a regular coffee can and as a tall as a toddler. The party guys had filled it with sand to create the world's biggest ashtray, and in the course of the semester it had gobbled up thousands of butts. It was disgusting, in other words, but the coffee can was also so large that it actually couldn't quite fit all the way into the room's left hand corner—which left a gap for me. Once I wedged myself into this space, I could unobtrusively lean into the corner and sip my beer, bob my head to whatever was playing from the computer speakers, smile and nod amiably at whoever came over to stub out their cigarettes.

That was where I was positioned that night in November when Greta asked me what I was doing. I didn't know her name, but I recognized her. She was another freshman in my dorm, a short, wide-hipped, black-haired girl who I always saw with her glasses hanging from a green cord around her neck, but never on her face. In the halls she moved in a rapid stride and wore a serious expression; she dressed in long skirts with pockets; I'd found her intimidating before ever talking with her.

"Pardon?" I replied.

"I asked what you were doing."

I glanced at my beer cup, then back at her. "Drinking?"

"You're Peter, right? I'm Greta. I see you here every party and it makes me sad. It's like you're trying to get cancer as quickly as possible. So I thought I'd just ask you what was going on." She cocked her head in a gentle, teacherly way.

"I'm just standing." I was embarrassed. I was also annoyed. I wasn't bothering anyone and she was looking at me like I'd eaten all the paste in her second-grade classroom. I had done that once—it was tasty, Goddammit—and I didn't appreciate the reminder. "Someone has to go in the corner or not everyone can fit in the room. It's a small room."

"People call you the Ashtray Gnome," Greta said.

This was exactly the kind of thing I worried about, that I appeared to be as big of a dork and a loser as I actually was. Why had I gone to a college whose promotional literature had featured Frisbee Golf so prominently if I was never going to play Frisbee Golf? Why had I gone to college at all, if I couldn't bring myself to talk to anyone?

"Like a garden gnome, but for the ashtray," she explained.

"You know, I got it, actually. I made the connection. I stand by the ashtray like a gnome stands beside a garden. Can't I have a beer and relax?"

Greta grimaced and touched her glasses cord where it crossed her collarbone, and ran the cord between her thumb and forefinger. As it happened, she looked a little bit like a gnome herself; she was stout and round-faced like a gnome, and she was cute like a gnome. "I'm sorry. I hurt your feelings. I hope you don't think that everyone calls you that, just some people. My problem is, I can't bear not to come right out with it, you know? I was worried you were suffering. I have to be straightforward. I don't know how else to be. I'm part asshole."

"But I'm not suffering," I said, "I promise."

"Well, you look like it when you stand here by the Can and you don't talk to anyone and you don't even smoke. And so I thought, maybe he's waiting for someone to say hello, so I'll say hello. And now I'm glad I did."

"Thanks, I guess." I was lonely, but I didn't want to be someone's charity case. I had to hand it to her, though: she had busted through my reserve. For once I wasn't worried about being inoffensive. "It's nice of you to speak to the Ashtray Gnome."

"See: you're pissed at me," Greta said.

"No one likes to be pitied. It makes you feel pitiful."

"Well, I don't think you're pitiful. If anything I'm pitiful. I'm part asshole, remember? And I didn't just come over here to be friendly. I came over because I like the way you look." Greta reached out to touch my forearm, but someone leaned in between us to jam a cigarette out in the sandy pit of the Can.

The intrusion also obscured my blush of surprise, which was so hot on my cheeks I could feel it on the inside of my mouth. She liked the way I looked.

"And," Greta said, as the intruder drew back, "I was thinking you'd be absolutely perfect for the short I'm making for my Intro to Film class this weekend."

We ended up talking for a while, me on my side of the can, her on the other. Every minute or so, someone would interrupt, squeezing between us to kill a cigarette. They'd stub their butt in the sand and retreat, and we'd keep going. I told her about how much I liked my classes, especially Intro to Art History and Composition. Greta said that was great, she was a total geek, too. "I have a really cool microscope."

I admitted I was impressed: she was a total geek.

"You know, I had a feeling you'd be normal," Greta said. "Some people are just so amazing at college, it's a little intimidating."

"Are you saying I'm not amazing at college?"

"I'm saying we're not amazing at college."

"I'm terrible at college," I said.

Where she was from it was all nail salons and football and rushing to get from one place with air-conditioning to another place with air-conditioning. I said where I was from it was all road-side crosses.

Her thumb and forefinger wandered up and down the green glasses cord. "With all this smoke flowing up between us, I feel like I'm seeing you in flashback, or having a vision of you in the future."

"Maybe you are," I said, hoping for the latter.

Greta's short was called *Stranger Danger*, and we shot it the next morning, a Saturday, on the tarmac playground of the college's daycare center. It was

a two-hander. I was cast as the Stranger. The other part, the Kid, was played
by a professor's daughter, who was seven or eight.

The way Greta's story went the Kid played around on all the equipment,
sliding on the slides, swinging on the swings, springing on the tin cow with
springs for feet. But every time she started to enjoy herself, she'd look and
see me—the Stranger—lurking at a different spot on the playground. After
the kid played a while, alternately enjoying herself and being disturbed by
my presence, she finally summoned up her courage and yelled the only line
of dialogue in the short, "Go away, you freak!" In the next moment there
was a shot of the empty space where I had been, the End, roll credits. All
I had to do was wear a black coat and a black fedora and stare menacingly.

"Am I supposed to be Death or a pervert?" I asked Greta.

"Does it matter?"

"Yes," I said.

Greta stroked her glasses cord thoughtfully. "Well, I was thinking
Death, but it works either way. Whatever feels right."

"Okay," I said, "I'm Death." There was a three-person crew—camera, sound, lights, everyone rotating when it was their turn to direct their
short—and I repeated this for their benefit. "I'm not a pervert, I'm Death."

"Sure thing, ace," said the bored and hung over guy in sunglasses who
was hoisting the boom mic.

Greta worked a lot with the professor's kid. The most important aspect
of the performance was the Kid's reaction to seeing me.

"What makes you nervous?" Greta asked, and the kid, four and a half
feet tall in a bright blue raincoat like a girl in a storybook, happily confessed, "Mice make me nervous. I don't like all of their little legs."

Greta nodded. "Little legs are the worst. Okay. When I say, 'Action!',
imagine a mouse on your forearm, and then, the moment the shot ends, I'll
yell, 'Cut!' and you blow on your forearm and picture the mouse turning to
dust and blowing away and never bothering you again. Can you do that?"
The girl said she could and as far as I could tell, she did a great job.

For the three or four hours that we filmed, I hardly felt like myself at all.
I got lost in the fantasy of my Death self, circling around the playground,

trailing sulfur, dragging my feet because I had the idea that I usually traveled by floating from place to place, and I wasn't used to putting my feet in shoes. Between shots, I watched Greta, moving from angle to angle in that sharp, downhill way she had, hands jammed in the pockets of her ankle-length corduroy skirt. I found myself involuntarily rubbing my thumb and forefinger together, mimicking her habit of stroking the cord that hung her glasses.

Every time I did a scene, after she called, "Cut!" Greta told me I was the best and she owed me. "I may be part asshole, Peter, but I never forget a favor!"

I told her it was no problem. "I have an appointment to be standing behind a smoldering coffee can later tonight and every Friday and Saturday night going forward, but otherwise my calendar is open. You've got me all day if you need me."

She laughed at that and I thought—well, you can guess what I thought. Not wedding bells or anything, but maybe a walk later on, maybe dinner together in the cafeteria, maybe a kiss.

It was overcast, the gray sky putting the bare branches of the trees into relief, but rain never came. Construction paper suns with smiling faces hung in the windows of the daycare center. The gab among the members of the crew was affably sarcastic, lots of jokes about how nice it was to not be working on a big budget production for once. We devoured a tray of spicy beef patties that the professor had brought. I pushed my co-star on the swings and she told me I was a good freak.

Then it was over.

Greta called, "That's a wrap! Thanks, everyone!" She gave me a hug—"Super appreciate it, Peter!"—and they hurriedly started to pack up the lights and the camera.

"Hey, what are you doing later?" I asked her.

"Sorry, can't talk," Greta said, snapping shut the latches on the camera. "Now it's somebody else's turn to shoot their film. Thanks again, though!"

Five minutes later I was alone on the playground. The symbolism was almost too much.

———— • ————

That night I lay in bed, shining the beam of Andy Patek's flashlight on the ceiling. He'd left it behind along with everything else—bedding, drawers of folded clothes, pens and unused notebooks, and the poster of the cartoon beach bum, NO SHOES NO SHIRT NO PROBLEM. Because it was a black light, with the lights in the room on, the circle of the flashlight against the whipped polystyrene surface was a fizzy white ball inside a faint purple halo.

As usual for a Saturday night, there was a rager going at the Party Room. I wasn't going to go, though—in fact, I didn't think I'd be going there again. On the one hand, I knew I was being petulant, but on the other, when a child tells you that you're a good freak, sometimes it pays to listen. I'd always had this idea that I'd find my tribe in the next grade, in the next level of school.

Why did I want that so much?

I really did like my classes. And I liked rewriting my papers and doing the extra reading. And I liked searching in the narrow stacks in the basement of the library for the books in the bibliographies, and checking out books that no one had read in fifty years. I even liked sitting in the study carrels, alone with the hum of my bloodstream, the world silenced by the earplugs that I'd found in an unopened pack in Andy's desk. If I already liked those things, I didn't see why I couldn't like them more. I wasn't, I told myself, saying goodbye to the world in a huff because a girl had pretended to like me so she could get me to be the joke in her short film and then blown me off; I was making peace with the world because the world didn't want me, and standing beside the Can for two nights a week wasn't getting me anything but a lung full of second-hand smoke.

College was where you figured out who you were, and tossed out your old pretensions once and for all. Life didn't turn you into a grown-up. You made yourself one.

Also: fuck everyone, and especially and most of all, fuck Greta.

I had busted my ass for a scholarship. My father framed houses for a living, and he had the melanomas to prove it. My mother drove a school bus.

I didn't need anybody to tell me that I acted weird. I knew I was different from the three guys in the Party Room, who could afford to drink until five in the morning because grades were irrelevant to them, because their parents paid their way. They could light money on fire and stub out the half-burned bills in the Can, what did it matter.

Okay, maybe I was in a little bit of a huff.

I clicked Andy Patek's black light flashlight on. It was small, the kind you'd probably find in a display by the checkout in a hardware store. Maybe he'd bought it on impulse, thinking it was a regular flashlight. I wondered where he was now. I clicked the black light off. I wondered where his head had been for the three weeks he'd been my roommate. I clicked the black light on. I guessed it probably worked okay as a regular flashlight; it certainly made a bright spot, that white circle with the purple corona. I remembered him going on in his anxious, spacey way about caring for his fellow man, facing the scary future. What he was worried about had been gibberish—there'd been that stuff about the Yellow Brick Road or whatever it was—but I didn't doubt his conviction. He'd cared, all right. I clicked the black light on and thought, with bitter satisfaction, that maybe that had been at the root of his problems, the caring for his fellow man. I clicked the flashlight off again.

The three beef patties I'd eaten that afternoon had started to move around in my stomach. I could feel them knocking against each other in slow motion, like bumper cars with sticky wheels.

There was a brisk rap on the door. "Peter?" Greta called. "Are you awake?" A second sharp rap on the door sounded. "Peter? Wake up!"

It would have been easier to ignore her, but I was always doing the easy thing, sticking myself in the corner, hanging back.

"Fuck off!" I called.

I listened: I didn't hear her shoes retreating. I knew she was standing there on the other side of the door. She hadn't seen it coming, me wising up to the bullshit.

"Are you okay?" Greta asked. The gung-ho had drained from her voice. "I'm sorry if I woke you up." She sounded concerned, but I didn't believe it. "Sorry I was so brusque, but I can't talk when I'm focused on something and we had to rush off to film another—"

"Fuck off!" I called again. "Don't bother me anymore!"

A minute passed, then a second minute. I didn't hear anything else. Did she think she could stand outside my door all night long? I threw my legs over the side of my bed, marched to the door, and yanked it open.

She was gone. She'd left a message on my dry erase board. *Call me or come by if you want to talk - G*, it read, followed by her phone number and her room number on the third floor. Below that was a *P.S. Thank you again for your help*, and a heart.

Down the hall, I could hear music and voices from the Party Room, smell the cheap beer and cigarette smoke. I stepped backward and shut my door.

Soon, I began to feel sick.

Along with the movements in my stomach, there was an acid taste rising up my throat, as if I'd swallowed a few butts from the Can along with the professor's spicy beef patties. It was no less than I deserved. I lay in bed in a fetal position, clutching Andy's little black light flashlight. I could apologize to her, but I couldn't undo what I'd screamed through the door. I'd shown her who I actually was: lonely, afraid, young, needy.

My stomach started to shake like it was coming apart on reentry.

I bolted from bed, rushed from the room, and made a split-second decision to bypass the nearest bathroom on the fourth floor and go all the way down to the single-toilet bathroom by the laundry room in the basement, where I could have diarrhea in privacy. I hustled past the Party Room, burst through the miasma of smoke and beer and tinny jam band rock, and bounded down the stairs, one flight after another. I was unbuckling my belt when I hit the basement stairs. I made it into the single-toilet bathroom, slammed the door shut and shoved my pants down, and thumped down on the ring just in time.

I don't want to get into the details, but it was unpleasant, rank, stinging, and I hoped that there was no one on the other side of the wall in the laundry room to hear my groans. Beware of strangers bearing tinfoil trays of spicy beef patties. That it could have been worse—I could have actually shit my pants—offered no comfort. When the bar is that low, it's time to stop keeping score.

After, I stood at the sink and used the graying surfboard of soap in the dish to wash my hands. I splashed some water on my face. The coolness against my skin brought a measure of clarity:

I'd blown it, and I needed to apologize, and to never bother Greta again. I was the bullet, and she'd dodged me. With that settled, I could get down to the more wide-ranging business of not bothering anybody else for the next four years. I wasn't fit company. I belonged in the deep stacks of the library, away from humans.

The single fluorescent bar above the sink buzzed, flickered, buzzed, and went off entirely.

The small, windowless room was thrown into full darkness.

This didn't alarm me even slightly. I knew the door was directly behind me to the left. I reached a hand back, sidestepped, found the wall, and slid my fingers along until I found the door and the knob. With what I'd just done to the toilet, it occurred to me that the blown light might be for the best, keeping people away until the stench cleared, which should only be in another year or two. In fact, it might have been my stench that blew it out—

Except it was dark in the hall, too. The dorm had lost power.

In the blind stillness I could smell the ozone of the laundry room next door and the cement damp of the basement hall floor. I still wasn't concerned. I guessed that the stairs were about twenty feet straight ahead. I could walk that far without any problem, sliding my hand along the wall—but I didn't even need to do that. I had Andy Patek's black light flashlight. In my hurry to make it to the bathroom, I'd jammed it in my pocket.

I took it out—it was about the size of a candy bar—and clicked it on. The ultraviolet beam cut a purple cone out of the dark.

Instinctively, I swung it to my right, from where I'd come, through the open door of the bathroom. Strange thing: Irregular spots of bright yellowish paint were sprinkled on the floor around the toilet. It took me a second to realize that I was looking at dripped piss, the phosphorescence highlighted by the ultraviolet.

I brought the flashlight forward and the beam found the stairs at the end of the hall. I made my way, following the narrow, purple lane.

It was only as I went up the stairs and emerged onto the first floor that I became aware of the sound—there was just the scrape of my shoes on the cement and nothing else. The door to the basement stairs was propped open, and gave onto the dorm lounge. I waved the flashlight from side-to-side.

There was nobody watching television.

This stopped me. College students keep truckers' hours. Even at four in the morning there was always someone in the lounge, stretched on one of the three couches arrayed around the wide-screen television, checking out a movie or a show.

But then again, why would anyone hang around in front of the television if there was no power?

I walked to the couches, thinking that maybe someone was lying flat, hidden by the couch back. There was no one, but the black light showed an octopus of yellow spatter on the center cushion. I couldn't help reflecting, briefly, on all of the cop shows I'd seen on television, those scenes where detectives used black lights to probe for murder evidence. I was a different kind of investigator, discovering that you should never walk in bare feet in a dorm, and, worse, as I'd long suspected, that people were screwing all over the place.

I moved the flashlight to illuminate the conference tables and chairs at the rear of the room. They were empty. I spotted the analog clock on wall. Battery-powered, it was steadily eating up time, the second hand moving smoothly, the hour and the minute telling me that it was 9:32. I glanced at my watch and it had the same time.

Across the lounge, right in front of the door, the black light found another flash of phosphorescence. I could see immediately this one was different, longer and wider. The black light possessed a horrible draw. You knew that you'd probably be sorry once you knew what you were seeing, but until you knew, you had to keep looking. As I approached, the lunatic possibility that groups of people were having incredibly messy sex in front of the dorm's entryway occurred to me. Who? When? For God's Sake, why?

I remembered Greta saying that she'd thought I'd be normal. I wished she was there with me, because this was not normal, and I wanted to commiserate. I could picture her pinching the cord of her glasses and giving me a wide-eyed look that asked, "Are we the only sane people here?" Unfortunately, I'd been a sour prick.

I arrived at the spot. It was a yellowish swatch about a foot wide. Definitely not sex, at least not as I understood it. It appeared painted, brushed on, with faint drag lines. The yellow streak trailed from the door, to the stairwell, and up the middle of the stairs, like a phosphorescent carpet runner.

I extended the toe of my shoe into the spill of the black light and rubbed it lightly over the edge of the illuminated yellow. There was no smear, no squeak of dampness. I moved the light back-and-forth along the trail. I imagined hauling something heavy, letting it slide along behind me, a duffel bag or laundry sack, bump-bump-bump down the stairs and along the hall. In theory that would be the right kind of movement, but I didn't see why it would leave a phosphorescent stain.

I went to the stairs, following the yellow, and began to climb.

Up on the second floor the quiet seemed more worrisome. The power might have knocked out everyone's computers and stereos, but along the second-floor hall all the doors to all the rooms were closed, and I heard no voices.

I'd been perplexed, then flabbergasted, but now I felt uneasy. It felt like I was alone. But how could I be alone? Why would everyone leave because the power went out? Not for a single moment did I consider the possibility that I was dreaming, because I was not dreaming. The building smelled stuffy, damp and dusty at the same time, like a summer cottage after being shut for the winter. I happened to look at my watch again: 9:35. I had an urge to stride to the nearest door and bang my fist against it, but the thought of my roommate was sternly prohibitive. Wouldn't that be a story? The two crazy guys who had roomed together; both of them taken away by the men in white suits before the first semester, and now rooming together again at the University of Shoes Without Laces.

The yellow continued up the stairs into the darkness. It tugged on me, wanting to explain itself. My shoes squeaked on the rubber stair treads. No, not dreaming.

As I followed the streak up the stairs to third floor, the black light fell on a patch of fliers—for a protest, for a meeting, for Spanish tutors—taped on the wall. A chaos of ocher fingerprints marked the fliers. Some of the prints dragged, as if the fingers had swept across the papers. I didn't like this, I didn't like the suggestion of invisible hands, of invisible fingers pressing and sliding. It made me think of those odd sensations of the skin, tickles and tingles, and I imagined my body covered in yellow handprints.

The flashlight was slippery in my palm.

My eye settled on a flier. It showed a guy in a beach chair. NO JOB? NO PROBLEM! SAVE A LIFE! It was for a life guard job at the college pool. The guy in the beach chair had been cut from a magazine. He was a movie star. By the black light his smile was sinister, like he might enjoy letting you drown.

I jogged up the stairs and tripped over the lip of the third-floor landing, banging my shin hard. I sprawled out flat, skinning my knee through my jeans and banged my elbow, but held onto the flashlight.

As I got to my feet, the arm of the black light pointed up: waves of ocher dust unfurled across the ceiling. I played the light over the dust, and it sparkled, misshapen lungs clenching and unclenching. I cast the light down. Ocher dust splashed silently up from the floor, rolling over my shoes and around my ankles without sensation. I brought the light up and saw sheets of ocher dust begin to curl from the walls.

Ahead, the yellow swatch extended about three-quarters of the way down the hall, stopping in front of a door.

I took a couple of steps. To my right a door was slightly ajar. The letters of the names pasted on the door—JAMES & MARLON—were a woozy green in the black light.

"Hey, anyone know what's going on with the lights?" The question escaped my mouth before I could reel it back. My voice sounded meek, the voice of the fourth-grader I had been long ago, when I told the bully who knocked off my Marlins cap, "I'm going to be someone and you'll be sorry you weren't nicer to me!" Now I was afraid, and I knew it. Again, I thought of Andy Patek, this time of him starting to cry over the fucking muffin, the fucking cranberry muffin, acting like it was bomb, like it might kill him.

I pushed the door and pointed the flashlight into the room. The desks, the computers, the beds, the jacket draped over the back of a chair, the shoes on the carpet, all leaped out in contrast to the dark, glaring whitely, unstained by phosphorescence. A lava lamp-style screen saver sent oozy bubbles across the monitor of an open laptop. I stepped all the way in.

"Hello?" The beds were empty, the chairs were empty, the closets— both standing wide and revealing rows of clothes without their bodies— were empty. I turned the light on the computer. The time in the corner of the screen read, 9:40 PM, and the battery read, 99%—which made perfect sense. The power had been out for only about ten minutes, so the computer's battery life had hardly been used.

Behind the computer was the window. I went to it. It should have looked out onto the quad, but it was the bottom of the ocean on the other side of that glass, a black that had never been touched by sunlight. The moon I had seen earlier that evening was gone. I realized that everything else was gone: the stripped late fall trees, the flagstone paths, the massive pompadour of limestone that the college's founder had shipped from his ancestral home in Sussex and planted in the center of the quad a hundred years ago, the chapel and its stained-glass windows, the old observatory and its silver dome, the daycare center and the paper suns that looked at the playground and the playground, too, and the library and its books and my favorite carrel, and the bathroom in the Physics Building where they said a girl had hung herself after acing her final, and the little attic in the History Building where a custodian found a box containing dodo bones, and the Frisbee Golfers, and the girls in white shorts, and the folksingers, and the friends eating pizza in the dining hall, and every recycling bin overflowing with crumpled beer cans and pages from the student newspaper.

"Go away, freak!" the Kid said, and perhaps Greta had directed her so well, it actually worked. I was far, far away. I was the dorm's sole passenger as it moved through distant galaxies.

I turned, the sweat on my face and neck chilled, to move back toward the hall. It seemed safer suddenly to be on the yellow path. I caught a flash in the mirror on the inside of the open closet door and came up short.

The mirror was lit—cleanly, brightly lit by incandescent bulbs—and in its reflection was a guy I vaguely recognized: frothy orange beard and sleepy eyes, James or Marlon. He was in the room, a step or two behind me, rolling up the sleeves of his shirt and nodding his head to some inner song. He paused, sniffed. "Huh, what's that," he said to himself, and sniffed again. He frowned and walked past the edge of the mirror in the direction of the hall to check. The mirror snapped dim as he left it and, in the next instant, I felt slightly jostled, as if by a moderate gust, or the knock of a shoulder.

Comprehension varies. A prodigy hears Etude in E Major once through and proceeds to play it on their toy piano with their fat little fingers. You're assigned to the office in Barcelona for six months and it's not until the last day, in a taxi on the way to the airport to return home, that your brain delivers you a full, polished sentence, Spanish-to-English, the driver saying into his cell phone, "I just have to drop this asshole at the airport and then I'm done with my shift." And then, most things, we never do learn; our education is spotty and life graduates us too soon.

But what I thought I had managed to grasp, as I walked the last few steps of the streaky yellow, black light path on the third floor of my abandoned dorm, as the ocher dust rose to my thighs and sifted down from the ceiling and unspooled from the walls, was that I was somehow inside of time and yet outside of the world. The clocks were moving, the batteries had juice, and the echoes of things were phosphorescent. One of my peers had given me a ghost shoulder, our dimensions momentarily hitting crosswise. My knee and my elbow and my shin ached where I had hit them when I fell.

I had no idea what it meant, but the yellow streak on the floor was the only way I could see to go.

Another three steps took me to the place where it ended in front of a door.

In the black light's tunnel of visibility the yellow streak on the floor blazed gold, flashed like a lightning bolt, and vanished.

I waved a warding hand, blinking against the swirl of blues and reds storming my sight. The black light jerked over the door: GRETA & TONI'S ROOM! I recognized the number from the message she'd left on my white board.

I wondered if I should go in. It had led me here, after all . . . Hadn't it?

But the streak was gone.

I felt a loosening, an indistinct sense of things coming back together, relief. I moved the black light around and sighted dusty ocher sneaker tracks going in the direction I'd come from. The ocher dust that had been flowing along the ceiling, floor, and walls, had abruptly evaporated. I turned back and shone the light past Greta's door, where the hall was—trembling.

I watched as a section of floor at the end of the hall peeled away, like a section of birch bark, and was sucked into nothing, leaving a black gap that was black like the world I'd seen through James and Marlon's windows. Part of the wall followed, torn off like wrapping paper, to reveal darkness beneath. Whatever this place was, it was coming apart. The flashlight buzzed and flickered. It was running out of juice. The dark closed and opened, closed and opened around me with the failing light, and I knew I had to hurry.

I ran after the tracks and away from Greta's door.

My feet dashed the prints, exploding them in silent puffs. The sneaker tracks climbed the stairs, and I chased them, sensing things unwinding behind me, vanishing into the sparkling dust and breaking away in chunks that were yanked away in a draft that I couldn't feel. I made it up and then onto the fourth landing, past the tomb of the Party Room, and finally, to my own door. I threw it open and leaped inside, and slammed it shut behind me, shut it on the nothingness on my heels.

The black light beam shot forward and caught Andy where he was seated on his bed with his hands on his knees beneath the poster of the beach bum. My roommate looked up at me, his eyes fully yellow without any pupil, and spoke with his mouth full, "I'm telling you, man, there's nothing to be afraid of, so long as you keep stepping right and true, stick to that golden way." Crumbs fell from his mouth down his shirt. He grinned, happier than I'd ever seen him. He'd washed and combed his hair.

The room's lights came on. Startled, I dropped the flashlight on the floor, and it went rolling across the floor. An alarm made rapid, piercing chirps. I heard the muffled rumble of panicked voices and running. There was no one on Andy's bed. The air in the room was wavery, and I could smell smoke.

It started, forensic investigators would quickly determine, in the Can.

For days or weeks, somewhere down in the Can's belly of sand and cigarette butts, an ember had been smoldering, a hot core biding its time, worming its way to fresh fuel, and growing larger. In the school newspaper a sophomore witness recounted seeing a jet of flame suddenly belch from the Can and light up the curtains that hung in front of the window in the corner of the room. In an instant, the walls, the posters, bedding and books, were all burning, and everyone was pushing from the room.

————•◆•————

The smoke in the hall was thickest to my right, in the direction of the Party Room. A guy in nothing but underpants with a marijuana leaf on the ass ran past me, pale gut jumping, a laptop tucked under one arm. That was the way to the fire stairs. I ducked low and followed him left.

There was a stifling grittiness to the air. I clamped my mouth, but the fumes went up my nose, stinging and peppery, making me wheeze and cough. Rivers of black smoke were running along the floors and ceilings and walls. Music was still playing from people's rooms, filling the spaces between the alarm's chirps with guitars and drums and swooping popstar vocals. The cacophony was huge, but I could still hear my own inner voice saying, I don't want to die. I don't want to fly through outer space all alone in an empty dorm. This freak doesn't want to go, not yet, please not yet.

Marijuana underpants crashed through the red emergency door. I shouldered through ten steps later. There was a crush on the stairs, but it moved quickly, and we passed by the emergency door on the third floor and then the one on the second floor. The last door was wedged open, and I stumbled into the almost-freezing cool of the November light, crunching onto the frosty grass of the quad, dizzy. I felt the smoke rip off me, as if I'd just gone careening through a massive cobweb.

"I'm okay!" someone wailed. "I'm okay!" Another person was weeping. Another was dry-heaving. I heard a girl say that she was never smoking again.

I sat down in the grass. I breathed. I looked up at the dorm, at my window, thinking, madly, that I'd see Andy—but there was just a gray fog behind the panes. My eyes sank downward, to the lit window beneath, the one on the third floor, the one that, I knew—just knew from my one visit, like that prodigy who plays Etude in E Major after one listen—was the where Greta lived. Smoke filmed the light, muting it to a putrescent, spoiled gold. I realized that it hadn't been dust that I'd seen in the blacklight during those lost minutes outside of the world: it had been the echo of smoke.

The frost under my jeans had melted, dampening my seat. My shin ached and so did my knee and so did my elbow. "Fuck," I said.

She was in there. I knew it. That's what it had all been about, what

Andy Patek's black light had shown me. I was going to have to go back in. I was going to have to try and save her, and I might die. I might really die.

Still. What choice did I have? If I didn't, I was already dead anyway.

I got up.

When I found Greta, she was collapsed in the corner of her room, huddled and wheezing. Her eyes were bloodshot and she was dazed. I'd wrapped my T-shirt around my mouth and somehow made it to her. I can't prove this, but I think maybe all the time I spent standing in the smoke by the Can worked like training for running into a burning building.

"Peter, what are you doing?" she said.

"No time," I said, and grabbed her under the armpits and pulled. Her head lolled back and she stared at me, upside down. Her voice was groggy. "Peter . . . The dorm's on fire . . . You know that, right?"

"It's okay," I said. "Andy told me I could do this if I was right and true."

Greta frowned at me. "Well, then, if Andy said."

The smoke was up to my thighs, it was flowing down from the ceiling, making a curtain; but somehow I was getting spoonfuls of air into my lungs through the cotton of the shirt, and I wasn't afraid, because I knew how to go. In fact, as I pulled Greta along the hall, and down the stairs, and outside, I was making the path, making the streak, the golden way, leaving it for myself to find later on, before, wherever that was.

And we lived. We got out.

So probably you want to know what happened to Andy Patek? Me, too. If I ever track him down, I'll let you know. On my birthday, someone mailed me a cranberry muffin, but I think that was just Greta fucking with me.

I'm not crazy. I know I hurt my elbow and I know I hurt my knee and I had a hell of a bruise on my shin that lasted for weeks. I know that Greta lived, that I dragged her down the hall, down the steps, and out the door, and that we followed the invisible path, that we stepped in gold.

NO WAY. NO OTHER EXPLANATION? NOT MY PROBLEM.

Suffice to say, if there's one piece of advice I can give you, it's this: stay in the light.

With Footnotes and References

by Gar Anthony Haywood

Parnell's father was a hard man. One would have thought a net worth of $240 million would make him a little less so, but a man didn't make a quarter of a billion dollars by playing nice with people.

Andrew Bennett knew how to make a dollar, in and out of corporate real estate, and he was filled to the brim with lessons to convey. Over the course of his twenty-two years, Parnell had heard them all, but the two that had stuck more than any of the others were, "stand by your word" and "never be the biggest loser in any deal."

The first bit of advice was tired and old, of course, just like Andrew had become himself, but it had its merits. Making good on your promises always seemed to reassure people that you could be trusted with their hearts and their money. Women, business partners, investors—they all lapped it up with equal zeal. But Andrew's second admonition was more confusing than trite, because how could you make money without occasionally losing more than the other guy? Wasn't that the simple math behind every deal gone south? Only after he was well into his teens did Parnell begin to understand what his father meant, and why it was important: Fall if you must, but always leave the hardest landing for someone else.

And Parnell always did. In this way, he earned his father's affections honestly. He worked hard and made smart decisions. If he partied like a fiend and ran through his monthly allowance—a generous eight grand—as if frugality were a mortal sin, his personal life at least had produced no public embarrassment for the family. In short, he was a fine son and only child, and neither his father nor his mother had any reason to believe he would ever prove a major disappointment.

He wasn't perfect, however. When he wasn't busting his ass to achieve a desired outcome, he was cutting a fine-edged, well-calculated corner to accelerate it. Parnell disliked the word "cheat"—it made his little indiscretions sound more desperate than inspired—but he knew that was the technical term for what he did. And that was okay. Because whatever word you used for it, Parnell never circumvented the rules of order just for the sake of it. He cheated with purpose, to seize on a unique opportunity or to save his precious resources of time and energy, and even his father could find very little fault in that.

Except as it applied to Parnell's college education. Andrew Bennett would not have been happy to learn that his son was gaming the system in any fashion to make his way through the University of Southern California. Business was war, where rules were made to be bent and broken, but education was sacred. A degree from the old man's beloved USC was an honor to be earned through blood, sweat and tears, not guile nor influence. Money could get you in, there was nothing wrong with that, but if it bought you a single step up after your first day of classes, the paper behind the framed glass on the wall wasn't worth five cents. It didn't matter what the discipline or who it impressed. Because it had been purchased under these very conditions, the diploma on Andrew's own office wall—USC Marshall School of Business, Class of 1990—was one of his most prized possessions, and he wanted—he *demanded*—nothing less for his son.

Parnell admired his father's viewpoint but found it too hypocritical to be taken seriously. College was no different from big business, it was all the same game of win or go home, and pretending one was more honorable than the other was a joke. Parnell had done all the work and made all the sacrifices necessary to gain acceptance into Andrew's alma mater, no small or uncostly feat in and of itself, but hell if he was going to spend the next four years of his life following his father's fanciful, starry-eyed playbook. He was his own man and he had his own way of doing things. He lived life on the edge and kept friends of all stripe, some of whom he found nearly as frightening as he did entertaining. And yes, he paid someone to write a paper on occasion.

Someone who knew the subject backwards and forwards and could be counted on to meet a deadline, and produce something for twenty-five hundred that hadn't been cut and pasted from online sources. Somebody nearly as smart as Parnell was himself, but who had far more to lose if their arrangement ever came to light.

Someone like Megan Deene.

Megan knew the type. She'd seen guys like Bennett all her life.

Smart. Funny. More money than God and twice the confidence, nearly all of it misplaced. Parnell was prettier than most but his M.O. was the same. Work hard right up to the point of discomfort, then pay somebody smarter to take you the rest of the way home.

That she was smarter than Bennett, Megan had no doubt. Just their typical, barroom banter over beer and appetizers was proof enough of that. But being smarter than most of the male students at USC and damn near all the women wasn't a prize that came with any cash award, and unlike Bennett, Megan had to find every dime of her tuition on her own. There was no Daddy or Mommy back home in Spartanburg to cushion her fall when what she owed and what she earned, working a half-dozen freelance gigs at once, failed to balance out at the end of the month. So she was left to do what she had to do, superior intellect be damned: Play the commoner and attend to the needs of Bennett and his blue-blooded ilk—for a price.

And that price was about to go up. Parnell didn't know it yet, but Megan had decided her latest term paper for him was worth more than the $2,500 she had been charging him up to now. "Vinegar and Oil: Ethics and Mobile Application Design" may not have been her finest work for Bennett, but it had been the most exhausting, and Megan was all through killing herself for his benefit without being adequately compensated. This paper was going to cost him four grand, and every paper hereafter.

He wouldn't like it, but what was he going to do? Write a sixty-page paper of his own overnight? Not likely. Though he probably could, were he properly motivated. That was the great irony of it all. Parnell didn't *need* Megan's services, not like the other losers she dealt with; he was only paying her to do work he could just as easily do himself out of sheer laziness. Megan didn't understand it, she had never understood it. Nothing else about the boy suggested such sloth; he appeared from every other angle to be industrious and self-sufficient, if wildly unscrupulous. And yet, here he was, outsourcing classwork to a poor girl like Megan, dropping more on a single paper than she could keep in her checking account for more than six hours.

She knew she was taking a big chance, changing the terms of their agreement without warning. Bennett would be furious and would threaten to write his own paper, at the very least. But that was as far as his anger would take him, because he didn't have the stomach for much more than talk. Megan was sure of it. Bennett had an edge to him, yes, but at his core he was soft, incapable of ever taking things to a physical level. This wasn't true of all Megan's clients; there were some she'd never dare cross in the way she planned to cross Parnell tonight. These guys would cave Megan's head in first and consider the consequences later. She'd seen plenty of their kind, too, over the years, and always handled them accordingly.

Bennett knew a few such crazies himself. His boy Ronnie Fetters was a prime example. Parnell's cast of party-animal friends was an eclectic bunch, to be sure, but Fetters was an outlier, a Black Mamba in a pit of garden snakes. He didn't belong in Bennett's circle, but he was there just the same. Megan could only imagine Parnell kept him around for laughs.

She wondered how much laughing Bennett would be doing after their meeting tonight.

The way it usually worked, Megan would email Parnell the first twenty pages of a paper under a generic title, just to prove she was on track, then exchange the remainder for $2,500 in cash over morning coffee at an off-campus Starbucks. But this time Megan wanted to close the deal in the early evening at the Leavey Library, and Parnell immediately thought he knew why: a man couldn't raise his voice in anger in a library without making a scene.

Parnell wasn't surprised. Megan was smart and streetwise, and people like her never stayed in one place too long. Raising the stakes was no doubt part of every bet she ever made. Had she never tried to game Parnell at least once, even just a little bit, he would have been both shocked and disappointed.

Alone at a table in Leavey, they made quick work of the small talk and got right down to business.

"I didn't bring the paper," Megan said. She showed Parnell the courtesy of not smiling.

"Yeah. I noticed that."

"I've been doing some thinking, and I've decided we need to renegotiate."

"That's funny, because I was thinking the same thing."

"You were?"

"Yes. At least, in this particular case. The item's not bad, but it's not up to your usual standards, and it's well below mine."

Megan's eyes flashed, and now she did smile, but not with any amusement. "Excuse me?"

"I'll give you two bills for it."

She waited for him to go on, but Parnell was done talking.

"Two bills?"

"Frankly, I'm being generous. I won't presume to suggest you weren't trying this time around, but your reliance on redundancy and run-on sentences was somewhat appalling. Very unlike you."

"You're fucking insane. If anything—"

"You were thinking of asking for more than the usual twenty-five. Of course you were. But my offer's two bills, just the same. Take it or leave it."

He did everything short of crossing his arms and lighting a cigarette to show her how serious he was. She sat there and watched him wait, doing a burn so slow he almost couldn't see it. But she was on fire, all right. If he couldn't see the heat coming off her, he sure as hell could feel it.

"Fuck you. Write the paper yourself. Good luck with that."

"I won't need luck. Just a few cans of Red Bull to make it through the next forty-eight. But thanks."

He started to stand.

"You're bluffing," Megan said.

Parnell laughed and settled back down in his chair. "Now, why in the hell would I need to do that? I've already got thirty pages in the bank. You don't think I can knock out another twenty-five in two days, and save myself a couple grand in the process?"

"You could, but you won't."

He almost found himself feeling sorry for her. "Megan. You're the one bluffing, not me. If I walk out of here without your promise to deliver the rest of the goods by eight tomorrow morning, you're not just kissing off two grand. You're kissing off every dollar you might have made from this arrangement in the future. End of the Bennett gravy train. Is that what you want?"

It wasn't because it couldn't be. Parnell had looked deep into the lady's background before getting into business with her and he knew how badly she needed the income he'd been providing. She wasn't going to throw it all away over five hundred dollars.

She pushed away from the table and got to her feet. Humiliation was a bitch, but starvation was worse. "Pay me. Now."

Parnell's eyes surveyed the room. There were cameras everywhere.

"Outside," he said.

A gun, Megan thought. *If I'd only had a gun.*

She would have killed Parnell for sure. That's how furious she'd been. And she was still furious hours later, curled up in a ball in bed like a war orphan, though now her ire was as much about her own stupidity as Bennett's double-cross. He'd thrown her off completely, changing the terms of their contract before she could do it first, and she'd never recovered her balance. How had he understood how weak her play was better than she understood it herself? She had entered the library thinking only in the short term, of a single sixty-page document and how desperate Parnell's need for it had to be, but *his* eyes were on the bigger picture, the one in which he held all the cards, not she. All Bennett had to lose by ending their working relationship was a couple nights' sleep, but Megan . . . However fair or unfair the fee, she had come to rely on the $2,500 Bennett was paying her to write a paper every six weeks or so, and she would have been hard pressed to find that money elsewhere.

Somehow, Bennett knew this—he'd probably always known it—and with that he had all the upper hand over her he could ever require. Servants were a dime a dozen, but masters were few. For now, Parnell held the power between them, and she either accepted his terms of service or dropped out of school to spare herself the indignity of being expelled.

She drew her laptop to her on the bed and emailed Bennett the rest of his goddamn assignment, vowing to someday make him wish he'd never heard the name Megan Deene.

"I say kill the bitch," Ronnie said.

"Don't be ridiculous."

"Ridiculous? What's ridiculous about it?" The big man was picking his front teeth with a chicken bone. "She can't be trusted. There's only one way to deal with people you can't trust."

"Actually, there are all kinds of ways to deal with people you can't trust," Parnell said. "And killing them is way down on the list. That is, unless prison food appeals to you."

"I ain't ever going to prison. People who go to prison ain't worth a shit afterwards. I'd make 'em kill me first."

"Death or prison. Same difference. Either way, you're fucked if you get caught. So let's just leave murder off the table for now, shall we?"

Parnell watched his friend light another joint, their third of the evening.

Ronnie's tiny apartment already reeked, so one more cloud of smoke would hardly matter. Parnell pinched the blunt between two fingers when it was passed and took a long drag, silently admitting something he could never tell Ronnie: He'd like to kill Megan Deene, too.

But that would be a gross overreaction that could backfire spectacularly. Ronnie was a thug in a Trojan lacrosse uniform who thought getting away with murder was just a matter of wearing rubber gloves and hiding the body in a ditch somewhere, but Parnell knew there was much more to it than that. You had to have the will to commit the act, first—something Parnell sorely lacked—and then you had to have a plan that was airtight, one the police couldn't penetrate no matter how many ways they tried. Given time, Parnell could come up with the plan, but time was a commodity he only spent on things that were essential. For now, there was no reason to think Megan wasn't a problem he had under control, and until she did something to prove otherwise, she was best left alone. Monitored closely and with suspicion, but left alone.

If she had the smarts he thought she did, he would never come to regret leaving the lady alive.

Megan tried, but she could never get over it. The way Bennett had played her just stung too much.

For a while, she had worried that she may have put herself in danger, making an enemy of someone who had powerful friends and more than enough resources to do her harm. But months passed, then a year, and her fear of Bennett faded to black while her resentment and outrage grew, festering like an open wound that refused to heal. Had that night at the Leavey Library been the last time she laid eyes on him, she might have been able to put the injury he'd inflicted upon her in the past, but she'd gone on working for him afterward, writing a paper here and there, taking his money without complaint. Never letting on that the sight of his face turned her stomach. Because every day was still a struggle just to stay in school and beggars couldn't be choosers about who was buying their books or paying their overdue electric bill.

Still, her anger lingered. It ate at her like a dog gnawing on a bone. And now, finally, it was time for payback. Graduation was looming; Bennett had never been more vulnerable. The few hundred he'd saved himself playing hardball with her over a single term paper was chickenfeed compared to the invoice she was about to lay on him.

Megan was the one thinking long-term now.

Ronnie didn't see Parnell's girl coming until she was practically at his table. She climbed up on the stool across from him and sat herself down, pretty as you please, smiling like she'd called ahead to ask permission.

"Hello?" he said.

They'd only seen each other once before that he could recall, here at Traddies last year, having a drink with some girlfriends. She'd drifted over to his and Parnell's table and Parnell had introduced them, explaining later who she was.

"You're Ronnie, right? Remember me? Megan?"

"I remember. What's up? If you're lookin' for Parnell—"

"Actually, I'm here to see you. You and I need to talk."

"We do?"

"Yes. But first, I'm going to order something from the bar. I'm starved."

"You're making a huge mistake," Parnell said.

Megan had called another meeting, this one at the coffee shop just outside the campus grounds where they used to conduct all their business. She didn't owe him another paper—only six weeks from graduation, his need for her services were a thing of the past—and she wouldn't tell him what she wanted over the phone, so he was left to guess what was on her mind. He showed up expecting the worst and she didn't disappoint.

"Am I? I don't think so," Megan said. "I think fifty thousand dollars to guarantee you aren't called into the Dean's office two months before you earn your diploma is just about right. In fact, I think it's generous."

She smiled to show she had used that word deliberately, "generous." That was what he had said he was being with her that night at Leavey, paying her two thousand dollars for a paper she thought was worth much more.

"The Dean's office? Why would I get called into the Dean's office?" He flashed her a smile of his own.

"Don't, Parnell. Fourteen papers in three years. I've got the emails, I've got—"

"Zilch. You've got zilch. Did you even think this through, Meg? You sent me Word docs with no titles and emails with no subject lines. Maybe I opened them, maybe I didn't. Maybe the emails went straight to my spam folder where I never even saw them. I always paid you in cash. Do I need to go on?"

"I have full copies of papers you submitted to multiple instructors under your own name, Parnell. Whatever else I couldn't prove, you'd never be able to explain your way out of that."

"I wouldn't have to."

"Oh. Because you're Parnell Bennett, right? And Daddy gives big bucks to the university. Is that it?"

Parnell shook his head, letting the grin on his face stay where it was. She didn't get it and probably never would. "I'm not going to pay you, Megan."

She shrugged. "Then you've just thrown away four years of your life for nothing."

He watched her stand up and back away from the table. "What are you going to do?"

"I'm going to go back to my apartment and hit 'send.' And if you were thinking about stopping me, you'd better get ready to do it yourself because your boy's not going to do it for you."

"My boy?"

"Ronnie's not your boy? I thought you two were buds. He thinks so, too. Though, after today, maybe not so much."

"You've been talking to Ronnie?"

"Call it a pre-emptive strike. Insurance against fatal injury."

Parnell had to laugh. Insurance *against*, the lady said. "Go on."

"I've just given you two choices: pay me or shut me up. You don't want to pay me and you don't have the balls to do what it would take to shut me up, so what's left? I did the math, Parnell. I got to Ronnie first."

"And?"

"He's not as stupid as you think. Or as loyal. He's not going to risk everything *he's* worked for these last four years just to silence me for your sake." She gave Parnell a moment to think that over. "Pay me, Parnell. It's the only move you've got."

She waited for him to say something.

"Okay. I'll sleep on it. But do yourself a solid in the meantime," he said, "and go check the rosters for the classes you wrote those papers for. I think you'll find them rather interesting."

Of course, she didn't follow. All she said was, "I'll give you 'til tomorrow, noon." And then she was gone.

". . . the rosters for the classes you wrote those papers for."

What the fuck was Bennett talking about?

She had him by the short hairs, of course he'd say anything to try and confuse her, but Megan couldn't convince herself he'd been talking just to talk. That wasn't Parnell's style. There was something in those class rosters she needed to see.

She spent most of the night in denial, eating and drinking like a fool, determined to celebrate the fifty thousand dollars of Bennett's money she planned to use to help pay off her student loans. But the minute she parked her car on the street outside her apartment building, she brought the class rosters up on her phone, unable to wait until she could crack open her laptop upstairs. To write the papers, she'd had to know the courses and the instructors, so finding the classes on the school site, and the roster of students assigned to each, posed no problem for her. It just took a little digging.

But her stomach was already turning by the time the first list appeared on her phone, because it had finally dawned on her what significance the rosters could possibly hold for her. Parnell's name wasn't on this list, and it wasn't on any of the others, either. He hadn't been enrolled in any of the classes he'd paid her to write papers for. In four of the seven, however, somebody else had been, someone they both knew, and his name leapt off Megan's smartphone screen like an icy bolt of lightning.

"Oh, Jesus," Megan said.

She was about to get out of the car when Ronnie Fetters jumped in on the passenger side. There was a knife in his right hand, maybe the biggest knife Megan had ever seen in her life.

"If you scream, I'm gonna kill you right here," he said.

Megan looked around in a panic, didn't see a living soul anywhere to save her. She took her chances and screamed anyway.

Parnell hadn't needed the money, but selling Megan's writing services to Ronnie and two other Trojans of his acquaintance had been a quick and easy way to pick up a little spending cash his parents never had to know about. A thousand off the top on each paper—Megan hadn't realized how underpaid she really was.

But the girl was shortsighted in so many ways. She thought Parnell was just a rich, lazy frat boy and that Ronnie was nothing but a dumb jock without ambition. She'd been wrong on both counts. There wasn't anything lazy about playing the middleman in a mutually profitable enterprise of your own invention, and not every muscle-bound college athlete lacked post-graduate intentions outside of sports. Ronnie was crude, to be sure, but his parents were nearly as well off as Parnell's and about twice as demanding of their son. Ronnie's father had plans for him to join the family business upon his graduation, and he wasn't going to be disappointed. He had two other sons besides Ronnie, each with degrees of their own, and Ronnie's only ticket in was a diploma from SC. Getting expelled from school was no more an option for him than it had been for Megan.

Now the poor devil had much bigger problems than expulsion to worry about. He'd wanted to kill Megan the moment he'd heard she was trying to game Parnell for more money—"*There's only one way to deal with people you can't trust*"—and now that she'd proven him right, he was going to put her in check in the most permanent way possible.

Parnell had been surprised when he didn't kill Megan last night, after she'd made the fatal mistake of trying to win him over to her side of a blackmail scheme of which Ronnie was the actual target, not Parnell. Ronnie had called Parnell right after, more just to say "I told you so" than to seek any advice. He'd already made up his mind what he was going to do, and when.

"I don't want to know any details," Parnell told him.

Because the details would not be necessary. It was past midnight. By now, Megan Deene was likely dead and Ronnie was still in the process of cleaning up his mess. All Parnell had to tell the 9-1-1 operator was that he feared a murder was about to be committed, and he thought he knew who was going to commit it. Maybe all of Ronnie's talk about preferring death-by-cop to prison was a lot of hot air, and maybe it wasn't. But Parnell figured it would be worth his while to find out. Either way, Parnell Bennett would not be the biggest loser in this deal-gone-all-to-hell.

Daddy would be so proud.

Penelope McCoy

by Nicholas Christopher

M y relationship with Penelope McCoy began and ended in the stacks of the rare book library. I could never have imagined it would result in my arrest for arson, and soon afterward, my leaving the college and moving to another state.

I was a Classics professor, specializing in the historians: Herodotus, Tacitus, Strabo, Livy. On the last Friday in March, at the end of semester break, I was in the cartography section, searching medieval folios for maps that illustrated the *Library of History* of Diodorus Siculus. One map, in particular, of the upper Nile basin that illustrated a portion of Book I. The stacks were silent. I heard the elevator doors open and close around the corner. Then the clacking of heels in the marble hallway that grew duller when the heels hit the ancient oak floor in the stacks. The woman who entered was a pale redhead with jarringly dark eyes—so black the irises and pupils were one—and a confident stride. Her shaved eyebrows were replaced by slanting lines penciled upward, her mascara was thick, and her lipstick was the same burnt-orange as her woolen coat, scarf, and leather gloves. She wore expensive French stiletto heels, yellow with red soles, that must have made for tricky footing on the icy streets. The temperature had not risen above twelve degrees for a week. The mounds of frozen snow from two recent snowfalls were impervious to the feeble heat of the sun.

The woman paused and cocked her head when she saw me, then walked right over. "Professor Varick," she said, extending her hand, as if it was perfectly natural that she should encounter me there. "Penelope McCoy. Archaeology Department. I thought I recognized you. I saw your debate with Shipman," she added in the same breezy tone.

That event, sponsored by my department four months earlier, was barely publicized and sparsely attended. For ninety minutes I debated a British academic named W.W.Y. Shipman concerning what he called the "fruitful inaccuracies" in Tacitus's *Germanica,* which I insisted were unfruitful errors best swept aside. Shipman believed that the mistakes showed the true state of Tacitus's mind—whatever that meant—and thus deserved analysis, however speculative. And so on. A forgettable evening, except that Penelope McCoy had not forgotten it.

"Shipman is a theorist," she said, "what I call a French poodle, slave to Derrida and Lacan. For his ilk, even misprints, generated at the book press, bear scrutiny. You disagreed, and said, 'No, misprints require a better copy editor.' "

"Even now," I replied, "that exchange sounds lame. I'm sorry you sat through it."

"On the contrary, I enjoyed the evening. I remember one comment you made in passing that Shipman waved away. You said that Herodotus, a prodigious long-distance traveller, had been dubbed the 'Father of History, Father of Lies' by lesser historians, but was in fact one of the great on-site investigative scholars of all time."

"Those lesser historians objected to his plumbing myths and legends for historical clues," I said. "They saw it as a diversion, not an enhancement. Herodotus gave us the word 'history' from the Greek *hystorie,* 'investigation,' as in scientific undertaking."

"So his critics were envious. And Shipman is doctrinaire. He dismissed mythology as 'ahistorical.' "

"It was bizarre that he reduced it to a pop-culture indulgence, lumping it with angelology and demonology. He lost me for good with that."

"He was stupid," Penelope snapped.

"He's a contrarian, so for him our debate was an opportunity to compete, not enlighten. Textured disagreements are not a part of his MO."

"By the end of the night I could've throttled him," she said angrily.

I was startled. I wondered if Shipman had really riled her or if she was just trying to impress me. There was an edge to her, a depth to her anger, that I wanted no part of. I knew that she had managed to engage me so easily—as had other people recently—because of my loneliness two years after the deaths of my wife and daughter. That was what brought me to the stacks every night and kept me up until dawn at home, poring over my research, fueling myself with coffee, and increasingly, with Scotch. That particular week was especially painful: during my marriage, it was the time of the year when the three of us would have found ourselves driving across Apulia or exploring a new island in the Caribbean. A lifetime ago.

I glanced at my watch. "Stacks close in ten minutes."

"Oh. I thought I had until eleven."

"Not during break. What were you here for?"

"A map of Thera," she said, without missing a beat. "I'm an Egyptologist."

"New to the university?"

"Since September." Her voice changed, as if suddenly she were reciting, not conversing. "I'm writing about Solon in Egypt, beginning with Plato's account of Atlantis in the *Timaeus*."

"Good luck." I began gathering my papers.

"How about a cup of coffee?" she said.

"Not a good time."

"Maybe next time," she smiled, and started for the elevator.

"What about the map of Thera?"

"I'll come back for it," she said over her shoulder.

The next time I saw her was two weeks later, the first day of the new semester, when she attended my lecture course. My graduate seminars were topped at twelve students. My lecture course in Xenophon and Thucydides, read in translation, drew undergraduates from across the college. Penelope McCoy approached me afterward. I had seen her in the third row the moment I got behind the lectern. She greeted me with a nod and held out my most recent book, *Strabo and the Asian Influence on Greek Geography,* and a pen. "If you would."

I took the book, opened it on the lectern, and signed the title page.

"No inscription?" she said.

I hesitated, then jotted down the date and *Good Luck.*

She tilted her head in disappointment.

The lecture hall was emptying. Three students were waiting for me to sign their registration cards.

"Excuse me," I said.

Tucking the book into her shoulder bag, she walked away without a word.

When I returned to my office, I couldn't find her name in the faculty directory. I telephoned the Archaeology Department and asked about their new hires, but the departmental secretary didn't mention her.

"We have a couple of European exchange fellows attached to the department," she said. "They come around for their mail, but not much else."

"Is either of them named McCoy?"

"Their surnames are Winder and Kleine. Wait." I heard her keyboard clicking. "Penelope McCoy was a master's candidate."

"Was?"

"She took a leave last year after losing her scholarship. I doubt she's coming back."

"She is back."

I saw her again two nights later, just before closing hours in one of the reading rooms of the main library. I was sitting alone at the end of a long walnut table.

She came up behind me casually, hand on hip, an open book in the other hand. She walked that way, hand on hip. I only saw her at the last moment, reflected in the dark window before me. Again she was wearing orange and red, a jacket and jeans this time that looked almost DayGlo against the dreary grays and browns of the reference shelves. And the same yellow heels.

"I need more information on Solon's assertions about the Nile, which I've only encountered in Herodotus," she said, as if it should be perfectly natural that she happened to be researching Herodotus and could thus segue into the next phase of our previous conversation.

"Are you asking what I might know about this?" I said.

She sat down across from me, smiled, and crossed her arms on the table. "I guess I am now."

I didn't find her smile appealing. Or her implying, in words and body language, that there was a connection between us. There was a hint of malice in her smile, a suggestion that because she was rich in guile, and at peace with that, she possessed a rarefied form of guilelessness.

"You're writing about the fire at the Great Library of Alexandria, aren't you?" she said.

"How did you know that?"

"I read it in an interview you gave to the *Herald Gazette*. February, 2018."

"And why were you reading that?"

"Because I'm interested in you."

"I'm not so interested in you, Penelope. I know you're not on the faculty."

She smiled. "Nice to hear you say my name."

"In fact, you're a degree candidate, no longer enrolled."

"I never said I was on the faculty."

"A degree candidate who lost her funding."

"And why were you checking on me?" she said, pleased to note that I had.

"This is the third time you crossed paths with me."

"It's a small campus."

"You've been seeking me out."

"Have I?"

"What is it you want?"

"Advice."

"About?"

"The fire at the Great Library, of course."

"You're joking."

"Not at all. I'd like your opinion as to who set the fire. Julius Caesar, early Christian mobs, or the Emir Omar?"

"All of the above. There were several fires over three centuries. Caesar's navy lobbed fireballs into the harbor during a sea battle. Christian mobs burned thousands of books and scrolls when they sacked the Temple of Serapis. The Emir incited his own book burning. There were plenty of guilty parties."

"Perhaps, too, a disgruntled scholar who betrayed Hypatia, the last Librarian?"

"I never heard that one before."

"After setting fire to the books, he turned Hypatia over to the mob that flayed her alive. She was a martyr."

"I know who she was. You haven't come to me for my opinion. What is it you really want?"

"Here's the thing: that *is* what I want. But we'll leave it for another day. Instead, I'd like to ask you to put in a good word for me with Professor Foxx. I believe I'm worthy of a scholarship."

"Ms. McCoy. I don't know you. And I'm not a member of Professor Foxx's department."

"Come on, a recommendation from you would go a long way."

I shook my head.

"I was going to send you my dossier, but wanted your permission first."

"Because you're a stickler for protocol."

"If I send it to you, will you at least consider whether or not I'm worthy? If the answer is no, just forget I asked."

"You could have written to me in the first place. Or mentioned this when you found me in the stacks. Surely you don't think I believe that was a coincidence?"

"Actually, it was," she said with a note of resignation.

"Fine. Send me your dossier and I'll take a look."

———— • ————

I never received the dossier. I didn't hear from her. Several weeks passed. It was an unseasonably warm April, and on the final weekend, our dean invited all members of the History, Classics, and Archaeology Departments to a barbecue at his house. Caterers in white jackets circulated with trays of wine and canapés. Tables had been set up across the lawn. There was a wet bar, buffet, and two large grills turning out hamburgers and kebabs. I got a glass of seltzer at the bar. I never drank anymore at professional functions. I couldn't be sure I'd be able to stop. The dean was holding court at the outdoor fireplace. Among the guests milling around him was Penelope McCoy. She was wearing a bright red dress, red-framed wraparounds, heels, and an incongruous pair of white gloves. Her face was attractive when you couldn't see her eyes.

I saw her before she saw me, or so I thought because a moment later she turned—not too quickly—and looked right at me. Then she came over, martini in hand.

"I thought you might be here."

"A safe bet, considering most of the faculty is here."

"I had a nice chat with Professor Foxx."

"I'm sure you did. I never received the material you were going to send."

"I sensed your reluctance. I didn't want to impose. Anyway, it turned out to be unnecessary. I think things are going to work out."

"Your scholarship is being renewed?"

"Not that. More important things."

"Like?"

She sipped her martini. "You don't drink, right?"

"Seldom." I drank alone now, always, and somehow, from her expression, I thought she must know this. But how?

"I'd like to ask you a personal question."

"That's a surprise."

"Very personal. Are you drawn to the fire at the Great Library because of the way your wife and daughter died?"

"Excuse me."

"Trapped in a fire, you know."

"Jesus. What the hell is wrong with you?"

"Oh no. I crossed a line."

"Whoever you really are, we're done. Don't ever come near me again."

"Or you'll call the police?"

"I will. And you can go to hell."

I backed away so I wouldn't slap her. Heading across the lawn for the street, I veered off to thank the dean's wife. When I glanced back, I saw Penelope McCoy standing by one of the grills. She knew I was watching her when she put down her glass, picked up a can of lighter fluid and a yellow fire starter and examined them with feigned curiosity.

My hands were shaking when I took out my car keys. At home I poured myself a double and put a frozen taco into the microwave. I never did eat it. I drank another double and dropped two Ambien. But I couldn't sleep that night.

My wife Rena and my daughter Kate were staying at the beach house we had rented for the summer. Rena was forty-two, Kate was twelve. It was late on a Friday night, and driving out from town to join them, I was delayed in traffic. There was an electrical short in the house's HVAC followed by a flash fire. The police initially suspected arson. They questioned me about my whereabouts at the time the fire broke out. They made inquiries at neighboring houses. But it was an electrical short. Unknown to Rena and me, pipes had burst in the house the previous winter and compromised the wiring. Rena and Kate were asleep in the two bedrooms. By the time they rushed into the hallway, both ends of it were engulfed in flames. I saw the smoke rising as I turned off the main road. By then, the fire was extinguished. I saw two fire trucks and an ambulance van. When I reached the house, two firemen were just entering with a stretcher. I jumped from my car and ran toward the door. A fireman intercepted me and tried to lead me away. *I don't think you want to see this, sir.*

But I did see it.

———•———

Four months after the dean's barbecue, on a stifling August night, I was in the stacks, working through the entries on Diodorus Siculus in a private edition—one of only two extant copies—of Herman Galoscz's *Notebooks*. Galoscz was a Czech philologist. His German was heavy sledding. I had not seen or heard from Penelope McCoy. The day after the barbecue, when I sobered up, I called Jay Foxx at the Archaeology Department. He told me that Penelope had never spoken to him or reapplied for her scholarship. She was gone, as far as he knew. At my request, he proceeded to double-check her status with the registrar and confirm that her university ID had been cancelled. Henceforth she would not be able to enter any university building. I told myself I should have done this months before.

She was far from my thoughts that August night. It was close to eleven, and the stacks had emptied out. I packed up my papers, put a hold slip into Galoscz's book, and went to the men's room. I had been reading for five straight hours. I cupped cold water onto my face. I toweled it gently. I combed my hair. *Tonight,* I thought, *I'll go to bed without a drink or a pill.*

When I returned to the stacks, the lights had been dimmed, the signal for closing time. I thought my eyes were playing tricks on me when I saw the can of lighter fluid and the yellow fire starter on the table where I had been working. On a nearby shelf, Galoscz's *Notebook* was burning. A neat triangle of flames. And there were several other such triangles around the room, on different shelves. They were growing larger, consuming the two- and three-century-old books on eighteen-foot shelves that were ready tinder. I ran to the fire alarm and broke the glass. The alarms went off. The smoke was getting to me, tightening my lungs. I staggered to the door. It was not locked, but jammed somehow. I banged on it. I shouted. I dropped to my knees, feeling the heat at my back, choking on the smoke.

When I opened my eyes again, I was lying on the floor of the library's lobby and a fireman was performing CPR on me. There was an oxygen mask beside my head. I coughed smoke. My chest ached terribly. My eyes were bleary. I sat up. The fireman gave me a drink of water. Other firemen were rushing in and out of the elevators with axes and fire extinguishers. Several campus and town policemen were standing around me. Their walkie-talkies were squawking. From what I heard, there was a lot of damage in the stacks, but the fire had been contained. Through the large windows, police cars and fire trucks were flashing red and blue lights. Students had gathered outside and were staring in. Some were snapping photographs with their phones. Two policemen pulled me to my feet, less gently than I would have expected. It was then that I saw a fireman holding up a plastic evidence bag containing the lighter fluid can and the yellow fire starter. One of the policemen spun me around. He pulled my arms behind me, and I felt cold metal on my wrists. As he snapped shut the handcuffs, I glimpsed a woman's burnt-orange coat flash in the crowd of onlookers, and then disappear.

"Penelope McCoy," I muttered to the policeman, barely recognizing my own voice as he guided me toward the door with a firm grip.

Tess and Julie, Julie and Tess

by Jill D. Block

I'm not sure how this works. I guess I should probably just start at the beginning?

I remember that first night, lying in the dark, listening to her breathe, wondering if she was asleep. I felt the corners of my mouth turn up in a smile. It was so weird, so unexpected, it was like I didn't recognize the feeling. I remember thinking that this must be what happy people feel like. Maybe this is how it feels when you aren't all alone. When you have a friend.

When I learned last spring that the freshman dorms all have double rooms, I decided that my roommate and I would be friends. She would be the sister I'd always wanted. And then, when we exchanged a couple emails? That's when I really knew. We were going to be best friends forever.

Tess was everything I'd imagined she'd be. She was pretty, really pretty, with green eyes and that thick straight shiny sandy-colored hair that you just want to touch. She had a nice smile and straight white teeth. And when she'd laugh it was like the most natural thing ever. Like it just welled up inside of her, and all she had to do was open her mouth and let it out. It made me realize that I always did this thing where I would hesitate, like I was waiting to see if other people thought something was funny, before I'd react. And then, when I would laugh, it always felt forced and awkward, too loud and too late.

Thank God, my mom was already gone when Tess and her parents arrived. I didn't want them to know that she had to work that day, so I just said we'd gotten an early start. I think I would have died if they saw my mom's shitty old Honda. At least I'd convinced her to wear regular clothes, and not her uniform, but of course we'd had a huge fight about it. It turned into the usual thing, about how I think I'm better than she is, and how Grandma is wasting her money paying for this fancy school when she could be helping my mom with the rent instead. It turns out it didn't matter anyway because we were the first people there, waiting in the car before they even opened the dorm and hung up the Welcome Freshmen banner. I told her that she didn't need to stay, that I would unpack and get set up myself. So she was already gone by the time other people started arriving.

Anyway, I helped Tess and her parents unload their car, dragging suitcases, a duffel bag and a floor lamp, up the stairs and down the hall to our room. I carried a laundry basket that was filled with shoes—slippers, sandals, sneakers, boots. The only ones I'd brought were the sneakers I was wearing. I almost blew it in the very first minute Tess and I were in the room. I told her that I'd taken my side of the room because I thought she was probably used to having nice things. She looked at me like I was crazy, like I'd just told her that I was a serial killer or something. I showed her what I was talking about, that the desk on my side of the room was messed up, stained by a permanent marker that had bled through a piece of paper, probably years before. But I told her that I didn't mind, that it didn't bother me. She was like yeah, whatever.

Tess's parents introduced themselves to me as David and Gwen, which was really nice. I'd kind of been hoping they'd tell me to call them Mom and Dad, even though I knew it was ridiculous. It was way too soon for that. They did invite me to join them all for dinner that night, at a restaurant near their hotel.

There was one other thing that happened that night, that almost ruined everything. After dinner, David and Gwen drove us back to campus. They said that they were going to leave early the next morning, and be out of our way. They got out of the car to say goodbye to Tess, telling her how proud they were of her, and that she was going to do great, and that she would make tons of friends and learn so much. And I was just standing there like an idiot, feeling like I was eavesdropping on this private family moment, but not wanting to go inside until I had a chance to tell them thank you. So then, when David was giving Tess a goodbye hug, Gwen came over to me and smiled. She said that they were so happy that me and Tess have each other, and she hugged me. And I started to cry. It was just some tears at first but then, when she didn't let go, I started sobbing, out loud. Really loud. Big, gasping, choking sobs. I never cried like that, but I just couldn't keep it in. It felt like everything she'd just said to Tess she was saying to me, too. It was nice to be hugged by someone who really meant it.

I could tell that Tess thought it was weird that I was crying, so I said something about being a little homesick, which couldn't possibly have been less true. But what else was I going to say?

So anyway, yeah. It was like my dream was finally coming true. But actually, to really make you understand, I think I should start at the real beginning.

This was like two years ago, the beginning of my junior year in high school. I'd waited in my room until things had quieted down, and then I went downstairs and into the kitchen. It wasn't the first time my mom and dad had a fight like that, yelling and throwing things, but this seemed different, worse than before. I remember thinking that it was going to be hard to clean up and act like it didn't happen.

The place was completely trashed, way worse than I'd expected. The big pot, the one my mom called the Dutch oven, was on the floor in a red puddle. He must have thrown it against the wall because there was a dent, like a punch, but with a big splash of spaghetti sauce running down the wall. Chairs were knocked over. There was water and broken glass all over the place. It looked like he must have picked up dirty dishes out of the sink and smashed them on the floor. I had to be careful where I stepped.

I went into the living room and saw that the front of the TV was smashed in. When I stepped on something hard with my bare foot, I picked it up to see what it was, turning it over in my hand. It took me a minute to realize that it was a bloody tooth. I felt like I might puke.

I was about to start cleaning up when I heard something that made me look out the window. There was my mom, standing in the driveway, naked. She'd been in the tub when my dad got home. She wasn't even trying to cover herself. The only thing I could really see when I looked at her was this giant triangle of black hair, down her thighs and up to her stomach. She held her hands in front of her bloody mouth, like that was what she needed to hide.

Even though I couldn't hear what she was saying, I could see that she was talking, yelling, crying. My dad opened the car door and got in. Good, I thought. He's leaving. But when he started the engine she ran around behind the back of the car and stood there, so he wouldn't be able to back out of the driveway without running her over. I don't know what I was hoping would happen, but I didn't move.

I saw the guy from across the street standing at the end of his driveway, holding his phone to his ear, watching. I opened the front door a crack, and I could hear my mom. She was wailing, apologizing, flopping her naked body over the trunk, banging her fists on the car. She was so sorry. It was all her fault. She should never have spoken to him that way. She was begging him to stay. Please don't go. That was when the police car turned onto our street, with its lights flashing. And as messed up as that was, all I could think about was how embarrassing it was that the cops and Mr. Wagondale from across the street would know that my mom didn't shave down there.

Anyway, that was the moment when I decided that I would do whatever I had to do to get in to college, and that as soon as I finished high school, I would leave and never come back. And once I was gone, wherever I went, I would start over. Someplace where no one would know me, where I could be anyone. Where I wouldn't be the girl with the trashy family who had no friends.

So, yeah. Getting Tess as my roommate was pretty much my dream come true. It was really happening. My new life was finally beginning. Those first few days were the happiest days of my life.

That night, after we got back from dinner with her parents, we met a bunch of the girls on our floor. We were in a Quad, which was four double rooms, a little common area, and a shared bathroom with three stalls and three showers. It was so easy to get to know everyone since we already knew each other. "Hi, we're Tess and Julie." I kind of liked the idea that people might not even be sure which of us was which, like it didn't really matter who was who. Tess and Julie. Julie and Tess. Everyone seemed nice, but I was so happy that Tess was my roommate. I could tell that we were a perfect match.

The next day we had orientation, and at lunch they gave each of us a little piece of paper with a number on it. When they told us that we were being split into groups for the rest of the day to do these dumb team-building activities, I switched numbers with someone who had the same one as Tess. I mean, why would they have put us together as roommates if they didn't want us team-building together?

There was a scavenger hunt, and we did this thing where, using just some newspaper and plastic straws and rubber bands, we had to make a carrier thing that was supposed to protect an egg so it wouldn't break when we dropped it out a window. Of course our egg broke. And then there was a trivia night after dinner. I was really resistant at first. I didn't care at all about bonding with these people. I had actually been thinking that maybe Tess and I could ditch the team altogether, but it seemed like she was kind of into it. Anyway, it ended up being fine. Our team was pretty terrible at everything, but everyone seemed like they were having fun.

This one kid, Jason from Los Angeles, was pretty annoying. He wouldn't leave Tess alone. It was like he decided he was in charge of her or something. I tried to get him to back off, because I knew she was probably too nice to do it herself.

After trivia, we went back to the dorm and hung out for a while with Tamara and Kelly, whose room was next door to ours. A little while later Karla and Dana came by, too, and eventually Bonnie and Beth got home. It was cool, like we were this group of friends, but with these best friend roommate couples. We all agreed that night that we were cool sharing our stuff with each other, and that we didn't need to lock the doors to our rooms. That way, if any of us needed something from someone else's room, we could just go get it. It was the first time I ever really felt like I was a part of something.

That night, everyone was talking about prom, and their high school boyfriends. I made up some stuff about a kid named Steven, but I said we'd only gone out for a little while and that I'd broken up with him before the prom. It wasn't that big a deal. But then Tess started talking about Jason, the kid from our team-building team.

She was like oh, he's so cute and funny and smart. I guess he was kind of cute, but the only reason she thought he was so smart is because he was good at trivia. So what? So he knew who was whose vice president. And everyone was like oh, it's so cool that his father is in the movie business. I don't even know when he told her this part, because I was pretty much there the entire time, but I guess he was listing all the famous people he knew. Like, just from living out there. And plus, he went to school with a bunch of kids with famous parents. I was like big deal, meeting famous people doesn't make you famous, and everyone looked at me like that was such a terrible thing to say.

Anyway, that night, after we got washed up and ready for bed, and we all went to our rooms, Tess was still talking about Jason. It was weird how, after just a few hours, she already seemed like she knew so much about him. Like, that he plays golf and tennis, and Rome is his favorite city, and how they'd hired someone to drive his car all the way from California just so he could fly here *and* have his car. It was like she'd totally lost interest in me.

I guess that's why I ended up telling her about my dad. I wasn't planning to. I mean, my whole thing was that this was my chance to start over, clean, where no one knew me or who I used to be. But I couldn't help it. When we got into our beds and turned out the lights, it just came out.

Well, not everything. Not the part about him getting arrested for beating up my mom. And not the part about the cops finding drugs in the car. I wanted to tell her just enough that she would think I was interesting. So I told her that he was killed, which was true, and that it was because he'd been working on what turned out to be the biggest drug bust in the state. Also true, sort of. I didn't lie, but I guess I made it seem like he was a cop or a DEA guy or something, and not a small-time dealer who got killed in prison for ratting out his supplier.

I asked her please not to tell anyone about it. I liked the idea of the two of us sharing a secret.

The next few days were pretty great. Registration was crazy because there is this huge rush with everyone on their computers the minute it opens, and classes keep getting filled up and closed before you have a chance to sign up. Luckily, Tess and I were in our room doing it together on two computers at the same time and we ended up registering for most of our classes together. The only one we couldn't take together was French. She already had like six years of it, and she tested into an advanced class. She loves everything French. She said that she's already planning to go to Paris junior year to study at the Sorbonne. At first I was thinking I'd sign up for something that met at the same time as her French class, so our schedules would be the same, but the idea of spending a semester in Paris with her seemed so great I decided to take Elementary French Intensive instead.

Once classes started, we started to get into the routine. Most days, all eight of us, our whole Quad, would go to lunch and dinner together, but for breakfast it was usually just me and Tess. Breakfast was the best part of my day.

One day after my French class I went back to our dorm to look for Tess. We had talked about going to the bank to open bank accounts, and I thought maybe we could do that before Psych. The door to our room was partway open, and for some reason I decided to wait for a minute, before I went in. I stood in the common area, outside the door where they couldn't see me, listening.

I heard Bonnie say, "Me and Beth and Karla and Dana were talking, and we all think that there's just something weird about her."

"You mean Julie?" Tess asked.

And Bonnie goes, "Yeah. Just, you know, how she's always, like, hovering. Do you know what I mean? And it's like she's always just there, watching and listening, but she never has anything to say."

And Tess said, "Come on. She's not that bad."

"No?" Bonnie asked. "Well, she gets on my nerves."

So then Tess was like, "Yeah, I guess I kind of know what you mean. I mean, yeah, she's weird, but she's harmless. Did you know her father was killed?" Even though I asked her not to tell anyone.

And then Bonnie said, "Okay, that's really sad. I didn't know that, and now I feel bad. But do you think maybe sometime we can hang out without her?"

I turned around and walked down the hall, stepping carefully to make sure my sneakers didn't make a sound. I didn't take a breath until I got to the bathroom, went into a stall and locked the door. What is wrong with me? Why can't I just be normal? I bit my lip so I wouldn't cry out loud, but there was no way I could stop my tears. Hovering? Watching and listening? Fuck her. What does she ever say that's so important?

I stayed in there for almost ten minutes, trying to figure out what I had done wrong. What was wrong with me? Why didn't Tess stick up for me? I replayed the conversation over again and again in my head. She's not that bad. She's weird, but not that bad. Was that what she said? There was something else, too. That I'm harmless. Harmless? What did that even mean? I took a deep breath and closed my eyes. I told myself to forget it. Pretend I hadn't heard it. If I had gotten to the room five minutes earlier or five minutes later, I never would have heard a thing.

I came out and stood in front of the shelves where we left our shower stuff so we didn't have to carry it back and forth from our rooms. My soap and shampoo were just on the shelf, but some of the girls had their stuff in these plastic baskets or boxes. I picked up Bonnie's shower caddie. It was a pink plastic bucket, like a little kid would take to the beach, and it had her name written on it. I took it back into the toilet stall with me, and without really thinking about what I was doing, I unscrewed the top of her shampoo bottle and poured it into the bucket. Then I did the same thing with her conditioner. I opened the plastic containers that had her soap and toothbrush in them, and dumped them into the bucket. Then I put the empty bottles and boxes all back in the bucket, just like they were before, but now everything was sitting in like four inches of goo.

When someone came into the bathroom, I sat down on the toilet and lifted my feet up so you couldn't see my sneakers to know who was in the stall. I saw through the crack that it was Kelly. I waited for a couple minutes after she left, and then I came out and put Bonnie's shower caddy back on the shelf. I looked at myself in the mirror. My eyes were red and puffy, but I figured if anyone asked why I would just say it's allergies. As I walked out, I stopped for one more second. I took Bonnie's toothbrush out of her caddy and dropped it on the floor.

I went back to our room, and Dana was there, too, with Tess and Bonnie. We all acted like nothing happened, like they hadn't just been talking about me behind my back. I asked Tess if she still wanted to go to the bank, and she said yes. I guess no one noticed that my eyes were red.

The next morning at breakfast, Tess asked me if I wanted to go downtown after class. She said she just felt like walking around a store that wasn't the school bookstore. I said yes, and that I was pretty sure we could take the Main Street bus. She said oh, that's okay, Jason was going to drive her. And then she corrected herself. Drive us, I mean.

The three of us went and it was fine. We got ice cream, and walked around the mall for a while. He's okay. Kind of arrogant, but nice. And I couldn't blame him for liking Tess. Everyone liked her. It was just that she's *my* roommate. So shouldn't I get some kind of priority or something?

Driving back to campus, with me in the back seat like I was their kid, Tess was talking about a girl she knows, Lucy, who is the older sister of a kid she went to high school with. Lucy is a senior and lives in an apartment off campus with two other girls. I thought it was weird that Tess knew someone from home and had never even mentioned her before and here she was talking all about her and her apartment. Anyway, she said that Lucy texted her to invite her to party she and her housemates were having the next night. I assumed she was talking to me, maybe Jason, too, but me for sure. But then, all of a sudden, she and Jason are making plans to go out for dinner together first, at some restaurant that he knows about. And they never even turned around to look at me, to see if I want to go, too. That's when I figured out that I wasn't invited. Obviously.

The next day was Saturday, and we all went to brunch in the dining hall. After that we did some homework in our room. Our first essay for Expository Writing was due Monday. The assignment was to write about an object of personal importance aside from its monetary value. Tess said she knew right away what she was going to write about. She showed me a white ashtray that had Café de Flore written on it in green script. She said it was from her favorite café, and that she got it when her grandmother took her to Paris for her sweet sixteen. I ended up writing about my dad's eyeglasses, which were the only thing of his I had. I'd gotten them after he died, and I brought them with me because I knew that if I left them at home my mom would have thrown them out. Parts of my essay were more like creative writing, but it was true that he used to wear them all the time and that I could still picture his face just by looking at them.

After that, everyone from the Quad came into our room to help Tess decide what to wear for her big date with Jason. It was so annoying. It made me think of that scene in Cinderella when all the mice and birds help make her dress for the ball. Big deal, they were going out for brick oven pizza and then to an off-campus keg party. I mean, give me a break.

While Tess was getting ready, I told her I wasn't feeling well. It was true. I was nauseous, and my head hurt. I got into bed and under the covers even though it was only five o'clock. I was kind of hoping she'd at least ask me if I needed her to stay with me, but she didn't.

A little while after she left to meet Jason, Tamara came in to say that everyone was going to dinner and was I going to come? I pretended that I'd been sleeping when she came in, and that I woke up just enough to say that they should go without me.

I lay there for a while, feeling really sick and sad. This whole thing was so unfair. I didn't get it. Everything had been going so great until that jerk Jason from Los Angeles showed up. And stupid Bonnie. None of this was my fault. I hadn't done anything wrong. I was the exact same girl that Gwen hugged goodbye that first night, saying how happy she was that me and Tess had each other.

And what was Tess's problem, anyway? What kind of friend would leave her sick roommate home alone? What if I was really sick? What if I needed to go to Health Services? Was I supposed to walk there alone? All the way across campus? How was she going to feel if there was something really wrong with me? I guess if I died, Bonnie could be her best friend.

I couldn't stay in bed anymore. I felt like I was going to snap, or scream, or something. I was hot and sweaty, and my heart was beating really fast. I just wanted to smash something. I saw Tess's stupid Paris ashtray on her desk. Without even thinking, I picked it up and threw it down on the floor as hard as I could. Instead of smashing into a million pieces, like I hoped it would, it bounced on the linoleum floor and rolled under her bed. I tried one more time but the same thing happened. It wouldn't break. I sat down at my desk, breathing hard, trying to calm myself down. That's when I figured it out.

I knew that they wouldn't be back from dinner until seven at the earliest, so I had plenty of time. I first went into Karla and Dana's room and looked around. I didn't know exactly what I was looking for, but I kept thinking about that assignment for Expository Writing. An object of personal importance other than for its monetary value. But what I was looking for was something of personal importance *and* monetary value. I would know it when I found it. Not a laptop. Not the gold medal Karla won for diving. I picked up Dana's headphones. Not exactly right, but close. I thought about Bonnie's shower caddie. It was weird that no one ever said anything about that. This time it needed to be something that would be noticed, that couldn't be ignored.

I went to Tamara and Kelly's room. Tamara had a big collection of Beanie Babies lined up on the shelf over her desk. There must have been twenty-five of them, and she said she'd left a bunch at home. Some of them were probably antiques, but who besides Tamara really cared about Beanie Babies? I opened Kelly's closet and looked inside her jewelry box. That was it. Her diamond earrings. Even though she usually wore them all the time, she'd taken them out when she asked if Tess wanted to borrow them for her date with Jason. Tess said no, that she would be too afraid of losing them.

I picked up the earrings and left, stopping in my room before going to

Bonnie and Beth's. I closed the door behind me, and slid the empty suitcase out from under Bonnie's bed. I opened it up and put Kelly's earrings, Dana's headphones, Tess's ashtray and my dad's glasses in the zipped inside pocket. Then I closed the suitcase and slid it back under the bed.

I went to my room. I still didn't really feel well, so I got into my bed, back under the covers. It was done. I had taken care of everything, and now it was just a matter of time. All I had to do was wait.

Except that it didn't work. Obviously, right? Or I wouldn't be here. I figured that eventually people would notice that stuff was missing. And I was right, but it all happened way too fast. Kelly noticed her earrings were missing right away. And since I'd been alone in the Quad the whole time, I was the prime suspect. Plus, they had somehow already figured out that I was the one who messed with Bonnie's shower caddie. They never even had to search our rooms. Once they confronted me, I told them yes, it was me. That I did it and everything was in the suitcase under Bonnie's bed.

They said that there was going to be a hearing, but it would be a few days until the Honor Board was ready. It was only the second week of school, and I guess they weren't expecting to have to deal with a disciplinary issue so soon. Anyway, I couldn't stay in the Quad because everyone hated me so much, so they made me stay at Health Services, starting that night. I was gone before Tess even got home from the party.

They told me that I could arrange to have people speak on my behalf, but weirdly, the only person I could think to ask was Gwen. I would have had to ask Tess for her mom's phone number, and even I knew that was crazy. So I just went by myself and said yeah, I did it.

No one was interested in pressing criminal charges. I guess it probably helped that I had always intended that the stuff I took would be found and returned. But they said that I had violated about twenty different provisions of the Honor Code. So they kicked me out, effective immediately. The good thing is that they refunded my tuition.

———•———

I looked up for the first time since I'd started. I had never talked for so long before, and especially not about myself. I almost couldn't believe that she was still sitting there, still listening.

"Thank you for sharing all of that with me. I bet it isn't easy to talk about."

She was kind of pretty. And young for a doctor. Younger than I would have expected.

"I look forward to working with you, Julie, and I think that we will be able to do a lot together."

She looked kind of sad, but that made sense. It was a sad story. I smiled at her.

"You covered an awful lot, which was very helpful. I'm sure you saw that I was taking notes." She sort of nodded toward her pad and pen. "But aren't you leaving something out?"

"Oh," I said. "You mean this?"

I lifted up my bandaged arms.

"Can you tell me about that?"

"It's nothing," I said. "Really. They said it's superficial."

"Superficial."

"Yeah. I mean it's not like I was trying to kill myself or anything."

"You weren't trying to hurt yourself?"

"No. Definitely not. I mean, yeah, I did it on purpose. And I knew it would hurt. But I wasn't trying to injure myself."

"Then why—?"

"Once I knew I was getting kicked out, I needed to figure out some-place to go. I couldn't go back home. No way. Coming to a place like this was the only thing I could think of. So this?" I lifted up my arms again. "This was just to make sure I'd get in."

Why She Didn't Tell

by John Lescroart

"Come on, Roger, be real."

"I've never been more real in my life."

He knew he could intimidate with a look. He'd destroyed dozens of arrogant, smart-ass doctoral students any number of times, in any kind of setting—in the middle of lectures, close up in seminars, during office hours. The power was right there, in the eyes, in the creases around the eyes.

Marian Chance moved his hand from her thigh.

He put it back, moving it higher.

She put her hand on his hand. He covered it with his other one.

"You know how attractive you are, don't you?"

"Roger, please."

They were on the low couch in the condo—in her and Scott's condo. In the living room, with sliding glass doors out to a balcony overlooking the Rose Bowl route on Orange Grove Avenue. Bougainvillea bloomed outside the window. It was early dusk, warm, still light outside, the glass doors open.

Roger's mouth was on her neck. "Please what?" His hands, their hands, went to the inside of her leg. "Please this?"

"Do you want me to scream?"

"If that's what you want to do."

"The neighbors will hear. Someone will come."

He smiled. "No kidding?" It was a horrible smile. "Someone will come?"

She went to push and slide away, but his hands held her against him. His other hand undid a button on her blouse.

"No," she said.

"Your skin is so smooth."

"Please. This isn't right."

She was thirty years old. She'd been married for three years and had had a lot of lovers—maybe too many—before meeting Scott. But before, no matter what, when she'd said no, it had been no.

Now no wasn't working.

She pushed, struggling to move away, trying to figure it out. Was Roger really doing this? Was Scott's mentor and doctoral advisor going to rape her?

He undid another button and his hand moved down, along her stomach. She sucked in a breath, unexpectedly giving him an opening under her skirt.

"There," he said. "That's it."

The hand on her leg moved up farther, moving under the elastic and lace. What good was her underwear doing her? It was as though she was wearing nothing.

His hands held her down.

It had gone too far already. How could he stop now, say it was a mistake, he'd gotten carried away, apologize and walk out?

She pushed his one hand away, wriggled to get free of the other one. The movement made her slide down a little bit on the couch, onto her side.

He pushed her down the rest of the way, lying next to her, resting his weight on her. "There you go," he said. "There you go."

His hand worked his own belt and suddenly she felt him hard up against her leg, pulling her skirt away, her underwear over to the side.

"Oh please God, Roger. No."

He went to kiss her and she turned her head. But the hand under her, around her neck now, took her hair and pulled her around, facing him, his mouth against her. She bit his lip as hard as she could. "Ahh." A quick yank at her hair, his eyes wild with anger. Holding her down, a drop of blood forming on his lip. "Goddam, goddam!"

Her skirt was now all the way up, bunched while he pushed and pushed. Suddenly on her, in her. Pushing more. His face hovering over her, his eyes open, right there above her, a corner of his lip sucked in to catch the blood.

This couldn't be happening.

She turned her face into the couch, felt his mouth against her neck. Struggling one way, then another, pulled then pushed up against his mouth, hard against him, trying to hurt him again.

"Yeah," he said. "All right now. Now! Now!" Bucking four, five, six times, and it was over.

Rolling back he all but collapsed, lying still, breathing hard. "God, that was good." He traced a finger along the curve of her neck. "Best I ever had."

He stayed to finish the drink she'd made him when he'd first come in. The ice hadn't even melted down in the gin.

When he left ten minutes later, she went to the bathroom and turned on the hot water in the shower. It was still light outside. Shaking, she sat on the toilet, cleaning herself with a washcloth, squeezing every drop of him out of her. Numb, naked, unthinking, she walked into the kitchen and put the washcloth and her underwear into the trash compactor, then came back to the bathroom, with its full-length door mirror.

There were no marks. Her chest was blotched slightly, but she knew that that would clear up quickly. Her neck, where he'd been kissing her, showed nothing.

Her heartbeat pounded in her ears. She put a hand on her stomach, pushing in, half doubling over. Stop, she thought, just stop. Sucking in a breath, she straightened up. "Okay," she said. "Okay."

The water was scalding, hotter than she would have normally been able to stand it, but she washed her hair, then turned the heat down to rinse. She stood, hands propped on either side of the spray against the tile, letting the water run down through her hair, down her body. Head down, eyes closed, her legs weak, rubbery.

She put on the Turkish robe Scott had given her for Christmas. Back out in the living room, she stood for a moment looking down at the couch. A jasmine-scented breeze ruffled the bougainvillea. She couldn't imagine that it was still daylight. Too much had happened since she had come to Kaplan Hall to pick Scott up, after which the plan was that they would go out to dinner in Santa Monica.

But unexpectedly, Scott's advisor, Roger Crane, PhD, had been in Scott's tiny TA office when Marian had gotten there. In the publish or perish world of academia, he was on the verge of a major coup; his article on one of those ridiculous English major themes—"Hamlet as a Mannerist Work"—had been tentatively accepted as the lead, featured quarterly essay by one of those ridiculous, esoteric and yet oh so influential publications, Yale University Press's *Timeless Stratford*.

A huge coup!

The only problem was that Yale had sent the galley proofs to Dr. Crane earlier today, and the corrections—proofreading and vetting the text and the 142 footnotes in the forty-three-page essay, roughly one footnote per sentence of text—had to be submitted first thing tomorrow. Meanwhile, Dr. Crane himself had to be at the Teacher of the Year dinner tonight. There was no getting out of it. As the head of the English Department at UCLA, he couldn't plead out of attending; this was a huge fundraising gala and Dr. Crane had put together a table of ten—Trustees and their spouses—as his personal guests. He could not, at this late hour, bow out.

But that left his essay in need of a last and most perfect (Crane called it the "pluperfect") edit, and Crane was in Scott's office because he was the graduate student in the entire English Department whom Crane trusted most. This was a bit of an unplanned crisis, true, but Scott—if he could find space in his own grueling schedule—could single-handedly save the day. Scott had a future (he hadn't needed to say "finally") here at UCLA. As soon as he finished his thesis, and he was on the fast track . . .

There was really no alternative. Scott would be pulling a late one.

He was a charmer, Roger was. He hated to ruin their night's plans, but this favor was something that Roger would never forget.

And say, how about if he drove Marian home? Leave the car she'd come down here to pick up Scott in and save her the trouble of having to come and get him when he finished his edits sometime after midnight. Roger had been over to their condo before, at their open house when they'd moved in and he knew that he had to pass right by it to get to his own home.

What a generous offer, she'd thought. How could she refuse?

She shook her head, trying to clear it. Someone honked down in the street, a million miles away.

She knew she should do something, but nothing seemed feasible. Her stomach was still hurting, at the same time making her nauseous. She turned back away from the open window. Her cellphone was in her purse and she went to where it sat on the kitchen counter.

She couldn't get her mind around what had happened. It wasn't the way she'd ever imagined it—someone she didn't know pulling her into some bushes, or skulking in a darkened parking lot. It hadn't been anything like that.

She picked up the phone. Who did she think she was going to call? The police? Scott? Scott was still working.

She put the phone down. To call anyone would mean Scott's job—after three years slaving away already in the doctoral program. It was the only real academic position Scott had ever had, the only one he could get after being wait-listed at five other universities, and then the gig here at UCLA only because Roger Crane's father was a friend of Scott's father.

Otherwise, who would have accepted a guy who'd been in so much trouble, even if it was only for selling weed in college? All that was long ago, Marian knew, but people didn't forget.

She knew it hadn't just been a few joints, either. And he hadn't been near those people, that scene, since long before he'd met her. He was straight now, thank God, but back in the day, nobody had wanted to risk the commitment to Scott—until Dr. Roger Crane had stepped up and taken him on.

What was she thinking? Who cared about the stupid TA job? Who cared about the degree? Next to what had just happened . . .

She crossed to the couch again, intending to sit on it, but found that she couldn't make herself do it. The couch wasn't hers anymore. She settled down to the floor.

Her own drink, untouched, was sitting in a small pool of condensed water on the glass-topped coffee table. The water had run to the edge and when she sat on the floor, jostling the table, the surface tension broke and the water dripped onto the rug. She sat cross-legged and rubbed the water into the rug for a moment. The she slugged back her own gin in two quick gulps.

At last she grabbed the two glasses—hers and Roger's—and brought them over to the kitchen. Opening the trash compactor, she dropped them in. She pushed the button and heard the satisfying crunching sound. Then she got the window cleaner and paper towels and went back to clean the glass table top.

Outside across her balcony, dusk had finally progressed. The sky was still blue but Venus was up.

Her damp hair suddenly sent a chill through her and she went back to the bathroom to wrap a towel around it. Opening the medicine cabinet, taking down the bottle of valium that Scott had needed for his back spasms last year, she shook out a few of the pills and washed them down with water from her cupped hands, then dried her face on the robe's lapel.

Back in the bedroom, she pulled the curtains and lay down on the bed.

It was almost dark.

She closed her eyes.

Scott was next to her. She bolted up. It was light again—a strong gin and four valiums equaled morning.

"Scott!"

He appeared naked in the bathroom door, half his face lathered. He'd already showered—his hair ruffled from drying it. "Hi," he said. "A little tired last night, were you?"

It started to come back. Say something, she told herself. *Say something!*

But he had already turned back, always in a good mood in the morning, singing a Kenny Chesney island song aloud now that she was awake.

Still in the robe she'd slept in, she got out of bed and came to the bathroom doorway. Scott was shaving, paying attention to the whiskers around his dimple. Pulling at his skin, his mouth every which way, he said, "The shower water's all warmed up. Why don't you hop in and I'll get the coffee going?" He stretched his skin some more. "Did you have a nice talk with Roger?"

There. *Now!*

But Scott kept up the patter. "I'm sorry I was so late. These fucking academics, I tell you. It would be nice if they planned ahead. I mean, they've known their deadline at Yale for a month, maybe more. And still, they send us the galleys yesterday? Are you kidding me? So we get to the last minute and it's total madness."

He rinsed the last of the lather from his face, splashed on some aftershave.

She came up against him then, opening her robe against his body, holding him, smelling his good smell.

Could last night really have happened? Yes.

Yes. She had to tell him.

"Scott."

"Shoot!" He cocked his head at the noise from the street, a heavy machine grinding. "Garbage. Friday."

"Wait!"

He was pulling on some jeans. He glanced at the digital clock next to the bed. "What?"

Once he took out the garbage, there wouldn't be any evidence left. It would only be her word against Roger's.

Light-headed and weak, she crossed back to him again. "One last hug."

"Will do. But let's hope it's not really the last." He went to her, gave her a quick embrace, then bounced young and carefree out of the room.

She heard him pull out the trash compactor bag.

Her feet wouldn't move. She was terrified that he'd see something. But how could that be? He wasn't about to go through the garbage, was he?

But she had to make him see what was in there. How could she explain? Would he ask about the two glasses? The wet washcloth? Would it look like she was trying to hide that stuff, somehow, as though she were guilty of something?

But in any event, he would have to see it eventually, wouldn't he, if he was to know, if he was to believe her?

She had to let him know before he saw anything on his own.

She had to just tell him the truth.

Her cellphone chirped next to her bed. Automatically, she stepped toward it just as she heard Scott open the front door, going out with the garbage. The door closed behind him.

She picked up her phone. "Mar, it's Nan. I forgot if you said you needed a ride in today."

Marian sat down on the bed. Was she really planning to go to work? How, today, could she teach kids anything?

But Nan was going along, life was going along. Like nothing had ever happened.

She didn't remember whether or not she had told Nan she wanted to drive in with her. Did Scott still have work to do on Roger's article? Did he have something he needed the car for today? And if he did, would he have time to take her out to school?

And Nan was offering.

"Sure. That'd be good."

"Quarter to eight?"

"Okay."

Here was Scott, back inside. She put her phone down on the bedside table and heard the front door close again behind him. The garbage was gone. Scott opened the sliding doors to the balcony and she caught a whiff of the jasmine. Down below them, out in the street, the grinding noise of the truck abated as it rolled away.

In the bedroom doorway, Scott appeared. "Just made it. Who was that?"

"Nan. Volunteering to drive us in. So the car's yours if you want it."

"Great. I've got to be in early anyway to finish up the Hamlet. That Nan is a godsend."

"Yes she is."

Scott gave her a worried look. "Are you all right?"

She sighed. "I think so. Just a little tired maybe."

"With all that sleep?" But he came over next to her, put his arms around her, kissed the side of her face. "What we need is a couple of days off together, you know that?"

"That would be so good." Her eyes met his for a second, then she had to look down. "I love you."

He rolled her back onto the bed, playful as a puppy. Her robe fell open and he growled his wild beast growl. It was a joke between them. They had jokes.

"Do I still look good to you?" she asked, wondering how in the world there could be no sign of it. None at all.

"You look beautiful," he said. "Completely beautiful." He glanced back at the clock. "What time is Nan coming?"

She told him and he moaned and sat up, mock pouting. "Dang. That pretty much gives us no time. You'd better go get in that shower. And maybe I should take another cold one myself."

She smelled the jasmine again, the sweet smell of innocence.

She knew that as soon as she told Scott, that innocence would be forever behind them. And here he was now, his sweet self next to her. She reached over and put an arm around him.

She had to tell him. Every second was making it less and less believable. She knew that. And then with the force of a blow it occurred to her that he might not believe it. He might not believe her. There was no sign of any struggle, and he knew she'd had a lot of men before.

He gave her a friendly pat on the back, then stood up, humming again. Happy.

She got up behind him and went to turn on the shower.

What if he didn't believe her? Or mostly believed her but thought she might have flirted a little with Roger. After all, she had invited Roger in, made them drinks. It would be an easy thing to think.

And if she said nothing, then what? Would Roger do anything again? If he did, if he even tried, she'd know what to do next time. She'd get physical, make him hurt her, leave a mark so there couldn't be any doubt. Then call the police.

Immediately. She saw that that mattered. You had to act right away.

Now, this time, she had to admit, it didn't even look to herself like she'd fought him. And she had. Hadn't she? She was starting to doubt herself. Had she fought hard enough? But if she'd fought him harder, might he even have killed her? That's what it had felt like.

The shower water ran down over her again.

Scott hadn't seen any sign of it on her. She looked down at her body, clean and unmarked.

Last night was when she should have done something, she told herself. Right afterwards. She should have called Scott and told him then. Have him come home, get together with the police. She'd missed her chance.

Scott brought in a glass of orange juice and put it on the sink's counter. "A magic elixir for the lovely princess," he said.

"Thank you." Then: "Scott?"

At that second, the egg timer rang in the kitchen. He held up a finger. "One sec."

Then he was back, holding a towel for her. "Okay. What were you going to say?"

She stepped into the soft, dry towel, in his arms, and leaned into him. "Nothing," she said. "I forget. I guess it wasn't too important."

Foundational Education

by Seanan McGuire

M ost of the people Eloise had gone to high school with had entered
senior year with a list of colleges as long as their arm, organized according to "dream colleges"—the alma maters they were reasonably sure
they wouldn't be able to get into, but still had to try for, to fulfill whatever
point of family honor was at stake—and "safety schools," which were universities they didn't really *want* to go to, but would lower themselves to attending if they absolutely had to. El's list had begun and ended with a single
school, U.C. Johnson's Crossing. Her guidance counselor had called her
single-minded focus both "brave" and "a little foolish," trying to convince
her to add at least a few more of the U.C.s to her list. Steadfast, Eloise had
refused.

After four years of being one of the only scholarship students—or, as
her classmates liked to remind her on a regular basis, "charity cases"—at a
college magnet high school, Eloise had grown very good at refusing. The
people with their lists, they didn't seem to understand, or maybe didn't
care, that every application came with an associated fee, or that some of
them were a lot dearer than the U.C. system's seventy dollars. Their parents
had deep pockets and open checkbooks; they were willing to pay anything
to secure the future for their precious children, whose only accomplishment in life to date had been germinating in the right class of womb.

Eloise lacked any such advantages. She'd been admitted to Graystone
Preparatory because the district required them to take a certain number

of "gifted students" from the rest of the district if they wanted to retain their accreditation; she'd studied for most of eighth grade in order to pass their tests, recognizing Graystone as her only clear path out of the poverty that had claimed her parents, hot tar around their feet, sucking them down into the darkness, and was already primed to claim her siblings. Graystone had been a rope, and when it was thrown, not at her, but in her general direction, she had grabbed hold and hung on for dearest life, unwilling to concede for even a moment to the idea that she was going to drown with the rest of them.

All the scholarship students were like her, clinging as hard as they could to the potential of a future that had never been a promise, not for a moment, not for them. The only other student from her neighborhood had been a girl named Heather, silly and sweet and an incredibly gifted artist. Sometimes Eloise wondered what schools Heather would have applied to, if she would have been more ambitious, or if they might have been roommates Freshman year. Dwelling on the past never changed anything, and there were never enough ropes to go around.

Even if there had been, all the ropes in the world couldn't summon application fees out of the ether. So Eloise stuck stubbornly to her single school plan, knowing all the while that if she got turned down, all her hard work would be for nothing. She paid her seventy dollars, scraped together a quarter at a time, and she sent off her paperwork, and she waited. And she waited. And just as she began to feel like all was lost, she received her invitation to the promised land in the form of a fat white envelope that *smelled* of money, crisp vellum paper and expensive ink from a printer that had never once received a "cartridge low" warning in its electronic life. Eloise held it balanced across her palms, staring down at it. Her future was inside. For good or ill, it was set. All that remained was to bring it into the light.

The sound of the envelope ripping was almost obscene, like the sound of a wedding dress being torn. Eloise closed her eyes as she worked the letter out of the remains of its protective sheath, unfolding it by feel before she opened them again.

The words seemed to swim, black against white, until she blinked hard and forced them into inexorable focus.

Then, slowly, she smiled.

Orientation took place on campus, naturally; that was what the incoming freshmen needed to orient themselves to, after all. Eloise had been there before. All the Graystone kids had, even the ones who were bound for Harvard, or Yale, or Miskatonic, choosing the splendors of the Ivy League over the down-home delights of the state school system. This was the first time she'd been present as a student, though, as someone with a *right* to be there, not a visiting high schooler doing a project for the Model United Nations or the mathletes. Eloise walked slowly, face tilted up so that the shade from the live oaks lining the path fell across her eyes, turning day into gentle twilight. She had already received her orientation packet and her new student paperwork. All that waited now was the arrival of her tour guide.

"Um, hello?" The voice was light, hesitant, and about an octave higher than Eloise's own. She lowered her head and opened her eyes, gazing at the curly-haired blonde in front of her. "Are you Eloise Field?"

"I am," Eloise allowed.

The blonde beamed. There was no other word for the expression; it was like watching the sun figure out that there was a way out from behind the clouds. "I'm Karen," she said, in a giddy chirp. "I'm your campus guide today. I understand you're joining us from Graystone High?"

It seemed a little odd that the campus tour guide should know which high school she was coming from, but only a little; Eloise had never been through a college orientation before, and couldn't say what normal looked like. "I am," she replied, with a bob of her head. "Is it just us today?"

"Oh, we'll have a few more students for the walkthrough, but you looked new—not that that's a bad thing! We were all new once, right?" Karen chuckled, a little uncertainly, like she expected Eloise to argue.

"I had some questions about this map," said Eloise, extracting the offending piece of paper from her packet. "I've been trying to find my way to the residence halls—they're marked right here—but no matter which way I turn at the library, I never seem to find them."

"Oh, I can help you with that, absolutely. Where do they have you bunking?"

"Abbot."

"Abbot Hall? That's a good one. They don't take many freshmen. It's a quiet place, study-oriented, no real nightlife to speak of."

Eloise nodded. "It was one of the only dorms covered by my financial aid, which seemed a little odd to me, but I don't have anything to compare it to," she said. "I'm glad to hear that it's a good one." On some level, when she'd seen the restrictions on the available residence halls, she'd been concerned that this was another case of "good enough for the poor people, not good enough for the people who actually matter." That was a train of thought she'd encountered more times than she cared to consider during her high school years, where zip code and parental income were all, and intelligence and ambition were almost shameful.

"One of the best," said Karen happily. Karen seemed to be one of those people who did everything happily. Karen probably went to the doctor for vaccinations happily, and thanked the nurse who stuck the needle in her arm. It would be easy to like her. It would be even easier to hate her. Heather would have found a way to do both at once. "I bunked there for my first year! Abbot is a wonderful place to stay while you get your bearings and learn how to navigate the campus!"

"If it's so wonderful, why did you change residences?"

Karen waved a hand airily. "My number didn't come up until late in this year's housing lottery, and by that point, all the single rooms in Abbot were taken. They set a certain number aside for incoming freshmen, which makes it difficult for existing students to get in. But don't worry! Your RAs will be people who are already familiar with the hall, and can help you get situated."

"Oh."

"Come on, now." Karen beamed as she started walking, gesturing for

Eloise to follow her. "The rest of our group is going to be waiting on the quad!"

The rest of their group turned out to be four more students as new as Eloise. Three of them had the languid, satiated look she associated with her high school classmates; they were the pampered housecats of the academic world, and like all housecats, they still had the potential to be killers. She watched them carefully. The fourth was a tall boy, so thin he seemed almost like he would disappear if he turned sideways, with the same restless, wary air that she saw whenever she looked into her own mirror. Another scholarship student. He was also the only one of the four rooming in Abbot Hall. Eloise smiled at him and said, "It'll be good to see a familiar face around the building," which seemed to settle his nerves somewhat, even as it did nothing for her own, which were on high, screaming alert as Karen walked them around the campus, pointing out the spots they would need to know—the library, the cafeteria, the bus depot—and steered them away from spots that were better left avoided.

"We're a reasonably safe campus, but no place is guaranteed to be a hundred percent safe a hundred percent of the time," she said, waving at a dark corner formed by the intersection of two buildings. "There have been muggings at Disneyland. The best way to stay safe is to stay aware of your surroundings, and not go wandering around alone at night. I don't care how many self-defense classes you've taken or how fast a runner you are, I care about you enjoying your time here with us in a safe and productive way that doesn't need to involve the police."

The three housecat children of the open wallet laughed dismissively, all of them clearly confident that they had nothing to worry about; Eloise and the paper boy, whose name was Charles, took careful note of the limits of the dangerous places, skirting around them as broadly as Karen did. Every space came with unwritten rules as well as written ones, and knowing those rules could be the difference between not only success or failure, but survival or . . . not survival. None of Eloise's academic efforts to date had actually carried the possibility of death as a consequence, but that didn't mean she was going to let herself get sloppy now, not when she was so close to being done with school forever and stepping out into the world on a supposedly even footing with everyone else.

The tour concluded at the edge of campus, where the residence halls loomed in silent invitation to come closer, come see where you're going to live until the school year ends, come put yourselves into our hands. "For those of you living here with us on campus, move-in is next weekend," said Karen, still happily. "Your RAs and building managers will be happy to help you get situated. Charles, Eloise, I know you're in Abbot; that's the pinkish building on the corner. Marcus, I believe you're in Filbert. That will be the green building on the opposite corner."

The other two housecats, freed from the indignity of living in student housing, smirked as they exchanged a look, clearly glorying in their own superiority. Eloise suppressed a surge of hot disdain that felt almost like hatred. She couldn't start hating people for having more than she did now, not when she was standing on the cusp of four years of insufficient scholarships and financial aid. If she was lucky, she wouldn't wind up working in the cafeteria. There was nothing wrong with having a job, but she wanted to work off-campus, where she wouldn't have to face the prying eyes of her peers. Everyone told her college wouldn't be like high school, that people were more tolerant of differences, that she'd be able to pick and choose her social group, but so far, she'd seen nothing to support that. The presence of the housecats was proof enough that nothing ever really changed.

"And that's the end of our tour," chirped Karen.

Eloise pulled out her phone as she turned to Charles. "Since we're going to be neighbors, can I get your number?" she asked, and offered it to him, watching as he laboriously input his information. Then she smiled, said, "I'll text you," and walked away before the housecats could offer to exchange information—assuming they would. She didn't want to know them that well. She just wanted to go.

Charles was standing in front of Abbot Hall with a cardboard box in his arms when she arrived for move-in the next weekend, all her worldly goods jammed into the back of her grandmother's old station wagon. She pulled into one of the last open parking spots and climbed out of the car, planting her hands at the small of her back as she stretched. No one had been available to help her carry her boxes out of the house, and she already ached. Abbot didn't have working elevators, one more small sign of ableism in academia, and she wasn't looking forward to carrying her things up three flights of stairs.

"Eloise!" called Charles, waving. "My parents are inside, getting me checked in. You can meet them if you want. I—" He stopped, peering at her conspicuously passenger-free car. "Are you on your own?"

"My parents aren't so sure about this whole 'college' thing," she said, trying to sound like it didn't bother her, like she was the one who'd suggested they stay home watching football and drinking beer on the day she moved onto campus. "Mom's probably already painting my room. She wants a craft room."

"Oh," said Charles, sounding a little puzzled. "Well, Dad and I'll be happy to help you carry your things in."

"I can't let you do that," protested Eloise. "I'm on the third floor."

Charles snorted. "If you don't let us do that, Mom's going to have my hide for being ungentlemanly. Come on. Let me be a good neighbor?"

Reluctantly, Eloise nodded. "I guess that would be okay," she said. She'd done this to herself, she knew, when she'd asked him for his number. She'd been trying to be friendly, not friends, but sometimes the distinction could be a fine one, and it would be nice to have more people to help her move in. Maybe having a friend again wouldn't be so bad. She'd been lonely since Heather had . . . gone away. It didn't have to change her plans, now or ever. Charles was in Abbot with her, incoming student too poor to buy himself anything nicer. He'd understand.

His parents were nice enough people. His father was built along the same cadaverous lines as he was, while his mother was pleasantly plump, and bustled around the men in her life like an aggressively friendly barnyard hen, more than willing to take Eloise under her metaphorical wing once she realized the girl was on her own. In what felt like no time at all, Charlie and his family had all her things upstairs, positioned in her half of the double room she was going to be sharing with some other incoming student, who had yet to put in an appearance.

"Thank you so much," said Eloise once they were finished and standing back out on the lawn, her new parking sticker blazing neon pink in the back window of her station wagon, her back aching like it was on fire, but all of her boxes in their new homes, ready for her to unpack them and begin her new life.

"Don't thank me too much," said Charles. "I don't have a car. I'm going to be asking for a lot of rides."

Eloise laughed, and somehow, the day had been perfect, despite all the reasons it shouldn't have been, despite all the little things that had gone wrong. She was a college girl now. She was on her way.

A month later, Eloise was a lot less sure she'd made the right choices. Her roommate, a pleasant physical education major named Martha, snored like she thought she was being graded by the decibel, and had solidly rebuffed polite suggestions that she look into a sleep study or something to figure out why. The food in the cafeteria seemed determined to find as many innovative new ways of being both starchy and as tasteless as possible; Eloise was starting to think that the fabled "freshman fifteen" came entirely out of the campus vending machines. And the housecats were everywhere.

In the freshman class. In the upper classes. Populating the sororities and fraternities that thrived in the admittedly small but still present off-campus Greek Row. Getting a job on campus marked you instantly as a scholarship student, and opened you to being treated like a mouse by the rich, bored, lazy students who had come to the state school because they couldn't get admitted anywhere else, and who thought grades were something to be purchased at their leisure. Getting a job off campus was virtually impossible; they had all been snatched up by more experienced students before the midpoint of the summer, and the few openings were things she either wasn't qualified for or had less interest in doing than she had need for money.

Grimly, she thought that if this situation continued much longer, cleaning cages at the pet store might start to seem appealing.

She marched through her classes, turned in her homework, took her tests, and pushed herself to excel in all areas, knowing how fragile her position was, and would be until she took steps to secure it. The days shortened and turned colder, plummeting into fall, until October arrived with the scent of spices and dried leaves, and substandard pumpkin pie began appearing on the cafeteria menu. Eloise unpacked her sweaters, bundling herself into them, and allowed Charles to walk her to class in the gloaming, neither of them happy with the idea of her being out alone after dark.

Some of the housecats cornered her one night on her way to the door after Poly Sci. "Look at the little nerd," one of them said, his tone a perfect mirror for all the boys who'd tormented her in high school, until they'd figured out that there were other, softer targets available, targets who didn't work as hard to both blend in socially and stand out academically. Eloise had always been the darling of her teachers and, when that wasn't enough, had other ways of protecting herself. She smiled at the boy who'd spoken, lips thin, and waited silently for him to step out of her path.

He didn't. Instead, he leaned over and put a hand on her shoulder, leaning closer. "Abbot can't be nearly as nice as the backseat of my car," he said, earning snickers from his friends. "Want to take a look?"

Eloise shrugged his hand off, and continued to smile her tight, cold smile. "It's almost October," she said. "I'll remember what you look like." She pushed through the group and opened the door, stepping out into the night where Charles was waiting.

He gave her a curious look. "What took you so long?"

"Just updating some lists," she said.

October began in thunder and rain, the heavens gaping wide and pouring their contents onto the paths and buildings of the Johnson's Crossing campus. Eloise, still in her pajamas, waited for her roommate to leave, having already emailed her professors to tell them she wasn't feeling well and would be missing class. The cocoa she'd made the night before had cooled, untouched, on her bedside table. Charles had taken his cup with him when he left. If she had any regrets about what she was about to do, they centered on Charles. She would have been happier if it hadn't been him. But it always had to be someone. Her freshman year of high school, it had been Heather. Heather had been sweet and funny and fun to spend time with, she'd eaten cheese sandwiches from the cafeteria almost every day, and Eloise still missed her even after all these years.

The rain poured down outside the window. Eloise slid out of bed and fished the container of salt from beneath her pillow, carrying it to the center of the room. Cleaning up was going to be annoying, but all her research had failed to find any better approach than the traditional circle of salt studded with iron nails. Sometimes the old ways were the best. They'd been tested and refined and written down by the survivors, after all.

She poured the salt. She stepped into the circle, and spoke the words. The air grew sweet and treacle-thick around her, stilling utterly. And the shadows puddled in the corners of the room flowed together into a column that twisted itself into something very like the shape of a man, and nothing like the shape of a man at all. It was amorphous, terrible to look at, painful to exist in the presence of. Eloise gazed upon it, unflinching, and extended a hand holding a single sheet of paper on which a list had been written. Some were names; others were descriptions, down to details of the clothing those people had been wearing at the moment they became candidates for this day's work. All were scribed in red-brown ink that flaked in places, leaving plain paper behind.

"The sacrifice has been made, or you wouldn't have come," she said, voice still as a stone. "These also are yours, to take at your leisure."

"The same as before, then?" asked the figure. Its voice, in contrast with its appearance, was honey-sweet and smooth, difficult to turn away from. It had to have some lure with which to catch the fish, or it would never have cast its hooks into the world. "Your time here will be well-fortuned. You will prosper and thrive. Your studies will be fruitful, and your days will be lonely, for the taint of my service will linger on your flesh."

Eloise closed her eyes, trying not to think of Charles. Sweet, energetic Charles, who would never see graduation, thanks to the generous dose of amanita she'd mixed into his cocoa the night before. It was a tragedy and a shame. It was a necessary evil. Like Heather before him, he would make sure she got to where she needed to go.

The housecats walked through their lives with all the advantages in the world. Was it really a crime for her to do what she could to secure an advantage of her own? And all it cost was her immortal soul. A small price to pay to make the Dean's List.

"Agreed," she said, and opened her eyes, and watched as the figure split back into its component shadows and disappeared.

The outbreak of food poisoning on the U.C. Johnson's Crossing campus which claimed the lives of twenty-seven students was eventually traced back to the pumpkin pie in the cafeteria. Classes were cancelled for a week. Charles's mother cried on Eloise's shoulder while Eloise patted her arm and made what she hoped would sound like soothing noises.

The academic year went on.

Goon #4

by Tod Goldberg

Goon Number Four hasn't been able to take a shit since landing in Dubai—which was, when? Yesterday morning? Jet lag has him all fucked up. He'd flown commercial, which was a bad sign. If you can afford a goon, get a private jet. Twenty-some hours with layovers and delays, and then Goon Number 7 picked him up at the airport, drove him to the Monaco Hotel, told him he'd be back in ninety minutes, so get showered, look fucking presentable, he was on the clock now. So Number 4 checked in, went up to his room, got out of his Adidas sweat suit, scrubbed himself raw in the shower—before he did a job, he always shaved all the hair off of his body, which made him look more menacing, but also he wasn't about leaving his DNA all over the fucking place—changed into the black Armani suit he got at the outlet stores in Cabazon, about thirty minutes from his condo in Palm Springs.

He picked at a plate of fruit. Drank a bottle of water. Checked his email on his encrypted phone. His sister Jackie sent him a proof of life photo of his cocker spaniel Thor, Jackie holding up a newspaper next to Thor's head, except Jackie had photoshopped it to say *Ruff You Were Here*. Jackie was a good sister. The only family he had left. "Don't you know yet," she said when she dropped him off at the airport, five a.m., not a soul around, "if you have enough money now?"

"For what?"

"For whatever."

Now, sitting in the front seat of a blacked-out Suburban, a locked brief-case on his lap, two other blacked-out Suburbans riding behind him in the arrow formation, the Arabian Desert streaming by, Goon Number Four found himself contemplating what "whatever" might be, while also scanning the horizon for . . . a Starbucks, if he was being honest, or a bush. Somewhere discreet. Because it turned out, he did have enough. This could be his last real job.

"How much longer?" Number Four asked.

"Twenty klicks," Number Seven said.

Klicks. Four seriously doubted Seven had ever been military. Four did two tours in Iraq, another as contract black ops, and he wasn't saying klicks. "I didn't ask how far," Four said. "I asked how long."

"What's the difference?" Seven said. Definitely not military.

"The difference is the difference between time and distance," Four said.

"Speedometer is in miles," Seven said. "Now you want me to do math?"

Four looked up into the rearview mirror, met eyes with Goon Number Three. This wasn't their first job together. Last time was in Peru. A fucking bloodbath on the streets of Lima. Time before that was a private security thing. Walking around Coachella in shorts. His own backyard, since he lived in Palm Springs. Easy job. Making sure no one put hands on someone's daughter and her friends, ten sorority girls up from USC, each with a Tri-Delt tattoo on the small of their backs, angel-wings strapped over their shoulders, all of them rolling on Molly. Not exactly storming Fallujah.

"Stay frosty," Seven said. "Two o'clock."

Four looked at two o'clock. Nothing but desert. At *eleven o'clock*, however, there was a trail of dust being kicked up from three Hummers moving at an intercept angle. This dumb fuck. He was going to get them all killed. He couldn't even tell time.

"Any idea what's so valuable in the case?" Three asked.

"Nope," Four said. It wasn't heavy, so it probably wasn't cash or gold bricks. These days, if something was being handed over like this, it was usually technology. Four's specialty, in situations like this, was to be the guy who walked up with the briefcase, set it down, took a step back and mad dogged everyone else until the case was popped. It wasn't hard work. Most of the time, everything went fine. The other 35 percent of the time, yeah, maybe he shot a guy, slit a couple throats, broke arms and legs, gouged out eyes, set fire to a mound of corpses, but that was growing rarer these days. You wanted to kill someone and had the cash to hire a bunch of goons, you also had the cash to get a decent drone.

Which made Four wonder about something. He opened up the moon roof, scanned the sky. Triton drones coasted at 65,000 feet, which was basically outer space. If he was getting blown up from outer space, that's just how it was going to be.

"Close that," Seven said. "Sand makes my asthma go nuts." He took a Kleenex from the center console, blew his nose. "Intercept in four klicks."

"Easy on that klick shit," Three said. He was checking the clip on his AK. "We get out of this situation," Three said to Four, "I'm going to buy a boat, park it off the Oregon coast, and become a private detective. Find missing cats for little old ladies. What about you?"

"I'm going back to school," Goon Number Four said.

"To study what?" Goon Number Three asked.

"Whatever."

"Just don't study history," Three said. "It's just war, war, war, genocide, war. In that order." He leaned into the front seat to get a better look at the Hummers coming their way, since the windows in the back were blacked out. "This is not good. Must be a tracker in here." He tapped his earpiece. "Comms are dead."

"I scanned the case," Goon Number Four said. "It was clean." He paused. "What about art?"

"That could be cool," Four said. "Tracker is somewhere in this ride or else they would have come up behind us. No sense coming from where we can see them." He glanced at Goon Number Seven, then back at Four, motioned to the floor, so Four put the briefcase on the ground. "How far until intercept, boss?"

"Two klicks," Seven said, which is when Three put a bullet in his temple. Goon Number Four grabbed the steering wheel. Three reached around and opened the driver's side door, shoved Seven out, the Suburban caught his body under the back tires, slowing the truck down enough for Four to slide into the driver's seat. He looked in the rearview, saw one of the trail cars thump over the body, too. Three got up next to Four, put the briefcase on his lap. "Do you draw?" Goon Number Three asked.

"Isn't art mostly on computers now?"

Three held up a finger, tapped his earpiece again. "Copy that." He turned to Four. "Hard right . . . now!" Four yanked the wheel to the right, just as a missile impacted with the Hummers, blowing them to oblivion. "Well, whatever you do, don't ever say *klicks* in the real world, copy?"

"Copy."

It took Goon Number Four two weeks to get home, his sister picking him up at the Palm Springs airport at noon on a Tuesday. "You look like shit, Blake," Jackie said when Goon Number Four got into her car. It had been a good long time since he'd heard his actual name. Long enough that it sort of jarred him. "What happened to your left ear?"

He ran his fingers over the ragged stitch job he received to reattach a chunk of cartilage. "A fight."

"With what? A dog?"

"Yes."

"Did you get a rabies shot?"

"I'm clear," he said. "How's Thor, incidentally?"

"He missed you," she said. "He's at PetSmart getting pretty for you."

"Did you do that thing I asked?"

"It's in the glove box."

Blake popped open the glove box. It was filled with black and purple chips from the various Indian casinos in town. He kept a great deal of his cash in casino chips these days, stashed in safe deposit boxes. It was just easier. And portable. He needed to move a quarter of a million dollars, he didn't need to bother with a wire transfer. But that wasn't what he was looking for. "What about the other thing?" he said.

"It's in there, too, in the envelope." Blake found what he was looking for, a slim manila envelope, opened it up, dumped the information on his lap. "You'll need to get a student ID in person, but that's all of your registration materials. I couldn't get you all the classes you wanted at the times you preferred. I guess there's priority registration for returning students."

"No worries," Blake said. His sister had signed him up for classes on Mondays, Wednesdays, and Fridays at the College of the Desert, the local community college. He'd driven by the campus a thousand times, marveled at the slick glass structures they'd erected for students who couldn't get into a four-year college, never thinking he'd end up there himself. He'd taken the GED and gone right into the armed forces for twelve years, which had then dovetailed into this goon work he'd been doing for the last decade. The upside was that he got to travel all over the world, made a lot of money for standing in the background, arms crossed in front of him, eyes behind sunglasses, looking bad ass. But of late his back and knees had begun to trouble him, doctors telling him he was about five years from needing a knee replacement, he needed corrective glasses to see at night, and he'd had a persistent prostate infection for a month in fucking Colombia, standing in a jungle like an asshole, needing to piss every nine minutes. This goon shit had an expiration date, turned out, and there was no health plan or retirement program. Fortunately, he'd invested and saved, Jackie told him to buy Facebook in 2012, since she was dating someone in the company at the time, and then he had chips around the world. Lots of chips. "What do I need to know?" he asked.

"I got you whatever was still open. Mostly big general education classes." Made sense. She'd signed him up under his own name, which he supposed was fine. He had passports and birth certificates for about a dozen other pseudonyms. But he only had actual high school records as Blake Webster, since no Afghani warlord was going to check to see if one of his fake names had passed Algebra II.

He had four classes. English Composition, Western Civilizations, Math, and then something he didn't recognize.

"What's JOUR 121?"

"Oh," Jackie said, "yeah, I thought that might be fun for you. It's working at the college radio station."

"Doing what?"

"I guess learning how to be a DJ? Or maybe a talk radio host? You could be like that asshole with all the conspiracy theories."

"Which one?"

"Yeah," Jackie said. "Him."

They came to a stoplight. On the corner was MillionAir, the private airstrip Blake often flew out of. How many times had he walked off of some sheik's Gulfstream G650 with someone else's blood still under his fingernails?

"Are you really doing this, Blake?" his sister asked. "Do I get to stop worrying about you dying?"

"I'm still going to die," Blake said, "but I'm probably not going to have to kill anyone for a while. Does that make you feel better?"

The light turned green. "A little."

That next Monday, the start of spring semester, Blake showed up for JOUR 121, his ten a.m. class, promptly at 9:30 a.m., because when you're a goon, you recon. The class was held in a classroom inside the radio station offices, located across the street from the main campus, next door to a sprawling Mormon church and a gated community called Rancho Del Sol. It looked to Blake like maybe the college had bought a house, did a light remodel, and then built a radio tower in the backyard. He'd seen a similar setup at a Sinaloa stronghold in Mexico, where the bosses basically ran their own private radio, TV, and Internet network, though the College of the Desert's setup wasn't nearly as nice.

You walked in, there was a classroom filled with Macs on your left— Blake thought it probably used to be the garage—and then a couple studios for the DJ down the hall in what used to be the living room, dining room, and family room, the house from the seventies, back when people had family rooms. Other side of the house were faculty offices, a lounge, two bathrooms. There were emergency exits in every room. Whole place was maybe 2,500 square feet and could be attacked from about twenty-nine different angles. A totally unsafe spot to conduct an op . . . but Blake guessed it was probably fine for learning.

The classroom tables were set up in a U, so Blake took a seat against the southern wall, giving him a view of all the entrances and exits. Took out his Smith & Wesson tactical pen—it was a ballpoint, but it was made of aircraft steel, the cap was sharp enough to pierce a sternum, with enough force, and/or pop out a car window, and it weighed over a pound, so if you held it in your hand and punched someone in the face, you'd collapse their fucking skull—and a pad of paper.

And then waited.

A woman in black jeans, black boots, a black scoop necked T-shirt, and huge black sunglasses came into the classroom in a flustered rush, dropped a book bag and a laptop on the podium at the front of the room, then spilled her full, giant Starbucks cup on the ground, coffee splashing all over her, the podium, the whiteboard, and, Blake was surprised to see, even the low, cottage cheese ceiling. "Shit fuck motherfuck cocksucker motherfucker," she said and then hurried back out, returning a few moments later with a roll of paper towel, only then noticing Blake. "How long have you been sitting there?"

"Twenty-three minutes."

"So you saw that whole production?"

"Yes."

"And you didn't laugh?"

"It didn't seem funny."

"It's always funny when your professor spills coffee all over herself at school," she said. "It's what makes going to school worthwhile." She stood on one of the chairs. "Help me here so I don't break my neck while I clean off the ceiling." All six feet, five inches and 245 pounds of Blake stood up then and the professor seemed visibly surprised. "Check that. You get up here. I'll make sure you don't break your neck."

Blake had some experience cleaning spatters of fluids off of hard-to-reach places, so it was no big deal. Back when he was starting out, he did a month working for a Latvian oil scion/two-bit gangster named Vitaly Ozoles who was constantly losing his shit and shooting someone in the face. Since Blake was the lowest goon, he'd have to drag the body out, bury it, then come back and clean the room up, so he had a whole checklist, literally, that he kept in a utility closet in the warehouse which housed Vitaly's fleet of a dozen cars. This was a significantly easier job. He climbed up on the chair, took his KA-BAR knife out of his cargo pants pocket, scraped the latte-stained cottage cheese pellets off into his hand, then got down, dumped it all into the garbage.

"Thank you," she said. She extended her hand and Blake shook it. "I'm Professor Rhodes, but you can call me Dusty. That's what everyone calls me, as you probably know."

"How would I know that?"

"From the . . . radio? Dusty Roads? The Morning Zoo on KRIP?"

"I don't listen to the radio."

"Well, we'll fix that," Dusty said. "And what's your name?"

"Blake," he said.

"No last name?"

Blake wasn't used to giving a stranger all of his details, but he guessed she probably had a roster, anyway. "Webster. Blake Webster."

"You'll need a different name for the radio," she said. "Your name makes you sound like that guy you went to high school with who still lives in the same town and is now assistant manager at Del Taco."

"I did grow up here," he said.

"Oh," she said. "What do you do for a job?"

"Goon," he said. "Assassin. Private security. Depends on the assignment."

This made Professor Rhodes laugh. "Can you imagine? What a life that would be." She gazed at Blake for a moment. "I hereby christen thee Blake Danger. How about that?"

"It's not my favorite."

"Well, Blake Danger, do me a favor, that giant knife you have there? Could you go ahead and put that away? Zip it in your book bag?"

"No problem," Blake said. He dropped the knife into his bullet-proof backpack. It was made from tactical-grade Kevlar, not like the crap they sold actual students. His pack could stop a bullet from an AK, whereas the kids he saw walking around with the bulletproof packs they sold at Target, those were only good for stopping 9mm shells.

"And if you don't mind me asking," she said, "why on earth did you bring that to class?"

"In case someone tried to kill me," he said. The classroom was beginning to fill with students.

Professor Rhodes smiled. "Okay then, Blake Danger," she said. "Take your seat."

"Bro, you're swole as shit." Blake looked to his left. There was a kid, maybe nineteen, sliding into the chair beside him. He had on a Warriors jersey, a non-bulletproof backpack, shorts that hung off his ass, flip-flops, and was chewing on a straw. "You do keto?"

"No," Blake said. He didn't spend a lot of time around young people, generally, so this was going to take some getting used to. Strangers didn't usually talk to Blake. Blake didn't usually talk to strangers. That was his whole thing.

"Cool," the kid said. "What're you in for?"

"In?"

"Like, what do you want to do? I'm on that sports tip. I can talk for hours about any sport. Throw one at me. Anything. I got it down now where I can have a hot take for thirty seconds on any sport. My radio name is Down-to-Go. Get it? So try me."

"Jai alai," Blake said.

"The fuck is that?"

"National sport of the Basques," Blake said.

Down-to-Go just stared at him. "The fuck is a Basque?"

Before Blake could answer, Professor Rhodes got up to the podium. "Okay everyone," she said, "welcome back. I see some familiar faces. We're going to have a fun semester, I promise. For the newbies, it's cool if you call me Dusty, since I've seen too many of you on Friday nights at the Red Dawn acting like a fool, and you've seen me, too."

This got half the class to laugh. Blake had never been in the Red Dawn before, but he knew where it was: across from the Lusty Lady Strip Club on Perez Road, an industrial section of Cathedral City. Not that he'd been in there, either, but next door to the Lusty Lady was a storage facility owned by the Mexican Mafia. The kind of place where they tied a motherfucker up before they drove him out to the desert. Red Dawn, meanwhile, was the kind of bar where eighties cover bands played on Tuesday nights, or where people like a local rock DJ might spin their favorite eighties dance hits for people born in the aughts. Blake didn't go out much. All the bombing he'd been around had left him with low-grade tinnitus.

"I'm not spinning there this term, so you're all safe," Professor Rhodes continued. More laughter. "All right, I'm going to pass out the syllabus and then we'll get started getting comfortable on some of the equipment, so everyone fire up your computers and load GarageBand. Down-to-Go, can you help any of the newbies with getting their mics set up? We're going to get everyone talking day one. Just like if you were coming out of a coma."

For the first six weeks of classes, Blake Danger found it fairly easy to keep up. His English composition class was pretty fun—the professor had them writing poems and short essays about their childhood, which Blake liked doing, since it reminded him of things he'd forgotten, like his third and fifth stepfathers, who were the same guy—and Western Civ was fine, except that half his class had never heard of Mesopotamia before, whereas he'd spent a decade there, blowing shit up, rebuilding it, and then blowing it back up again. Math was math. But JOUR 121 was where Blake found himself actually making friends and learning new things. He'd started out hating the sound of his own voice, but Professor Rhodes had forced that out of him by having him do a podcast project where he interviewed people who lived in his gated community about their lives. He'd gone door-to-door with his iPhone and a mic and asked each person the same five questions—*Where were you born? What was your first job? Who was your first love? What is your first memory? What is the most beautiful thing you've ever seen?*—and then he edited it all into a tight package, with voice-over and sound effects, like he was doing This American Life, a show he'd never heard of a few weeks prior, but which made him feel more comfortable about his own speaking voice. He didn't sound like Ira Glass or David Sedaris and that was fine.

The sound of his breathing still really bothered him, however. He detected a slight whistle coming from his nose. He'd fix that.

Funny things was, it wasn't like he knew his neighbors beforehand. In fact, he'd practiced not knowing them, avoiding eye contact whenever possible, and now here he had this assignment . . . and Blake was a man who took his assignments seriously, so he'd emailed the entire HOA asking for volunteers and was surprised that almost everyone wanted to talk. "There's nothing people love more than opening up about themselves," Professor Rhodes had told him early on in the process. "You won't get them to shut up now, is the problem."

And it was true. Blake couldn't go to the mailbox now without getting drawn into a conversation about HOA politics.

The grass should be greener.

The pool should be warmer.

The short-term renters should be shot.

It was only a matter of time before Blake was put up for office, because he agreed with everyone, on everything.

He'd emailed his assignment in the night before. So when Professor Rhodes walked up to Blake that morning in Beeps Café, the shitty coffee joint on campus, and asked if she could join him, he was both nervous and excited. *Had she listened? Did she want to talk about it? Was he any good?* She was dressed in what Blake had come to realize was her uniform—the same all-black getup she'd worn on the first day of class—including the sunglasses, which she kept on.

"I need you to tell me something honestly," she said to Blake.

"Okay," he said. "I'm ready." *She hated it. Dammit.* He knew it. *She's going to ask me if I even graduated high school. I'll have to tell her I took the GED. Shit.*

"I wouldn't ask this if you were one of the kids, by the way," she said. "And maybe I shouldn't be asking you, regardless, because of FERPA or HIPPA or OSHA or, I dunno, KE$HA." She leaned toward Blake, like she was waiting for him to laugh, but Blake was feeling like he might throw up. *I fucked it all up.* "Anyway. I'm not loaded up with friends in this place, so, here we are. You seem like a nice person. Are you a nice person?"

"I try to be," Blake said. "But I often fail."

"Right. That's what we should all be doing, right? Trying to be nice people." She cleared her throat. Then took off her sunglasses. "Can you tell that I have a black eye?"

Professor Rhodes's right eyeball looked like a stop sign, but the skin around it was the same color as the rest of her face, which Blake realized was a trick of make-up. Concealer, powder, enough foundation to hold the Taj Mahal.

"No," Blake said.

"Really?"

"No," Blake said again. "It's clear you have an eye injury. It's not clear that the injury extends to the rest of your face. But looking closely, I see some swelling and slight discoloration. Someone sees you, they're going to know that you hurt yourself, but they aren't going to know *how* you hurt yourself. But if you start to sweat," he drew a circle in the air around her eye, "there will be questions."

"I can't be walking around this place looking like I got into a fight," she said. "That's how adjuncts lose their jobs."

"Did someone hurt you?"

She put her sunglasses back on. "I've been taking self-defense classes," she said. "This seventeen-year-old girl who works at the yogurt shop across the street? Sprinkles? She kicked me in the face like we were in a cage match. And then I sort of . . . lost it. And then she kicked me again." Professor Rhodes shook her head. "I'm the only person who has ever taken a self-defense class and got beaten up *in the class.* Unreal, right?"

"Self-defense isn't about winning. It's about surviving. You don't want to get kicked in the face, you need to learn how to fight, not how to defend yourself."

"You ever see *Play Misty for Me?* The Clint Eastwood movie about the DJ?"

"Is this one of those movies with the chimpanzee?"

Professor Rhodes thought for a moment. "No," she said. "Could be. I don't think so. Anyway. It's terrible. Clint's a DJ and he has a fling with one of his fans, she starts calling him all the time, there's another woman, blah blah blah, murder, murder, etc."

"I mostly watch documentaries."

"The point is, I'm in a situation with a stalker. It isn't to the *Play Misty For Me* level yet, but it's the only cultural touchstone I have, so there you go."

"This stalker," Blake said. "Do you know him?"

"Her," she said. "She works here."

"At the college?"

"Yes," she said, "you'll love this. Campus security. She walked me to my car one night, then a couple nights later she shows up at Red Dawn, not a huge surprise, right? Like, small town, people hang out wherever, but then two nights after that, I'm here on campus to watch a play—*Noises Off*, which was terrible—and she sits down next to me in the auditorium. Then she starts calling in and winning contests at my other job on KRIP. Duran Duran tickets one week, Robbie Knievel tickets another week, free pizzas, whatever, just so she has a reason to show up to the station. Everything short of calling in to request 'Every Breath You Take.'"

"She asked you out?"

"Yeah, that first night. Real casual. I didn't think anything about it. Asked if I wanted to meet up for a bite sometime and I was like, *Yeah, sure, sometime.* It was late and I wanted to go home. Then she's at Red Dawn and she's like, How about tonight? And it's loud, so I can't quite figure out what's happening, so I say, Sure, yes, later. I get off work, it's three a.m., I'm dead, and she's sitting on the hood of my car, waiting for me. Just a real creeper vibe, so I went back inside, had one of the bartenders walk me out, and I guess that pissed her off. So now I just see her everywhere, but she doesn't actually speak to me. Which is creepy, yes?"

"Have you talked to the university about this?"

"Do you know what I get paid for teaching here? Fifty bucks an hour. That's a hundred and fifty bucks a class. That's it. I go to HR and complain about a campus security guard stalking me by, you know, following me around campus, you know what they're going to say? She's doing her job. And then fall semester will roll around and I'll be out of a job for causing problems and then I'll be replaced by that twerp from KDZT. Mike on the Mic in the Morning? You know him?"

"No."

"It doesn't matter," she said. "So now I'm in self-defense classes and Buffy the Yogurt Slayer kicked my ass. I might burn down Sprinkles."

"Don't do that," Blake said.

"Yeah, that would be obvious. Can you do that for me?"

Blake considered this. "It will take me some time," he said. "Tell me about this stalker." Blake said. "Does she have a name?"

"Annie Levy. And she's not a campus cop. She's just, like, a woman on a bike with a flashlight."

"Okay," Blake said. "That's a problem I could solve for you."

"In addition to burning down Sprinkles?"

"Yes."

Professor Rhodes cocked her head at Blake. "That would be inappropriate," she said. "Since you're my student."

"I could drop your class."

"No, no," she said. "There's only ten weeks left in the semester, that would be crazy." She paused. "But say you took care of this problem. What would that entail, exactly?"

"Well," Blake said, "I could either kill this person, hobble them permanently, or encourage their behavior to change by suggesting that I might kill or hobble them."

"Uh-huh," she said. "And what would this cost me?"

"Cost you? Nothing."

"I'd want to pay," she said, "for ethical reasons."

"If I killed this woman," Blake said, "that would be more than you could afford. And I don't typically kill women. Hobbling, we could negotiate a price. Payment plan if need be. A stern talking to, I'd call that $500."

"Would you take that on a Starbucks gift card?"

"Money is money," Blake said. "I understand you'd probably be worried about a trace on it, so yes, a gift card would be fine."

Professor Rhodes sipped her coffee. Took a deep breath. Sat back in her seat. Let out a chuckle. "Can you imagine? If only it were all so easy," she said. "Anyway. Whatever. Thanks for listening, Blake Danger. It's probably nothing. Just an annoyance to deal with."

"Do you really only get $150 per class?" Blake asked after a while.

"Yep," Professor Rhodes said. "I mean, it's fine, whatever. It's my side gig. Well, it's my other side gig. But I'm not working at Red Dawn this semester, because of this whole stalker shit. Plus, I got super tired of running into students there. Now that weed is legal, it's less fun to illicitly get high in the bathroom and then watch your students attempt to get their mack on to old New Wave songs."

"If teaching pays so little," Blake said, "why do it?"

"It's not about the money," she said. "It's a calling. Either you love to teach or it's a job. I love to teach. Simple as that."

"I don't get that distinction."

"There's not something you love to do?"

"No," he said.

"No? How is that possible? You just sit at home in the dark all day? There must be something."

Fact was, he did like sitting in the dark. If his tinnitus was bothering him, he'd sit quietly in his living room, lights turned down, white noise machine droning in the background, Thor on his lap, reading on his Kindle. Blake thought for a bit. "Walking my dog," he said. "I like seeing him see the world."

"Well," Professor Rhodes said, "then maybe you should start a professional dog walking service. Imagine how much joy you would get from that."

"How does one *imagine* joy?" Blake said.

"You see, not to be overly personal? But this is what I hate about people." She took down the rest of her coffee. "I wouldn't feel right existing only for myself. I have zero money. I have a job playing music for a living at a radio station whose signal is literally thirty-five square miles. But they let me play what I want, which is pretty cool, right? Because maybe you'll hear a cool song and buy an actual physical CD or record and some starving artist somewhere makes a buck. And then I teach these couple classes and maybe I get some kid who has no idea she has any talent and I'm the first person, ever, to tell her that she does. And then she maybe goes to a four-year college, gets a degree, wins a Pulitzer Prize. I don't know. Whatever. Just gets a decent job that makes her happy. If I played a small role in that? I can imagine joy from that. Even if I only get $150 a class."

"I've offended you."

"No," she said. "If you really feel that way, then you need to make some changes, Blake Danger. That's my advice to you, as your teacher. It should be easy to imagine joy."

"My line of work," Blake said, "it's often about making other people feel good. But I don't get a lot out of it."

"What is it you do, exactly? You told me once."

"I'm a goon," he said.

"Is that how you think of yourself?"

"It's what I am."

"We all feel that way sometimes," she said. "Look, I'm not trying to tell you how to live, Blake Danger, I'm just telling you how I live. Maybe you just need to figure out a way to give back, even if it's not in the scope of your job."

This made sense to Blake. "Is that my assignment?"

"It's your *mission*," she said. "I want graphs and tables and all that. Keep a list. Update it daily. Extra credit if it becomes a super cool podcast."

Professor Rhodes pulled out her phone, checked the time. "Oh, shit, we're going to be late. Can I tell you something?"

"You can."

"I don't want you to take this the wrong way," she said, "but I listened to your homework in the car coming over here and I think you could do this professionally." She grabbed up her book bag. "Oh shit," she said, quietly. "Don't raise a fuss, but my stalker is pretending to peruse the pastries."

"Where? On a watch face."

"Does it matter if it's a.m. or p.m.?"

"No," Blake said.

"Three o'clock."

Blake looked to his right. There was a woman in a security uniform with her back to Blake. She was about five-six, long black hair tied into a sensible work ponytail, flashlight on her belt. Blake could dispose of her in ten seconds.

"Walk with me," Professor Rhodes said, "in case I need you to kill someone."

Stalker Annie Levy lived in a second-floor garden apartment a mile from College of the Desert. The complex was behind a guard gate, which meant absolutely nothing to Blake or anyone else who wanted to do some bad shit. A guard gate made the people inside feel safe. It merely told criminals that they'd need to hop a fence if they wanted whatever they were after, so after Blake followed Annie home, he got online, found out her exact address, parked his car at the Whole Foods a block away, and then slid over the block wall fence of 1 Roadrunner Place, the luxury apartment complex with twenty-four hour security . . . if you walked up to the front door. Everywhere else was wide open, if you had a step-ladder or some upper body strength.

Blake was dressed as un-intimidating as possible. Tan cargo shorts, a blue T-shirt, a white Nike sweat-wicking golf hat, a fanny pack, his iPhone set to record sound. That he had zip-ties, a blackjack, and a Sig in the fanny pack would be of some concern if a cop or a security guard searched him, but Blake didn't see that happening.

A cop or security guard might stop him. But no one was searching him.

Blake made his way up the stairs to Annie's place, nodded at a man walking down. He was in his early sixties and dressed in a ratty white tuxedo jacket, a bow tie loose around his shirt collar. So many people around Palm Springs wore cheap tuxedos for their jobs at restaurants that Blake thought it made the value of black tie functionally worthless these days, except in places like Monte Carlo, where people really followed certain fashion rules. Blake had tuxedos in storage around the world, because he was too big to get a rental, so he had one in Paris, one in Phnom Penh, one in Brisbane, one in Sao Paulo, one in New York, one in Chicago, one at home. Need be, he was always one call away from getting his clothes overnighted to him, no matter where in the world he was. Being a goon meant not worrying about whether or not you had a tux. You had one. It was on the way. You had to stand in the background while your boss played pai-gow for the Hope diamond, you were ready.

"Pardon me," Blake said to the man, who was now at the bottom of the stairs, Blake on the landing outside Annie's door, "can I ask you something."

"You just did," he said, like he was the first guy to ever say that.

"Does your job give you joy?"

"Do I look happy?"

"Not really."

"And I'm already ten minutes late," he said.

"Would you be interested in six lightly used tuxedos? You'd need to get them tailored."

"Yeah," the man said, "leave them and an envelope filled with cash at my door, Mr. Bond."

Easy enough.

Blake waited for the man to get into his car and drive off before knocking on Annie's door. "Who is it?" she said. Blake could tell she was staring at him through the peephole. Different situation, he'd shove his Smith &

Wesson tactical pen through the hole, come out with her eye. It wasn't going to be like that today.

"You don't know me," he said.

"Why are you at my door?"

"I'm here to talk to you about stalking Professor Rhodes."

Silence.

"You're freaking her out," Blake said. "You'll be surprised to learn she doesn't suddenly want to go out with you now. In fact, it's the opposite. She's actively training for the moment when you come close enough to her that she can break your arm, or leg, or skull. Personally, I think breaking your pelvis would make more of a statement, but Professor Rhodes is a pacifist."

Silence.

"I've been training her. Take a good look at me. I look familiar because you saw me with Professor Rhodes today."

Silence.

"What I want to tell you, Annie, is that your behavior is *your* choice. Professor Rhodes's reaction to your behavior is *her* choice. And she has chosen to hurt you until such time as your behavior stops. If you understand this, knock once on your door."

Silence.

And then . . .

Knock.

"Good," Blake said. "I understand you're worried about your job now. You should be. You should quit." Blake unzipped his fanny pack and took out a stack of purple chips from the Spa Casino in Palm Springs, waved the stack in front of the peephole. "You should also move. But we're not unreasonable. This is $5,000 in chips, which is double your take-home salary for a month. This should give you some breathing room as you start your new life. You have one week. Knock if you understand what this gift entails."

Knock.

"Good," Blake said. He set the chips down on her welcome mat. "Now, I assume you've dialed 911, that would be smart of you at this point, but have not yet hit send, so I'm going to leave. If you bother Professor Rhodes ever again, I will take that money back in blood. You don't need to knock if you understand that, because Annie, I hope you are the kind of person who does not understand such a thing. Now. Before I go. I want you tell me something. What do you think of when you imagine joy?"

"I don't understand," Annie said.

"Yes you do," Blake said. "Think."

"Okay," she said. Blake could hear the fear in her voice. That was good. "Monument Valley. The vastness of it all. I like standing in the vastness. I don't worry about anything."

"Good," Blake said. "Move there. Never come back. If this is all to your liking, knock for thirty seconds."

Knock. Knock. Knock . . .

Blake was already back over the wall by the time Annie was done knocking. Still, he sat in his car and watched 1 Roadrunner Place for the rest of the night, waiting for the police to show up. They never did.

When he got home, he had two things for his list. The audio was a little muddled, but he could fix that in GarageBand.

The week before finals, some two months later, Blake had to spend three hours helping to produce Machine Gun Kelly's show, *The Second Amen.* It was the one conservative show they had on the campus radio station. It ran on Sundays at noon, timed for folks leaving church, and it was hosted by this guy named Kelly Stevens who'd gained local fame for transitioning from being the buttoned-up weatherman on the ABC news affiliate to habitually losing Congressional elections. Each week he'd have on some whack job who had a story to tell about how guns had positively affected their lives, Machine Gun Kelly eventually saying, "Well, you must have said amen to God and then amen to your gun, am I right?"

Blake's job that day was to sit across from Machine Gun, work the board, hit a shotgun sound effect button and then to periodically pretend to be engaged by the topic Machine Gun was discussing with his guest, all under the auspices of learning radio production. Apparently, a big part of working in radio was feigning interest.

"You were great today," Machine Gun told Blake after he'd finished interviewing a chef from the Marriott in Indian Wells who'd personally cooked for Oliver North. "I know it probably hurts your Libtard sensibilities, but you showed some real professionalism. I had that kid Down-to-Go in the other day. That did not work. But you, you're a person who understands might makes right, I'd guess."

"I understand it," Blake said, "but that doesn't mean I adhere to it."

"You don't have to," he said. "Everyone else adheres to it around you. No one wants to piss you off, even if you're not aware of it. And so the world has probably been opened up wide for you most of your life." He looked over his shoulder and then rolled back in his chair and closed the studio door. "Off the record. I'm not your teacher now. I'm just a guy in a bar. I bet you've gotten all the pussy, money, and power you've ever wanted, am I right?"

"Were you ever my teacher?"

"What?"

"Are you employed by the college?"

"Not as a teacher, no," he said. "But I'm right, aren't I?"

"No," Blake said.

"It's natural selection. But all of you beta males out there, you won't admit to it. You, you're a beta, but you present alpha. Me, I present beta, all 165 pounds of me, but I'm all the way alpha. Right? We can agree on that?"

"I agree with exactly nothing you're saying," Blake said.

"Fair. Fair. But if we're really two guys in a bar, and I've pissed you off more than I seem to have, I've got the equalizer." He lifted up his shirt and showed Blake the butt of his gun. He had what looked to be a shitty little .22 shoved into his khakis. That was also his thing. At the end of his show, he'd say, "Follow me on Twitter @MachineGunKellyForCongress, but don't follow too close, because I'm always packing."

"You're aware they make holsters now."

"A good guy with a gun still needs the element of surprise."

"I don't think it's legal for you to have that on a college campus, is it?"

"Is it?" Machine Gun Kelly asked.

Blake's cellphone buzzed with a new email. It was from Professor Rhodes. He'd turned in his final assignment to her, so maybe she wanted to talk about it? The subject said: COME SEE ME. "Are we done here?" Blake asked.

"I'd love to have you work on the show over the summer, if you're interested," Machine Gun said. "I dig your energy. I'll talk to Dusty about getting you some extra credit. Though I'm sure she'll be giving you whatever grade you want. Now that's a door I'd like to open, am I right?"

Blake came around the board and stood in front of Machine Gun Kelly. Then, in one motion, he grabbed the .22 out of Machine Gun's pants and shoved the rolling chair across the room, Machine Gun slamming into the soundproof wall with a thud. Blake popped the magazine out, put it in his pocket. Cleared the chamber.

"What the fuck!" Machine Gun Kelly said.

Blake examined the .22. It was a shitty Smith & Wesson. $200 at Walmart. "You ever shoot this at a real person?"

"What?"

"You ever shoot this tiny little metal object at a living creature? Or no?"

"No."

"Don't ever try," Blake said. He popped the slide off the top of the gun, yanked the spring out of it, removed the barrel, dropped it all on the floor, tucked the bottom of the gun in his fanny pack. If you couldn't field strip a Smith & Wesson in fifteen seconds, your goon card could be revoked. "In my line of work, if someone flashes their gun at you, that means they are willing to kill you. Are you willing to kill me?"

"What? No."

"See, that's why a good guy with a gun is useless. Unless you're a bad guy, you're really not prepared to kill someone." Blake smiled at Machine Gun Kelly. "Now. I'm not going to kill you. But if you ever flash your gun at me again, I'll put a hollow point directly between your eyes."

———— •◦• ————

Professor Rhodes's faculty office was located in what Blake figured was probably the old laundry room, what with the tile floor and the exhaust vent in the ceiling. She was sitting at her desk with AirPods in her ears, her eyes down. Blake knocked on her door, even though it was open. She looked up, slid one of her AirPods out, set it down on her desk. Clicked something on her computer.

"Blake," she said. "Sit down." He did as he was asked. She handed him the AirPod. "Is this you I'm listening to?"

Blake slid the AirPod in. She clicked her mouse. Blake heard a mechanical voice say, "If you bother Professor Rhodes ever again, I will take that money back in blood."

"Yes," Blake said, "that's me. I applied a filter on it, for legal reasons. I have the original if you need it, for my grade."

"*For your grade*? No. Blake. I don't need it for your *grade*." She clicked her mouse again. "This whole file you submitted. This is all you?"

"Yes," Blake said. "I completed my assignment."

"There's audio of you burning down Sprinkles."

"No one was hurt."

"Jesus fucking Christ," Professor Rhodes said. "And this is you speaking at an HOA meeting? Is that correct?"

"Yes," Blake said. "I was elected President."

"Did you actually *shoot* a short-term renter?"

"No," Blake said. "I shot *at* a short-term renter. Intentionally missed. Again, no one was hurt."

"Over the course of the last two months," Professor Rhodes said, "I've received about $15,000 in poker chips. Sometimes they come in the mail. Sometimes they're in my car. Sometimes I open my purse and there's a stack of black chips in there. Am I to presume that those are from you?"

"Presume? No."

"Blake," Professor Rhodes said, "there's an audio recording of what sounds like the robot from *Lost In Space* breaking into my car and filling the glove box with poker chips. Are you telling me that wasn't you?"

"I'm telling you not to presume." Blake leaned forward. "Part of what my aim was, obviously, was for this to be serialized and then maybe it's revealed who I am after I'm already gone. I wanted to discuss that with you. I know you can't appear in student work, but I thought it would make for an interesting post-script."

"Do you intend to disappear?"

"Well," Blake said, "eventually I'd like to pursue my BA. So this would be a two-year long project, I guess."

Professor Rhodes pushed back from her desk, got up, closed her office door. Stood against it for a moment, then sat down next to Blake, but scooted the chair back a few inches. It was something Blake noticed people often did with him. They'd sit close to him . . . and then feel like they were too close. "Is Annie . . . dead?" she whispered.

"No," Blake said.

"Because I haven't seen her."

"That's good. That's what you wanted. Mission accomplished." He scooted his chair closer to Professor Rhodes. She scooted back. He scooted closer, grabbed the arms of her chair, pulled her toward him. They were friends now. She didn't need to be afraid. "I want to talk to you about an idea I had. I keep hearing my classmates talking about how they can't afford student loans, which is stopping them from going to a four-year college. What if I began to offer private loans? I'd draw up contracts and everything. I wouldn't charge these exorbitant rates like other lenders. It would be fair and honest. Provided people paid the loans back on time. That would give me joy. Do you think that's something you could help facilitate?"

Professor Rhodes shook her head. Very slowly.

"No, no," he said, "I suppose that would violate the student-teacher contract if you were involved in the money side. Well. Never mind that. I have a friend from Chechnya with some experience in this field. Anyway. Thank you, Professor Rhodes. You have taught me a great deal. *There's nothing people love more than opening up about themselves.* You were absolutely right."

About Our Contributors

Thirty-something years ago, **Jill D. Block** received a too-thin-to-be-good-news envelope from the College of Her Choice. She figures she will forgive them for it any day now. In the meantime, she graduated from Clark University, where she wrote some stories, and from Brooklyn Law School, where she didn't. And then she closed a whole lot of commercial real estate transactions before remembering that she is, in fact, a writer. If she had it to do all over again, she'd probably do it all over again.

Nicholas Christopher is the author of seven novels, including *A Trip to the Stars* and *Veronica*; nine books of poems, most recently, *Crossing the Equator: New & Selected Poems* and *On Jupiter Place;* and a book about film noir, *Somewhere in the Night*. He lives in New York City.

A former adjunct instructor at Hofstra University, **Reed Farrel Coleman** is the *New York Times* best-selling author of thirty novels. He is a four-time recipient of the Shamus Award and a four-time Edgar Award nominee.

Tod Goldberg is the *New York Times* best-selling author of over a dozen books, including *Gangster Nation, Gangsterland, Living Dead Girl*, and the Hammett Prize finalist *The House of Secrets*. His nonfiction and criticism appear regularly in the *Los Angeles Times, USA Today*, and *Wall Street Journal*, and a recent effort was chosen for *Best American Essays*. Tod holds an MFA in fiction & literature from Bennington College and is a Professor of Creative Writing at the University of California, Riverside, where he founded and directs the Low Residency MFA in Creative Writing & Writing for the Performing Arts. He lives in Indio, CA with his wife, Wendy Duren.

Jane Hamilton has written seven novels, including *The Book of Ruth*, *A Map of the World*, and *The Excellent Lombards*. Through the years she has occasionally taught at the college and MFA levels. The deep secret of any teacher, she figures, is that one learns far more than the students themselves. She's grateful for the peep into the academy—and then, how great to be able to flee.

A. J. Hartley (aka Andrew Hart) is the bestselling author of twenty-three novels for adults and younger readers spanning multiple genres—mystery, thriller, fantasy and science fiction. Recent work includes *The Woman in Our House, Cold Bath Street*, and the *Steeplejack* trilogy. As Andrew James Hartley he serves as the Robinson Professor of Shakespeare at the University of North Carolina, Charlotte, where he specializes in performance theory and practice. His academic books include studies on dramaturgy, political theatre, and the stage history of *Julius Caesar*, the play which he is currently editing for Arden.

Gar Anthony Haywood would love to paraphrase what ex-Los Angeles Laker Elden Campbell once said, when asked if he'd earned his degree at Clemson: "No, but they gave it to me, anyway." But Gar never attended Clemson, nor any other four-year university. He has won the Shamus and Anthony awards, however, and dropped in on every community college in the state of California.

Owen King is the author of the novel *Double Feature* and co-author of the novel *Sleeping Beauties*. He is a graduate of Vassar College and the Columbia University School of the Arts. Go Brewers! Go Lions!

Joe R. Lansdale is the author of fifty novels and hundreds of short pieces. Writer-in-Residence at Stephen F. Austin State University in Nacogdoches, Texas, he is a member of the Texas Institute of Letters as well as the Texas Literary Hall of Fame.

John Lescroart dabbled with three majors in three universities before he settled in for six quarters of English Literature at UC Berkeley en route to a cancelled graduation ceremony to protest something which must have seemed important at the time.

David Levien is a proud graduate of the University of Michigan who enjoys suffering every fall during the Wolverine football season. He is currently making the Showtime drama *Billions*, which he co-created, and has written four novels in the Frank Behr series, the most recent being *Signature Kill*.

Peter Lovesey's main achievement at Reading University was persuading a beautiful psychology student to marry him. It turned out that Jax was a mystery fan with a mission of her own: to persuade an Eng Lit graduate to make a killing out of crime. After more than sixty years of marriage and almost as many books, the plotting hasn't yet turned personal—or so they would have us believe.

Seanan McGuire is the award-winning author of more than forty books and a horrifying number of short stories. Currently, she writes *Ghost-Spider* for Marvel Comics, as well as various novel-length and other projects for her prose publishers. Seanan lives in the Pacific Northwest, where she cohabitates with some terrifyingly large cats and a bunch of deeply creepy dolls.

Warren Moore holds a PhD in English from Ball State University, and since the university has not asked for it back, he guesses he'll keep it. He is Professor of English and Creative Writing at Newberry College, in Newberry, SC. At various points, he has been a member of the MLA (Modern Language Assoc.), MAA (Medieval Academy of America), and MWA (Mystery Writers of America.)

David Morrell has an MA and PhD from Pennsylvania State University. His master's thesis explores Hemingway's early style. His doctoral dissertation is titled *John Barth: An Introduction*. For sixteen years, he taught in the English department at the University of Iowa, most of them as a full professor. His *New York Times* bestsellers include the classic espionage novel *The Brotherhood of the Rose*, the basis for the only TV mini-series to air after a Super Bowl.

Ian Rankin began writing his first Inspector Rebus novel while he should have been researching his PhD in Scottish Literature at the University of Edinburgh. He never finished the PhD but did finish the novel. He now has several honorary doctorates and degrees which he singularly failed to work for, and was recently Visiting Professor of Creative Writing at the University of East Anglia. While a student, he belonged to many clubs but no secret societies.

Tom Straw, a UCLA dropout, is the author of seven *New York Times* best-sellers under the pseudonym Richard Castle. He recently completed his tenth mystery novel, this one under his own name. An Emmy and Writers Guild of America Award nominee, he was most recently head writer and an executive producer of *Nurse Jackie*.

許素細 **XU XI's** recent titles include the novel *That Man In Our Lives*, the memoir *Dear Hong Kong: An Elegy for a City*, and two collections—*Insignificance: Hong Kong Stories* and *This Fish Is Fowl: Essays of Being*. She has been a Writer-in-Residence at universities in China, Sweden, Hong Kong, the Philippines, Iowa, and Arizona, that might have been better served by Monkeys. But she has taught writing for around two decades, mostly at the graduate level, and does hold an MFA in fiction from the University of Massachusetts at Amherst. In 2018, she was named Faculty Co-Director of the International MFA in Creative Writing & Literary Translation at Vermont College of Fine Arts. She also co-founded Authors At Large for the writing life beyond the darkling halls.

Lawrence Block is the editor of *The Darkling Halls of Ivy,* but evidently couldn't be bothered to write a story for it. This resonates nicely with his duties as Writer-in-Residence at Newberry College, where he sits around watching other people write. He's been identified as a man who needs no introduction, and that's exactly what he's getting here.

Contact Lawrence Block

Email: lawbloc@gmail.com
Twitter: @LawrenceBlock
Facebook: lawrence.block
Website: lawrenceblock.com

My Newsletter: I get out an email newsletter at unpredictable intervals, but rarely more often than every other week. I'll be happy to add you to the distribution list. A blank email to lawbloc@gmail.com with "newsletter" in the subject line will get you on the list, and a click of the "Unsubscribe" link will get you off it, should you ultimately decide you're happier without it.